I0818257

The Ancient Scroll

The Ancient Scroll

Tom Morris

A Journey of Destiny

Book Seven

Walid and the Mysteries of Phi

Wisdom/Work
Published by Wisdom Work
TomVMorris.com

Published 2021

ISBN 978-0999481325

Printed in the United States of America

Set in Adobe Garamond Pro
Designed by Abigail Chiaramonte
Cover Concept by Sara Morris

To Ed and Don and Bruce.
And To All Those Who Have Hope.

Contents

I

Early Morning

Egypt: Many years ago.

To be more precise, it was 1935. The Golden Palace was glowing in the first rays of the early morning sun. Dozens of staff members and kingdom officials were already at work in many parts of the building. Gardeners outside tended to the grounds before the heat of the day would arrive. Walid and Mafulla were sitting together having breakfast where they always shared the first meal of the day. The head butler knocked lightly on the door and glanced into the room to say, "Excuse me, Your Majesty. Good morning. Do you have everything you might need?"

"Yes, Kular, thanks for checking on us," Walid replied. "Please, tell the kitchen how much we're enjoying the new breads they sent up."

"Yeah, they're really good!" Mafulla added. "And that jam. Amazing."

"Excellent. I'll pass on your compliments," Kular responded, and then looked back at Walid, and said, "Oh, I almost forgot. When you're done, the documents you've been waiting for will be on your office desk for a signature. They were just delivered."

"Ok, great. Thanks for the update. See you soon," Walid said, and the royal butler did a single nod of his head, as an abbreviated bow, and ducked back out into the hallway, closing the door quietly behind him.

Mafulla put down his cup of steaming black coffee and looked up at his friend. "I'm really glad you didn't move into the king's rooms."

"What? Oh. Yeah. There was no way I was going to do that." Walid picked up another piece of the still warm bread swirled with cinnamon and fruit. He dipped a knife into the soft butter and spread it across the bread. Without any reason, he traced a circle on top of the bread. He said, "Where I am is good. I like my room."

Mafulla continued, "There sure was a lot of pressure at first, with some people pushing for it, really urging you to move in."

Walid then used the knife tip once more to draw a vertical line through the circle on the toast as he pondered this and said, "Yeah, I know, but it really didn't feel like pressure. I knew everybody meant well by their suggestions, and almost insistence, that I should take all my stuff into Uncle Ali's rooms. But at the same time, I just felt like it was wrong. I wasn't about to do it. I mean, sure, I'll use the sitting room for meetings, which only makes sense, and his office for stuff that needs to be done there, like the papers I have to sign this morning. And, you know, I'm fine with us eating in the dining room there like usual, especially for evening dinners and when we have visitors and official meetings over lunch. But I'm not going to move in there and sleep in his bed like it's mine. He's just … away for now, right? It's not like we have any reason to believe it's … anything … that's at all permanent."

Mafulla took a deep breath and let it out. "It's all so crazy and strange. But, yeah, everyone seems to agree that we should think of him as just sort of mysteriously away for now, doing something that I guess needs to be done, whatever and wherever it might be." He was quiet for a second and then added, "Otherwise, somebody would have known, don't you think? Some Phi would have had a strong feeling, if it was … different from that."

"Yeah, maybe."

"What do you mean, maybe?"

"Well, the king is the king. I mean: he's so much more advanced than anybody else. It could be that if he—you know—made the great transition … he would just slip from this world to the next without anyone sensing anything. It might be sort of like walking quietly and invisibly from one room into another. Maybe he was so close already—in his spirit, I mean—that we wouldn't have known, none of us. Not even Hoda or Masoon." Walid's eyes grew moist with the thought. And then he tried to stop his mind from moving any farther in that direction.

"I guess it's possible," Mafulla said. "But, in every other case, somebody's always known stuff like that, and even stuff that was not nearly as big."

"True."

Mafulla seemed lost in thought for a second. Then he said, "I think Hoda for sure would have known. She's really advanced, too, like the king. So, even if it was really subtle, her abilities are equally amazing. And she's just as puzzled as we are. But, she's not worried or pessimistic or distraught, and I guess we shouldn't be, either."

"Yeah, and we've got a lot of reasons to think the Maayufs would also have known," Walid said. "I don't know of anyone more senior than them in what they know."

"Good point. But would they have said anything?"

"I think so. They've always been up front and honest about difficult things, news that's maybe hard to hear or deal with." Walid took a deep breath. "It's just all so confusing," he said. "I've got this swirl of feelings and forces going on inside me, like grief and fear and blankness, and hope, and shock, and, you know, resolve, or determination or something—to do whatever I'm supposed to do until all this gets figured out."

"I guess it's stuff like this that the king was preparing you for during your original trip across the desert," Mafulla said, adding, "you know, hard stuff, confusing stuff, scary stuff."

"Yeah, everything that makes an oasis within us necessary. And I've been using a lot of what he taught me. He really helped me create a place of calm and rest and peace inside that I can go to almost all the time. Otherwise, I don't think I could be doing any of this right now."

"Yeah, it's just wild. Here you are in the role of king, for now, as hard as it is to believe. And I think you're doing a pretty good job."

"Thanks." Walid said.

"Yeah."

Walid then added, "It's like we're living in this bizarre dream where everything's gotten turned upside down."

"You got that right."

"It's crazy for sure, but I really do feel like it's temporary."

Mafulla took a sip of coffee and said, "It's been two weeks already."

"Yeah, and a very long and strange two weeks."

"You know what's really weird?"

"What?"

Mafulla now had his mouth full and chewed a few more times before swallowing and saying, "Think about how many people would love to be a king, how many kids dream about it, and now you are one, and there's been absolutely no point at all when you said to yourself, 'Wow, this is great. This is awesome. I'm the King of Egypt.'

"That's so true," Walid commented, plucking a fig from a nearby bowl. "Nothing in me has ever thought of this as a good thing, in any way at all. How could I? And, you know, by contrast, when Uncle Ali became king, he was really happy, and we all were, to the max. I've never seen so many people so excited when the news came out."

"Yeah, you're right."

"It was a huge celebration."

"I remember the feelings everybody was having, all the dancing in the street and the food and people yelling like their favorite team had just won a championship." Walid nodded his head and said, "It was wild."

Mafulla thought for a second and began to reflect. "I guess most first days as a king aren't really like that at all."

"Oh, yeah?"

"Yeah. In one way it happens, of course, battles have been fought and a lot of people have had to die for a new guy to become the king of a kingdom. And the new king, if he's a decent person at all, has got to feel pretty bad at some level about what's had to happen to make it possible, and all his friends and followers who have maybe died."

"I think you're right," Walid said. "Unless he has no empathy at all, and no sense of the value of human life."

And then Mafulla continued, "Or, and I suppose this is more common: The former king passes on and the heir, normally a member of the family, like his son or nephew or something, becomes king and, you know, is really sad, I would think. And he then takes on the new role and duties of being king with maybe a bunch of grief and uncertainty and worry and responsibility all mixed up together."

"Yeah, unless it was the heir who killed the king."

"Good point. That seems to have happened pretty often in history."

"It's bad. People get really messed up about power. And so they'll sometimes do anything to get it. Sons, daughters, wives, brothers, uncles, nephews, and friends have all killed kings just to become the king, or queen."

"You're right."

"And, in that situation, there can hardly be the sort of celebration we had when Uncle Ali retook the throne here. There's got to be a lot of anxiety around in a palace where massive intrigue and murder just happened. The killer's got to be looking over his shoulder all the time, I mean, in addition to whatever regret or at least inner conflict he should also be feeling."

"Yeah."

"Any kind of celebration at all would take place with a bunch of negative stuff in the backs of everybody's minds."

Mafulla swallowed his food, sipped more of his morning coffee, and added, "I guess, however it happens, it's usually death in some form that spurs a transition from one king to another."

Walid said, "And yet for us, it's just a totally unexplainable disappearance, a sudden vanishing, which is a really big part of what makes it so strange and, you know, extra unsettling."

"I agree. I thought we had seen strange things before—well, we have seen a lot of crazy things—but this is bizarre in a whole new way, and I'm still pretty shook up about it, even now."

"Me, too," Walid said.

Mafulla thought for a second. "I'm just glad Uncle Reela gave you the great advice about how to move forward and deal with everything."

Walid coughed and said, "Excuse me." He coughed loudly a second time and cleared his throat and said, "Wow, I swallowed wrong." He then coughed once more, loudly and forcefully.

"Are you Ok?"

"Yeah, I'm good." He croaked out the words and sipped some water.

"Well, don't even think about choking to death. Ok? I'm really not ready to take over around here. So, please, stay healthy."

Walid laughed and cleared his throat and said, "I'm Ok now." He took another drink of water and put the glass back on the table and said, "But, what you just said about Reela: You're so right. He came to the rescue, for sure. It was the perfect advice. I don't know what I would have done without it. I mean, for him and Hamid and Masoon to be serving officially as three vice-regents, basically taking care of the day-to-day stuff so I can still go to classes and just be fourteen is great. That kept all this from being a total disaster."

"Yeah."

Otherwise, I could see the headline now: Idiot Boy King Messes Up Everything."

Mafulla laughed and said, "Really." Then he added, "It's odd, but they're all doing such a good job, it's sometimes like nothing has changed."

"Yeah, you're right. It's weird. Almost every day, at some point, I sort of expect the king to come walking out of his rooms and call us over, or for Kular to tell us that he's waiting for us in his office and wants to see us."

"I have the same feeling pretty often," Mafulla said. "I really miss him, and … you know, your dad, too."

Walid mumbled, "Thanks," and grew silent, and then said, softly, "This would all be a lot easier with dad around." He looked up and saw Mafulla's expression change and said, "What? What is it?"

"What do you mean?" he responded.

"You look really strange all of a sudden, like you just felt sick or shocked or worried."

"I sort of felt a wave of something," Mafulla slowly answered. "In my gut. Something's happened."

"What?"

"I don't know. But it's got to be something really big."

"Is it bad?"

"I don't know what it is. It's just something super strange and big."

"In the past, I would have said: We need to go tell the king."

"I just did," Mafulla replied.

"Oh. Yeah."

Thousands of miles away, a clock in the distance chimed once. A man's mind rose slowly from the deep and came to a first small spark of consciousness, and then it floated with a bare thread of awareness almost untethered to his body just a moment before his eyes would spontaneously open. It was dimly dark around him and a little cold. His entire torso jerked and then shivered, almost as if by reflex.

He was on some sort of smooth hard surface that he could feel as if it was pushing into the side of his left leg and shoulder and also, though more gently, up against his back. Within three or four seconds, his eyes began to adjust to the darkness and he became aware of a faint flickering of illumination coming from somewhere. His head hurt. But then, that passed. He felt like he had just been through the longest and deepest sleep of his life, but a sleep of struggle at first, a state that was not at all restful. And yet, it apparently had been followed by something almost like a twin brother of nonexistence, a cessation of thought and being. But he had somehow, in some way just now, in this moment, re-emerged as a living, sensing, and embodied soul.

He began to move, ever so slightly, and he ached like he had been in the same position for days. Every muscle seemed to be nearly frozen in place. By sheer willpower, he started to break the inertial stiffness that had kept him, until now, from moving and falling off the narrow ledge that apparently held him up. A vision flashed into his head. He was on the edge of a platform of some sort above a bridge in fog. His body was in the same position. And as he awoke in the vision, not knowing where he was, he began to roll off the hard surface a brief moment before a fall that would most certainly mean his death. But in the middle of the roll, at the first split second of what was to be the plunge, something caught him and the vision vanished. And here he was right now. He was here, and not falling, and not dead.

It wasn't actually a ledge that he was now on, or the platform of the vision, he suddenly realized, but a bench of some sort. He groaned aloud, but softly, and struggled to sit up, grasping with his right hand the smooth, curved surface under him, moving his body slowly, and pushing against what he could now see was dark wood. He coughed twice. The muttered words, "Where am I?" hardly made it into real consonants and vowels and, as an extended sound, barely escaped his dry lips. A deep nausea came over him and passed.

He slowly and almost painfully managed to come to a sitting position, but he was still bent over with his head in his hands. Another spark of mental vision, like a bright bolt of lightning, a huge flash, tore through his brain. "Oh!" This was louder. He had no idea what had just happened. But whatever it was, it jolted him into a higher state of consciousness that came with a greater awareness. He was still not completely awake in a normal way, but more out of the dark muck of fog and confusion than he had been a second before. He put his left hand on the bench underneath him, and now his right hand, and he moved sideways with great difficulty and sat up a little straighter, squinting and trying to focus his eyes.

He wasn't on an ordinary bench, but a dark church pew, one of dozens in what must be an empty religious sanctuary of some sort. He looked around what seemed to be a fairly large silent space, and noticed that the source of the faint glow that kept the room from total darkness was up in the front of the place. He could now see three candles flickering. They were in glass candlestick holders, and were standing on a table of some sort, on what looked to be a white cloth.

The thought ran through his head, "What is this?" And then he noticed for the first time in the semi-dark his own clothing. He was wearing a dirty, torn robe of what might once have been fine cotton. Even in the dim light, it looked awful and like it, or he, had been in a bad fight, or even a battle, or that he had been wearing it for a very long time in extremely rough circumstances. There was a big rip in the right sleeve, and several short rips on the left side. There were stains of unknown origin. His hands were darkly marked and grimy looking, and they felt almost encrusted with something. There was a wound of some sort on his left hand that had healed, at least mostly. He found this curious but, strangely, not confusing. It was as if none of what he was taking in could in the least confound his expectations, because at that moment he realized that he had none at all. Apart from these nearly random sensations, his mind was mostly blank.

Nothing can seem strange if nothing seems normal. And a sense of what's normal depends on memory. The man on the pew became oddly aware at that instant that he had no feeling at all for what would or might be normal. He just took it all in, as if he had been created on the spot and these were his first seconds of life and consciousness in whatever world he was now a visitor.

"Oh, my goodness, hello." He heard a surprised voice and then a sound of footsteps coming in his direction. A man dressed in a slightly wrinkled white shirt and dark trousers was approaching him with a silver stick of some sort. As he came closer, the light glinted off the slightly tarnished surface of the item he carried, and its shape could be made out. It was a candlesnuffer, or what some would call an extinguisher. And he somehow knew that.

The three candles were still burning low up front. Then, the man again spoke.

"I'm … Robert Archdale, Reverend Archdale to my older congregants and some of my more formal neighbors, but just Bob to most."

The man on the pew looked up at him with no inner reaction at first. This unanticipated person, who seemed to have appeared from nowhere, was speaking in what touched the man as a kind, gentle tone of voice. He was not a threat. And then the voice continued.

"I'm glad to have you here in my church, even at this late hour, or I should say, this extremely early hour of the morning."

The newly awakened man was silently taking in what he was hearing. He still had not spoken or made any gesture in response. He was nearly immobile, just sitting, simply there.

"May I ask your name?"

The man then roused himself and spoke in a bit of a hoarse voice that rumbled up from deep in his throat and seemed to cut through a coating of something thick. "Sorry," he said. "What was that?"

"May I ask your name?"

"Oh. Yes. But, it seems that nothing … comes to mind."

"You don't remember your name?"

"No, it … appears that I … don't."

"Oh."

"At least, not at the moment. I'm … a bit blank."

The minister took a step closer and looked the man over as well as he could in the dim light. "Have you had a problem, or have you been in an accident of some sort?"

"I'm … not sure." The stranger looked from the minister's face, back down to his own arms, and then again up to meet the reverend's concerned gaze. "It seems like I might have been. I just woke up."

"Would you mind if I turn on some lights? I'd like to get a better look at you and make sure you're Ok, that you haven't been badly injured in some way."

"That would be fine," the man said. "I appreciate your concern."

Reverend Archdale walked briskly up the rest of the aisle and to the door in the back of the room, which may have been at the front of the building itself, and he first checked the door, shaking the handle and its mechanism. It was locked up tight, as he had left it many hours earlier, before he had retreated into his study for his nightly time of reading and reflection. He then flipped on the light switch next to the doorframe, and several bulbs came alive throughout the space, offering much more illumination, but still not the brightness that might have been expected.

In the new light, it was clear that the room wasn't nearly as big as it had seemed earlier. It looked old but well kept, and had a subdued combination of tan painted walls and dark wood trim. It even smelled old, but not unpleasantly bad. From the faint aromas in the air, the man could tell that many candles had been burned here before. A scent took the edge off the age of the place.

"Let me look at you more closely, my friend." The minister was back already and bending over now to scrutinize his unexpected guest. The man sat still and quiet, allowing a careful visual examination for several seconds.

"Oh, my. Yes, I see. It does seem as if you may have experienced some form of great difficulty. Do you remember how you got into the church?"

"Not at all. I just came to consciousness a few minutes ago, as if from a deep sleep. My body was stiff. It felt like I'd been here a long time."

"I see. It could be that someone brought you here for help. But the only door on this side of the building had been locked for the night, many hours ago, and it's locked now. I think all the other doors are also locked. It's a bit of a mystery."

"I wish I had answers for your sensible questions."

"No, no. That's perfectly fine," Archdale said. He pondered all this for a moment and then gently sat down on the pew a few feet from his visitor and said, "Please forgive my prying, but you have a distinctive accent of some sort."

"Yes?"

"I don't think I've ever quite heard it before."

"That might have been a useful clue for us, if you had heard it in the past, I would think."

"Yes, it might have been, indeed. As it is, we have a bit of a puzzle on our hands, it seems, and any clue could help. Tell me, if you don't mind, anything you can remember—anything at all."

A kaleidoscope of images flew through the man's inner vision, but so quickly that he couldn't grab one long enough to see what it was. "A tumble of things, of scenes, and maybe people come to mind," he said, "but nothing I can recognize or remember distinctly or label with words." His mouth felt very dry.

"No worries. It will come."

"I seem to be terribly thirsty. Do you have any cool water?"

"Oh, yes, indeed. Let me fetch you something." The minister got up quickly and walked over to a front corner of the room. "Just a second," he said and disappeared through a door.

Within a minute or so, although the man on the pew had no sense of the passage of time at this point, the reverend was back, with a glass in his hand, and he offered his visitor the water. "Here, drink as much as you need. There's plenty more. It's on the house."

"What? Oh." The man at first sipped gently, and then drank more.

"I hope that helps."

"Thank you. Yes. It does, a lot." The man looked at Archdale and said, "You have a distinctive accent, also, it seems to me."

"Well, that's what everyone here keeps telling me. But I prefer to think that they're the ones with the accents. They just can't seem to acknowledge it. I don't know if it's stubbornness, or perhaps overweening pride—the devil's cologne, I like to call it. Either can prevent a proper self-knowledge." Archdale said this with a little shadow of a smile playing on his face. Then he added, "I'm from North Carolina, which is pretty far from here."

"In the United States?"

"Yes."

"And we … right now … are we also in the States?"

"Yes, in New York City, in the state of New York."

"Really? This is true?"

"I wouldn't joke about a thing like that."

"What am I doing in New York City?"

"That's a question I ask myself at least once a week." Archdale paused and then said, "Look, would you like to get cleaned up?"

"What?"

"I have a small apartment in the back of the church. It's where I live, and if you'd like, you could bathe and change clothes. I think I can find something in your size, or close enough. It will be better, at least, than what you have on now. I mean this in terms of condition, not fashion. We collect clothing and other necessities for those in the surrounding area who have little of their own."

"Oh. Certainly, yes, that would be very kind of you. I'd love to wash up and perhaps wash away the thick coating of amnesia that seems to be clogging my brain at the moment."

"It couldn't hurt to try a bath, then. Insights have been known to be attracted by water," Archdale replied, and smiled.

"Perhaps, like Archimedes in the bath, I'll have a Eureka Moment," the stranger said with a slight smile himself.

Archdale thought to himself that this man knows the story of an ancient Greek mathematician and words like 'amnesia' and seems quite intelligent, despite his addled, scruffy appearance, and his obvious memory issues. He then said aloud, "Come, I'll show you where you can clean up, and maybe that will help. Unless you think you need to see a doctor first."

"No. Thank you. I feel no such need."

"You could have had a knock on the head."

"There's ... no pain right now."

"You're sure?"

"Yes."

"Well, if you do decide you'd like to be checked out, I can help with that. It's a bit past one in the morning, or likely one-thirty by now, but there's a hospital not too far away, and a member of the congregation works there. He lives only a couple of blocks from here. We could easily wake him, I think, and with his help get you examined within the hour, I would guess."

"No, no, that won't be necessary. But, I do thank you. I think I'll be fine—whoever I am, and whatever counts in this situation as fine." And with those words, he slowly stood up with a groan and steadied himself with a hand on the back of the pew in front of him.

2

A Clue

"Uncle Leem, you have a serious worry frown on your face." Ibrahim Hadad had walked into the front room of their home and noticed that his favorite senior detective was reading the morning newspaper with an intense focus and an almost sour expression. "What's the matter?"

"Oh, it's just some world events far away, things I wish were even farther."

"What's happening not quite far enough away?"

Leem sighed and said, "It's Germany. That Hitler's a disaster. He's going to create a big catastrophe. I can just feel it."

"Ok. I've read something about him. He's their leader now, right?"

"Yes, unfortunately, and the evidence is that he's a very bad man, completely power hungry, and already keen on shooting people who disagree with him."

"Oh, my. That's awful."

"Yes. I have a troubled sense about the future of the whole mess going on there."

Ibrahim said, "Why? I don't know much about it."

Leem folded the paper, put it down, and replied, "I'm afraid that this one man, Adolf Hitler, is determined to act out a very dangerous kind of craziness on the biggest world stage, to satisfy his own warped emotional needs, and that at some point, it will eventually have damaging effects on us in North Africa, and around the world."

"Why do the Germans have a man like that in charge in the first place?" Ibrahim sat down in the chair opposite his uncle.

"They're a highly intelligent and educated nation, good and strong in many ways, but they've just been through some hard economic times and they've experienced a sense of national shame, or even of deep humiliation, following the big war. Some say that Hitler's a strangely charismatic type who has people almost hypnotized with wild claims and outrageous promises that they're desperate to hear. When he speaks in public, apparently the response to him is pandemonium. He touches all the right buttons in people's emotions—or, at least, in enough people to cause a real problem."

"That's unfortunate."

"Yes, and this is sadly the way it often goes in politics. People who seek power learn to say what others want to hear. And the masses allow themselves to be led along, listening and seeing what's in front of them quite selectively. They blind themselves to the true nature of the one who's constantly and expertly manipulating their feelings. And there's always some sort of disaster that results."

"I guess that's why King Ali was always working so hard to educate people to see through guys like that," Ibrahim said.

"Yes, his goal from the start was to move us in the direction of true democratic governance, and that requires an educated electorate composed of citizens who can exercise sound judgment. Otherwise, people fall for the claims of passionate demagogues like Hitler."

"What's a demagogue?" Ben had just walked into the room and heard the tail end of what Leem had been saying.

"Oh, good morning, my boy. We were just talking about world politics. A demagogue is a bad leader, a person who wants to run a nation for the sake of his own power, and who manipulates and deceives others to get his way. He often creates terrible trouble for everyone."

"Oh. That sounds bad."

"Yes. A demagogue is always bad."

"So, who's the leader you're talking about?"

"He's a man named Hitler, Adolf Hitler, and he's in the country of Germany, a very long way from us here in Egypt."

"Good. I'm glad he's not around here." Ben walked up to the table and said, "I'm hungry."

"Oh, yes, of course you are. I've eaten already, a little earlier. There's bread and jam and some fruit that's still out. You and Ibrahim grab something, and we'll get you off to school in just a bit."

A few miles away, Walid and Mafulla's good friend and classmate Haji Afah had just walked up to the front door of Khata El-Noor's home. His heart was beating faster than normal. The Silver Sabre was in a state of high anxiety, far outside his sphere of comfort. And he was a little unsure of what he was planning to do. So, he hesitated and just stood there for a few moments. Some simple but beautiful piano music was coming from somewhere inside. A small dog a few houses away started barking. Haji's mouth suddenly felt dry and a wave of something like dizziness shot through his head. He said to himself, in the quiet of his own mind, "Come on. Come on! This should be easy." He took a deep breath and knocked on the door.

No one came. After a very long fifteen seconds, he knocked again, this time, louder. Within maybe ten seconds more, the door opened, and Rama El-Noor broke into a big smile. "Haji! What a nice surprise! It's so good to see you! What can I do for you on this fine morning?"

"Hi, Madame El-Noor, it's good to see you, too." Haji's heart jumped up and banged on his rib cage several times. He throat seemed to tighten up. This was much worse that confronting bad guys with guns. He took a deep breath and said, "I was just walking to school and thought maybe I'd come by and see if, you know, your daughter Khata might like to walk along with me—I mean, just this morning. We could talk about some school stuff."

Rama continued to smile, knowing that their house wasn't exactly on the most direct route for Haji to take to the palace school, and also that he usually walked with his nearly constant companion, Malik. "Come in and I'll let Khata know you're here. Her friend Ara is with her in the music room. They usually walk to school together."

"Oh," Haji said, feeling suddenly very disappointed.

"But I'm sure they'd love to have your company."

"You … think so?"

"Yes, I'm certain of it. Come on in."

Just as Haji stepped through the doorway, Khata and Ara came bounding into view inside, with their book bags slung over their shoulders. "Haji!" Khata exclaimed. "What are you doing here?"

Rama interjected, before he could respond, "He was just passing by and thought he'd check in to see if anyone wants to walk to school with him. And I'd say he'd be an ideal morning escort, if you ask me."

"Yeah, we'd love to have you as our companion," Khata said.

"Sure," Ara chimed in enthusiastically, and then shot a quick glance over toward Khata. She then looked back at Haji and said, "Actually, I'd like to ask your opinion on something we talked about in class yesterday."

"Oh?" Haji responded.

"Yeah, but we can talk about it on the way."

"Ok."

Khata leaned over to her mother and gave her a kiss on the cheek and said, "Alrighty then, we're off, all three of us!"

"Have a great day in class!"

"Thanks, Mom."

"Yeah, thanks, Rama," Ara said with a big smile.

Khata said, "We'll see you later."

"Yeah, see you later, sometime," Haji said, a bit sheepishly.

After calling out a couple of reminders to the girls, Rama stood at the door and watched the three students walk toward the street and then turn in the direction of their daily trek to school. She smiled inwardly and said in a low voice, "Well, well."

Not so far from there, in the palace, Walid and Mafulla made their way down the hallway to the office where the new but probably temporary king could quickly sign those papers Kular had mentioned. Then, they would have a little time before class to kick a ball around outside. When they got to the doorway, they could see that Masoon was already inside, sitting at the desk, writing.

"Oh, hello, Your Majesty," Masoon said the moment he noticed them, and he quickly stood up in order to bow slightly to Walid. "Good morning, Mafulla."

"Hi Masoon," Mafulla said.

Walid added, "Please, don't get up. Sit and continue what you're doing. We're just here for a minute so I can sign some papers."

"Take the desk," Masoon suggested.

"No, that won't be necessary," Walid replied. "I'll just pull up the chair on this side and grab the papers. I think I only have to sign my name four times, maybe five."

"As you wish, Majesty," Masoon said and waited for Walid to sit before he took his own seat again.

Walid then said, "Mafulla, could you get the door? The three of us need a minute."

"Sure," he replied, and then added, "Your Majesty." In the old days, Mafulla would have used that phrase for Walid only with a certain mirth, or friendly irony, or clear Mafoolery in his tone. But after the events of the recent past, he could speak it now in true seriousness. He closed the door behind him, and then sat in one of the other available chairs, facing Masoon at an angle. The top general looked up expectantly at the two of them and then focused on the king.

"I have something to ask you," Walid said.

"Certainly. Anything."

"Ok, I think I know what you'll say, but I'm going to pose you with a possibility anyway, to get your opinion, which you know I value very highly. It's something that's been weighing on my mind."

"You're getting my curiosity up," Masoon said.

"Well, you know our history as masked crime fighters around town."

"Yes."

"We've had quite a run as The Golden Viper and Windstorm."

"One word, of course," Mafulla added.

"What?"

"Windstorm—one word."

"Yes. One word," Masoon acknowledged, and added, "The newspaper can't reliably seem to get it right."

"Sad but true," Mafulla said.

"So, we've had lots of crime fighter adventures in the past, but of course, our situation has just changed considerably," Walid added.

"Indeed."

"Yes. Well. I'm planning on having a talk this afternoon with Haji and Malik about the whole thing."

Masoon sat quietly, listening, and nodded his head slightly.

Walid continued, "And, I think—but I really want your view on this, your totally honest opinion—I think that maybe, somehow, this thing is supposed to continue, just now and then … the masked crime fighting, I mean."

"You do?"

"Yes."

"You mean, for Malik and Haji."

"Well, yes, for them, but … also for us, as well."

"For you?"

"Yeah. And I wanted to know how you would feel about that."

"Oh. I see. Well, this is … surprising … quite unexpected, on one level," Masoon said. "With your being now … the King of Egypt, of course, the ruler of one of the most ancient and important nations on earth, and with there existing no precedent in all of human history, as far as I know, for the sovereign leaders of major countries who live and work under the scrutiny of the entire globe to put on masks and run around with their friends for the purpose of stopping thugs and petty thieves from plying their trade on the city streets of their capital, I would have to give you the opinion that, by now, you might have come to expect from me."

"Ok, ok, when you describe it like that," Walid replied, completely embarrassed that he had even brought it up.

"Actually," Masoon said, "I think it's not a bad idea at all."

"What?" Both boys said this at the same time.

"If you feel that you should do it, you'll have my wholehearted, and of course, clandestine, support."

Walid's mouth actually fell open. "Ok, this is not at all what I had anticipated."

Mafulla said. "I need to sit down."

"You are sitting down," Walid pointed out.

"Oh, yeah."

"You ... really, think this is Ok?" Walid said in a voice of great hesitation.

"Yes. I do."

"Could I ask ... why?"

"Sure. And I'm a bit surprised that you're so surprised. You know who I am. And I know who you are. I know your training and your powers, at least those that have been developed to this point. I know that you would never do such a thing at present, and in the near future, except in the company of a fellow Phi."

"That's true," Walid said.

"And I understand how this, in the past, has gotten you out of the palace, around the city, and among the people."

"Also true."

"I think Ali has always secretly wanted to join you in these wild adventures, but his age and commitments and stature in the kingdom, not to mention the fact that he's been, from day one, so recognizable—all these things would have made it much more difficult for him than it has been for the two of you."

"I always thought the king would be great at it," Mafulla said. "We'd be total amateurs compared to him."

"I sort of wondered about that, from time to time," Walid admitted.

"You imagined the king joining in?"

"Yeah. He did seem to enjoy hearing about our escapades, although he used to caution us pretty often about being careful."

"I know he did," Masoon replied. "And from what I've seen over time, you've indeed become more cautious and more skilled in what you've done while masked."

"Yeah, we've gotten better at it," Mafulla said. And then he asked their mutual trainer, "Why haven't you ever done something like this?"

Masoon smiled and said, "When I was young, I suppose I had my own version. But I lived in smaller villages, as you know, and there were no sand masks or secret identity names back then, which, in a way, is too bad. But then, in another sense, in a little village, such things could never have worked. And yet, I still managed to do some good deeds, and stop some bad characters—and now and then, even anonymously."

"Well, why didn't you continue?" Mafulla asked.

"I think it's something like a developmental stage, almost like a part of your Phi training that you take on yourself, to put into action what you're learning to do, along with what you're realizing about yourself. You act as you have and as I did in order to make your first efforts toward physically assisting others in a way that only a trained Phi can. But then, as you grow older, you eventually come to use your talents in other ways and you know that the younger generation will likely be out on the streets, doing their part to keep people safe. It's a changing of the guard. It's the normal flow of life."

"That makes sense," Walid said.

"I know you've learned a lot about people and situations while doing this," Masoon said.

'We have," Mafulla agreed.

Masoon continued. "As you've moved around the city, and gone into action now and then, you'd grown and matured, and you've brought away knowledge about how people live and what they struggle with that will help you now and in the future. A king should understand his people. So should a prince. And even a duke, or earl, or whatever."

Mafulla smiled and glanced over at Walid and said, "That seems right." He thought for a second and looked back at Masoon and said, "But maybe now that Walid's the king, he should be a little more careful and let me be the heavy muscle of the outfit." And of course, as he said this, he did a little pose, flexing his right arm, which was not nearly as skinny and funny looking as it once had been, but was actually pretty impressive at this point. Still, the other two laughed at his silliness, as he had hoped they would.

"You guys are a good audience," he said. And he added, "Feel free to leave a little extra when you pay on the way out." They both shook their heads, as he added, "Hey, remember, I've got a very hungry mouth to feed."

"Meeting over," Walid said.

"Just be extra careful now, Your Majesty," Masoon counseled. "That's what Ali would tell you if he were here to advise you."

"I will. Thanks, Masoon."

Mafulla looked at Walid and said, "Good thing you have such an awesome bodyguard." And with those words, he did his famous double-eyebrow jump.

"Yes, it is, but I can't be with him all the time," Masoon said, with a serious expression.

"Ha!" Mafulla said. "Very funny. You stepped on my joke and squashed it."

"It's good that we can still goof around and laugh, I mean, after everything that's happened," Walid said.

"Yeah," Mafulla agreed.

"It's because of who you are and what you know," Masoon commented.

In his small New York City apartment at the back of the church, Bob Archdale sat at the kitchen table under a dim light, reading his New Testament, in the book of Galatians, as he waited for his guest. At that moment, the man came out of the bathroom, looking much better and wearing the rumpled khaki trousers and slightly creased white cotton dress shirt that Archdale had given him. But he was still barefoot.

"Oh. You look good," Archdale said. "How do you feel?"

"So much better, there are no words for it," the man replied. "Thank you for the hot bath and these clean clothes."

"I'm glad to do it," he said. "Did you discover any evidence of injury, any cuts or bruises or pain spots?"

"No, none at all."

"Good." Archdale paused and glanced down at the man's feet. "I forgot to give you shoes."

"Not a problem."

"No, no, I'll have something here. Any follower of Jesus who doesn't have a pair of sandals around, at least, is seriously slacking off."

The mystery guest smiled. "Anything will be fine."

Bob excused himself for about half a minute and came back into the room with a simple pair of dark reddish brown leather sandals that looked like they might fit perfectly. He handed them to his guest. "We're about the same foot size, I think."

"Yes. So it seems." The man took them, slipped them on, and said, "Thank you again. I'm just sorry to have kept you up so late."

"Oh, no, think nothing of it. I often stay up late to read."

"What are you reading?"

"I was just now engrossed in the New Testament, the book of Galatians, chapter four. Are you a spiritual man, my friend?"

"Yes, I am," the stranger answered.

"Oh, well, that's nice to know, and it's also our first piece of real information about you that goes beyond your appearance."

"Indeed," the man said. "You snuck up on me with your question, and the answer just came out, as if I knew my own history."

"This is progress," the minister replied. "Let me ask you something else, Mister—Oh, I'm sorry, your name has slipped my mind."

The stranger laughed and said, "Good try. Very good, but still, nothing leaps out in that regard. Yet, there actually was a name earlier."

"What do you mean?"

"There was a name that came into my head while I was bathing and my mind was otherwise blank, at total rest."

"What was the name?"

"Santiago."

"Like the city in South America?"

"Yes. Wait, how would I know that? That's a second piece of information to pop out of a mind otherwise operating under what seems to be a total freeze of remembrance."

"Excellent. Of course, your linguistic memory seems completely intact. You're using language well."

"That's true. And it's interesting."

"And in our conversation earlier, you remembered the old story about Archimedes and the bath. But much else may be blank. And yet, now, we already have more to go on. You know some history and a bit of world geography."

"Yes."

"They say that even in serious cases of amnesia, or memory loss, access to the most commonly used information like language may yet remain, stored in a different way in the brain."

"I see."

"So, do you think you're from Santiago, Chile, or that Santiago might be your name?"

"I have no idea."

"Still, it's progress."

"Yes, it is, however minor."

Archdale gestured to the chair across from him. The stranger nodded and pulled it away from the table and sat down. He looked at the book that was open in front of him, facing his host. "Would you tell me more about your reading?"

"Sure. It's one of the letters in the New Testament traditionally ascribed to the Apostle Paul, the Letter to the Galatians, or to the people in a group of churches located in Galatia, which scholars think was somewhere in central Asia Minor, an area long before settled by Celtic people who retained many of the features of their original culture and language, even in Paul's day. But I'm going on too much."

"No, no, it's interesting. What passage were you most recently reading, in particular?"

"Oh, actually, when you came in, I had just read one of my favorite verses: 'When the time had fully come, God sent forth his Son.' I love that concept: When the time had fully come. The original Greek phrase, if I remember correctly, was used in those days to refer to a period of ripeness, or to the moment when a pregnant woman was ready to give birth to her child."

"Oh? I suppose that is a moment of fullness or completion, when things are just right and something important is about to happen."

"Yes, and what I love so much about the phrase is that it represents things as having a proper time, maybe even a perfect time. We grow impatient, or despairing, wanting something ahead of its time. We can't wait. We stress ourselves over it. We push. We seek to force things. Or, in the opposite direction, we find ourselves totally surprised and unprepared for something whose ideal time has snuck up on us and caught us off guard. Things are ready, but we aren't. We think we need more time. We say to ourselves or to others, 'No, not yet!' and because of that, we may not be able to react well and take advantage of the opportunity being presented."

"Yes. That's common, in either direction, as you say, to be out of synch with the grand, unfolding progression of things."

"Oh, I see I have a fellow philosopher on my hands. It's another clue. Good. I could use someone to talk with about such matters. And maybe the time has fully come for that. I believe that it's one of our challenges in life to be sensitive to when things are ripe, when the proper moment for something has arrived."

"That's a very sensible perspective, and wise."

"So, when the time had fully come, the author says, God sent forth his Son—no sooner, and no later, than the perfect time. And, for Christians, this is an important claim. But for everyone, perhaps, there is a broader perspective here that can be endorsed."

"I see, and I completely agree," the stranger said.

"I'm not surprised."

The minister's guest then said, "Things happen when they should happen. And if we can be properly poised and ready, we can take advantage of the perhaps unique opportunities they then present to us, chances that might never, in the same form, come again."

"Indeed. And maybe, just maybe, your being here in my church, mysteriously asleep on a pew this very evening, or early this morning, is one of those things that has happened exactly when it should."

"Do you think so?"

"Yes. I do. Just don't insist that I give you an adequate reason for that conviction. I have an intuition, but not an explanation."

"We'll simply allow that intuition to stand and do our best to live up to it." The man in khakis smiled again and added, "We just need to figure out what exactly has happened in such an odd way, and why."

"That's correct. That's our key mystery to solve, I suppose."

"In addition to the basic matter of who I am."

"Yes, in addition to that."

"I know this may sound strange," the visitor said, "but even though I apparently just woke up from a long time of sleep, or at least some form of deep unconsciousness, I feel very tired. Where do you think I might sleep for a few hours? Is there a place nearby?"

"There's a place right here, out back. The church has a small detached cottage—tiny, actually, where our caretaker used to live."

"Where's the caretaker now?"

"He moved away to be with family, and we've been too poor as a church to replace him with anyone skilled enough to be of help to us."

"I see."

"So, if you'd like, you can feel free to use the empty rooms."

"That would be very kind of you."

"The place is really small. So measure the kindness accordingly."

The stranger smiled again. "The biggest need I have right now may easily be met by a place that's small. And I'd prefer to measure the kindness by the size of the need it meets.""

"All right, then, my good man. Let me find you the key."

"As long as it's no trouble."

"None at all." Archdale got up, opened a drawer in a kitchen cabinet, rummaged around a bit and said, "Yes. There it is."

He walked over to his guest, presented him the key, and said, "I think all the bed covers you need will be there in the cottage, in a closet. It's just out that door, and straight ahead toward the back of the grounds, not many feet away. You'll see it. There's a stone path. The key unlocks the door."

"Thank you, my friend."

"You're welcome. Now, despite the hour, I should be up by eight or eight-thirty and back here in the kitchen for breakfast. I'll also be doing some early reading and study. Whenever it's good for you, please come and join me. You can start the day with some hot food."

"That sounds nice, and very hospitable of you," the stranger said, and he made his way to the door.

"We'll solve your mystery, my friend."

"I hope so."

"Until tomorrow, and ... until I have another name for you, I'll say goodnight for now, Mr. Santiago."

The man smiled and, with a quizzical look on his face, said, "Goodnight."

3

Obsession

Khalid was sitting on the edge of his desk. The session had been especially satisfying today. For the past hour, the boys had enjoyed a lively discussion of their latest assignment. Now, their teacher wanted to make a general point about a number of the readings they had been assigned recently and had talked about in class.

He said, "Ok, look. Allow me a bit of transition: Let's think about some of the books we've read in the past few months, some of the old and new classics of the western world, especially, that we've examined. There's a theme that comes up again and again, it seems, a very important theme." He then paused dramatically, and looked at each of the boys, whose expressions ranged at the moment from curiosity to perplexity to, in at least one case, complete blankness.

"What's the theme?" Set asked.

Khalid raised one eyebrow and pursed his lips and waited about five seconds longer, just to stretch out the pedagogical moment. And then he said, simply, "Obsession."

Mafulla was always ready for an opportunity such as this. He instantly commented, "Good. I really want to hear about this. It's … something I can't stop thinking about, no matter how hard I try. I mull it over day and night. It's really the theme of all themes, don't you think? I can certainly never get enough of it as a topic—never!"

"Ok," Khalid said.

But Mafulla had to go on, "No, no. Really. It's just that I happen to be oddly fixated on this particular idea, this concept of concepts, and, you know, I have to admit that I'm totally fascinated by it, maybe even a little bit addicted to pondering it, night and day. It never gets old to me. You might even say that, on this subject, at least, if not others, I'm genuinely and totally …"

"Silly to the point of absurdity." Walid cut off the obvious culmination they could all see coming, and finished his sentence for him, eliciting a few chuckles and nods from around the class as a result.

"All right, Mafulla, we get it, and thank you, Walid," Khalid said, with an almost exasperated half-smile, as a couple of the other boys grinned at the dependable Mafoolery. Then their teacher went on, "It's indeed an important and fascinating topic. Think about it. In the ancient Epic of Gilgamesh, what was King Gilgamesh obsessed with? Jabari?"

"The ladies!" That got a few laughs from around the room.

"True, but what else?"

"Himself?" Jabari replied.

"Yes, and … meaning what?"

"He was sort of obsessed with his own interests, with getting his way, with whatever he wanted. And he also seemed obsessed with his superiority to other people—you know, with being special and different in his physical strength and appearance, and in his position as king. And he was obsessed with what all that could get for him."

"Very good. Anything else?"

"Well," Walid said, "I remember that when Enkidu, his new best friend the gods had sent, suddenly died, Gilgamesh got pretty obsessed with the reality of death, and the possibility of immortality."

"Correct. And that obsession drove the rest of the story." Khalid paused for a moment again, and said, "So, how about the great warrior, Beowulf?"

Malik responded, "He was maybe obsessed with his own power and skill as a warrior, with his ability to do impossible looking things all by himself, and, likely, I'm guessing, with his reputation and status in the eyes of others. The whole glory and honor thing."

"Excellent insight," Khalid replied. "What about Don Quixote?"

Bafur raised his hand and when Khalid looked his way, he answered, "Don Quixote was obsessed with, I guess, a fantasy lifestyle of great and exciting exploits that he had read about in lots of books."

"That's right. Now, Haji, how about Victor Frankenstein?"

Haji hesitated for a second to think, and then said, "Um. He was certainly obsessed with his dream of creating a human life, through his knowledge of science."

"And probably," Malik added, "like Beowulf, I'm thinking, he was equally obsessed with what he imagined would be his reputation or great fame if he succeeded with that goal."

"Good. Very good! What about Captain Ahab, in Melville's big story Moby Dick?"

Jabari said, "I think Melville himself was obsessed with whales and whale blubber."

"You may have a point, there," Khalid said, "but what about the character, Ahab?"

Set said, "He was totally obsessed with an adversary, one enemy, the great white whale, and in particular, he was obsessed with revenge."

"That's right. Now, let me ask a different question." Khalid looked from face to face around the room and said, "What do we learn about obsession from these stories?"

"It … always leads to problems," Jabari said.

"Yes. It always leads to problems. And, what else?"

"Gee, this is weird," Walid paused and ventured to say, "It

sometimes can strangely lead to transformation, and even to some form of genuine greatness."

"For example?" Khalid asked.

"In the Gilgamesh story, the obsession with death and immortality ends up transforming this guy who had been a totally self-absorbed and out-of-control leader and, as a result, he begins to see his life in a new perspective. And he becomes a great builder for his people, actually concerned with the city and the welfare of his subjects, in addition to his own."

"Yes." Their teacher let this sink in for maybe five seconds and then said, "So, what does this show us about obsession?"

"It can be good or bad?" Mafulla answered.

"It's dangerous," Jabari added, "but it can sometimes spur people on to amazing stuff, and huge accomplishments."

Khalid nodded and said, "Obsession can be, in a sense, an extreme form of interest, and a strong, intensely focused version of value-recognition, or value-attribution, as well as of appreciation, direction, commitment, determination, and persistence. It's a huge source of ongoing motivation."

"Value-attribution?" Jabari said. "What do you mean by that?"

"Well, let me answer by contrast. Value-recognition is seeing or recognizing something's importance. Value-attribution is deeming something to be important, or even conferring importance on it by your thoughts, feelings, attitudes, and actions."

"Oh, Ok, I get it. The obsessed person does either to an extreme."

"Yes, and as a result, that mindset can fuel difficult achievements. If you set a goal and attribute to it great value, and to some extent you're even obsessed with attaining it, that can often motivate you to overcome extreme challenges, and persist through almost anything."

Set quickly said, "And it can also demotivate you from anything else, from anything other than the obsessed focus."

"Say more on this."

"It can create a blind, monomaniacal way of thinking, oblivious to needs like balance and to the wide range of values represented by things and people in the world around us that fall outside the narrow borders of the obsession."

"Exactly. Yes. And because of that, obsession can be a dangerous and powerful friend, on occasion, or an outright enemy—depending on the degree of its intensity, its precise role in your life, and the way it affects your proper needs." He paused for a moment and then said, "Consider this. In art and sport, and occasionally in politics and business, we sometimes use the phrase 'a magnificent obsession' to identify what was behind an extraordinary feat of accomplishment that was otherwise seemingly impossible until it happened, and perhaps still a little so, even then."

"Interesting," Malik said.

But Khalid wasn't finished. He said, "Now, let me ask you this: What's the difference between obsession with a person and loyalty to that person?"

"Well," Set answered, "among other things, loyalty is a virtue, and a virtue is always good to have, in any circumstances."

"Is loyalty always good, in absolutely any circumstances?" Khalid asked.

"Sure, isn't it?"

"What about loyalty to the wrong person, or to the wrong cause, or for the wrong reason, in the wrong circumstances, or to a wrong degree?"

"Oh, wow, you sound like Aristotle talking about anger. He asked those same sorts of questions."

"Yes."

"Can you say more?"

"Sure. Aristotle, in the discussion you refer to, was trying to show that there are situations in which anger can be healthy or useful, and others in which it's bad and harmful, and that deciding which it is in a particular case requires answering exactly such questions. This is the challenge of wisdom. In parallel, I'm suggesting here that there are situations in which loyalty is misplaced, or unhealthy, as well as, of course, the obvious times and circumstances when it's good."

Set's face showed intense concentration. He said, "Ok, so loyalty is sometimes unhealthy and obsession is often unhealthy. But also, they're just different things, right?"

"Yeah, they're different," Mafulla replied. "Loyalty is faithfulness, or fidelity to a person or a group or a nation or a cause; but obsession is mostly just about fixation and narrowness," he offered.

Khalid asked, "Could you be obsessed with a person but not loyal to that person?"

Set said, "Maybe. I mean, sure, since they're just different things. You could be obsessed with a person and do stuff that scratched your own itch, because of the obsession, despite it's being bad for the object of your obsession. Loyalty means acting, or at least trying to act, in the interests of the person or cause or nation you're loyal to."

"That's right," Khalid said.

Set continued, "And it can certainly go the other way around. You can be loyal to a person or cause without being in any way obsessed."

"Yeah," Jabari said, "There's a big difference between the interest and support that's always part of loyalty, and just some out of control crazy intense focus."

"Why did you even ask about these two things?" Set wondered. "I mean, if loyalty and obsession are so different."

"Because obsession can sometimes look like loyalty, but it's different. It can occasionally appear to be a normal yet strong commitment, but it goes way beyond that. It can be dressed up as an extreme form of consistency, but it's not that, either. And I wanted you boys to know this, because obsession sometimes gets disguised or masked by other things, and confused with them, and even excused by them, but it's different. It's distinctive. And it can be very dangerous."

Bafur had his hand up. "Yes, sir," Khalid said, nodding at him.

"Why is it a theme in so many of these classic western books?"

"Maybe because it's so common in life," Haji ventured.

"But is it really that common?" Malik turned and asked his

friend, as well as the class. "I mean, how many truly obsessed people do we know?"

"I'm obsessed with good food," Bafur said and got some laughs.

"Walid's obviously obsessed with Kissa," Mafulla said, and got even more.

"Hey, remember what Khalid said. It could be a path to greatness," Walid answered, and got a laugh and a quick thumbs-up from Malik.

"Yeah, but it's a path to greatness that's filled with danger," Jabari intoned, and he looked at the class in general, going from face to face. "I mean, first you're harmlessly obsessed with a wonderful young lady, and then, boom, you're married. And before you know it, you're doing boring kid jobs again like taking out the trash and washing the dog. Soon, you end up with a new obsession: finding some way to get out of the house and go see your buddies." Then he looked back at Walid and grimaced and said, "Just kidding—sort of," and wiggled his ears for anyone who was looking.

"Food for thought," Walid said, with a smile.

Bafur sighed. "One more mention of food and I'll have to excuse myself."

"Seriously, though," Walid commented, "it is dangerous."

"Food? Maybe so, but I'll bravely take my chances," Bafur replied.

"No, obsession, my friendly gourmand." Walid said."

"Oh, 'gourmand'—that's impressive," Mafulla commented.

"Yeah, it is. Most people don't know the concept at all." Bafur was certainly impressed.

Walid smiled, and then he grew serious and thought for a few seconds and said, quietly, "You know, the guy Santiago, the guy who gave us all such trouble, was totally obsessed." He looked at Khalid.

That got everyone quiet. And Khalid responded, "Yes, Juan Osvaldo Santiago was apparently quite obsessed with acquiring power—more and more power."

"And look where that ended," Haji remarked.

"Yeah, with his own destruction, apparently," Mafulla commented, and then added, "Or at least his sudden removal from the scene of his obsessed pursuit."

"But, he did die, right?" Bafur asked. "That's what my dad said, and that's what the newspaper reported."

"Well, maybe, yeah, we sure think so," Walid answered.

"But, there was no dead body at the scene?" Bafur asked.

"No, there was no body, no corpse."

"I just don't get it."

Walid looked over at his teacher, and he nodded ever so slightly. So he said to Bafur, "It was actually a pretty complicated set of circumstances, very complex and strange. And the senior people who were on the scene, or who quickly arrived, judged it to be a situation where the guy was, most likely, dead and gone, removed from the palace and our world. I was, unfortunately, sort of in the middle of it, and that's what I thought, too. But the man had apparently suffered such a tremendous and unusually devastating type or level of injury that there was no physical body left for us to see and examine to absolutely confirm his death—you know, like if he had been completely blown to bits by a hugely powerful bomb or totally eaten by some gigantic wild lion or something. He was just done away with, according to all the senior people like Masoon who were sort of more acquainted with what had happened. Dead and gone."

"And the king was … just gone?"

"Yeah," Walid said.

"And not dead. Just gone."

"Not dead, and temporarily gone, at least, for now—from what we can tell. But there are some big mysteries yet to be solved, for sure. There are things yet to be revealed."

Mafulla noted his friend's words with a split second of serious regard, and then added, "We're all hoping these mysteries can be cleared up soon, but we're trying not to be … you know, obsessed about it all."

Throughout the room there was an unspoken appreciation for how Mafulla's cleverness could sometimes work to bring things back to where they should be. His little remark acted as something like a turnaround to get their minds once again on what they had been talking about.

And at this point, Set wanted a bit more general understanding of the issue that Khalid had brought up. He said, "One more thing, please: I want to get clear on this. How does this mental state of obsession, the thing that's sometimes responsible for forms of high development and maybe even greatness in some people, also lead to terrible harm or even self-destruction in other people? How can one thing have such different effects for different people?"

"That's a good question. But, actually, it can lead to both results in the same person, in the same life," Khalid explained. Then he thought for a second, and said, "The fierce focus of obsession that can allow for almost superhuman results in one thing can obliterate from people's minds many other things that they need to consider in order to keep their lives healthy and balanced and viable."

"Obsession can distort things terribly," Walid then suggested. "The person who has an obsession can end up living in a world of fantasy that gets him completely out of step with reality, and sets him up for terrible consequences that he can't see coming."

"Yes, and we're all vulnerable to that, to at least some degree. That's possibly why it's highlighted by many great authors as something we should be wary of, and extremely cautious with," Khalid said. "It comes in many forms, and disguised as many other things, but it's always dangerous."

He let this thought resonate for a moment and then said, "Notice that all the books we've mentioned were about men who thought of themselves, and wanted to think of themselves, as important."

"That's really true," Malik said in a tone that showed he found this insight to be deep and meaningful.

Khalid nodded and went on. "Obsessed people tend to crave a sense of superior value for themselves and to cling to anything that makes them feel important. By contrast, a classic Chinese philosophical text, *The Tao Te Ching,* has in it a wonderful antidote, the simple sentence: 'Accept your unimportance.' It's a statement I've always loved." He looked around at various faces and said, "Accept your unimportance. The first time I read that sentence, I laughed out loud."

He then paused and added, "It's strange. An obsession with your self and your own sense of importance can lead to an obsession with almost anything else, in apparent service to the self—but in fact, gravely endangering the self unless massive caution is exercised. And quite typically, an obsessed person is not a master of caution. That's the last thing that obsession would allow."

Mafulla sighed aloud and said, "It's too bad."

"What?" Walid asked.

"Unfortunately, I find it extremely hard, and maybe impossible, to even consider a self judgment and personal value of unimportance, in any measure, in my own case. And forget about my accepting it."

"That's Ok," Jabari shot back. "Don't worry. The rest of us have long ago accepted it for you." When Mafulla looked over at him with an expectant expression, Jabari gave his friend a big, stretched out grin and his best version of the famous double eyebrow jump, and that made some of the others laugh. "We'll keep it safe for you, this sense of your vanishingly small importance in the grand, cosmic scheme of things, and we can turn it over to you whenever you need it."

"Ha!" Mafulla was impressed. He added, "It may be a while."

At a great distance from Khalid's class and this lively discussion, in Berlin, Germany, it was at present a cloudy and gray, misty day. There had been some heavy rain, but it had stopped an hour earlier. The thick overcast that remained blocked most of the light that was normal at this time of day. Down a back street not far from the center of power, behind an old wooden door framed by a nondescript stone doorway that lacked even a street number, there was a long, wide, dingy hallway leading to a room where a recently launched secret project was being coordinated.

Only twelve people were involved in the enterprise. There were two teams of four each in the field, with four more individuals working in this mostly hidden headquarters, one of them a senior advisor to friends of the Chancellor.

At that moment, a man sat behind a large, dark ornate wooden desk and another individual, whose coat glistened with moisture from outside, had just taken his seat in a chair opposite him. The visitor spoke briskly and with a bold tone of authority to his counterpart behind the desk. "Exactly where are we now? How far along?"

"One team is in New York City and the other is in Cairo."

"What's the status of each?"

"The American team has been in position for over a week. They've set up a small office, thanks to our men on the ground who were already there, and they've begun their investigation, following the initial leads we provided them."

"And the Egyptian team?"

"They arrived four days ago."

"What was the holdup?"

"We had fewer helpful contacts in Cairo. The way had to be prepared. But everything's being worked out."

"Success is required in this venture."

"I understand."

"I'm deadly serious."

"I know."

He now spoke slowly and emphatically. "Nobody announces a one thousand year timeline who doesn't expect to see it through."

"We won't let you down."

"You can't let us down."

"It's in the most capable hands we could gather. The operatives are all highly trained experts, the best we have."

"How soon do you think we'll have some results?"

"The extensive background research has helped a lot. The field investigation from this point may take days or perhaps weeks, but no longer. Then, the retrieval itself should go quickly."

"Good. Get it done as soon as you can."

"We'll not disappoint you. Things will be done quickly."

"I can't stress enough the importance of that. You need to make this happen with no delays."

"I will. You can be sure of it."

The man with the questions and demands looked into the eyes of his colleague for a moment and then silently rose, turned, and left the room. As he walked out through the door and down the hall, he pondered the fact that only fifteen people knew of the existence and nature of this special team, as well as what it had been tasked to find and bring to Berlin. And of that number, only three were not actually members of the team. Just four people altogether were aware of the full reason for the mission. But soon, he thought to himself, the whole world would know the results, very soon. And then, everyone would learn and come to understand why their supreme leader, with his enormous vision for the world, had been secretly but completely obsessed with this one thing. And the world would be amazed.

At his home in Cairo, Shapur Adi sat at his personal desk and slowly opened a large, light tan leather bound box that he had gently placed on the center of the desktop mere seconds earlier. At that moment, his wife Shamilar walked in and saw what he was doing and laughed and said, "You and your scrolls!"

Shapur looked up and smiled. "Yes, I am a bit obsessed!"

"I actually love it that you finally have a hobby. Once upon a time, you were almost all work and no play!"

"I am a father, thanks to you, and so there has been some play. You may remember seeing me with certain smaller individuals."

"I said, almost."

"Yes, well, my little medical emergency changed all that."

"It did. I've seen the change and I admire you for it."

"Thank you. But, isn't it too bad that it so often takes a crisis to show us what's valuable in life?"

"It is too bad, but it's better than nothing's ever having that effect."

"That's for sure," he said.

Shamilar looked into the box and gestured toward the contents of the elegant looking container. "How many do you have now?"

"I currently have a new total of six ancient scrolls in my collection."

"You know, I'd never realized that scrolls like these could be in private hands. I thought they were all collected by museums."

"Well, many are—those that are considered to be of importance as cultural artifacts tend to get snatched up by museums. But once you start looking into it, you can find some pretty incredible examples that fall through the cracks, so to speak, that never catch the attention of the professionals, for one reason or another. Then, a guy like me can come along and begin a collection."

"It's surprising to me, whenever I think about it, how you got each one, and without having to spend a lot of money on them."

"Yes, it's almost like my love of them began to attract them to me," he commented. "There have been so many coincidences! A casual conversation will lead to a chain of unlikely events and … I end up with a new scroll!"

"Has Mafulla seen them all?"

"He's seen only four of them. Two are new, since he was last here," Shapur explained.

"I bet you can't wait to show him the new ones," she said.

"You're right. I think he'll really like them. One's Egyptian and the other's Sumerian and both are, apparently, quite ancient."

"We're turning this place into a regular museum," she replied.

"Yes, but without all the nosey visitors and organized tours, and clamoring street vendors outside, which is good."

"And without, unfortunately, the admission fees, which is bad," she pointed out, wagging her finger. And, at that, he laughed.

"I could use the fees," he said. "They would allow me to get many more scrolls!"

"Or a new dress for your wonderful and deserving wife," she responded, holding up the hem of the old one she was wearing.

"It's too bad you can't wear scrolls," Shapur said, in fun.

"Well, roll them out, and let's see."

At that, he laughed again and said, "We do have fun."

"Yes, whenever we can," she agreed.

"When's Mafulla coming by?"

"I think tomorrow."

"Good. I do believe he'll like these recent acquisitions. Each one is interesting, and, like I said, they're both pretty old."

"As old as you?"

"Yes, and even a touch older, believe it or not."

"By a few years?"

"Or a few thousand—I'm considerably younger than I appear, you know."

Shamilar laughed. "Yes, we often mistake your wise look for age."

"An understandable error, I would say."

"Yes." Shamilar then paused for breath or two and then said, "To be serious for just a moment, I don't think I've ever thought to ask what originally got you interested in this new collecting. It seems to have evolved without my realizing at first that it was even going to rise to the status of a real hobby. How did you pick scrolls, of all things?"

"Well, it's hard to say," he answered, "except for the fact that, at the end of my time in the hospital, and right after that, I starting thinking about such scrolls now and then, and even seeing them in dreams. It was probably from something I had read along the way. I've always been interested in history, and these scrolls are like precious items that have floated down the river of time, right into my hands. They make the past so vivid. And you just never know what you're going to find on one of them, once you start looking."

"I guess that's right," Shamilar said, adding, "I suppose it's a special feeling to hold in your hands something that's been around for hundreds, or even thousands, of years."

"If I can hang on long enough, you may have that feeling yourself one day, my bride," he joked.

"Stop! I'm being serious."

"I am, too. I actually think that, as my skin continues to age and dry out, I'll start looking and feeling more and more like the ancient papyrus and occasional old parchment I'm collecting. And they do tend to last. So one day, perhaps, you can collect me."

She shook her head and sighed loudly. "Silly man."

"Just don't box me up too soon."

"You and Mafulla are just alike."

"Give or take a thousand years," he said.

"Yes, give or take."

4

A New Job

Leem Hadad was sitting at his desk in the small offices of the Cairo Detective Agency at Number Four Giza Way. He had a cup of coffee on the desk and was reading the two remaining stories he had not yet had a chance to look over in the morning's issue of *The Kingdom Daily News*. Initially, he had glanced back at the article on Germany, but it bothered him too much to think about it any more, so he turned his attention to national and local events. And yet then, the first piece he began reading turned out to be about a cultural exchange mission involving some minor officials and scholars from Germany who would be visiting the city for a time. Oh, well, he thought. So it begins.

But he read on and quickly came across a few other new forms of unpleasantness being reported. There was apparently a group of people saying that the king's sudden disappearance from town was part of a conspiracy to undermine Egypt's sovereignty. They were a fringe element of the local political scene and few in number, but they could be noisy and troublesome for the government to handle. He shook his head: Crazies abroad; crazies at home; and new visitors now to connect the two in cultural exchanges. Wonderful, he mused.

The old investigator then pondered the current story a bit more as he refreshed his coffee. The way the paper had presented recent events, everyone knew that there had been a plot against the kingdom led by a man named Juan Santiago, and that this man had been killed in a terrible confrontation that took place inside the palace. They read that the king still had to accomplish some things for the sake of the nation, to tie all this up, and that a suddenly necessary secret mission would most likely keep him out of the capital for a while. In the meantime, readers had been assured, the prince would be standing in for the king, and the king's top three aides would take care of the day-to-day affairs of the palace and the kingdom as they usually did, working side-by-side with the temporary young monarch, Walid Shabeezar, who was of course widely known as the very capable and extremely well-prepared nephew of His Majesty, Ali Shabeezar. Not much was said about Walid in the paper during this reporting, and his actual age wasn't mentioned, thanks to favors being done for the palace. The whole tone of the news about these events seemed calibrated to give the impression of continuity, stability, and some degree of business as usual at the top of the nation.

King Ali would be out of the kingdom and unable to make any public appearances for a while, readers had been told, but otherwise, the affairs of state would continue to be run smoothly from the palace and the various government offices reporting to the palace. The managing editor of the paper had actually agreed to let Reela Adi help craft the article reporting all this, and had been told in return that the entire government was now in his debt and would go out of its way to be helpful with his needs in the future. The full story about what had taken place with Santiago and the king was known by only a few people, representing the tightest concentric circle around the events themselves, while in each more removed circle of friends, family, and government staff members, much less of the complete account was known. No one wanted to alarm the general population over what might or might not be the ultimate story that was still playing out. The typical transparency of this monarchy was now, as a perceived necessity, tinged with circumspect prudence and a cautious wisdom.

As Leem contemplated what he had just read, bringing to mind the additional details he had been told about these recent events, Ibrahim came through the office door with a big smile. "Uncle, good news!"

"Excellent! I could use some good news after too many minutes of reading the mostly bad news that dominates the paper today. But, let me guess: I've been nominated for Detective of the Year." he said.

"No," Ibrahim laughed, "but you deserve it. I didn't know there was such an award."

"There isn't, as far as I know, but there should be, don't you think?"

"Yes. We should create it. And you certainly should be the first recipient."

"You don't think that would look like suspicious favoritism?"

"Not to anyone aware of your many investigative virtues and great accomplishments."

"Well, Ok, then." He cleared his throat and said, "I'm both humbled and gratified by this marvelous award. I would like to thank you and everyone who made it possible." Leem playfully said all this in the tone of an awards speech. "Now, what's the real scoop?"

"I think I'm making some progress in our new missing person case."

"I'm glad to hear it," Leem said. "What's happened?"

"I was at the Blue Camel with Ahira while he ate a late breakfast. And I was telling him about the case, since it's the first one where I've been the lead investigator. And a writer from the paper who was at the next table overheard me and interrupted my tale, introducing himself, and saying he'd love to do an article about it."

"Really?"

"Yes, he said it was a classic love story that everyone would enjoy."

"That's quite a break," Leem said.

"Yeah, I know. Practically everybody in town will read the article and someone will surely know the man I'm seeking, or at least know something of his whereabouts."

"How much of the story did the writer hear? I didn't mention it earlier, but I was able to read only the first page of the lady's letter to us before I turned it over to you. I was so busy last week that, once I realized it was a simple missing person case, I knew you'd enjoy pursuing it on your own, for once."

"You were right. I'm enjoying it a lot already. And, as to your question: Well, I told Ahira that we had gotten a four page, handwritten letter from this lady who said she was eighty years old, and that she had met a dashing young soldier when she was only a girl, and how kind he seemed and how handsome she thought he was. But the army took him away and she didn't hear anything about him or from him for a long while after that. Nonetheless, she says, he was in her heart, and she was apparently in his. Two years later, they met again, seemingly by accident, and it was as if no time had passed at all. She felt a special spark, but there was an obstacle with her family. Her mother wanted her to marry the son of her father's business partner, for financial reasons, and the mother said he was also much more religiously suitable, whatever that meant."

"So, what happened?"

"Military service took the young soldier away once more, and the two of them occasionally corresponded back and forth. Then, a year later, the young lady received a letter from her soldier proposing marriage. But she had just become engaged, quite reluctantly, due to the insistence and strong intervention of her mother. And when she told this to her absent love by return letter, he didn't write back. She thinks that, due to a clear nobility of spirit she had seen in him, he didn't want to break up the family or cause her any more pain than she was already feeling, as was apparent in her note to him."

"I see."

"And then, time passed. She was married, though not happily, and had three children from the union. But then, not long ago, she lost her husband of all these years, who, she said, had been a difficult man and a harsh taskmaster in the household. And now, nearly a year later, she said she has been having dreams of her old love, the soldier, and feels moved to find him, wherever he might be. She explained that, since his last known address was in Cairo, she decided to contact us with her need."

"How did she learn of us?"

"I don't know. She didn't say."

"Is she in the area?"

"She's living in Alexandria right now."

"Ok. She may have spoken with someone who knows about my new work here. Did she give us any clues about the man being sought that might help us?"

"She said he was of medium height, strong build, and that she thinks he served in the Fourth Division, First Regiment of the army. She said he had a patch on his uniform that indicated this. She gave his name, and his sister's name, and some other details."

"Remind me. What age would he be now?"

"I'm thinking about eighty-four or eighty-five."

"So, he may be …"

"Yeah, no longer with us."

"But then again, there's always hope."

"Yes. I really want to find the guy and reunite these two. If he's still breathing, I'd love to get them together, at least so they could speak again, as friends. Her letter was so sincere and from the heart and sweet."

"Good! I feel the same way, now that you've told me the details. Everybody loves a love story."

Ibrahim smiled and said, "Especially if it can have a happy ending, thanks to a little detective work!"

"And also thanks, perhaps, to a story in *The Kingdom Daily News*!" Leem said, with a laugh.

"Yeah, and that, too."

"When the time is right, things happen."

"True."

There was a knock at the door behind Ibrahim. He turned and took a couple of steps toward it and opened it quickly. Right away, Leem heard him say, "Oh, hello. Please, come in."

"Hello," a soft-spoken, older man said, looking almost surprised to see the younger man there at the door.

Ibrahim said, "Welcome to the Cairo Detective Agency."

"I … hope I'm not interrupting anything important," the man said, meekly.

"No, no, please come on in. I was just speaking with the senior detective here, about a case I'm working on, but I had finished my report right before you knocked."

"If you're sure," the man said. He looked quite hesitant.

"Yes, positively sure. Do come on in," Ibrahim opened the door wider and smiled at the visitor, gesturing him into the room.

"Greetings. What can we do for you today, my friend?" Leem asked as he slowly stood up from his desk chair to greet their guest.

"Oh, yes. Greetings to you, as well." The man slowly came through the door. He was dressed well, but his clothing appeared old and more than a little worn. He had a certain sort of threadbare formality both in his choice of garments and in his demeanor. He looked over toward Leem, and then back at Ibrahim, and said, "I didn't know where to go for some information I seek, and was walking by just now and saw your sign and remembered that you're here. And I wondered if you might be able to help me."

"Please, have a seat," Leem said, gesturing to the chair in front of his desk. "Tell me what you need."

"I don't want to be any trouble," the man replied.

"No, no, I have no other appointments or pressing business right now, and I'm eager to be of help in any way I can," Leem responded.

"It's very kind of you," the man said, and slowly sat.

"Now, what's the issue that brings you to us?"

"Well, I just wondered if you might have heard something about the recent power outages."

"What outages?"

"The ones that have been happening during the past few days."

Leem looked slightly puzzled and said, "Where exactly have these outages been occurring?"

"Why, around here," the man replied, looking a bit perplexed himself. "Haven't you noticed them?"

"No, I can't say that I have."

Ibrahim spoke up and said, "I haven't seen anything, either, and this is the first report I've heard about such a problem."

"Oh. I didn't realize. I see. There have been several disruptions to our electrical service in the neighborhood during the past three days," the man said. "Of course, it's not the most reliable thing in the world, in the first place. Lights will flicker now and then, but that's normal."

"It's true," Leem agreed.

"But in these instances, the power has vanished for several minutes at a time, and in one case, for almost an hour."

"Where exactly has this been going on—or off, as the case may be?"

"Two blocks away, where I live, and over a larger area, I've been told. I assumed that you would have been experiencing it too, and that, being a detective agency, you might have checked it out and discovered what's causing it, and how long it might continue."

"What's your address?"

"214 Garden Lane."

Leem wrote it down on a pad in front of him. He said, "Could it be that any of your neighbors might also have had these outages in their homes?"

"Oh, yes, everyone I've asked. That's why I assumed it was a broader problem, at least in this part of town."

"Have you reported it to the authorities?"

"I tried to, but the people I spoke with were not very helpful."

"I see."

"I was just hoping you might have some information about it."

"Not at present, but would you like us to look into it for you?

"Oh, I wish I could afford to hire you to uncover what's going on, and find out how much longer we'll have to endure this unpredictability, or else how it might be fixed, but I'm afraid that personal finances right now would not allow it." The man smiled in an almost embarrassed way and said, "I have a younger cousin who's a private detective and I know what the rates are, at least in Alexandria, and would assume they're roughly the same here in Cairo. I simply stopped by as a neighbor. I hope that's all right. I wish I could offer you a new job to pursue this, but it would likely be a fairly uninteresting task for you, and yet still unaffordable, at least in the present, for me."

"You say you have a cousin in Alexandria who's now working as a private detective?"

"Yes. He was a policeman for years, but he wrote me that when his boss retired, a man he admired a lot, he thought he'd try something new, in a related field."

Leem laughed and said, "Well, if he was a city policeman, I was his boss. I'm the one who retired."

"No!"

"Yes. What's your cousin's name?"

"Baadi al-Sum."

Leem laughed again and said, "I knew him well. Where's he working now?"

"The Delta Detective Agency, there in the city."

"Good people—I know the founder," Leem said, and nodded. "May I ask your name?"

Yes, I'm Nasser Alexander."

"I'm pleased to meet you, Mr. Alexander. I'm Leem Hadad."

"Oh! Chief Hadad! You're Chief Hadad?"

"Yes, but retired."

"It's certainly an honor to meet you. I had no idea. I'm so sorry to have disturbed you and taken your time with my little neighborhood problem."

"No, no, please, allow me to look into it for you, as a small gesture of appreciation for your cousin's fine work through the years. I think it will be a very small job for us, and there would be no charge to you."

"Oh, that's very gracious of you and quite unexpected, but thoroughly consistent with your reputation, if I may say so."

"Thank you. I'm glad to be of assistance."

The men talked for a few more minutes and when Alexander had to leave, Leem walked him through the door and onto the sidewalk outside, promising that he would be in touch soon with the information he sought.

In the small rectory kitchen of The Wesleyan Chapel in New York, Reverend Bob Archdale sat at the table and read, while he was having coffee along with two scrambled eggs and toast. There was a knock at the back door. He called out, "Come in, please."

The door opened and his unexpected visitor from the night before walked in, smiling. "Good morning, sir."

"Good morning to you, my friend, Santiago," Archdale said. "How did you sleep?"

"Very well," the stranger replied, and he smiled at the name. "The bed was firm and comfortable. And I couldn't hear any of the city noises until after I had enjoyed a nice long sleep. I woke up totally refreshed. I must thank you for that."

"Oh, it's my pleasure to be of help."

"Yes, I know. It means a lot to you, whenever you can help other people," the stranger said. "And it should. This is one of the purposes for our lives, to be kind and useful to each other."

"Yes, indeed. And you've sized me up well, in our very short time of acquaintance."

"And yet, with all your enjoyment for helping others, you need to be careful with your time and energy."

"What do you mean?"

"Your work has been draining on you lately. I can tell. Especially since you've been called on to help your own family, I think quite recently, in a difficult matter."

"How in the world do you know that?"

"I have no idea. It just came to me."

"Well, you're right on all counts."

"I see."

"You seem to know much more about me than yourself."

"Indeed. It's quite odd."

"Have you experienced any more realizations since we last talked?"

"Well, I do feel that I have a mission here, a purpose of some sort."

"You mean, on this earth?"

"Yes, but to be more specific, I mean, in this city, in this particular neighborhood, and perhaps even in this church."

"Oh, I see. Well, that's very good in more than one way. Good for all of us, of course, but good for you that you're perhaps on the verge of remembering more about yourself."

"So it seems. I have robust hope."

"That's the best kind to have."

"Yes. I agree."

"Oh, I just realized … please, forgive my absentmindedness. There are some clean plates and cups and a glass over there next to the sink. Grab whatever you need and I'll cook you an egg or two if you'd like. There's juice also and coffee."

"It's not too much trouble?"

"None at all."

"Well then, that would be very nice. Thank you," the stranger said as he turned to the sink and reached for a plate and cup.

"Let me get the pan hot," Archdale said, rising from his chair, and moving toward the small stove.

The man being called Santiago happened to look for a moment at the water handles on the sink there in the kitchen of the rectory, and spoke up to say, "By the way, I should tell you that the little sink was stopped up, out in the cottage."

"Oh. I'm sorry. It's been so long since anyone used the cottage. I didn't know. I'll see if I can have someone come and look at it."

"No need. I fixed it."

"You did?"

"Yes, it was easy. And the door lock was not working quite properly, so I took care of that for you as well. It was the least I could do in return for your kindness."

"You fixed the lock?"

"Yes."

"Well, first of all, thank you very much. But, secondly, we have here more clues. You're a man who knows how to fix things. I have to admit that, unfortunately, I'm not." He thought for a second and said, "You could be a plumber or a locksmith."

"Or a jack of all trades, as I think some would say."

"That would be even better. There's a lot around here that could use a little work."

"It would please me to do the work," the stranger said. He then added, "I had a feeling you might ask."

"Really? Ok. How about this? And of course, I don't mean to be presumptuous here. You could be a famous medical doctor from one of our leading hospitals, or a top scientist, or a great leader of men, for all I know, but ... if it would interest you, for a while, until you regain your memory and get back on your feet, I could offer you a new job here, a small one, but needed, as you can see, just helping to repair and keep up the place, in return for bed and board and a little cash. I'm afraid there's not really a budget available for the amount of help we need."

"Bed and board?"

"Yes, a common phrase in our country that means your housing and food. I think I can also provide you with ... five dollars a week. It's not much, but we don't have much."

"Actually, that's a kind and generous offer," the stranger said. "I hate to disappoint all the other potential employers out there who may have their hearts set on acquiring the skills of a possible surgeon or scientist or great leader of men to do whatever they might need to have done around their homes or workplaces, but ... I accept."

Archdale laughed and said, "Very good! And it's only for as long as it suits you. When you feel better, or think for any reason that you should leave, your work here will be over. And I'll be deeply grateful for your help."

"That's an interesting addendum to the offer, and very fair," the man said. "I appreciate your lenient conditions."

"Excellent, so … you're hired!"

"Thank you. That's good. When I woke up this morning, the last thing I expected was a new job," the man said. "But, of course, these days, I hardly know what to expect. Life is a series of adventures, it seems."

"Yes. Yes, it is."

5

Unsettling Developments

Walid and Mafulla sat watching Masoon and Hamid do an extremely intense workout. Mafulla exhaled loudly and turned to his best friend and said, "I have such a long way to go."

"What do you mean?" Walid asked.

"There's such a long path from where I am to anywhere near their shape and skill level. Compared to these two, I'm just a beginner."

"Well, sure, of course, me too. But you sound discouraged about it."

"Yeah, a little, or maybe a lot, actually. It just hit me in a new way how much farther along these guys are than us."

"They're a lot older. And they've been at it a lot longer."

"True. But it can be sort of overwhelming to think of the huge gap between where I am and where they are."

"Look how far we've come in such a short time."

"Yeah, it's been pretty amazing. But I'm not improving nearly as fast now."

"The king, I mean, Uncle Ali, says that progress in anything is never smooth and constant. We plateau. We slow down. We sometimes even go backwards. Then we get new momentum. We just have to hang in there and not give up."

"I guess. Thanks, coach."

"Look. Here's a thought."

"What?"

"Suppose you found a magic bottle with a powerful genie trapped inside. You rubbed the bottle the right way and the guy popped out and gave you three wishes."

"Ok. First, why is it a guy?"

"I don't know. It just is."

"Why couldn't it be a very beautiful girl?"

"I have no idea. But the point is the three wishes. He gives you three wishes."

"Just three?"

"Just three."

"Why not four, or five thousand?"

"I don't know. That just seems to be the rule in genie stories."

"I would wish for more wishes."

"That's what everybody says. But I'm pretty sure it's the one wish you can't make. It's null and void. Prohibited. Genie Rules."

"Oh. See? Even the magic genie scenario is disappointing me today."

"Just forget the number of wishes for a second."

"Ok. Continue. I'm listening."

"Suppose you were really feeling bothered about how far you have to go in your Phi training and that this was really on your mind when the genie appeared. And so, for your first wish, you said, 'I wish that right now, in the next moment, I'll be as strong and powerful and as Phi-skilled and physically developed as I'll ever be.' And then, suppose the genie waved his hand at you: Zap!"

"I like the zap."

"Good. And as a result of it, you instantly were taller and heavier and really well muscled, super cut, totally fearsome looking, and at the maximum strength and skill you'd ever be, right then, at that instant."

"Cool. That would be totally awesome."

"But would it?"

"Of course. What do you mean?"

"Let me ask you something. Do you enjoy the training we do?"

"Well, it's really tough some days, but, yeah, sure."

"Do you like the overall process of learning some new thing, working on it hard and failing and trying it again and still falling short, and then getting it right for the first time, and finally growing stronger and more skilled and being able to do something you've never done before? Do you like that challenge, and the feeling of getting better that the process gives you?"

"Yeah, absolutely. I enjoy that feeling all the time—the sense of real accomplishment that comes from the struggle."

"How about when you, on your own, set a new goal and try to attain it and fall flat, like when you shoot for a new personal best while lifting weights and don't get it? How does that make you feel?"

"It used to get me down, but now I think about it differently, thanks to something Masoon said to me one day."

"What do you think now?"

"I think, hey, I'm failing forward—I'm at least trying hard, working on a new goal and I'm on the path, and failing at first is a step along the way and it's even proof that I'm pushing myself. And most people don't even try. But now I've got the new goal in my sights, and eventually I'll get there, and all the failures along the way will have been worth it."

"So you've learned to like that feeling, when you overcome lots of failures on your way to a physical goal that you've set for yourself?"

"Yeah, and I even sort of like the first part now, I mean, trying something I can't yet do."

"Why?"

"It focuses me. It lets me know where I am. And what's next. It's like a stretch where I try to get into new territory, and not quite getting there means learning my current limits and knowing they won't last long if I work hard enough. And also, I know how it's going to feel when I finally get it. And I love the anticipation. It's good in itself."

"I totally agree. All the stuff you've just said, I feel the same way," Walid explained, and then added, "Well, though, here's the problem. After that day, the day of the genie transformation, you'd never have that experience again with any physical challenge or warrior technique or Phi skill goal—never, for the rest of your life."

"Oh." Mafulla looked a bit surprised.

"Yeah, there'd be nothing to hope for, aspire to, or work at in the physical realm and in the realm of Phi power and skill, ever again. You'd already have all that you'd ever get, right then, at that instant."

"Oh, yeah."

"No more fighting for a new physical stretch goal. No more feeling of accomplishment that comes from the struggle, no more such great anticipatory joy for a future development, ever again, for the rest of your life."

"Yeah. Wow. I hadn't thought of it like that."

"So, maybe it wouldn't be as awesome as you assumed."

"No. You're right. It would be sort of a very surprising, unexpected, big, gigantic let-down, in that respect."

"Yeah, it would be. And that's why it's not a bad thing that there's such a gap between where we are and where Masoon and Hamid are. We're here to grow and develop and there's joy in that."

"Oh. I get it. Ok. This is true. That's a very different perspective."

"And, guess what?"

"What?"

"There's probably a gap for Masoon and Hamid as well."

"Come on."

"Yeah, that's why they work out so hard. Even they are getting stronger and growing and experiencing the great anticipation of the next level."

"Wow. Yeah. I guess you're right."

"Gaps can be good."

"Yeah, I see that now."

"So, do you feel better?"

"Yeah, I do. And I suppose that makes you the real magic genie."

"Very funny. And you didn't even make a wish."

"So, I still have three?"

"No. You wish. But back to my point: I just hope now that you're looking forward to the next little success you'll have in overcoming your current state of tremendous weakness." Walid grinned.

"Well, it's not tremendous."

"Compared to these guys? You're pretty close already?"

"Well, no."

"Then you have a lot to look forward to, don't you?"

"How come you're the smart one today?"

Walid laughed. "I need to have a day, now and then."

"Ok, today is officially yours. But don't get cocky. There's still a gap, a tremendous gap."

"What do you mean?"

"Between you and me, my friend, in the realm of the mind."

"Ha!"

"But you shouldn't get discouraged, either. You have much to hope for, aspire to, and work at."

"Ok. You're making me eat my own words now."

Mafulla now laughed and said, "It's good for brain growth and humility enhancement."

Right then, Masoon looked over and called out to them, "Now, you two. Come over here. We have a challenge for you."

As they stood up, Mafulla said to Walid, "All right then, gap erosion time."

Walid replied, "Even if it starts with gap confrontation failure."

Mafulla smiled and said, "Bring it on."

A bit later on, and elsewhere in the palace, Leem Hadad thanked the guard who had escorted him to the office and, knocking lightly on the edge of the doorframe said, "Thanks for seeing me, Reela," as he tentatively poked his head through the door.

"Nonsense! You never have to thank me for a visit. Come in. I'm always glad to see my favorite detective."

"You're too kind. But I know how busy you are."

"Never too busy for you. Sit, sit," Reela said, as he stood up from behind his desk and gestured to a wooden chair facing him.

Leem came the rest of the way in and took a seat as his host had indicated. Reela also then sat down again and said, "So, how are things at the agency and with the family?"

"Excellent," Leem replied. "All is well. Ibrahim is doing a great job at work, and his social life's flourishing. Ben loves school and is a great member of the family in every possible way."

"That's all very good to hear," Reela said with a big smile.

Leem nodded and said, "I'm just so sorry for what you've all been through recently here at the palace, with the tragic death of the king's brother, and the unexplainable disappearance of the king himself, along with the transition of leadership that it's entailed."

"Yes, thank you. We've all been deeply mystified by these recent events and we've struggled to carry on as best we could. It's not easy on any of us, but Ali had everything around here running so well and smoothly that it hasn't been hard for us to keep most things going in his absence."

"How's Walid adjusting?"

"As well as you can imagine. He's smart and resilient and has all the right attitudes about the current state of things."

"I would expect no less of him."

"Yes, we're quite blessed to have a young man of his talents in the position to take on certain roles around here, until Ali returns."

"Indeed," Leem said. "Indeed."

"Of course," Reela said, "I'm sure it's all had a deep emotional effect on Walid, nonetheless."

"It would have to," Leem agreed, in sympathy.

"He keeps up a brave front and works hard, but I know that the return of Ali would be not just a joyful moment for him, but a true and tremendous relief at every level."

"We all hope for the best in that regard," Leem replied.

"Yes," Reela said, and then asked, "Would you like some coffee or tea while we talk?"

"Coffee would be nice, if you have any," Leem responded.

"The new man just brought me some, minutes before you arrived," Reela said, and he got up to fetch a couple of cups. Pouring from a pot on the table behind him, he said, "So, what in particular brings you to see me today, my friend?" He turned and placed one of the cups, sitting on a saucer, on the desk in front of his guest.

"Actually, a very small matter in the grand scheme of things," Leem answered. "But I was hoping that a word from you might help."

"Certainly, anything I can do is yours for the asking."

Leem took a sip from his cup and said, "An elderly gentleman visited my office earlier and asked for my help in discovering the cause of a problem he'd been experiencing. I've made official inquiries in the past couple of hours, but haven't been enjoying much luck in getting answers. I thought you might be able to help me."

"I'm glad to. So, what's the nature of the problem, and who are the recalcitrant individuals whose arms I may be able to twist for you?"

Leem laughed and said, "I didn't know you were an arm twister."

"Yes. I can be quite troublesome to those who give my friends trouble. And I happen to be especially well positioned at present to get action from even the most reluctant kingdom functionaries."

"Good! Well, I've had some trouble with the utility people, or the electric power people, to be more specific, and the government office that regulates them."

"Oh, well then, I have good news: There are some imminently twistable arms in both places, so fill me in on the details."

"The old fellow who visited me is related to a man I knew well in Alexandria, a truly good guy who served on the police force for many years, a man I could always depend on, and a recipient of several awards over the years. He's now a private detective, too, having retired from the force, apparently right after I did. It was an older cousin of his who stopped by without even knowing of the connection, which became clear only during our talk."

"What brought him to you?"

"He lives a couple of blocks away from the office and saw our sign, and just felt like he should stop in to ask a question that he's been asking other people in the neighborhood without getting any answers. And so far, all I've been able to do is to replicate his experience."

"And the problem or question is what?"

"Yes, the problem is that he's been experiencing several electrical power outages in his home over the past few days, and neighbors of his have had the same experience. And he can't find out what's going on, or why, or when it might come to an end. He stopped by, seeing that we were detectives and thinking that if we had undergone the same problem or knew about it, we might have answers for him."

"And it sounds like you don't, yet."

"That's correct."

"Had you experienced the problem yourself?"

"No. We'd not had any of the disruptions in the office, or at least not during normal business hours when we were there, and none at home, so it was the first we'd heard of the problem."

"I see."

"He said many neighbors had complained about it, but no one knew what was going on."

"So, you went to the power people?"

"Yes, and they said that, to their knowledge, service had been normal. They were unaware of any problems in their provision of power. They said everything had been functioning well on their end and there was no reason in the system for what I was reporting."

"Interesting."

"When I tried to ask more questions, I could tell that the gentleman speaking with me was out of time or patience with the subject. So, from him, I experienced something like an attention outage." Reela laughed, and Leem continued, "As a result, I got nowhere."

"He could send out a crew to do some inspections and then repairs if needed," Reela said.

"Well, I assumed so, but it was not an offer he made. And when I suggested it, he said that he would write up a note on the matter, but that he couldn't guarantee anything. Then, I visited the government office overseeing utilities and got no help there, either."

"Wait a minute," Reela said. He suddenly looked very serious, and even worried.

"What is it?" Leem asked.

"Do you remember Carlos Sanchez, the director of the main intelligence agency in Spain, the man who visited not long ago?"

"Yes, I do."

"At the meeting we had with him, the meeting the king arranged, where we were both present, he said something about power outages."

"He did," Leem replied. "And, until this very moment, I hadn't remembered that. It hasn't even crossed my mind. And it was something about Santiago, wasn't it?"

"Yes. He said that our former enemy would not typically stay for very long in urban settings like Cairo, because his presence would cause strange phenomena like power outages and electrical disruptions in the immediate area around him."

"He did say that, and it sounded a bit outrageous at the time."

"Yes, but we all kept an open mind about it," Reela commented.

"We did," Leem agreed.

"And when Santiago finally came to town and onto palace grounds and into the palace itself, there was the mysterious and unparalleled incident with the king, which was even stranger."

"Yes."

"He and the king both disappeared from the scene, vanishing completely."

"I heard this, too."

"And we assumed he was dead, gone from this world—Santiago, I mean."

"But now," Leem said, anticipating Reela's thought.

"Yes, but now, with what you're telling me," Reela said, hesitantly, and dropped off in thought for just a second.

"It could be," Leem picked up on the idea and went on, "that he's alive and back, somehow, in the city, and in the area near my office, and it's his odd presence that's causing these disruptions."

"Yes. It could be. We actually have no conclusive proof of his death. Some of those present had serious reason to believe it, but not anything like proof. And there was no body."

"What of the king?"

"Fortunately, we have absolutely no evidence of death in his case, at least, apart from his sudden disappearance. And, knowing him as well as we do, buttressed by the assurances of those closest to him, we've been operating on the hopeful assumption that he's still alive, but somehow, and for some good reason not yet known, he's just … unavailable to us at present."

"So, there was an encounter between the king and Santiago and something happened, and they both mysteriously disappeared, and one is presumed dead and the other is assumed to be alive."

"But we could be wrong in one of our assumptions. And we know that. Assumptions are often dangerous. But, there were vast differences in the two men. And, due to how others present felt in the situation, they intuitively drew those conclusions."

"I see. But could you say any more?"

"Only that there was a deep relief without grief, and a sense on the part of some very intuitive, sensitive, and trustworthy souls that one powerful person had left the world, but not two."

"Well, what do you think we should do now, in light of the strange thing that Sanchez told us?"

Not too far away from the palace, the students Khata and Haji were walking down the street. This time, it was just the two of them, and both had just laughed at something. Khata then said, "It was really nice for you to offer to walk me back home this afternoon. It's good to have someone to talk to along the way."

"Thanks. I'm glad. When I passed by your classroom and overheard Ara say she had to stay late with Hoda to work on a project, I thought maybe you'd still like some company."

"You were right. I don't enjoy walking alone, even in the middle of the afternoon like this. I usually get one of the girls to come with me, but they were all occupied today, so you really came to the rescue."

"Good," Haji said. And then he suddenly had no idea what

to talk about. It was like his brain froze and became blank. But, fortunately, Khata asked him a question before too much time had passed.

"Where's Malik today? You guys usually do stuff together all the time, and almost always after school."

"We do. But he had to help his dad with something this afternoon. So I was sort of cut loose, which is good, considering that I got to be the walking-home hero of the day."

Khata laughed again, as if this was the most normal, comfortable thing in the world, to be sauntering down the street with a boy that she knew had at least a bit of a crush on her, but who had never said anything to her to indicate more than a casual friendly interest, like he might have with any of the girls at school. And yet, he did seem to pay her more attention than the others, and she had caught him looking at her quite a few times in social settings. And now, they were having a second walk together in one day, which was interesting.

At that point, they were passing a row of nice shops of various kinds. Many of the front doors were open and patrons could be seen inside. This was a wealthier part of town, generally, and the stores were more upscale than most. There were several foreign shopkeepers as well as native Egyptians along the street, and mid afternoon was a fairly busy time for them. The main marketplace in town was the opposite. Mornings were the busiest there, and afternoons saw lighter traffic. But in these shops, and in two cafes along this part of the avenue, the ladies and gentlemen who lived nearby tended to do the most visiting and browsing and buying in the afternoons.

Khata slowed her pace just a bit. She said, in a lowered voice, "Haji, did you notice the Antiques and Antiquities Shop we just passed?"

"Not really," he answered.

"There was a sign on the door that said 'Closed' and that's really odd for this time of day."

"Oh, yeah?"

"I've never seen that before. And I walk by here every day. I also caught a glimpse of what I thought were maybe two men inside the shop, and I have a bad feeling about it all."

"You do?"

"Yeah, pretty bad, actually."

"Ok, let's go around the block and see if there's a back door to the place."

"What can we do?"

"I'm not sure yet, but we should at least check on the situation."

"Have you seen any city police around?" Khata nearly whispered at this point.

"No, not on the whole walk so far," Haji answered her.

"Are you sure we should try to do anything?" she asked.

"Well, no, I'm not sure, but I think we should at least have a look, since you say it's unusual for the shop to be closed, and because of the feeling you had when you saw those guys in it."

"Maybe I'm wrong. I'm not advanced. I'm just a beginner, really."

"You're pretty advanced, naturally."

"But I haven't been trained for very long at this point."

"True, but Layla's a great trainer."

"Still."

"Don't worry. We'll be careful."

"Are you sure?"

"Yeah. Absolutely. If everything's fine, then great, we've just tried to be helpful. But if there's trouble, we'll get help or something."

"Ok, I guess." They were walking as they talked, and now rounded a corner.

"Good. I thought I remembered an alley back here. We can just go to the back of the shop and see if there's a door or window or anything, and any sign of something bad going on."

"Yeah, but we should be careful, really super cautious," she said.

"No problem. I agree. Tell me if you see or feel anything else."

"Oh," she said.

"What? You look almost pale, all of a sudden."

"I just felt something … something very big and really bad, something maybe even evil."

"What do you mean?"

6

The Shop

Over the door, an old sign said, "The Wisdom Shop: Groceries, Dry Goods, Books, and Curios. Ian Wisdom, Proprietor."

"Here we are."

"This is it?"

"Yes. It's by far my favorite store in the neighborhood and, maybe even in the entire city." Bob Archdale held open the door for his new parish handyman. "Before we even begin to look around, I want you to meet my friend, Ian, who owns the place."

Just inside the door, there were rows of fresh fruits and vegetables on tables or stands, right and left, waist high. Behind them were aisles of canned goods and packaged foods. There was a smell of fresh ground coffee in the air, and other aromas intermixed with that. Something was cooking somewhere. Next, back and to the left, was an aisle of candy and toys, close together. Behind them, some tools sat on a shelf. To the right, farther back, a few racks of clothing could be seen. It was an old-fashioned general store of a classic sort, right in New York City. Four or five shoppers were in various parts of the establishment, either browsing or selecting items for purchase. Archdale looked around and caught a glimpse of his old friend standing toward the back and busy at something. "Come this way, follow me," he said to his new companion, and walked toward the proprietor.

"Ian! Ian, old man! There's someone I'd like you to meet."

The individual being addressed turned around and instantly had a big smile on his face. "Reverend Bob! Your Holiness!" he boomed out. "Greetings!"

"Greetings to you, my friend," Bob answered.

Ian Wisdom had a chubby, ruddy face, with light brown hair thinning considerably and flying about on his partly balding head. He was of medium height, with a little more weight on his torso than his current size of clothing could easily handle. Raising his bushy eyebrows and arms heavenward, he exclaimed, "Welcome as always to my personal sanctuary, my cathedral of helpfulness! Come in, come in!"

"We are in," Archdale said, with a smile and a laugh.

"No, I mean a good deal farther in, or at least far enough that you'll feel like you have to buy something before you can courteously make your way out," Wisdom joked in his hearty British accent, as he waved at the visitors to come on back to where he stood.

"I always buy something," the reverend responded.

"Yes, I can count on that, despite the relative penury of the clergy. There's inevitably a purchase."

"I can resist everything except temptation."

"Oscar Wilde—or his character, Lord Darlington, in Act 1 of his great comedy, Lady Windermere's Fan."

"Goodness! You certainly know your fellow Brits well! And it's an irresistible quotation, as you might imagine, for a man of my profession."

"Well, that's fine as long as you don't bemoan your own failures in the face of temptation. As Darlington says in the same play, "We are all in the gutter, but some of us are looking at the stars."

"Very nice," Archdale said. "I'm truly impressed."

"I'm equally impressed that I can depend on your financial support every time you come through the door, whether it's from a weakness of the flesh or a strength of the spirit, manifested by a natural fascination with all things excellent and extraordinary—as befits a man with his eyes on the stars, and beyond."

The minister laughed and said, "You always have something

that whets my appetite or piques my curiosity." Then he added, "But before any personal money changing takes place in your fine temple of retail today, let me introduce you to a new parish employee and friend, our long-needed caretaker and handyman, Santiago."

"Hello there, Santiago, I'm Ian Wisdom, and I'm pleased to meet you," the proprietor said, as he reached out to shake the hand of the new potential customer.

"My pleasure, entirely," Santiago said. He added, "Not many men are named for one of the two greatest qualities."

"Oh?"

"Yes, wisdom and virtue, which, as an old proverb has it, are like the two wheels of a cart."

Wisdom nodded his head and said, "Very nice. I like your proverb, and I thank you. But let me ask: Santiago—is that your first name or your last?"

"Possibly, neither," the visitor said, adding, "But it's my most recent."

"An unexpected answer, indeed!"

Archdale explained, "My new friend here and fellow worker just suddenly showed up last night in the strangest way, through locked doors and windows and lying fast asleep on a pew in the church. When he awoke and we had a chance to speak, he had the most extreme case of amnesia you can imagine."

"My goodness! Is this the God's honest truth?"

The handyman nodded and Archdale said, "It is! Our new friend couldn't even recall his own name."

Wisdom looked at the man with an expression of great surprise and fascination. "Indeed?"

"Yes. Reverend Archdale speaks the absolute truth," Santiago said. "I awoke, as from a sleep of death, and at first no wiser than a newborn. I couldn't tell him or myself my own name."

"I see. But, then, where did you get the fine name of Santiago?"

"Your old friend allowed me to take a bath and clean up. And while I was relaxing for a few moments in the tub, with my mind in total repose, the name 'Santiago' just occurred to me. It simply popped into my head with no clear significance attached."

Archdale jumped in and said, "We don't know if it's actually his name or the name of his home city, or that of a good friend or acquaintance, or what his favorite dog is called, for that matter. But, with no other obvious options available to us, aside from random naming, we've been using it as his own appellation, first or last."

"Probably not the first, and, as I say, possibly not the last," the man added.

Wisdom smiled and replied, "You may then find yourself soon fancying such additional manly options to complete the picture as 'Robert' or 'Ian', since you have now become acquainted with these other fine names as lively possibilities."

"Yes, now that you mention it: Robert Ian, or Ian Robert, either one, might make for a better introduction than the mysterious single name of Santiago," the stranger joked, in the spirit of the Wisdom's remark.

"I think Santiago makes for an excellent family name, a fine, solid last name," Archdale said.

"So, perhaps, we need a first name," Wisdom opined.

"Yes, I'm certainly open. Do you have any suggestions?"

"How about Carlos?" Ian looked back and forth from Archdale to the man with one name. "Carlos Santiago. That has a certain natural sound to it, don't you think?"

The handyman then pronounced it slowly. "Carlos Santiago. Not bad. But it rings no bells."

"Marco." Wisdom tried again.

"Also nice, but no."

"Rupert. Or Winston. Maybe Winston."

"Now, you're just being silly," Archdale broke in and said. Santiago smiled.

"Winnie for short."

"Stop. This is serious," the reverend chided him with mock severity.

"Sorry, old duck. I'm just in a mood today."

"A mood that often enlivens you, I'd say," Archdale commented.

"So people tell me. What do you think, Juan?" Wisdom looked at his new acquaintance, eyebrows raised high.

"Juan," Santiago said, with a bit of surprise and a new look on his face. "Juan. That's a possibility, indeed. Juan Santiago." He bobbed his head slightly, back and forth, and a bit side-to-side, as if considering it favorably. "That somehow sounds better, and even possibly right. It strikes me as oddly familiar."

"Really?" Both Archdale and Wisdom responded, roughly at the same time.

"Yes. It could be the name of a terrible outlaw in the news, for all I know, but we can use it, as long as you two promise to keep me out of trouble, or jail."

"We'll do our best," Wisdom said. "But really, do you think your given name might indeed be 'Juan'?"

"Possibly so," Santiago said. "It truly is the first thing that's seemed at all familiar. It has … a strange resonance."

"Well, for our present purposes then, and until we learn otherwise," Wisdom pronounced, almost as if he were uttering an official decision, "the name of 'Juan' is hereby recognized for you, effective this day, in the presence of these witnesses, with all the powers vested in me as proprietor of this establishment, and so on, and such and such. It's nice to meet you, Juan."

All of them laughed, and the handyman said, "I thank you. It will be at least convenient to have a full pair of names to use until the mental fog clears and my past becomes accessible once more."

"And, who knows? We may have this little fact right," Wisdom said, with real optimism in his voice.

Archdale looked at his new friend and said, "You don't quite strike me as South American, Central American, or even Spanish. But that's neither here nor there. What do I know? We'll use what seems to work. And it does sound good."

"That's indeed a … sound approach," Wisdom added, lifting up a finger to punctuate his point.

"True Wisdom," Archdale retorted.

"I thank you, dear sir," Ian replied with a little chuckle. "And I especially thank our friend here, who shall not remain nameless, despite still being somewhat anonymous around the edges."

In the upscale neighborhood within Cairo where Haji and Khata had been walking home together, the boy moved quietly and quickly down a narrow alley behind the stores, and Khata followed close behind him. There were no other people in sight at this point. The alley was used mainly for deliveries, typically in the early morning hours. As they approached the right door, Haji could see that it was slightly ajar, almost closed but not quite. With his ear up to the opening, he could now hear voices. A man spoke harshly and in a thick accent. "Where are your scrolls?"

"I told you," a voice answered, "I sold them recently."

"Who bought them?"

"I don't reveal such things. It's a private transaction."

"You must tell me."

"I'm sorry, I can't."

Haji heard what sounded like a hard slap and a grunt. At this, his body tensed and he put his hand on the door, but Khata grabbed his elbow from behind. He looked back and she shook her head no as he felt her concern, and her words enter into his mind, "I'm not ready for this." There was a sound of a quick scuffle and a distinct click, as of a revolver being readied for use.

"Tell us now, or die here for your secret." It was another voice. "It's your choice."

"No, no, please."

"You have three seconds, and now two."

"Ok, Ok. It was another merchant."

"Who?"

"Adi. Shapur Adi."

"Who is he? Where's his shop?"

"His store is in the marketplace, one of the two main avenues. Anyone can point it out. Don't kill me."

"If this is not true, if we don't get our scrolls, we'll come back and you'll die then. I promise you that. Tell no one we were here. No one! When someone finds you, say that a criminal tied you up, here to rob you, but he heard a noise and ran. That's your story."

"Whatever you say. I promise."

"And if you're lying to us about the scrolls, you won't escape giving us the truth later, very painfully."

Haji grabbed Khata's arm and pulled her quickly away from the door. They were only a few feet from another merchant's back entrance. If it was also unlocked, they could get fast shelter. Haji tried the door and shook it and it opened. He guided Khata inside. It was dark and it was some sort of storage room. They got into it just a split second before the two men left the back door of the antique shop and came toward their hiding place.

Haji had left their door cracked just enough to be able to see the men if they walked by. As it turned out, they passed the door too quickly for him to get a good look at them. But he did notice that they were both light skinned, like northern Europeans, one with brown hair, one with lighter hair and taller. They also dressed as westerners, in dark jackets, light shirts, dark pants, and dark shoes. It was just a flash as they walked by, but Haji at least saw something. He looked at Khata and held his left index finger to his lips to signal continued silence. He noticed then that she looked afraid. After about three seconds more, he whispered, "I'm sorry. We have to follow them."

"Are you sure it's safe?"

"No, I'm not, but we have to. That's Phi."

"Ok."

He slowly pulled the door open and, hearing nothing, said, "Be causal." With those words, he took Khata's hand and led her into the alley again. No one could be seen, at first. He said in a low voice, "Quickly," and lightly pulled her in the direction the men had been going. Then he released her hand and walked fast, ahead of her, to the corner of the end building. From there, he could see the two men getting into a dark blue car a block away. He whispered more loudly, "We're going to lose them!" Haji then jogged across the street in their direction, trusting that Khata would be close behind.

The car pulled away when he was still some distance behind it and moving more quickly toward it. He stopped and watched to see where it would go. It didn't proceed in the best way to take the men directly to the marketplace. It turned too soon. But they could still go that way. Khata stepped up beside him, silent. He said, "We have to warn Mafulla's dad and the Sakat brothers who watch their shop."

"What about the poor man here?"

"What?"

"The man in the store. It sounded like they tied him up or something."

"Oh! You're right. We have to go back and check on him. Maybe he even has a telephone we can use." Haji glanced over toward the shop, and then looked back at Khata and said, "Are you Ok?"

"Yeah, yeah, I am," she replied. "I was just a little scared for a minute. It looked like we were going to get involved in something I'm not ready for, yet."

"I'm sorry, I just have these instincts to run right in," he explained. "You were right. We shouldn't have gone in to try to break it up."

"They had a gun."

"Yeah, at least one."

"And we don't."

"True. But we have skills."

"I'm just starting."

"That's easy to forget. I mean, you spoke to me with your mind."

"Yeah, Ok, but still, we did the right thing."

"I agree. Let's go check on the man."

They walked fast back to the alley and all the way to the door, which was closed but not locked. Haji opened it cautiously. It led straight into a darker part of the store. A storage room was off to the right. He stepped inside and projected his voice: "Hello?"

"Who's there?" A frightened voice called back in a near whisper.

"Were friends to help," Haji answered and walked in, looking around.

"He's over there," Khata said, pointing ahead and to the left. They made their way between some shelving and lots of items that were for sale and, coming to an aisle, saw the owner sitting on a wooden chair, his hands tied behind him and a rope around his mid-section.

"Help me," the owner said. "There were men here who tied me up."

Haji got straight into action, untying him quickly. "Did they rob you?"

"No, they were just looking for something, for items I sold days ago."

"What were the items?"

"A couple of old scrolls."

"Who were the men?"

"I have no idea."

"You never saw them before?"

"No," the elderly owner said as he removed his hands from the rope Haji had untied, and then rubbed his left wrist.

Khata, who had been standing back, now stepped closer and spoke. "You're bleeding." His jaw had been cut.

"I'm Ok."

"Are you sure?"

"Yes."

"These men: Were they foreigners?"

"Yes, Germans." He stood up slowly.

Haji said, "You know German accents?"

"I once lived there for a short time, in Munich, long ago."

"We need to report what just happened. I'm Haji Afah. My father is Masoon Afah."

"General Masoon? You're General Masoon's son?"

"Yes. We happened to be walking by and saw something suspicious and wanted to check on you."

"I'm so grateful you did. But I'm also glad you didn't come in when those men were here. Who knows what might have happened?"

"Yes, who knows," Haji said, but meaning something quite the opposite of what the old man had in mind. "Do you happen to have a telephone?"

"What?"

"A telephone."

"Oh, yes, we had one installed last week."

"May I use it?"

"Certainly. You know how it works?"

"Yes."

The man took Haji over to his desk where the phone sat silent. Haji picked it up and waited. He did something that Khata couldn't see.

"Where are you calling?" she asked, and he held up his hand.

Then he said, "Operator? Yes. Market 1618, please."

"Who's that?" she whispered.

"Mafulla's dad, at the shop."

"How did you know the number?"

"Mafulla just had a phone installed there, too, a month ago, and he chose the number for it. It's his favorite number, he said."

"1618?"

"Part of the golden ratio."

"What?"

"Shh."

"Mr. Adi?"

"Yes?"

"This is Haji Afah, calling with urgent information."

"Haji? Is everything Ok? Is Mafulla all right?"

"Yes, he's fine. I'm calling about you and your shop."

"What's the matter?"

"There are two men who may be coming there soon to try to take from you some scrolls."

"What?"

"I was walking by the Antiques and Antiquities Shop across town a few minutes ago. Do you know the place?"

"Yes, I do."

"Two Germans had just come in and roughed up the owner, looking for some scrolls."

"Oh, my."

"And they threatened his life, and he finally said he had sold them to you and didn't have them any more."

"Oh, no."

The elderly man, who was standing close by, listening to this, said to Haji, "Tell him I'm so sorry. Please, forgive me."

"The man says he's so sorry. He asks for your forgiveness."

Haji paused in silence, listening, and looked at the man. He said to the shop owner, "He understands." Then he turned around and looked out toward the window and spoke again into the phone, "Mr. Adi, those guys may be on the way right now, or later today, or tomorrow. They could be violent. So please, as soon as you hang up, go get the Sakat brothers. Tell them what I've told you."

"Ok, I will."

"I'll call dad and let him know what's going on."

"My wife is at home with the kids. Are they safe?"

"Yes. I think so. We'll alert the house guard as well. The Sakats will radio it in."

"Oh, good."

"But, please, go across to the Sakats this very minute."

"I will. I just have a few things to put up. Thank you, Haji."

"You're welcome. But this is important. Mr. Adi, when you put down the phone, just put down anything you may be holding and walk out the door now with no explanations to anyone. Don't do anything first. Leave the shop right away for help."

"Yes. I promise you, Haji, as soon..."

The line then went dead.

7

Three Phi

A dozen soldiers from a top army commando unit were out on the streets wearing dark green Cairo Water Works uniforms and going door-to-door to speak with residents. Reela knew that any obvious police or military presence might alert an enemy, if there was one in the area. Strangers in civilian clothing moving around door to door could also catch the attention of any wary adversary. And even electric utility uniforms might alarm their old nemesis, Juan Osvaldo Santiago, if he was alive, back in Cairo, and hiding out in the area of the outages. This strange man reportedly avoided living in cities at least in part because of the strange effect his presence was believed to have on electric currents. In the highly improbable scenario that he was the cause of the recent problems, he would likely be aware that any official search into the matter might create immediate difficulties for him. So, the simple ruse was that Water Works men would be neither feared nor suspected in any way. They could question neighbors about all their utilities and recent service without sending any signals that might spook a monster of legend in the area.

Many people, in response to the men's inquiries, were confirming the recent interruptions in electrical power and several said that they remembered the day the problems began. The soldiers were also asking about whether anything else out of the ordinary had happened at the time of the first outages, or on any day shortly prior to that. So far, throughout the morning's interviews, no one could recall anything too different or unusual.

Because of the remote chance that this problem might be due to the surprising presence of a highly dangerous enemy, three fairly advanced Phi—Walid's good friends, Paki, Omari, and Amon—were in charge of the operation. Masoon had personally assigned them to the duty, in consultation with Reela Adi. Masoon firmly believed that the likelihood of Santiago's being behind the problem was remote, but that, nonetheless, extreme caution should be exercised. He reasoned that if this dangerous, power hungry man was indeed alive and again present in Cairo, he would likely be causing problems much more severe than simple interruptions in the electrical supply. And in addition, Masoon speculated, it would make little sense for him to have reappeared in this way with the king still missing, given how they both had initially vanished together. But he understood Reela's concern and thought it should be taken seriously. Caution and safety should always lead the way.

After many hours of canvassing the neighborhood, Omari happened to be with two of the men when they received an interesting piece of information. A homeowner they were speaking with said that in his recollection, two days before the first outage, some new people had moved in across the street from him. It seemed not to be a traditional family, he reported, but four adult men dressed in western, or European, clothing. A truck had brought their belongings, among which were many large boxes that looked unusually heavy, given the apparent struggle of the men to unload them and carry them into the dwelling. Another neighbor then reported that the apartment they moved into had previously housed a big family who had all recently relocated to the kingdom of Iraq.

When Omari and the men crossed the street to knock on the door of the apartment in question, there was no answer. No one seemed to be at home. He made some notes on the address and what they had been told, and then they moved on to the next residence with their same questions. The information and this place got Omari's attention a bit more than most, but at first not strongly.

By now, neighbors had told them of many things that had happened when, or right before, the outages began. Two young women in the neighborhood had new suitors coming by, and the visits had begun around the time of the power problems. Three families apparently had new pets, two of them large dogs, and they had arrived on the scene at about the same time. A dark sedan had been observed going up and down a couple of the streets several times in recent days. And it was a car never noticed before by a couple of the older men in the neighborhood who often sat outside to talk, or by several of the ladies who now also reported it. One kid had been flying a new kite recently. A few teenagers had been getting into trouble of various kinds in the past week or so. Omari made notes on all these things, and he knew that the other groups were most likely collecting similar reports that they could all compare and analyze by the end of the day.

A physical inspection of the local power lines was going on at the same time that the teams were out in the field with their questions. No clear problems had been detected in the lines, poles, or transformers. Nasser Alexander had no idea of all that was happening in response to the simple inquiry he had made in Leem's office. But something important might be going on in the area, and both Leem and Reela were determined to discover what.

At about this time, Walid was in the king's sitting room, reading a long report. It was a complicated document full of technical details on kingdom agricultural production and trade, and he was growing tired. The school day alone had taxed his mind enough, he thought to himself. But this had to be done. He needed to get through it.

Just then, however, Mafulla opened the door and walked in. He was the only person Kular would allow to come into any of the king's rooms unannounced. The head butler knew the special relationship between the two young men, and understood how important it was during this difficult time. Walid looked up at his friend and said, "Save me from this report."

"You're officially saved. We're needed at my dad's shop."

"Why? What's up?"

"I have no idea, but we have to go there now."

"Both of us?"

"Yeah. Abandon kingly things for an hour and come with me."

"Ok. Is it one of your feelings?" Walid put down the report and moved it over to the side of the desk.

"Yes."

"Like yesterday morning?"

"Sort of, but there's no time to talk about it right now. We need to go immediately and get there fast. Can you set up a ride?"

"Sure. Do we need more Phi?"

"There's no time, I'm telling you. Believe me. We need to leave now." Mafulla looked very serious and even agitated.

"Ok." Walid stood up and shouted out, "Kular?"

"Yes, Your Majesty." The butler poked his head through the doorway.

"Please call down to have a truck waiting for us at the back entrance with four senior palace guards, as soon as possible."

"Right away."

"Come on," Walid said to Mafulla and began to walk quickly toward the door.

"That's more like it," Mafulla said. The two of them passed through the door and Kular's office, down the hall, toward the closest stairs, and kept going with a fast stride.

"Here," Mafulla said and reached out his hand to Walid.

"What?"

"I got your sand mask."

"You did?"

"Yeah, and I have your gun."

"Boy, at least we're prepared. You really think something that bad is happening?"

"I just tried to call the shop and the operator said we couldn't get through."

"There was no answer?"

"There was no connection at all. The line was dead."

"Odd."

"Yeah."

Just then, they were approaching a palace guard Walid recognized. He bowed as they drew near and said, "Your Majesty."

Walid said, "I need you to do me a favor."

"Anything, Sire."

"Go tell Bancom to radio the Sakat brothers and alert them that something may be happening at the Adi shop. Have them go check."

"Yes, Your Majesty. Right away."

"As quickly as you can."

The man nodded and jogged down the hall off in the direction of Bancom's office. Walid and Mafulla continued on, full stride, across the palace, through the long hallways, down a staircase, and out the back entrance. A truck was waiting.

"Naqid!"

"Your Majesty! When I heard of your sudden need for transportation and senior guards, I thought I'd come along."

"Great. We need to get to the Adi shop in the marketplace as fast as possible."

"Is there trouble?"

"We don't know yet. There might be."

"I have three men in the truck already, and two more on standby."

"If it's quick, bring them."

Naqid whistled loudly and motioned toward the truck. Two more guards came running from a nearby door. They did short bows to Walid and Mafulla, which always both surprised and gratified Mafulla, and then they followed Naqid's direction to get into the covered back of the truck with their colleagues. Walid said, "We'll ride in back. Drop us half a block from the Adi Shop. Keep one man in the truck and position the others in the back alley behind the store."

Naqid gave directions to the driver and hopped into the covered back with Mafulla, Walid, and the guards who were already sitting on the benches there. The truck pulled away and accelerated through the side gate, out onto a city street, and headed in the direction of the big market. Mafulla explained to all the men in back that he had a history of intuitions about family members and that he had just experienced an odd feeling that something might be wrong at his dad's store. He had often been right about such things, he reiterated. And so, to be safe, they were going to check on his dad. But weapons should be at the ready because similar past situations, unfortunately, had always required force. The men nodded. They had all heard about Masoon and his unusual intuitions, which were legendary among kingdom warriors. Naqid had a policy to choose as palace guards only top military men with great respect for the deeper mysteries of our lives.

After mentioning weapons, Mafulla pulled out Walid's revolver and handed it to him. The guards were all a bit surprised, but as a result, they understood the seriousness of the situation on a new level. Mafulla then showed Walid that his own was tucked into his belt. Within just a few more minutes, they were at the destination. The brakes squeaked as the truck slowed and pulled over to the side of the street. "Send the men out first," Walid said to Naqid. "Take them around back. And wait there for a signal. But don't let anyone leave the building." Naqid nodded and did as he was asked, walking quickly down the rest of the block and then up the side street and onto the alley that would take them to the back of the building. The afternoon lull at the marketplace made all of this easier. Few people could be seen on the street in either direction. None were close.

Mafulla said, "Mask on and Reverso flip time." He and Walid clicked over their watch cases, waited a few seconds, donned their sand masks, and jumped out of the back of the truck to head to the front door of the shop. But, suddenly, they heard a voice calling to them.

"Guys! Hey!" Haji was jogging toward them from down the street.

"Haji?" Walid turned and looked at his approaching classmate.

Haji said, "Yeah." Then, he turned to Mafulla, "I called your dad and warned him, but then the line went dead."

"What?"

"I called from the Antiquities shop where the guys had tied up the poor owner and were after the scrolls and found out that your dad had bought them."

"I ... don't know what you're talking about," Mafulla said, puzzled.

"Your dad's in danger from a couple of German guys with guns. I'll tell you more later." Haji said, and without any further questions or words of explanation, they all turned and ran toward the shop—three highly experienced crime-fighting Phi together. The phrase 'one for all and all for one' at that moment flashed through Haji's thoughts and he felt confident they could prevail over any opposition.

In his own shop in New York, Ian Wisdom smiled broadly and said to his visitors, "We're not busy now. Why don't I give you the grand tour of this place? Bishop Bob, of course, already knows his way around, but I'd love to acquaint you, Juan, as my newest potential customer, with the wide range of our fine merchandise."

"Very good," Santiago said. "If we have time?" He looked over at his new friend and employer.

"Yes, yes, absolutely!" Archdale said, "We have all the time we need. We're at your disposal, Ian my friend. I haven't been in the back room in some time, and would love to peek in to see what's new."

"Oh, well, yes, of course, but first things first," the proprietor replied. He looked at Santiago and pointed out, gesturing around them, "As you can see, we're a general store, which is rare enough these days in the city. We started as a small grocery. But the neighborhood was not being well enough served in other ways, so I expanded my initial business concept, and my stock. We first branched into hardware, perhaps a bit of a strange combination in its own right. But many people would come in for food items in those early days, and would happen to mention in conversation that they needed a light bulb, or some screws, or a pair of pliers, or a hammer. So we began stocking basic hardware items as well. You can see the relevant section over there. And, as the new handyman for the church, I hope you'll take full advantage of our stock and good prices."

Santiago nodded his approval of what he saw, at even a brief glance. Archdale said, "We do need a couple of things. Don't let me forget."

"Excellent!" Wisdom replied, and then continued, as he waved his hand in the proper direction. "As you can see, we added clothing to the mix. At first, some gardening gloves and aprons got into the hardware supplies, and then we just kept on going. Of course, most things start small, and this was no exception. Some very basic boots and shoes and socks, work pants, work shirts, jackets, gloves—such items got us started, and then we stocked more things, as needed."

He paused for a second and added, "A retired couple from the neighborhood, Charlie and Ella Hawkins, came in a while ago to help me out, part-time, Charlie with the hardware, and Ella with the clothing, and that freed me up to expand a bit more. The shop next door closed down when the owner passed away and his family didn't want to run it. So I bought the space and knocked out a wall over here to incorporate the space into my growing empire." With these words, he led his visitors through a doorway and into a small bookshop area.

"We stumbled into the book business. At first there were mostly cookbooks and handyman guides to home improvement and manuals on sewing and gardening—just practical things to supplement what we were already doing. It made sense. But I'm a lover of history and of reading generally, so the collection began to grow."

Santiago smiled and said, "It's very nice, and quite unexpected."

"Yes," Wisdom replied. "We can't be all things to all people, but we're getting close. In here we sell mostly used books, and some new. We have some strong titles in fiction, history, business, and, in honor of the Archbishop Archdale here, some hefty tomes in religion and philosophy—not exactly hot sellers, for the most part, but books that a few enjoy. There are some fairly intellectual types and even a few writers in the neighborhood, who are always also avid readers."

"I didn't know that," Archdale replied.

"Yes, it's quite a mix here of people and professions in this part of town." They were walking slowly through the bookshop area, and then Wisdom said, "Now we can go into the famous back room, where some proprietors with no actual propriety would run gambling parlors or sell whiskey, but where we have a few bona fide antiques and historical artifacts." He unlocked a door along the back wall, pushed it in, and flipped on a light switch. "We open this up only by request. There's not a lot of walk-in business for it, but we do have some regulars who appreciate the things I'm able to find."

It was a room of moderate size, not at all small. And on several tables and shelves, a variety of items were to be seen. There were weapons from what Wisdom called "The somewhat unfortunate but perhaps inevitable War of Independence here," and from the American Civil War, as well as things from other wars, expeditions, and times.

"We have some fine antiques from Europe," Wisdom said, directing their attention to a few small clocks and pocket watches, and a variety of vases and wooden boxes. "And, we're most fortunate to possess some true antiquities from the middle-east, and even northern Africa."

"Oh. That part of the world is of great interest to me," Santiago said. "It's a fascinating part of the globe."

"Your memory is indeed coming back, however slowly," Bob replied.

"Yes, it does seem to sneak in a new moment of remembrance every now and then," Santiago replied.

"What's the source of your interest and fascination?" the minister inquired.

"Of that, I have no idea," Santiago chuckled.

"Progress often comes in small doses," Archdale reassured him.

Then Wisdom walked over to a shelf and said, "We even have some of our older books back here, as well, so that they won't be overly handled by the more casual browsers." He turned to the man he now knew as Juan and asked, "Do you read any other languages, sir?" And, as he spoke these words, he handed him a very old looking book, bound in leather, with gold accents on the cover.

"Ah, Don Quixote, the Man of La Mancha," Santiago said. "The masterpiece by Cervantes—one of the great novels, perhaps the greatest of all. Is the main character a divine visionary, or a deluded fool?" He took the book very carefully and opened it up. "Yes, I seem to be able to read the Spanish quite well." He turned a few pages and said, "I love this passage about his companion, Sancho Panza." He then looked up at the other two men and said, "So, obviously, I've read this before, and I know it. More clues."

"Very nice," Wisdom said, and handed him another, more ancient looking book. Santiago put down the first thick, heavy volume, and took this one in his hand, a smaller book, but not by a lot. He opened it to the middle and said, "Oh. Arabic. Oh, my. Yes, yes, I see."

"You can read that?"

"Yes, I can. This is philosophy. And the language is old."

Archdale spoke up and asked, "How do you know Arabic?"

"I have no idea. But I do."

"There are some Arabs in Spain," Archdale said.

"Yes," Santiago replied.

"The plot thickens considerably," the minister remarked, clearly impressed. And he was right. But he couldn't possibly know that the plot was about to get much thicker, and quite soon. The unexpected events and fearsome antagonists he would have to face in his own church would not, like Don Quixote's adversaries, be denizens of his own imagination, but real and sudden threats to them all.

8

Tied Up

In Cairo, at Khata's house, Ara was sitting on the side of her bed. "I can't believe what you guys went through! You were both so brave!"

Khata had just told her the whole story about walking home from school with Haji, and how they stopped at the Antiques and Antiquities Shop to help the owner. She responded, "Well, I didn't feel brave. But, thanks, anyway. Haji was the brave one. And it was such an ordinary afternoon, except for the fact that I'd had a strange feeling for most of the day."

"Really?"

"Yeah, and then more than the feeling got strange."

"So Haji actually rode home with you in a taxi?"

"He did. One happened to come by, and he wanted to get me home and then go to the Adi Shop fast, and the house was on the way."

"Aren't you worried about him?"

"Actually, I am, a lot really, but just on one level. I wish I could have talked him out of going to where the bad guys would be, but when he was on the phone with Mr. Adi and the line went dead, well, that pretty much did it. He said he had to get there and help out if help was needed."

"But you said the men had guns."

"They both did."

"That's so scary."

"Yeah, it was."

"Wait. I just realized something."

"What?"

"You said you're worried about Haji, but just on one level. What does that mean? I'd be totally tied up in worry! I mean I sort of am already. And you're being so cool about it all."

"Well, listen, Haji clearly knows how to take care of himself. I mean, remember, he and Malik helped break up the operation of all those animal thieves. He's strong, way beyond his age, and he's not reckless. He showed me he knows how to be careful."

"But still, he's our age," Ara said.

"Yeah, he is. And yet, I have a calmness about it."

"Well, I wouldn't be so calm if he was my boyfriend!"

"He's not my boyfriend."

"Oh, yeah? He thinks he is."

"What do you mean?"

Ara scrunched up her face and said, "I talked to Malik at school, and Haji kind of thinks you like him."

"I do like him, but I'm not sure about the boyfriend stuff."

"He's really cute and strong, and really nice."

"That's how a girlfriend talks," Khata said. "Maybe it's you whose boyfriend he is, or should be."

Ara blushed and said, "He's all Mr. Smitten about you, not me."

"Oh, yeah? I saw how he got so into the conversation with you on the way to school this morning. I think it's really you he's interested in."

"Stop it. I just happened to be at your house, and he didn't come over to my house to walk me to school."

"Well, we'll see."

"I wish we could see what's going on at the Adi Shop right now," Ara said, and she stood up and sort of paced around the room. I mean, really, we should do something, shouldn't we?"

"What? We can't do anything," Khata said. "And I'm pretty confident Haji will get help somehow before he goes barging into a dangerous situation. He knows the difference between courage and craziness."

"How will he get help?"

"He knows the Sakat brothers, and they're sort of like palace guards, but they're in charge of security for the Adi store. You know, they're the guys with the leather shop across the street. They can see what's going on there from their front door. And they keep a pretty good watch on Mr. Adi."

"Still," Ara said.

"Yeah, I know … girlfriend."

"Stop it."

The palace school library was quiet, especially this late in the day. Kissa and Hasina were sitting at a long table and doing some work while Khalid and Hoda were still in their offices grading the last of the essays they were going to be giving back to the students tomorrow. They would all walk together to the El-Bay home for dinner, and Layla would join them there. But they had maybe fifteen or twenty more minutes to work before the two teachers would be ready to go.

"Hey, you guys. I thought I was the last one in the library this late, but you're both still here?" Set walked up to the table and put down some books on the edge of it.

"Yeah, we're working away for another few minutes, until Hoda and Khalid are ready to go," Hasina replied.

"What have you been up to?" Kissa asked him.

"Just some research," he said.

"You'd better be researching young women and relationships," Hasina said, with a straight face.

"What do you mean?" Set was clearly puzzled.

"I shouldn't say anything," Hasina said.

"Well, you already have," Set helpfully reminded her.

"The gentleman has a good point," Kissa said.

"I mean, I shouldn't say anything else," Hasina clarified.

"About what?" Set asked, still completely perplexed at what she was getting at.

"I just think that a certain young lady has a lot more interest in you than you might suspect. That's all I should say, and I likely shouldn't have said even that."

"Who?"

Hasina pursed her lips and raised her eyebrows.

"Who's the young lady? And why do you think this?"

"I can't give out any more information, but I have my reasons for thinking you need to be researching the best stuff you can find about relationship wisdom, for the sake of a certain someone."

"Who? Who?"

"Do you hear anything?" Hasina said to Kissa.

"I thought I heard the Owl of Minerva, going 'Who-Who.' But nothing else, really," Kissa replied to Hasina and then turned to Set with a smile.

Set let out a deep breath and just said, "Girls." He picked up his books and then added, "Well, it's been really nice, as always."

Hasina replied, "Thanks for stopping by."

Set turned and began to walk away. "Oh, one more thing," he looked back and said.

"What?" Hasina asked.

"Say hi to the young lady for me. Greet her warmly and wisely."

Both girls laughed. Kissa turned to Hasina and said, loudly enough for him to hear, "See? She has good taste, matching his keen wit." Set just shook his head slowly and walked away. Girls.

It was less than five minutes later that Hoda came into view and said, "Ok ladies, we're ready to go."

At the Adi Shop, Mafulla was the first through the front door. Walid was close behind him, followed by Haji. At first, the place seemed empty, which at this time of day would not have been unusual. But where was Shapur? Mafulla scanned the room. Then he heard a groan from toward the back. He rushed in its direction. Walid heard it too, and had his gun at the ready.

They rounded a corner of displayed items, and there on the

floor, face down, was Mumar Sakat, with his hands tied behind him. The boys got to him instantly.

"What happened?" Walid asked, as he gently turned Mumar over.

"Where's dad?" Mafulla said.

"Oh, my head." Walid freed his hands as Mumar groaned again.

"What happened?"

"Sorry, Your Majesty. I think I was caught by surprise. I came in and saw a European looking man tearing things up in the back, and then before I could intervene someone must have hit me from behind on the head. I guess I was knocked out. Ouch. It's pretty sore."

"Mumar! Where's dad?"

"Oh, he's with Badar! Sorry. Your dad came over to the store and told us there might be trouble. Moments after he arrived, we got a message from Bancom that Shapur might be in danger, but I said he was safe and with us. Your father then told us about the telephone conversation he had with Haji and I ran right over to the shop, leaving him with my brother for protection. The men apparently came into the back of the store just as he was walking out the front."

"So he's Ok?"

"Yes. He wasn't even here."

Walid ran into the back room and opened the door. "Naqid! Have you seen any men around back?"

"No, Prince—I mean, Your Majesty—no one since we got here."

"Ok. They must have gotten away right before we arrived."

"Who, Your Majesty?"

"There were men here, dangerous thieves, minutes ago, apparently, who ransacked part of the store. Mafulla's dad was the only one working this afternoon, and he got out just in the nick of time before the men came in, searching for something they had planned to steal. They also knocked out Mumar Sakat."

"Oh! Should I send the men to fan out and look for the criminals right away?"

"Yes! Have them go in both directions up and down the main street out front. It may be two guys together, or they could have separated. At least one looks European, possibly both. But they might already be long gone. Have the men go quickly to look and then come back in five or six minutes, in case we need them for something else."

"Right away."

Walid turned back into the shop and saw Mumar standing with Haji and said, "Where's Mafulla?"

"He ran back across the street to get his dad and bring him in to see if anything is missing."

"Oh, Ok, good."

Just then, Mafulla came in with Badar and Shapur. "Mumar, are you Ok?" Badar asked, with an expression of great concern. He saw that his brother was rubbing his head and grimacing.

"Yeah, just embarrassed and a little sore, and with a headache."

"I'm so sorry!" Shapur said.

"No problem, I've got an impressive lump on the back of my head, but, otherwise, I'm fine, I think."

"Did you see anything before you were hit?"

"Only one man going through your desk, throwing things left and right. He was tall, with light colored hair, typically European in complexion and clothing."

"I see," Shapur said, as he made his way to the desk. "Oh, my, what a mess they made in a short period of time."

"They were apparently looking for something specific and whether they found it or not, they just took off," Mumar said.

"Scrolls," Haji added.

"Scrolls?" Badar looked confused.

"Yeah, I saw the guys earlier today at the Antiques and Antiquities Shop across town, you know, in that nice neighborhood not far from the palace."

"Yes. I know it. What were they doing there?" Badar asked.

"They had tied up the owner and were yelling at him and pointing a gun and demanding some scrolls."

"Very strange. How did you discover this?"

"I was behind the shop, and the door was open. I could hear it all. Under threats, the shop owner told the men that he had just sold some scrolls to Mr. Adi, and that's when they took off, apparently to come here, but maybe with a short detour elsewhere first."

"Why would they want my scrolls?" Shapur asked, puzzled. "I still don't understand."

"I have no idea," Haji replied. "They didn't say anything about it when I saw them earlier. They were just interrogating the poor guy."

"Did they see you?" Badar asked.

"No. My friend Khata and I were walking back from school, and when we passed the store and felt something was wrong, we went to the back door of the place and listened and hid when the guys left. We just caught a glimpse of them. So they don't know I heard or saw anything."

"Good," Badar said. "Can you give us anything like a detailed description of them?"

"Wait," Mafulla said. "Dad, where are your scrolls right now?"

"At home, they're all at home in the nice leather box I have for them. I've never kept them here in the shop."

"Where are mom and the kids?"

"At home." Shapur suddenly looked stricken. He said, "Oh, no."

In New York, Ian Wisdom was taking his visitors back through the rambling general store, returning to the front area where they had originally come in. But Bob Archdale suddenly spotted an old trunk sitting over to one side with books piled on top of it.

"Wait," Archdale said. "I've been needing a storage trunk for some of my things at the church. By any chance, is this old trunk under the books for sale?"

"I suppose it could be," Wisdom replied, as he stopped and turned to see what Archdale was talking about. "Oh, I see the one you mean. Sure, sure, I could part with that for a reasonable amount."

"How much?" the minister asked.

"Well, I hope this doesn't change your mind, and I'm afraid I can't possibly be convinced to come down any from this, no matter what you might say, but I could go as low as … absolutely nothing?"

"Wait. What do you mean?"

"Let it be my gift to the enterprise, my little contribution to the cathedral. It's about time I gave a little to the grand enterprise."

"No, no, you don't have to do that."

"I know I don't. But you've been sending several new customers into the shop, especially in recent weeks, and they've actually bought things, unlike many who come in here just to look. So, I think I owe you a gesture of appreciation."

"No you don't."

"Wait. Are you trying to bargain me up? You want to get the price higher?"

"Well," Archdale said.

"Ok, double it," Wisdom said with a grin. "Triple it, for all I care, you shrewd man, but take it out of here before this negotiation gets any stranger."

Archdale had to laugh. "Ok, all right, if you're sure. But it's very generous of you."

"The trunk's been here for a long time and no one ever asked about it before, so I've just been using it to display some books, as you can see."

"What will you use if we take the trunk?"

"Oh, we have extra shelving in the back."

"Ok, I feel better about it now."

"But, for the price I'm getting from you, I can't afford to pay anyone to clear off the books and dust it, or deliver it, so if you wouldn't mind doing all that yourself, it would be great."

"Certainly! Santiago and I can do it, if you don't mind, Juan?"

"Not at all, it's a pleasure," the handyman said, inwardly amused at his name. He then bent down to begin removing the books that had been sitting on the trunk. "Should I just put these on the floor?"

"Yes, in neat stacks for now. We'll make a place for them later."

Once all the books had all been taken off, Santiago bent down to examine the trunk. "Nice. Old, but sturdy," he said. "It's clearly seen some travel in its day." Archdale pulled out a handkerchief and bent over to begin dusting it off.

"Yes. It's a little banged up, but not bad. And, I'm sorry about all the dust," Wisdom said, "But no matter how much we clean around here, there's always more. It's a task worthy of old Sisyphus!"

"Yes, the church is exactly the same way," Archdale said. "Sometimes, it seems to me that one common purpose of every building is to collect and contain all the dust and dirt that, without the architectural filters and repositories we put up, would simply be blowing freely about the earth."

"That's a novel perspective," Wisdom said. "I like it, since it would counsel just opening the doors and windows and putting the brooms away to allow this cosmic purpose play out in its own manner."

"I'm often tempted," Archdale said. "But, Ian, now that we've made sure to leave you with as much of the dust as possible here, could we just grab the trunk now and take it back with us to the church?"

"Yes, thank you. If I recall, it isn't that heavy," he replied. "If you each take one of the handles at the end, it should be easily manageable for the short walk back."

"Again, I really appreciate this generous act of kindness," the reverend said.

"Glad to do it," Wisdom replied. "Remember me the next time you speak with the Almighty."

"You mean that bossy older lady who's been a member of my church forever?"

"You're very funny, for a man of the cloth."

"My cloth and I thank you."

Wisdom smiled. "Here, let me push back a couple of displays, so that you won't have any trouble getting the trunk out." He walked forward toward the front of the store and adjusted some display racks to give the two men a bit more room to carry their treasure home. But then, he froze.

Archdale and Santiago immediately saw what had stopped him in his tracks. At a cash register over near the clothing section, a man in a dark jacket was standing at the counter and pointing what looked like a small handgun at Charlie Hawkins, as he fumbled through the cash drawer. The man had a dark kerchief tied up around his mouth and nose. He grunted out some sort of command and was shaking the weapon at Charlie, who at that moment had apparently finished filling a cloth bag with cash and then handed it to the man.

Time seemed to slow down for all of them. They had now stopped in place, and for a second they couldn't believe what they were seeing. In that long, paused moment, they all heard the thief say, "Down on your knees!" And as Charlie, with hands slightly raised in a posture of surrender, began to bend his knees and kneel down, the robber leaned over the counter and pointed the gun closer to him.

Santiago could hear the hammer being pulled back on the pistol, a sound so slight that it didn't register with either Wisdom or Archdale, as they were all a distance away and now standing at an angle to the intruder, who had not yet noticed them. It could have been in the next split second, but it's hard to say with certainty that any time passed at all between that distinctive sound and a loud shrill shout of pain involuntarily emitted by the gunman, who immediately dropped his weapon, which fell to the floor. BANG! It fired as it hit, and that stunned everyone. Bob and Juan simultaneously set the chest down, in reaction to it. Charlie at first thought he had been shot. But the bullet went harmlessly into a large container of sand in front of the far back wall in an area of hardware and gardening supplies.

With another shout of pain and a streak of profanity, the gunman, grimacing and shaking his right hand, turned and ran toward the door and through it, out onto the sidewalk. Santiago stared at the man's feet as he ran and, at that instant, the fleeing thief tripped and fell, sprawling out hard on the sidewalk, the bag flying from his other hand. Before Wisdom and Archdale knew what was happening, Juan was through the door and bending over the man, whipping out his old black leather belt, newly acquired from the church, and tying it around the hands of the criminal, who was still face down on the pavement.

Coming to his wits, Wisdom immediately ran over to check on Charlie, and as he did, he bent down and scooped up the gun that had been dropped. Oddly, the metal felt exceedingly hot to his touch, but at this point, it could be handled without actual pain. "That's very strange," he thought to himself. "Very strange, indeed."

Reverend Archdale ran out the door and onto the sidewalk himself and up to where Santiago had just finished tying the man's wrists. "I need your belt!" Juan said.

"What?"

"Please give me your belt, quickly," he said.

"Oh, Ok, sure," Archdale replied, while removing his own, thin brown leather belt, and handing it to his new friend. Santiago roughly tied the man's ankles, with his own knee in the small of his back.

The man was groaning in pain and at that point said, "What happened?"

"You fell from grace, and then on your face. That's what happened," Archdale replied.

"But the gun!" the man said. "It caught on fire! It burned my hand!"

9

A Box and a Trunk

"Well, so far, no one has seen Santiago or any trace of him," Reela said to Leem, as they sat together in one of the palace parlors.

The private detective took a sip of his tea and replied, "Of course, whether we can even remotely believe such a wild claim or not, the last we knew of him, from what I was told, was that he was in possession of the famous Ring of Gyges discussed by Plato, the legendary invisibility ring. So I suppose it shouldn't surprise us that no one has yet actually caught sight of him." And, saying this, he smiled.

Reela replied, "That's what I heard as well. And you just never know. Some legends, myths, and ancient stories have a way of surprising us."

"But an invisible man?"

"Well, I suppose many of the important things in life are ordinarily invisible, in themselves. And science portrays the world these days as being much stranger than we could have imagined."

"Still."

"You just never know." Reela said and paused. Then he added, "But that alleged situation was before the big confrontation with the king."

"And yet no ring was found at the site of the confrontation, was it?"

"No, nothing was found. So, your somewhat playful point still stands. We have to keep our minds open to a level of oddness altogether commensurate with the monster himself."

"Yes, I suppose you're right."

"It's a strange business, for sure."

"Indeed."

"Here we are, looking for something or someone who might just be impossible to see."

Leem pondered this for a moment and said, "Well, I hope that's not what we're up against. It's hard enough to find the normally visible missing persons of the world."

"I would imagine you have plenty of experience with that," Reela commented.

"Yes, and we're working on such a case right now that's getting interesting."

"May I ask what it might be?"

"Certainly. There are no legends involved, but it's a good tale."

"Oh?"

"It's a job we're doing for an older lady who's trying to find a long lost love. He was a young soldier when they met, many decades ago."

"I see."

"With his name and some long remembered tidbits of where he was stationed during his military duty, we've been able to fill in a few more of the details."

"And you say it's getting interesting?"

"Yes, it turns out that, after his service, our elusive soldier may have become an archeologist, or perhaps an assistant to a well-known senior archeologist, working in various countries and remote locales in the middle-east."

"It's not the most common occupation," Reela said.

"No, it's not, and that's helping us to some extent," Leem added. "It seems that our mystery man might have been involved in bringing certain ancient artifacts into Egypt, whether legally or not. We're unsure at this point."

"Ah, that adds a twist."

"Yes, if it was illegal activity, then the man may not want to be found."

"But if it was legal, tracing the artifacts may help you to track him."

"Exactly. So, either things are worse or better than they otherwise would have been for our search."

Reela laughed and said, "So much of life is exactly that way."

"True."

"We often don't know whether our situation, as it changes, is improving or degrading."

"And we always hope for the best," Leem said.

"While preparing for the worst," Reela added.

"Absolutely."

A few miles away, things were tense. By the time that Walid, Mafulla, Haji, Mafulla's dad, Badar, Naqid and the other guards, except for one, had climbed into the truck for a quick ride to the Adi home, Mumar had gotten back to his shop to radio over to the men whose job it was to watch over Shapur's house, day and night. A single palace guard had been left behind to help Mumar keep the shop secure, in the aftermath of what had just happened there.

The truck went quickly down one street and the next, as Mafulla and his father tried not to worry. Surely Mumar could radio word to the guards near the house in time to get the family out and to safety. But the men who were in pursuit of the scrolls would have had a head start of at least a few minutes in what might be a desperate race to the Adi home. And as they all knew, minutes could be a disastrous advantage for violent criminals with a clear goal. And several precious innocent lives were at stake.

The truck pulled up right outside the Adi home, and all the men jumped out quickly to run toward the front and back doors. Mafulla, with two of the palace guards, made it first to the front door, and rushed through. He saw two men with guns standing in the presence of his mother and younger brother and sister just a split second before he recognized them as the neighborhood guards who were often posted down the street, within sight of the house. His heart spun instantly from sharp alarm to reassurance.

"You're all right?" Mafulla said. And as his mother nodded, he looked back and called out, "Dad! They're fine!"

Sammi and Sasha were clearly a bit overwhelmed at all the men coming in with guns, and Mafulla could tell that they were doing their best not to break out crying. "It's Ok, guys," he said. "Everything's going to be fine. We're just here to make sure everybody's safe."

As Mafulla said this, Shapur walked in and hugged the kids and then his wife. But Sasha was only five years old and still looked like she was on the very edge of shedding tears. Shamilar was now holding her hand and said to her older son, "What's the danger we face? These men just got here and have said only that there is a possible threat and they're here for our protection."

"Yes, I'm so sorry we didn't have time yet to explain," one of the men said to Shamilar, and then added, "But perhaps your son can do it better, with more complete information."

Mafulla said, "It's totally fine. I'm just glad you guards got here so fast. I really appreciate it." He looked over at Shamilar and said, "Mom, there are some men who are looking for certain ancient scrolls, and they went to the Antiques and Antiquities Shop near the palace to try to find them. They seem to have thought the scrolls would be there, but they weren't, and so the men tied up the owner and hit him and threatened to shoot him unless he told them where the items they sought could be found."

"Oh, my!"

"Yes. And under dire threats, he explained that he had sold his only scrolls to dad, and so they left and went to our shop."

"Violent men with guns?"

"It's Ok, because Haji, who had heard about all this, by a huge coincidence, or rather a blessing, had just telephoned and warned dad to go somewhere safe."

Shapur spoke up. "That's right. And I went over to tell the Sakat brothers, and the thieves snuck into the shop when I was gone and they knocked out Mumar Sakat when he came in to check."

"No!"

"And they ransacked my desk and cabinets and didn't find what they wanted, and they must have left just seconds before we got back there."

"My goodness!" Shamilar said. "Shapur, are you all right?"

"Yes, darling, I am," he said, as he walked up closer and put his arm around her. "I'm just glad you are, too."

"Why? Did you think they would come here?" she asked.

"Well, this is where the scrolls are," he replied.

"But do they know that?"

"If the men couldn't find the scrolls at the shop, and I own them, they would likely guess that they could be at my home," he said.

"And they know where we live?"

"Oh!" Shapur said, as he turned to Mafulla, then to Naqid. "They might have no way of knowing where we live."

"Really? Are you sure?"

"Well, they were just told about my shop and its location, and not about our home—is that correct?" He looked at Haji for some confirmation to justify his sense of relief.

Haji said, "That's right. We didn't hear anything said about where you live, now that I think about it. But couldn't they have gotten that information from your office?"

"I don't think our home address is written on anything there."

"So, that could be why they aren't already here," Badar said.

"But can't they still find out where we live?" Shapur asked.

"Anyone can find out anything with enough time and money, or threats," Naqid commented.

"So, what should we do?" Shamilar asked. "It sounds like they'll be here as soon as they learn of our location. And we know so many people, that may not take long."

"I'm scared, Daddy," Sammi said.

"Me, too," Sasha added. And, right then, as soon as little Sasha spoke, Mafulla thought he heard something outside the window.

Across a vast ocean, it was late in the afternoon. The church was quiet. A few people had come and gone during the day, some to pray, others to just sit in contemplation. Reverend Archdale had counseled two congregants who were suffering with various forms of trouble, and then had talked at length with a married couple who had been faced with a great difficulty. Few people ever came to him to share good news. It happened, and he always enjoyed it, but most people asking for time with him brought problems, heavy personal burdens that he would then seek to help them bear. It was not easy to end a day with so many big troubles weighing on his heart, and a heaviness of spirit that could trouble him through the night if he didn't do something to cleanse his heart and mind.

At the end of his last counseling appointment for the day, Archdale got up from the desk where he had been making notes, stretched his back, and wandered toward the kitchen for a snack. Sometimes, a bite to eat, and even going outside to provide a treat for the birds would be all that it took to restore his normal cheer. When he walked through the doorway to the kitchen, he was pleasantly surprised to see his new handyman and caretaker sitting at the table, reading.

Archdale said, "How's your afternoon been, my friend?"

"Less exciting than our visit to the Wisdom shop," Santiago replied.

"Good! That was quite an unexpected adventure."

"Yes, it was."

"The robbery was frightening," the minister said.

"It was also very odd at the end," Santiago mused.

"That business about the man's gun catching fire—who's ever heard of such a thing? And then, to see him simply fall on his face right outside the door where there was nothing to trip him."

"I was looking right at his feet when it happened."

"Of course, you, my friend, were certainly the hero of the day."

"Well."

"You jumped into action before the rest of us could even move, and tied up that man tight until we were able to fetch the police."

"It was all instinct," the caretaker said. "I had no time to think. I just found myself leaping into action."

"Well, I wish more of us could respond like that in a time of crisis!"

"At least, Ian got his money back," Santiago said.

"Yes. And we made it home safe with our new trunk. Thanks again for that help."

"I'm happy to be of assistance," Santiago replied.

"I see you're doing some reading," the minister observed.

"Yes, after completing my list of small jobs around the church for the afternoon, which went more quickly than I had thought, I decided to take a break and have a glass of water. And then I looked around at your books on the shelf here and picked one to peruse. I hope that was all right."

"Certainly."

"I actually found several of interest. This is your English translation of the ancient Chinese classic, *The Tao Te Ching.*"

"Oh, yes, I recognize the cover now. And my books are all yours while you're here, so avail yourself of them at any time."

"Thank you."

"You read things from many cultures, it seems."

"Yes. I find it fascinating that the best wisdom about life to be discovered across cultures and throughout very different times is so similar, deep down."

"My feeling exactly."

"People's lives seem so vastly different in various parts of the world, but human nature is always the same, beneath it all. And so the basic insights that help in one culture, will likely help just as well in another."

"I agree completely."

"I love the image of a wisdom river that runs for thousands of miles."

"Oh, I don't know that image," Archdale said.

"This ancient, winding river, in all its twists and turns, passes and feeds a vast variety of different plants, trees, and vegetation along its way, winding through forests and grasslands, high country, and low, and for the entirety of its span, it brings the same cool waters to all."

"Very nice."

"Yes, it's a wonderful image for the deepest insight, ever flowing, nourishing, and growing all those of us who would draw from its waters, whoever we are, wherever we live, and whatever our different circumstances might be."

"I like this a lot," Archdale commented.

"We too often focus on our differences, on what separates or divides us, while this single stream of truth and value could unite us all."

"I think your stream, your river, goes quite deep, and far."

"Yes. I agree. I gain the most from books like this that focus well on life and reflect on what can be learned from it and about it. Some of the most profound secrets available to us hide in plain sight." He thought for a moment and said, "Many important insights remain hidden to most people because, in contrast with our often superficial perspectives and expectations and prejudices, they can seem outrageous and false at first glance. For example, there is the truth that selfishness is self-defeating, or the insight that, as an adult, you must first give in order to properly receive, or the surprising fact that humility can be a source of power and greatness. Such perspectives can seem false to the superficial glance. But it's rather the surface illusions hiding these insights that are deceptively false."

"That's quite profound. You, my friend, are even more of a philosopher than I realized," Archdale observed.

"Thank you," Santiago replied. "I'm indeed a lover of wisdom. It's the greatest source of power on earth. I seek to find it, embrace it, and live with it intimately in everything I do."

"More clues!"

"That's true. I speak about myself now as if I were not mostly opaque to my own gaze and remembrance. And yet still, the rest is blank."

"I think you're gradually recovering from whatever clouded your memory and, even though it's not happening all at once, the improvement is going on all the time in small ways. I believe I can hear a new sense of self-confidence in your words and even see it in your face and your actions. You're coming back, my friend!"

"May you be right," Santiago said. "Of course, I'd like the process to quicken its pace. But I can be patient." He smiled.

"Good! Patience is a doorway to many things," Archdale said.

"It truly is."

"And faith helps, too."

"Yes, you're a man who has built your life around faith, it seems."

"I am." Archdale paused for a moment and then said, "Do you want to hear a short story?"

"Yes, that would be nice." Santiago put a piece of paper in the book he was holding to mark his place and then closed it.

Bob sat down in another chair at the table and said, "Once, when I was a young man, I was at the ocean, in southeastern North Carolina, not far from where I lived, walking on the beach. I was enjoying all the sights and sounds of the day—the graceful, but sometimes noisy, ocean birds, the white caps on the water, the wispy clouds decorating the bright blue sky. I saw a young porpoise jump up from the surf and gracefully return. I remember the sun was warm on my face that day. Then, suddenly, it occurred to me that I should try an experiment in faith."

"Oh?"

"That moment, I stopped in my tracks and looked down the beach along the line of the water off to my left, fairly straight and even for at least a mile or more ahead of me. Then I closed my eyes. I stepped forward in the faith that I could walk along the shore in a straight line without seeing, as I moved forward."

"How was this walk of faith?" Santiago asked, with a smile.

Archdale laughed and said, "I walked only about fifteen steps before I had to open my eyes to see where I was."

Santiago laughed. "I understand."

Archdale smiled and explained, "The inner pressure was too great. I gave in to my uncertainty. But then, I thought to myself, 'This is no good, I have no faith.' And I decided to close my eyes for fifty steps. That was my clear goal. I walked and I counted, and it was hard. I wanted desperately to sneak a peek at where I was. The desire to know almost made me dizzy. And that really bothered me. So, standing motionless for a moment and with my eyes still closed, I inwardly screwed up my courage and I said to myself, 'One hundred more steps with no sight, just feel: for one hundred more paces.'

"Oh, my," Juan said.

"Yes. I had to defeat this need in me. I had to have faith! So, I started walking forward again with my eyes still closed, and once more I began to count. At thirty more steps, I felt a new form of light pressure in my soul; at forty, more pressure; at fifty, my mind begged me to stop and I felt almost dizzy again but I kept going. The inner stress of the unknown grew with each successive step. And by the time I got to eighty paces, it was almost painful to put a foot forward again on that path I could not see. Something in my mind was begging me to stop and open my eyes. There was a lack of trust that was almost screaming out to me."

"What happened then?" Santiago said. "You were so close."

I was."

"Did you make it?"

"At ninety paces, my head nearly started to throb. I panicked. I thought, 'This is crazy!' But it was real. So I took a deep breath to calm myself. And I kept going. 'I'm stronger than this,' I said to myself. At one hundred steps, I stopped. I had made it. I opened my eyes, looking first at my feet. It was such a relief! I felt like a huge weight had been lifted from me. But when I looked up and noticed where I was, I was so surprised!"

"Why?" Santiago asked. "Where were you?"

"By a lake on the side of a mountain in Tibet."

"What?"

"I'm just kidding."

"Oh! You had me going there for a second."

"Thank you. I do my best. It wasn't actually anything so shocking, but it was a surprise. Unknowingly, I had been walking a crooked path, diagonally oriented to the water, moving ever closer toward it. Thinking that I was going straight and parallel to the water's edge, I had veered at an angle moving toward the surf, as if it had been calling me beneath my conscious awareness. Or it could have been the gentle slant of the sand down to the water, which was so gradual that I was altogether unaware of it at the time. But that very state of unawareness may have participated in allowing it to have an effect on me that I didn't feel. And that, I think, is why the great spiritual traditions have always stressed the importance of awareness."

"Very interesting. So, unaware of the forces that had been impinging on you, your path was diverted by them."

"Yes, I think so. And that may be a metaphor for the normal human condition. But, whatever the cause, I had gotten way off track."

"Just as you did a moment ago in telling the story," Santiago said with a straight face.

"Indeed. Touché!" Archdale laughed and continued, "In that moment of surprise in my real version of Tibet, where I had gone for a bit of revelation, on the beach, it came to me that, without any clear vision to guide us in life, we'll almost inevitably veer off course. We'll wander and get out of line, ending up some place we don't want to be. We can be pulled and nudged by any force that impinges on us, whether we're aware of it or not, and especially if we're not. But with our eyes wide open, we can much more likely walk a straight path."

"That's very wise. And what conclusion did you draw about faith?" Santiago asked.

"Ah. That was big for me. Authentic faith doesn't involve just blindly moving forward with no use of the resources you have available to you. Trusting providence doesn't mean refusing to use what you've been given. In fact, it's quite the contrary. Right then and there, I immediately said to myself, 'Bob, my good man, you should always look where you're going. Have a clear vision for your life that's inspired by the best you can learn. Pay attention to where you are. Consider where you need to be. Look for how to get there. Eyes wide open. Use what you have. And use it well. And then have faith that you'll receive whatever guidance and support along the way that you need.' The faith I was experimenting with that day with my eyes closed was really just a faith in myself, in my own abilities and orientation. And that doesn't work without also having faith in something greater as well, and a clear view of things."

"Very good," Santiago said.

Archdale continued, "I realized, standing so near the water, that blind faith is not what's asked of us in this life, but faith combined with clear sight, or faith with vision: a deep trust that operates with a full awareness of the mind and heart together."

"Nice," his guest said, nodding his head. "Very nice, indeed. I like your conclusions."

"Thank you, my friend. If I had continued my little experiment in blind faith, I could have walked right into the water, and the whole thing would have ended with a form of baptism I would not have expected!"

Santiago laughed and said, "Indeed. The whole story is a good one."

The minister admitted, "I've used it in sermons more than once over the years."

"I'd love to hear one of your sermons."

"In a sense, you just did. But, you're always invited to the official ones."

Santiago nodded with a smile. Then Archdale said, "I almost forgot. I was going to ask you if, later on, you could take a look at a part of the old trunk we just acquired from Ian. We may need to make a small repair."

"Sure. What's the problem?"

"One of the feet it sits on looks a little loose, and jiggles a bit.

I was wondering if you might be able to fix it before I open up the trunk and start loading it down with stuff."

"Sure. Let's take a look now," Juan replied, and he got up from his chair, as did Archdale. He picked up the book he had been reading and slid it back onto the bookshelf where it belonged. Then the two men walked together to the room where the trunk had been put down. The late afternoon sun fell precisely on the old item of storage.

Bob bent over it, and pointed to one of the tarnished pieces of metal on which it sat. He said, "See, here, it's one of the feet on the back. It's twisted a bit to the side and must be loose."

"Yes, I can see what you mean," Santiago responded, as he also bent down to look. "That should be easy to fix. If we can first turn the trunk over, I can get a better look, find out how it might be attached, and see what tools I need."

"Good idea," Archdale said. "Let's do it." He grabbed a handle on his side, while Santiago did the same on his end. They slowly turned the trunk first on its side and then on its top and were carefully putting it down when the reverend lost his balance and dropped his end the last inch or so. "Ow!" he exclaimed. "I'm sorry! That was clumsy!"

"Wait," Juan said. "I heard something inside it just as it hit the floor."

"I thought it was empty," Archdale said.

"I did, too. But something rattled."

"I hope I didn't break anything. Should we reverse the process and see?"

"I would normally want to go get my tools and fix the foot first, but in the remote case that we just overturned something containing a liquid, like a bottle of ink, or wine, or whisky, we might get a mess on our hands unless we check it right away."

"Whisky? Here in the church? That would indeed be a mess!"

Santiago laughed. "Oh. It would still be holy."

"What do you mean?"

"Wholly your fault."

Archdale laughed. "I agree. So let's turn it back over and check."

They did so, and heard a noise again, as of something that was now loose inside. It was not likely a bottle, but something else. And so Archdale immediately unlatched the lid on both sides and opened it for the first time. "Well, I'll be," he said. "What in the world?"

Santiago looked inside and saw right away what must have happened. He reached in and picked up a thin, dark wooden box, and said, "This was apparently under a false bottom the trunk has. Look, right there," he pointed. "This slat came loose, and the interior secret compartment gave up its contents when we overturned the trunk and dropped it just now. It didn't take much, so it must have been loose already, but this box then fell out. Look over here, at this."

"Oh, I see what you're saying," Archdale replied, as he peered into the trunk. They both now examined what originally would have looked like the bottom of the empty trunk, but a panel of it had broken loose and what had been behind it had, as a result, tumbled out when the trunk was upside down. What was perhaps long hidden was now suddenly revealed—a movement often seen in life.

"This long thin box was stashed in the trunk in a secret compartment, and it's light enough in weight that none of us suspected there was anything in here at all."

"I wonder what's in the box, and why it was hidden away like that?"

"We shall see." Santiago now turned the mystery box over and used his thumbnail to pry the lid loose, which he then removed. And they both were quite surprised at what they saw.

"My goodness," Archdale said.

10

The Discovery

"A scroll!" Santiago spoke what they both had just realized. "It looks very old."

"It does," Archdale agreed. "I've never handled such a thing. Should we take it out to see what it is, or maybe try to find someone who knows how to do that without damaging it?"

"I know how to handle it," Santiago said.

"You do?"

"Yes. We first need to put the box down on a table."

"Over here," Archdale directed him, moving to the side and clearing a place on his work desk.

"Ok." Santiago put the box down on the top of the desk, and gently reached into it, to take hold of the contents. "It's papyrus," he said. "First used by the ancient Egyptians."

"Is it delicate?"

"Outside of a very dry climate like Egypt, it won't do well over time."

"Oh."

"It may not be as old as it looks, due to possible humidity damage. Or it could be quite ancient."

"I wonder what it is." Archdale mused, and looked on as Santiago slowly slid the scroll out of its protective container.

"We'll soon see," Juan replied.

Then, taking hold of it with an extremely gentle touch, he began slowly and carefully to unroll it, a small bit at a time. He then placed a paperweight down softly on an unmarked portion of its leading edge as he delicately coaxed more from the roll.

"The first markings here are Arabic, aside from this place near the beginning of the scroll where it looks like the ink has peeled off, leaving a faint mark where it had been."

"Yes, I see what you mean," Archdale said, as he leaned forward, focusing his eyes closely at the spot to which Santiago was pointing. "It seems like a faint outline of the Greek letter Phi, with the circle and the vertical line through it."

"I believe you're right," Santiago said. "The mark is just barely visible, but it is indeed a Phi."

Archdale squinted at it and said, "Interesting. Can you read the Arabic?"

"Yes. It's an old, archaic dialect, but I can make out the first lines here. It says that this document is a companion to a master scroll, or book on the origins of the society or community … that's responsible for so many of the wonders of the ancient world. It will provide a key to reading the greatest secrets presented by that other document."

"Do you think this is authentic?"

"It certainly looks that way. It says also that no one should read on, except for the most senior members of the society."

"That's odd." Archdale said. Although, as he said this, he had a very strange, visceral sensation, almost of fear, that what they were seeing was more than odd, and perhaps even dangerous.

"Yes." Santiago answered simply. And he felt a sense of awe, and then a physical shiver go through him that he couldn't quite understand. "Something is strange about it. I can't quite say what it is. I feel almost as if there's a power here, in or through the scroll."

In a residential neighborhood of Cairo, inside the Adi home, there were at least two different conversations going on. But Mafulla was focused on a sound he thought he had just heard outside the nearest window. His father had moments earlier taken Badar and Naqid into another room to show them the scrolls he kept there. Shamilar was talking to Walid, and Sasha was holding the king's hand. Haji was across the room, chatting with young Sammi. Mafulla now took two steps away from his mother, Sasha, and Walid, who at first either didn't notice or didn't think to wonder what he was doing. Then he took a few more careful steps in silence toward the front door, concentrating all his energy on listening to anything that might be going on outside the house, and especially right beyond that window.

Only Walid then sensed that something might be wrong, and he softly said to Mafulla's mother the words, "Please excuse me for just a second," and he kissed Sasha's hand, which he then released with a smile, saying, "I'll be right back." At the moment, Haji didn't know that anything might be going on, because Sammi had just pulled him out of the room where they had been with the others. He said he wanted to show Haji something in his bedroom toward the back of the house.

Walid now moved across the living room, following his friend to the front door. But, as soon as Mafulla had reached that threshold and stepped outside a second or two ahead of his friend, he instinctively exploded at a full, frantic dash toward the corner of the house and around it. The soldiers out front near their truck momentarily froze in place out of sheer surprise, not knowing what they were seeing or what they should do about it.

The young king was as shocked as they were, but had the presence of mind to motion for them to follow his friend, along with him. He now took off and ran as well and put out his arm to grab the side of the house and help him make the abrupt turn at nearly full speed. As he came around the corner, he suddenly stopped and again was instantly puzzled at what he was seeing. Mafulla had a boy a little younger than the two of them penned up against the wall. The boy's dark hair was longer than most. He was dressed in the manner of an average, working class family. But his face and eyes looked wild. As Walid came up, Mafulla was just then saying, "What are you doing?"

"Nothing!" The palace guards were now in the boy's sight behind Walid with their guns out. Two of them glanced around in every direction. But they hung back a distance, to more fully assess what was going on.

"No!" Mafulla said. "What are you doing at the window of this house?"

"I live here!"

"No, you don't!"

"I live next door!"

"No, you don't."

The boy suddenly struggled, trying to break Mafulla's hold on him and, when he couldn't, he said, gasping a little for breath, "I live in the neighborhood. I was here to see my friend."

"Stop it now! Stop making up lies, and tell me the truth about what you're doing, or else you're going to prison, or worse, and you'll never see the sun again."

"I can't tell you!"

"You have to."

"Yes," Walid spoke up and said. "You have to. I'm Prince … former Prince Walid Shabeezar, and I'm now your king. I respectfully command you, in my role as your king, to tell us the truth, now, right now. No more lies."

The boy looked stunned, and then really paid attention for the first time to the soldiers with their guns, and after two seconds of baffled silence, he fell down to his knees, allowed to do so by Mafulla, who could see at this point that he was no longer trying to escape.

"Please, King … King Walid! Don't hurt me! Don't put me in jail! I'm sorry! I'm sorry!"

"What are you sorry for?" Walid asked.

"My grandfather told me to come here!"

"Why? For what purpose?"

"I'm supposed to find out where some scrolls are."

"Why would your grandfather send you to do that?"

"Do I have to tell you?

"Yes. You do."

"Ok. Ok. I was working in my uncle's shop today, and I was in a small storage room looking for something when I heard men come in and they started shouting at my uncle. And I peeked out the door and saw one of the men holding a gun. The other man shoved my uncle down on a chair and began tying him up while the first man yelled and demanded some scrolls. And Uncle Asham said he didn't have them. And they said they'd shoot him if he didn't tell them where the scrolls were, and one of the men hit him and finally he said he'd sold them to Mr. Adi, and they left. And I was still hiding, too afraid to come out."

The boy fell silent, as if reconsidering what he should say. Mafulla simply directed him with the words, "Go on, please."

The boy looked around at everyone listening to him and said, "Then, after a few minutes, I heard some other voices, from younger people, I think. But I was afraid to even look out at that point. And then my uncle was freed, and after everyone else left, he remembered I was there and called out to me and came to get me and checked to see if I was Ok. Then he told me what had happened. And he sent me home and I told my grandfather everything. And he said I should come here and look around and listen, if anyone was at home, to see if I could discover where the scrolls are, and if they'd been taken." The boy's words quickly tumbled out at this point. Mafulla's hand was still on his shoulder, in case he tried again to shake loose and seek to escape.

"Ok, Ok, this is better," Walid said. "Now, who is your uncle?"

"Asham al-Buri, the owner of the Antiques and Antiquities Shop."

"And who is your grandfather?"

"Elam al-Buri."

"What does he do?"

"He's retired. He stays around the house a lot. He reads. He talks about the old days when he was young."

"Why would he want to know about some scrolls?"

"I don't know."

"Tell us," Mafulla said, in a stern tone of voice, but with less harshness than before. "You must tell us."

"I would if I could! But I truly don't know! I'm so sorry! King Walid! Please forgive me. I didn't know that what I was doing would make anyone mad, or get me into trouble."

Walid said, "It's Ok. You can get up now. But tell me this, do we need to tie your hands and feet, or will you freely stay with us for a time while we figure this out?"

"I'll stay. I didn't know you were King Walid." He sort of bowed. "I'll do anything you say."

"Ok, good." Walid looked at his friend and said, "Mafulla, please take our friend here into your home."

"It's your house?" the boy said, surprised.

"Yes."

"Oh."

Mafulla took him by the arm and led him gently back toward the front of the house. Walid turned around and saw that Naqid had come out and had been listening.

"Did you hear all that just now?"

"Yes, Your Majesty."

"What do you think we should do?"

"I think we should talk to the grandfather right away to see what's going on. We need to learn what he knows."

"I agree. You and I can go with Mafulla and two of the soldiers. You choose them. Let's leave the other guards here with Badar and Haji, so they can protect the family while we gather more information."

Walid then turned back to the boy. "How did you know where the Adi family lives?"

"My grandfather gave me the address and directions."

"How did he know?"

"He didn't tell me. But he's lived in town for many years and knows lots of people."

"Ok, we'll find out. Right now, we need you to go with us and direct us to his house."

"Is he in bad trouble?"

"No, not necessarily. He may be in no trouble at all. In fact, he may need our protection so that the men who came to your uncle's store won't visit him with guns and hostile intent."

"Oh."

"We'll get in the truck out front and go there in just a minute."

"Ok."

"But first," Walid said, "What's your name?

"Nappi."

"Nappi?"

"It's short for a longer name."

"What's the longer name?

"Utnapishtim … al-Buri."

Mafulla said, "That's a very different and long name."

"Yeah, that's why people call me Nappi."

"It comes from a very old story," Mafulla commented.

"It does? What story?" The boy looked puzzled.

"The Epic of Gilgamesh," Mafulla explained. And then he added, "It's actually the oldest epic tale that we have in writing and comes from about four thousand, six hundred years ago."

"Wow. Who's Utnapishtim in the story? What does he do? Nobody's ever told me this."

"He's a very special, mysterious man who lives far away from most people, and he's a man the gods have favored and allowed to live forever. He has the secret of everlasting life."

"Really?"

"Yeah."

Walid thought that this connection was odd. But he got back to the matter at hand and asked, "How old are you?"

"Four thousand years."

"Very funny. You're pretty quick."

"Thank you."

"How old are you really?"

"Eleven," Nappi answered.

"You're big for your age," Mafulla said. "And strong."

"Yeah. Thanks."

"I'm sorry I had to get a little rough outside," Mafulla said. "My family is under threat from some people who are violent and who are trying to steal some scrolls from them."

"It's Ok, I understand. I'm Ok."

"Good.

Walid had just stepped back inside the house to see Badar and Haji. He wanted to make sure they knew what had just been learned and explain quickly the plan for what would happen next. Shapur and Shamilar also listened intently, and were glad that extra protection was being provided. He then said, "We don't think we need to move you at this point, because we have no reason to suspect the Germans know yet where you live. But they may gain that information soon, since, as we were saying earlier, you're not exactly a family of recluses. You're well known around town and, likely, somebody will spill the beans at some point, not knowing they're helping criminals."

Badar at that point added, "And if they do come here, they'll be surprised to find they're seriously outnumbered and outgunned. We'll take them into custody and then find out what's going on. They'll not get what they're after."

"You're right. It's a good plan," Walid said.

"And we'll keep everyone safe, meanwhile," Badar assured him and everyone else.

Walid replied, "Good. I'll let you know if we need to have everyone move to a more secure location, depending on what we find out in the next hour or so. Meanwhile, Mr. Adi, would you take a closer look at the recent scrolls, and write me some notes on what each one is, to the extent that you can tell?"

"Ok, sure, Your Majesty," Shapur said. "But again, I apologize about all the trouble. Who knew that a simple hobby could cause such crazy commotion?"

"You certainly couldn't have anticipated any of this. We'll figure out why it's happening, and exactly what's going on," Walid said.

Mafulla stepped in and said to both his parents, "I'm really sorry all this is taking place for you guys. We'll find whoever's behind it and stop them soon so you won't have to worry."

"Be careful, my son!" Shamilar said and walked over to hug Mafulla.

"I will," he replied.

"Walid—I mean, Your Majesty: Are you sure this is safe?" She turned and asked.

"Yes, thanks, I'm sure," he answered. "Both for us and for you."

"I trust you," she said. "Just take care of Mafulla."

"Mom," her son said.

Walid nodded to her with a smile and assured her, "I will, although most of the time, he's the one taking care of me." He looked around and said, "All right, we need to go now and see our new friend Nappi's grandfather." He and Mafulla walked back outside to join Naqid and the palace guards who would go with them to the place where they hoped to find some answers quickly.

"Nappi, what's your grandfather's address?"

"319 Village Way."

"That's not far from the Cairo Detective Agency," Mafulla said.

"You're right." Walid wrote down the address and gave the note to Badar, who had stepped outside to see them off. Within less than a minute, the truck was on its way to what would be a big surprise.

In the palace, Leem Hadad had just gotten up to leave Reela's office, where they had been sitting for the last bit of their time together. Their talk had gone on longer than Leem had thought it would, and he needed to get back to work on the case at hand. As he was about to leave, he said, "I want to thank you for all your time today, my friend. It's always enlightening when we have a chance to talk."

"It was good for me, as well," Reela said.

"Let's just hope that we solve the Santiago mystery soon," Leem added with a smile.

"Yes." Reela also smiled in response, and then, suddenly, his expression totally changed. "Oh! How could I have been so stupid?" He exclaimed this as he stood quickly from his chair. He held his forehead in his hand for a second and shook his head.

"What is it?" Leem asked.

"My brother! I need to go see my brother! I didn't think of it until this very second. Shapur can likely tell us whether Santiago's back!"

"What do you mean?"

"Didn't you hear? After his time in the hospital and the brush he had with the next world, he returned to this one with a new ability to see in his mind's eye wherever that miscreant might go."

"Oh?"

"Yes. It was very useful to us for tracking the man and trying to discern his intentions, back before the faceoff he had with the king and then disappeared, along with Ali. Shapur would have visions of Santiago and could see in the visions a small area around the man, however no more than a few feet in any direction, so we couldn't pinpoint exactly where he was, but it was still very helpful."

"How in the world was he able to do something like that?"

"We have no idea, but it certainly seemed reliable. The world is indeed a very strange place."

"I suppose you're right. But wouldn't your brother have gotten in touch with you if he had detected Santiago's presence back in town?"

"Yes, he would, if he had become aware of it. But it could be that he has to be thinking about Santiago, focusing on him, in order to have that strange experience of his immediate whereabouts. And most likely, the terrible man just hasn't entered his mind at all in recent days. I mean, why should he? We've all been assuming he's dead and gone."

"Good point."

"Shapur has probably tried to get the whole mess out of his mind and heart. It could very well be that he's done something to diminish any special awareness of Santiago that he otherwise might be having, since he has no idea that it might still be helpful and important to us."

"I see," Leem said, with keen interest. "So, perhaps, if you ask Shapur to focus his mind on Santiago, then he'll be able to tell us whether our adversary is somehow alive and still here in Cairo."

"Yes, because of his special connection or ability. And for whatever reason, that possibility hadn't occurred to me until this very moment. Hold up a second and I'll walk out of the palace with you. I need to go see him, and I have time before my next scheduled meeting."

"What would you think if I went with you?" Leem asked.

"That would be nice. We can go together. But I don't want to keep you from your work."

"No, no, in a sense, this may also be my work, and I have a strange feeling that we might learn something from the visit that will be helpful to me in more than one way."

"Oh?"

"Yes. Call it an old detective's hunch."

"Well, then, let's go," Reela replied. "Shapur may be home from work by now. We'll head first to the house. If he's not there, we can go on to the shop. There may be something, some window into the truth here, that's awaiting us both at one place or the other."

"It could be just the discovery we need," Leem said, with a strange sense of assurance about it all.

"Now that you speak in this way, I find myself feeling even more confident about it," Reela commented, as he ushered Leem out the door and they walked together at a brisk stride down the hall. "We'll take a palace car."

II

A Surprise Meeting

At the church in New York, the scroll had been put away for the time being. Santiago was going to examine it more closely, later on in the day. Reverend Archdale had to speak with his music director before the weekly scheduled choir practice. He wanted to add a hymn to the upcoming service. The new handyman was working on an inner door at the moment, fixing a latch that had been broken for a long time.

A young boy hesitantly walked toward him and then stood, watching him work. The boy must have been no more than five or six years old. He was quiet, standing about ten feet behind Santiago, and then he suddenly broke his silence by saying, "I know who you are."

Santiago turned abruptly around and said, "Oh, hello."

"Hello."

"What did you say just now, a moment ago?"

"I know who you are."

"You do?"

"Yes."

Santiago was amused by this and decided to play along. He said, "Well, I seem to be having a little trouble with some of that information right now. Can you tell me what you know?"

"You came here from somewhere else."

"Where did I come from?"

"Another place. A place where things are really different, and I think it's far away from here."

"What else can you tell me?"

"You have a job here."

"Yes, I do."

"You have power."

"Oh?" Santiago chuckled. "What sort of power?"

"Big power," the boy said.

A woman's voice could be heard in the hallway near the sanctuary. "Clark! Clark! Where are you?"

"I'm in here, Mamma, with the man," the boy turned and said.

"Come back here, son! We have to go now," the voice replied.

"Ok." The boy turned again to the handyman and looked at him, eye to eye. "I have to go."

"When you come again, we should continue our talk," Santiago said, still amused by the boldness of the little fellow.

"Ok. You have to do your work soon."

"Yes, actually, I have to fix this door right now. And you have to go, I believe."

"I mean your other work. Bye." The boy turned and ran to his mother.

Santiago called after him, "Goodbye, my friend." He thought about this odd encounter for a moment, and within the quiet of his mind said to himself, "That was unexpected and different."

Thousands of miles away, the royal palace car pulled up to the Adi home and stopped. Reela and Leem got out and walked to the front door of the house. Reela stepped up and knocked loudly and was surprised to see Badar Sakat, of all people, open the door.

"What's wrong?" Reela asked, right away. He knew the Sakat brothers well and was glad they'd been assigned by King Ali to guard the Adi store and the family, whenever they were in the shop. But there was another guard detail positioned at a house in the neighborhood here, and Badar would be present at this location only if he was needed for some extraordinary reason.

"Reela! Leem! Come in," Badar said and quickly added, "Everyone's fine here." He then took a couple of minutes standing just inside the door to fill them both in on what had happened, from the incident with Haji and Khata, on through the discovery of the boy Nappi. He explained that Walid and Mafulla had gone with the boy to question his grandfather about what his role or knowledge might be regarding the whole situation. They were seeking some sort of understanding as to what could be going on and why.

'What's the address?"

"I have it here on a piece of paper," Badar said. He walked over to a table and picked up the note. "Let me see. It's 319 Village Way."

"That's just a few blocks from my office," Leem commented. He turned to Reela and said, "Maybe we should join the men there after you speak to Shapur."

"Yes, that might be a good idea. Let me go see my brother." Reela walked back through the house and found Shapur. They talked for no more than two or three minutes. And then Reela rejoined Leem where he was now waiting outside at the palace car. He said, "No sign of the adversary for now. Let's go," and then, as he was getting in, he told the driver "We need to get to 319 Village Way, as quickly as we can." But then, a second before they pulled away, he lowered the window and said to Badar, "Stay alert, my friend."

At the address in question, Walid, Mafulla, and Naqid were right outside the front door with Nappi. Naqid said to the king, "I should follow our young man in with guards backing me up, and then, Your Majesty, when we're absolutely sure it's safe, you and Mafulla can enter."

"Ok," Walid replied. "Thanks." He understood the extra caution.

Naqid then sent Nappi into the house first and he called out, "Grandfather, I'm home and I have some visitors with me!"

Naqid followed him, and the two palace guards they brought along walked in right behind their chief but stayed several feet back. Elam al-Buri suddenly appeared in an inner doorway, armed, and with his old rifle half-raised toward them.

"Stop where you are!" He said this in a loud voice and then aimed the gun at Naqid. "Nappi! Come here! Get away from those men!"

"Palace guards!" Naqid said. "Egyptian military!"

"What?"

"Palace guards here just to speak with you!" Naqid said.

The man looked completely puzzled. "I thought you were thieves."

"We're the good guys," Naqid said, still not raising his own weapon. "We're chasing the thieves. We want to help you."

"What do you know of me?" the older al-Buri asked, hesitantly lowering his gun just a bit.

"We know you sent your grandson to check on Shapur Adi's house."

"What of it?" he said, a bit defensively.

"For what reason did you do that?"

"Why should I tell you?"

"Because, otherwise, we'll have to arrest you in front of him, and he's a good boy who shouldn't see that."

"I have this gun."

"Yes, and we have many more."

"There are three of you."

"There are more outside."

"Why? What's going on? Why is the palace guard involved in this?"

"Mr. Adi's son lives in the palace, in service to the king, and his family has been threatened. We have to be involved."

"You're really from the palace guard?"

"Yes. I'm Naqid Bustani, head of the guards."

"How can I be sure of this?"

"Look at us. How are we dressed?"

"Anyone can steal a uniform."

"The king himself is also here."

"What?"

"Put down your weapon and I'll ask him to come in."

"No, this is a stupid lie."

Nappi then spoke up and said, "He's telling the truth, grandfather. I've met the king. He's here."

Elam looked at his grandson and then at Naqid and the two guards behind him and said, "Ok. Ok. I trust my grandson and his words." He bent over and put his rifle down across a low table. And then he took a step back and spoke again to Naqid. "Show me then the most unlikely visitor I could ever have here in my house."

"It's clear, Your Majesty," Naqid said, turning his head, "You can come in." And at that cue, Walid walked through the door, followed closely by Mafulla.

"Oh, my goodness," Elam said. "Your Majesty!" He bowed deeply. "It's true! I'm stunned."

"You recognize me?"

"Yes, yes, Sire, I've seen your picture, and I've seen you at a distance once before when you were serving as the prince of the kingdom. I know you're stepping in as our monarch while King Ali is away. I have the greatest respect for you and your entire family."

"Thank you. You honor me."

"I'm sorry for my belligerence and distrust earlier. I didn't know."

"That's not a problem," Walid said. "It's natural. But we just have some questions for you. You may be able to help us."

"I'm shocked. I don't know what to say. But, please, ask anything."

The sun had almost completed its daily course, and the sky was now much less bright outside the small house where this conversation was taking place. Long shadows were starting to creep across the neighborhood. One lamp was already lit, before the unexpected visitors had arrived, and it helped to illuminate the room they were all in. "Could we sit down?" Walid asked.

"Oh, forgive me! Yes, please, it would be my great honor! Here, take the best chair I own!" The man bowed again and gestured to a stuffed armchair that was clearly old but comfortable looking, and positioned on the other side of the room.

"The rest of us are fine with the floor," Naqid said.

"And what am I thinking? I'm hosting the King of Egypt and his friends! May I get you anything? Tea? Cookies? Some fruit?" The man was obviously embarrassed by his initial hostility, and now seemed flustered in his sudden realization that this was an occasion instead for the best hospitality he might be able to offer. He sputtered, "Anything at all! Anything! Just say the word! I'm your servant."

"Thank you so much for your kindness, but we're fine," Walid replied. "There's no need for you to go to any trouble."

"I assure you, I don't normally greet guests with a rifle in my hand. I don't actually have many guests. Life has been upside down recently, and now your visit, it's so unexpected—and wonderful. I admire greatly your uncle, King Ali. I've always revered your family, which is what inspired me to join the military years ago, to help preserve the kingdom they had worked so hard to build in decades past. We've had difficulties in the meantime, as you know, but I always hoped the Shabeezars would return to bring back our former glory and dignity."

"I thank you for your kind words," Walid said. "While my uncle's away, I'm doing my best to carry on his vital work."

"Oh, yes! I'm sure!" al-Buri said. "I've read about his current absence from the city and your good work in his place."

"You were in our military?"

"Yes, Your Majesty, as a young man, Fourth Division, First Regiment."

Just then, Reela Adi appeared in the doorway, with Leem Hadad not far behind. He knocked lightly and said, "Excuse me. I'm sorry. May we come in?"

"Oh! Hello, Reela!" Walid said, and turning to his host asked, "Is it all right? These are friends."

"Oh, yes, Your Majesty! Any of your friends is most welcome," the man replied.

"Please, then, join us," Walid said, surprised to see the men. "Hello to you also, Leem. What brings you both here?"

Reela answered, "Your Majesty, We just visited Shapur and

found out you were all at this address. Something led us to come. There may be information here that we need."

"Interesting," Walid said, as he considered this. "I'm glad you're here."

"Are things still quiet at the house?" Mafulla asked his uncle.

"Yes, all is well there," Reela assured him. "More men have been positioned nearby as additional security."

"Good."

"We arrived only minutes ago," Walid explained. "Our host, here, was just telling us of his military service, Fourth Division, First Regiment of the army, years ago."

"Oh?" Leem said, now fully in the room as well.

"Please, have a seat," Walid said to the new arrivals.

"Yes, please sit," al-Buri replied. And then he said, "I was indeed in the army. But it was long ago."

"May I ask your age now?"

"Eighty-four," he answered.

"You look very fit."

"Thank you. I eat moderately and exercise. I try to take care of myself."

Leem looked over at Walid and said, "I'm again so sorry, Your Majesty, for interrupting whatever was going on here before we arrived. But what our host has just said could be of importance to a current investigation. May I ask another question or two?"

"This may be the reason we're here," Reela commented.

"All right, Leem, surely, but I need to ask our host something first, for the sake of time, if you don't mind."

"Certainly, Your Majesty," Leem said.

Walid turned to their host and said, "Do you know anything about the men, the Germans, who attacked your son in his shop today and then went to the Adi store to look for something?"

"No, I have no idea who they are."

"Do you know or even suspect what they'll do next?"

"No, Your Majesty. I'm sorry. I have no knowledge at all of these men or of their plans."

"Why did you send your grandson to the Adi home?"

"I wanted to find out what was going on, to protect my son from any further trouble, and myself, and Nappi."

"But why send him, then, in particular, to go snooping around?"

"An eleven year old boy would never be suspected of gathering information about such a matter. He could do so safely, I believed."

"And why to their residence, instead of the shop?"

"I knew the men would go to the Adi Shop, because of what my son told them. That was too dangerous a place to send Nappi. But I figured if he went to Shapur's home, he might hear something or learn something. It was not so likely, but I had to do something."

"To protect your family?"

"Yes."

"Ok, then, but you're sure that you have no information that would help us to locate the men now and arrest them?"

"I'm afraid not. I wish I did."

"All right. There must be another reason we're here."

"If I can be of help in any way, I would be honored."

"I'll ponder the situation for a moment. And, so, meanwhile, Leem, please ask whatever you'd like. Perhaps you hold the key."

"Thanks so much, Your Majesty." Leem turned back toward the man of the house. "I'm a private detective and I've been trying to track down a man about your age who also served in the Fourth Division, First Regiment, many years ago."

"Is he in some sort of trouble?" Elam asked.

"No, no, it's nothing like that," Leem said. "Actually, the newspaper is going to do a story about this soon. An old sweetheart of his, a lady who fell in love with him when she was young, has written us a moving letter about her desire to find him. They were separated by the needs of the military and kept apart by her family. But now, a long and difficult marriage is over for her and, as a widow, she feels a great desire to be reunited with this man, if only for a meeting to share greetings and memories. He should be about your age. I realize the unlikeliness of this, but I wonder if by any chance you may have known him, a man named Elam al-Buri."

At that, everyone in the room other than Leem and Reela felt very surprised and looked at Leem. "I am Elam al-Buri," the man said.

"What?"

"I am the man."

"My goodness," Leem said. "This is too big a coincidence." He glanced over at Reela, and then at the king.

Elam said, "I could not be more shocked, except by the presence of the King of Egypt in my own home, I suppose."

"You knew the lady of whom I speak?"

"Yes. The lady is Bara Husani, or that, at least, was her family name."

"That's the name she used to sign the letter, although she also mentioned that her married name was El-Ari."

"Yes, that was the name of the man her mother forced her to wed."

"I'm sorry," Reela said, "but, Leem, there is a piece of information we have about Elam that may be relevant to the king's presence here."

"Oh, yes. Elam, you worked for a time as an archeologist, didn't you?"

"Yes, I did."

"In that work, did you come into contact with any ancient scrolls? As you may know from speaking with your son, this is what's currently posing a problem for the Adi family, and is of great interest to the king."

"Yes, yes, I'm afraid I did. And I'm very sorry for any trouble it's bringing to you now."

"Can you please explain it all to us?" Walid asked.

"Yes, Your Majesty." Elam took a deep breath and paused for a moment before he began his story.

12

The Black Widow

The girls came into the classroom and saw a list that had been written on the blackboard.

Kingdom: Animalia
Phylum: Arthropoda
Class: Arachnida
Order: Araneae
Family: Theridiidae
Genus: Latrodectus
Common Name:
Black Widow Spider

As soon as Kit had sat down and read through it all and got to the end, she said, out loud, "Ewww. Gross." Then she turned to Bakat and said, "This gives me the shivers."

"Me, too," Bakat replied.

"Have you ever seen one?"

"Yes. Once. It was scary."

"The whole idea of these creatures totally creeps me out."

"Yeah, they're like these weird little super poisonous things, almost like angry aliens from another world."

"They make my skin crawl."

"As long as they don't crawl on my skin."

"Ha, yeah."

"Then, I'd just scream and die right then and right there, on the spot."

"Me, too."

"They wouldn't even have to bite me."

At that point, the most diminutive girl in the class, Cabar, came in with her books and said, "What?"

"Look at the board," Kit replied with an expression of near total disgust, gesturing in its direction.

"Ok." Cabar started at the top and read the Latin with concentration on the endings so that, at least in her mind, she would pronounce it all properly, and then, realizing what she was reading about, she finished aloud with the word, "Yuck. I think my insides just jumped."

Bakat said, "Us, too. How can words do that to us?"

"Yeah, it's amazing," Cabar said. "Words can do the work of things."

"I guess in a sense words are things," Kit replied.

"True, and sometimes they're powerful things," Cabar conceded. "Tools. Jewels. Weapons. Blessings. Curses."

"Ah, deep," Bakat said, impressed.

"Where's Hoda?" Kit now asked, to no one in particular.

"She'll be right here," Kissa said instantly, as she entered the room and overheard the question, crossing the threshold.

"Oh, Ok. Hi Miss Kissa."

"Hi Kitty Kat. What's new?" Kissa put down her book bag and sat down two chairs away from her slightly smaller, perky friend.

"Not much, except for thoughts of spiders."

"Oh, yeah?"

"Yeah, on the board."

"Oh."

"Did you hear about Khata and Haji?

"Just a few minutes ago."

"Wild," Kit said.

"Yeah. I'm glad they're Ok," Kissa replied.

Hasina walked in at that point, in conversation with Khata and Ara. Greetings were exchanged all around, and Kit again pointed out the blackboard, eliciting the expected reaction from Ara. But Khata and Hasina just nodded, looking serious.

At that moment, Hoda swept into the room.

"Good morning, all!"

"Good morning," a few of the girls responded, while others greeted her in different ways.

As their teacher put some books down on the big desk in front, Kit spoke up and said, "What's with all the evil, creepy crawly information on the board this morning?"

"Oh," she said. "Khata, please tell the class what you dreamed about last night."

"A black widow spider," Khata replied.

"Hasina, now, would you also please share the focus of your scary dream last night?"

"A black widow spider."

"Kissa?"

"The same."

"What?" Bakat said out loud. "Three of you had the same dream last night?"

"Four of us," Hoda said. "And, maybe not exactly the same dream, but dreams about the same thing."

"You, too?" Kit asked.

"Yes, and we don't know why. That's a little too much to be a coincidence, don't you think?"

"Yeah, for sure."

"And there were no stories in the newspaper about spiders, there was nothing on the radio, and no one we know had brought up the topic recently. Then, in one night, the four of us independently had black widow spider dreams."

"That's just crazy," Cabar said, adding, "and maybe a little scary."

"What happened in your dreams with the spider?" Kit asked.

"That's another strange element," Hoda answered. "None of us can remember anything that the spider was doing, or anything else going on in the dream, except for the presence of one item."

She looked over at Khata, who then said, "a radio."

"What?" Kit asked, puzzled.

"A large radio," Kissa added.

"A really big radio," Hasina said, "with lots of knobs and stuff on it."

Hoda explained, "Hasina came to our house this morning to walk to school with us, and she was the first who first brought up having such a dream. Kissa immediately chimed in and said she had dreamed the same thing. And since I had as well, I knew something was up. Then, this morning, Khata and Ara were waiting for me in my office and Khata told me what she had shared with Ara on the way to school, that she had dreamed of a spider and a large radio."

The girls just all looked perplexed. This was far too strange. Hoda explained, "So, I came in here right away and wrote what you see on the board before I went back to the office to put things together for class. I thought I'd better say something first thing this morning about the particular spider we all saw."

"Why? What do you think's going to happen?" Kit said with great hesitation in her voice.

"I don't have a clue whether anything's going to happen," Hoda said, "and even if it does, I don't know if whatever takes place will involve a real black widow spider, or maybe something that this creature is standing in for, or symbolizing."

"Oh, My Gosh," Bakat said. "This is giving me goose bumps in a new way already."

"There's no need to be alarmed," Hoda added in a soothing voice, "But I thought that it wouldn't hurt to have a conversation about this creature to start our day. And Khata showed me a few minutes ago a picture she had drawn of the spider in her dream. It looks just like the one the rest of us saw, so I wanted her to share her drawing with all of you this morning. Notice in particular the bright, colorful red hourglass marking that's characteristic of the spider, so that you could spot this particular one immediately, if you ever saw it."

"If and ever being the operative terms, I hope," Ara said, and then shuddered.

"Yeah, definitely," Cabar echoed. "With never being more than slightly preferable."

"As we pass around Khata's drawing for you to see, I want to tell you something about these spiders and how they operate." With these words, Hoda began her short lecture that kept the girls on the edges of their seats, occasionally voicing their disgust at what they were hearing. Kissa and Hasina then joined in, reminding the class of the day some time ago when dangerous spiders were released on palace grounds in a spot frequented by Walid and Mafulla and visited that very day, for a picnic, by all four of them.

"So we've already had enemies of the kingdom use poisonous spiders to try to sicken or kill representatives of the government," Hoda reminded them.

"Do you think something like that could happen again?" Bakat asked.

"We don't know," Hoda replied. "But anything's possible."

Earlier in the morning, long before the school day was to start, a group had convened in the king's large sitting room. Present were Walid, Mafulla, Haji, Malik, Masoon, Hamid, Naqid, Reela Adi, and Leem and Ibrahim Hadad. Hoda and Hasina's mother, Layla, had also been asked to attend, and they were actually the first to arrive.

Walid opened the meeting and used a few minutes to update everyone on the series of events that had begun when Haji and Khata approached the Antiques and Antiquities Shop on their way home from school the previous day. Leem, of course, had already told Ibrahim about the discovery of their mysterious former military man, Elam al-Buri, and the young detective was at once excited, and yet at the same time a little disappointed that it was not his own sleuthing that had resulted in a discovery of the man. But

Leem reassured him right away that, indeed, his work had been quite important, and that he was very proud of all that his nephew had done on the case. "All's well that ends well," he reminded his younger associate.

Today, Ibrahim would send a telegram to their client to share the good news and put her in touch with Elam, so that she could have the meeting she had longed for. He would also arrange for a reporter from the paper to be present to witness the great reunion and to speak with them both about it. The resolution to this moving tale would make a heartwarming second installment to the story the paper was already going to run, likely tomorrow, and readers would love it.

For those who had not been at Elam's home, Walid had important news to share. He said, "Mr. al-Buri, it turns out, during his military service, was exposed to some important Egyptian antiquities, right after they had been unearthed from an archeological dig in a nearby nation. How they got there is unknown, but it was his job to help return them to our National Institute of Historical Preservation, where they could be catalogued and kept safe as a part of our heritage. During this time, his immediate superior gave him some things to keep privately that he said were of no real national importance but still might one day be of financial value, just as antiquities. He was told to consider it a small gesture of appreciation for all the good work he had done. And, as a young soldier, he was thrilled to be personally recognized and rewarded in this way."

Masoon spoke up and said, "Excuse me, Your Majesty, but I would venture a guess that, among those items, were some scrolls."

"Yes, exactly. There were two scrolls, one clearly of Egyptian origin, and one written in another language that Elam suspected might have been used long ago in or around its place of discovery, the ancient city of Uruk, in Sumer, or Mesopotamia, but now known, of course, as the Kingdom of Iraq."

Hamid said, "That could be Sumerian, the world's oldest known written language, or the closely related language of Akkadian."

"Both quite ancient, indeed," Hoda remarked. "But, wouldn't it be unusual to see either of those languages used on papyrus scrolls?"

"Yes, it would," Hamid said and added, "since they both involve cuneiform script, descended from the very earliest proto-writing pictographs, and were typically inscribed on clay tablets by the use of a reed stylus, or hard pen. You don't typically see them used on scrolls of any sort."

"And Sumerian would have died out long before there came to be a use of papyrus," Hoda added.

"Yes, that's correct, but Akkadian evolved for a long time, and could have been used. And yet, in any case, my guess would be that a papyrus scroll from that area is written in Aramaic, which went on to replace many Akkadian documents, as early scribes copied and translated important writings into something less ancient and more widely accessible."

Mafulla said, "Aramaic was the language Jesus spoke."

Hamid replied, "Yes, although it was around long before his time."

Naqid then said, "When Shapur showed us the scrolls, he unrolled one a bit, and it may have been written in Aramaic. I've seen the language before. But I'm not sure, since it's not one I can read."

Walid said, "We'll get someone on that. We need to have the scrolls gone over thoroughly, I think, to see what we're dealing with and figure out why someone is trying to steal them."

Leem said, "I think I can find a trustworthy translator."

"Good. Thanks, Leem. Please do so as soon as possible."

"I'll get on it right after we adjourn."

Walid nodded and looked around the room and said, "Now, to continue with our update: We learned yesterday that the young Elam was told to put away both the scrolls he had received, and keep them hidden and safe, which he did. And then, some years later, he was contacted by his old officer, the man who had given him the items, and was informed that they could be dangerous to retain any longer, and especially to read."

"Interesting, and more than a little unusual," Masoon said.

Walid replied, "Yes. I agree. And, some time after that, he received a note from the now retired officer saying that, apparently, someone was looking for the scrolls. And then, in a very short time, Elam learned that this man, his former superior, had suddenly died under suspicious circumstances. Elam immediately hid the scrolls in what he considered to be an even safer place, outside his home. And years passed, then decades. But just recently, he started thinking about the scrolls again and wondering if they had indeed become worth anything, financially, as he once had been told. He retired as a carpet importer many years ago, and with his advancing age was in need of some additional income, and so he asked his son, now an antiquities dealer, if he could take the scrolls to sell. The younger man agreed, and that brings us up to the purchase of the items by Mafulla's father, and the events that Haji and Khata witnessed."

Leem looked over at Mafulla and asked, "Has anything else happened at your family's home?"

"No, fortunately," Mafulla said, adding, "But I'm a little nervous about it all."

"So the Germans have just disappeared?"

"Apparently, at least for now."

"We need to find these people before they do anything else," Masoon reminded everyone.

Leem offered, "I remember reading that we have some new German cultural exchange people in town. Should we locate them and set up an interview as a possible first step?"

"Good idea," Masoon said. "I'll have someone make enquiries. And I'll contact their embassy and our people about any recent arrivals."

"This may be nothing," Reela commented, "and may not be related in the least, but there have been some electric power outages in the neighborhoods near Leem's agency and, with Masoon's help, we've been canvassing the area to see what we can learn about possible causes."

"How did you get involved in a power company matter?" Walid asked.

"Leem was trying to discover the cause of the outages as a favor to a man in his neighborhood, but was getting nowhere with a couple of the relevant officials and he asked for my help. We talked about it, and then I remembered that when the head of Spanish intelligence visited us a while back, he suggested that the presence of our former adversary, the recently vanished Juan Santiago, in any urban setting could result in power outages without any other cause. So, recalling this strange tidbit of information, and wanting to make sure there hadn't been a reappearance of the monster of legend, I got even more involved in the matter than I had at first anticipated."

"Oh, my," Hoda said.

"Have you come across any evidence of Santiago?" Masoon asked.

"Fortunately, no. But in interviews conducted throughout the area, we did hear of various things going on in the neighborhood. And at the time, it meant nothing to me but we were told that some European men had moved into an apartment in that area about a week ago. Now as you know, there are many Europeans in our city, as there are people from other parts of the world, and they're here for all sorts of reasons. But it may be of interest to interview these new arrivals to see if, by chance, they might know anything about our problem, in light of the fact that the criminals, if they are indeed German, as it seems, share that broad geographic origin."

"I hadn't heard about this yet," Leem said, intrigued.

"The report came in less than an hour ago, earlier than expected, and this was just one fact among many in the document, but it happened to catch my attention." Reela thought for a moment and said, "I'll get someone on it right away, just in case there's a connection."

Masoon said, "Reela, if you can get me the address of those new arrivals, we'll use that information in connection with the embassy and cultural exchange people. I'll put someone on it today."

"I have the address right here," Reela said and took a piece of paper from his pocket.

"Excellent." Masoon reached for the note. "Your Majesty, if you could excuse me for a second, my assistant is outside the door with Kular. I'll give him this right now and have him make contact with these new arrivals. I'd like to get this in motion as soon as I can."

"Please do, Masoon," Walid said. The general got up and quickly walked to the door, where he disappeared for less than half a minute, returning then to his chair.

The king had taken a moment to ask Hamid a question. And then he turned and said, "On the other matter: Leem, you said you can find someone to translate the scrolls that are in Shapur's possession."

"Yes, Your Majesty. Right away. Today."

"Good. So, if you're doing that, and Masoon is following up on the cultural exchange people, the embassy, and the newcomers near the Cairo Detective Agency, I think we'll be doing all that we can right now for progress in locating the men we're after."

"Whoa!" Mafulla suddenly said and slapped the side of his chair, brushing at it vigorously three times, and then putting his sandal on something, while he twisted his foot.

"What?" Walid asked.

"A spider," Mafulla answered, and shuddered. "A small black spider. Jeepers. Sorry, everyone."

13

In The Night

It was three o'clock in the morning, New York time. The nearby streets were mostly silent and still. Only a couple of cars had splashed through puddles on the closest main avenue, a long block away, during the past hour. A thickly overcast sky blocked any light from the moon that would otherwise cast its normal nightly shadows on the empty streets. There was a lingering dampness in the air, a hint of mist, and a deep darkness shrouding everything.

The new church caretaker popped awake with eyes wide open in the pitch-black surroundings of his room. His mind was intensely focused. His senses were alert. He thought he heard at a distance the tinkle of breaking glass. He swung his legs over the side of the small bed and grabbed his pants, quickly slipping them on. His feet slid into his sandals and he tugged at the back strap of each, adjusting it over his heel. Walking to the cottage door, he stopped and stood and listened. Nothing. But a feeling beyond words put his hand on the doorknob, and he turned it and quietly opened the door. He saw a dim, flickering light through one of the church windows, at a distance from Bob Archdale's living quarters. It was the window of the pastor's office and study. Sometimes, Bob would be up in the middle of the night, reading or looking up something in one of his many reference books. But whenever he was doing that, more lights would be on.

Santiago closed the door behind him and walked across the yard, over to the window revealing the dim light. He peered into the room from the nearest corner of the glass, careful to keep himself from being seen by anyone inside. The bottom of the window was level with his chin, from where he was standing. He couldn't make out anything at first, but then movement in the interior room brought within his field of vision a man he had never seen, and then another. It looked like these intruders were searching for something. He backed up and swiftly but silently made his way to the back door of the church, a short distance away. He took out a key and slid it into the lock and slowly turned it and then the knob, almost noiselessly opening the door, whose hinges he happened to have oiled the previous day during a stretch of regular maintenance.

As Santiago crept into the kitchen, Reverend Bob appeared in the doorway from his bedroom, a bit startled from the noise he thought he had heard, but also silent. He had just that moment lit a small lamp behind him and he could barely see the older man, his caretaker and guest, but recognized him right away. Juan made a sign for quiet that he also saw and, coming close, he signaled with his hand for the minister to stay where he was, or go back a few steps into his room, but not to come forward any more. He then pointed at the lamp and did a short gesture with his right hand.

Archdale nodded his understanding. He backed up and turned out the light. The church had never been broken into in the middle of the night, except of course, for whatever happened to bring Santiago onto that pew in the sanctuary not long ago. But there had never been a threatening intrusion before. Bob Archdale was a man of friendliness and peace, and had never thought about how he would handle a situation like this. So he was relieved that his new caretaker and handyman seemed to know what to do.

Juan, now once again in complete darkness, took several steps in the direction of the hallway leading to the study. He remembered the boards in the floor that would groan with complaint if he put any weight on them. So he stepped over or around each, as he made his way toward the study. The door to that room had been pulled mostly closed but not shut. He could see the flickering candlelight inside from the small flame that was being used to illuminate whatever search was going on. The intruders might be unaware that there was anyone living on the premises. Or they could know that, but think they were being sufficiently quiet as to avoid detection from any resident who at this hour would be in a deep sleep elsewhere in the building.

Santiago could hear movement from inside the room, the shuffling of feet and the sounds of things being disturbed. He slipped off both sandals and held them in his left hand. Then he took one with his right hand and threw it high in the air down the hallway, far past the study door. The instant it hit, the sounds in the room stopped. The two intruders froze. One turned to the other and said in a whisper, "Maybe a cat."

The other man replied, "Yes, they prowl at night."

Santiago then threw the second sandal to the same spot. After about two seconds, one of the men stuck his head out the door, and looked in the direction from which the sounds had come. Juan had two small stones in his trouser pocket, little pebbles he had picked up right outside the front door of the church the previous evening. He suddenly remembered them and quickly pulled one out and tossed it even farther down the hall. It clattered to the floor and brought the man a little more out into the hallway, his back to Juan, peering into the dark corridor. As he moved farther out from the study door to check on the noise, the man slid a large military knife out from a sheath that was hanging on his belt. Juan saw it. He then silently tossed the second stone and timed his next move to correspond perfectly with the noise it would make precisely when it hit the floor. The intruder was focused so intently on the stone's noise that he hardly heard or registered the quick rustling of cotton fabric as Santiago rushed up on him from behind, grabbing his knife arm and taking the weapon before the man could form a thought about what was happening.

The shock of this was that the intruder was a well-trained military man, strong and fast in his own reflexes. But on this occasion, there seemed to be a split second delay in his reaction that he didn't even notice, and certainly could not have explained. The only thing he then knew was that he was in someone's powerful grip. The large handle of the knife was brought down hard into the back of his head, and this instantly left him unconscious, beyond any further knowing.

His partner inside the study, on hearing the subdued but inevitable sounds of the attack, pulled a black luger pistol from his belt and pointed it toward the door. Outside, Juan felt the weight and balance of the knife in his hand and flung it into the study so that it would be noisily embedded into the wall opposite the door. That distracted the gunman at the moment necessary for Santiago to enter the room, now unarmed. The gunman's head suddenly felt like it was exploding from within as he doubled over with a searing, disabling, and mind-numbing pain that seemed to blot out the possibility of conscious thought or deliberate action. But, as if it were the result of a decision made a single tick of the clock before the pain cascaded through his soul like a powerful gushing waterfall of misery, the man's body jerked slightly upward and his finger pulled back on the trigger that immediately could end all this.

A minute or so earlier, a lookout who had been staying outside the church building behind some bushes to watch for police quickly changed plans and came through the now unlocked back door of the building. He had caught a glimpse of what looked like a dark figure going in, and had seen a glow of light for half a minute from a side of the church where he had not expected it. He now had his own pistol out and ready for use, the same make and model being employed at that very moment by his besieged colleague in the pastor's study.

Entering through the kitchen area, this armed man quickly found Reverend Archdale, dressed and standing quietly inside the door of his bedroom. He was tense and worried, as he awaited a signal from Santiago that things were safe. Bob had hoped that the caretaker would simply be able to scare off any intruders who might have broken into the church. Maybe, he reasoned, the mere fact that they'd been discovered would alarm and frighten off the thieves or vandals who may have assumed that the building was unoccupied and unattended at night. Having no plan any better than hope, though, had rendered him vulnerable to this additional criminal whose access into the building had been now perhaps even less expected than that of his associates. The most recent intruder found the silent preacher unprepared to resist, and in no time at all had him tied to a chair.

Blocks away, Ian Wisdom was bound and gagged and tethered down in the exact same manner, but with more rope. For many hours, he had been confined to the sturdy maple chair on which he had been placed back in the closed-off antiquities room of his shop. He was once again conscious, and had been for what seemed like half the night, after initially being knocked out. And in a futile attempt to escape confinement, he had just now managed to turn the chair over and ended up lying on the cold linoleum of the floor, still tied to it and unable to move more than a few inches. Things often go from bad to worse. He had no thought of what he could do now.

The men had come in right before he had left for the night and had questioned him about a certain trunk in his shop. He explained that he had recently sold it and resisted their first efforts to persuade him to reveal the buyer. The men, however, were not to be refused. After various unpleasant actions on their part, he finally gave them the current location of the trunk, and prayed in his own way for the safety of his friend whom he now felt he had betrayed, but likely at the purchase of his own life. He had actually been kept alive, so far, in case his directions did not prove true and more information had to be extracted from him later on. Then he would be fully disposable.

Wisdom's employees, Charlie and Ella Hawkins, had been treated differently. They had both been killed instantly, and their bodies were now lying on the floor in the back of the shop. The Germans had shown no mercy to them, simply because that was their way.

Mercy springs only from grace. And it was a form of greed that's the opposite of grace, rooted in a sort of madness, that was the motive and mode behind everything these violent men were doing. In a quest akin to that of the mythical Prometheus, they sought to steal a form of fire from the gods—but in their case, to benefit only one man, not the whole of humanity, as was the claim in the myth. Of course, they expected to receive great rewards from this sole individual they served. Promises had been made. Glory, honor, and great riches were at stake. They had a focused and urgent job to do, and nothing could stand in their way.

Across a great stretch of sea and land, inside a beautiful home that was landscaped magnificently and framed by the very nicest neighborhood in Alexandria, Egypt, Bara El-Ari, the former Bara Husani, was thrilled to receive a telegram with the good news about her long lost friend and young love, Elam al-Buri. She shared the news right away in all its details with her son. He was every bit as glad as she was. She could not wait to get to Cairo for the great reunion. It was what she had dreamed about for years. And it was finally going to happen, in all its fairytale glory.

Train tickets had to be purchased, proper outfits chosen, and detailed plans made. The excitement was almost more than she could manage. Her son would go with her. He would be vitally important to her purposes for the trip. She would cable Elam himself and suggest that they meet together at Cairo's most famous hotel, and in the dining room for their first lunch in so many years. It would be a great place to linger over talk and memories full of emotions. Her son Ebar would otherwise occupy himself during the lunch, and things could proceed as she long had hoped.

In Cairo, on a street not far from 214 Garden Lane and the home of Nasser Alexander, the man who had first asked Leem Hadad about power outages in the area—in fact, just the short distance of a few city blocks from there, in a fairly good sized apartment that had been newly rented in the recent past, three men and a woman were having a tense conversation. But at the moment, there was only a pause of deeply frustrated silence.

One man cut through the charged atmosphere and addressed the woman. "Look, there's still plenty of time. Don't tell him we tried and failed. Tell him simply that we're taking all appropriate initial actions and getting closer. It's a complicated situation. But we'll get it sorted out, and we'll soon prevail."

"He doesn't want to hear vague and meaningless assurances. The transmissions aren't empty pep talks. You know this. He wants a report of real progress. But more than that, he wants a report of success, telling him the package is in hand, or on the way back."

"Yes. I know. But in a sense, we've made real progress toward that imminent success."

She stared at him and practically hissed, "He has no patience for progress. You know that, as well as I do. And he doesn't want there to be a trail of living witnesses. You should have killed the men, both of them. And I'll have to mention that when I check in."

"But, I had good reasons both times. And, tell me, why do we have to report in now at all? Every time we turn on the equipment, there's an interruption to the lights in the apartment, and I think the entire block, and maybe even more widespread than that. I've heard people talking at the local grocery shop. Somebody's going to figure out that we're the source of these power outages and then questions will be asked, and that could easily inhibit our ability to complete our work here. I'm sure of it."

A second man spoke up at this point and said, "I agree."

The third man then added, "The lady next to us told me that some city utility people have been on the street knocking on doors. It's good that none of us was here when it happened. Suppose someone saw something."

"And now the palace wants to have a meeting with us," the woman said. "That's the last thing we need at present, to be visually identified by officials of the monarchy."

One of the men remarked, "I guess it's the price of our cover story. When do they want to see us?"

"In exactly an hour."

"So soon?"

"Yes. So make yourselves presentable and we'll get this done and go back to work."

Another of the men said, "The Ambassador hasn't given them our location, has he?"

"No, he's not stupid. He won't do that."

"What about his staff?"

"They know nothing, except to refer all questions about us to him."

"Ok, good. That's good."

"We're too close now to let anything get in our way."

"Yes, but close is not something to brag about," the woman said, and then she began to mock the man's statement by speaking with a tone of great sarcasm, as she stood up and paced and gestured. "Close. You're close. The three of you, you're all very close. 'Did you shoot him?' 'I came close.' 'Did you win the war?' 'We were close.' You disgust me." Then she looked from one face to the other, lingering on each, and pronounced her next words very slowly: "Let me ask you this: Did you succeed and thereby gain the power to live through the coming week? Did you? Or are you going to say to me, 'We came close'? Let me make this clear: If you merely come close to success on this mission, my orders will be to end all your lives, and I won't just come close. I will have success."

She stared back at the man who had just spoken, and then again at the others. "I have orders," she said. And with those words, she slowly began to roll up the left sleeve of her shirt, and on the inside of her forearm, a couple of inches beyond her wrist, there could now be seen for the first time the tattoo of a black spider with a vivid red hourglass marking on it.

"We know," one of the men said, in a somber voice of both fear and disgust, mingled with a bit of desperate resignation.

"It's my job. It's the reason I'm here. I have to eliminate any source of failure, and any potential cause of it. It's my nature and training and purpose and … it's my … joy." She said the last word with a cold relish that sent a shiver through each of the men.

They didn't know how she did it, but her legend had preceded her. And there were more like her—not many, but enough to finish any job that she might be prevented from accomplishing alone, however unlikely that might be. The women were together named for Phylum Arthropoda, Class Arachnida, Order Araneae, Family Theridiidae, and Genus Latrodectus. And they were the leader's most feared group of assassins, or "problem solvers," as they were often called. The common collective term for their tight circle was hardly ever spoken. Their mark was almost never shown, as she was displaying it to her colleagues now, except as a serious and final promise of utterly unforgiving demands. The mere rolling of her sleeve was the most powerful and yet oblique threat she could possibly make. She was serious. And they were now on notice. They knew just enough to realize what her action meant for them. It was their last warning. There were rumors of supernatural powers, of cult rituals and mystical procedures, but mostly whispered tales of sudden and murderous effectiveness that no one could quite understand.

"All right," one of the other men said. "This is vital. We know. Lives depend on it."

She began to unroll her sleeve and extend the cuff again to her wrist, and as she buttoned it, she answered. "Yes, lives depend on it, and first of all, yours. So, if you don't mind, please, and I want to ask you politely: After our meeting at the palace, go forth with me, beyond any further considerations of what may or may not be close to effective, and just get the job done."

They all looked back and forth at each other and then they stood up slowly, and one of the men said, "What the leader wants, the leader gets." And they walked toward the door as she considered them.

In the Adi home across town, Shapur had just ambled into the kitchen. Shamilar was chopping some vegetables. She saw him come through the door and said, "Have you heard anything? When will they let us reopen the store?"

"They said later today. They have to finish the search for evidence."

"Did they put up a sign so our customers will know to come back?"

"Yes, they told me that it says 'Closed This Morning For Inventory. Open at Two."

"So, we're closed during the busy time and open for the slow time."

"Yes, but just on this one day."

"Well, whatever they have to do to keep us safe and catch these men is fine with me."

"I feel the same way."

Shamilar scooped the vegetables up and into a pot where a rich broth was simmering. "I'm going to have a good lunch for you today."

"Oh, very nice."

"Plus, I'll have a snack for us in a few minutes. You've been up so long already. Your breakfast was far too early this morning."

"You're right. You take good care of me," Shapur said. "I am indeed a bit hungry already. A snack would be nice."

"Good. I have something in the oven that should be ready shortly. And, oh, by the way, did you finish already with the scrolls?"

"Yes, everything I could do. The king just wanted a brief written description."

"Why did that guard come by with a message for you?"

"Oh, Hamid wanted him to tell me that Leem Hadad will be sending a translator to read the scroll that's in a language I don't know."

"When's he coming?"

"Shortly, I think. But the guard wasn't certain."

"What could be in the scrolls these men want so badly that they'd break the law to get them and harm innocent people along the way? I just don't understand, do you?"

"I'm still not sure," he replied. "The one scroll is Egyptian, and it's written in a fairly ancient form of Arabic. I can read some of it, but not all, and not even most. It seems to say that its contents, beyond a certain point, are keys to interpreting another scroll. Maybe that's the one composed in some other ancient language. And there appears to be a long poem, or something like a poem, but I couldn't make much sense of it. So, it's a mystery."

Just then a guard stuck his head into the kitchen and said, "I'm sorry, Mr. Adi, and Madam Adi, but a man is here to see you."

"What's his name?" Shapur asked.

"He says it's Hakeem."

"Is he a younger man than me? Strong looking?"

"Yes."

"Excuse me, my good wife. I should go see what brings our friend to us today."

"Please convey my greetings."

"I will." Shapur quickly walked through the doorway and followed the guard to the front room and up to the entrance door.

"Hakeem!"

"Shapur! Are you and Shamilar all right?"

"Yes, yes, please come in, my friend, but why do you ask?"

The man came through the door and said, "I went by your shop earlier and saw that it was closed, which I don't think I've ever witnessed before during business hours, and especially at the busiest time of the day for shoppers."

"Don't remind me."

Hakeem smiled and said, "We all hate to lose potential income."

"Yes. Indeed."

"I asked around among some of the other shopkeepers and someone told me that a man had been attacked inside the store. I feared it was you and had to come check on you."

"No, no, it wasn't me, but I thank you for your concern. It was a military man who was there guarding the store." Shapur said, adding, "Please sit and be comfortable," as he pointed to a nearby chair. The men then both sat down to continue to talk there in the front room.

Hakeem said, "There was a guard for your store? For what purpose?"

"Oh, ever since our son Mafulla and Prince Walid—King Walid—have been friends, we've had people watching our store and home to make sure we stayed safe from enemies of the monarchy. It was a great kindness to us done by King Ali."

"Oh, that's good," Hakeem nodded and replied. "It makes sense. But why was the guard attacked? Who would do such a thing?"

"Some men came into the store minutes after I had left and they were looking for some old scrolls I own. And the guard entered and saw one of them ransacking my desk, but before he could react, someone hit him on the head from behind."

"Oh, my."

"The shop is closed for the morning just so they can collect evidence that may help them catch the men involved in the attempted theft."

"So they were thieves?"

"Yes, in their intentions. But as it is, they got nothing."

"Good!"

The two of them talked a bit more and Hakeem asked when exactly the events in question had taken place, and Shapur told him, as accurately as he could recall. "Interesting," Hakeem replied. "I recall seeing a couple of men in western clothing about that time of day, coming out of the alley behind your shop. They walked quickly to a dark sedan and then took off the second they were inside."

"Were you at your shop?"

"Yes, right out front. And I wondered what the men were doing back in the service alley." He thought for a moment and added, "They could very well have been your thieves. But I was called back into the shop and didn't see anything more." Just then, Mafulla came through the front door, surprising both his father and Hakeem.

"Dad!"

"Mafulla! What brings you here when you're normally getting ready for school, or even starting your school day?"

"I just felt like I should come by." The boy turned to their visitor and said, "Good morning, sir."

"Good morning to you, young man."

"I'm sorry to interrupt. But is everything Ok here?" Mafulla asked both men.

Shapur said, "Yes, but why do you ask?"

"I just had a strange feeling."

"You're going to be late for school because of this feeling?"

"Walid and I took the day off to concentrate on the situation with the scrolls."

"Oh. I'm sorry to be putting everyone to so much trouble with my hobby!"

"No, no, it's no trouble to us at all."

"Well, you're missing school."

"Just today. And it's not a problem. I want to be of help. We need to rid the city and kingdom of these brutish people, whoever they are. It's certainly worth our time and energy."

"But ... what sort of feeling exactly was it that brought you here?"

"It's hard to say. I had a sense that something is about to happen and maybe you and mom and the kids should go somewhere extra safe."

"When?"

"Now. Or, soon."

"There's that big of a hurry?"

"Well, I'm not sure."

"Your mother is about to give me a snack. How about after that?"

Mafulla let out a deep breath of air and said, "Ok, but as soon as you're done."

"You think there's suddenly new danger?"

"Yes. There's danger of some sort, and soon. I'm not sure it involves you, or anyone in the immediate family, but it feels like it may involve either you or else someone who is close to us."

"This is not good. Oh, I almost forgot. Do you know my friend Hakeem?"

"No, I don't think we've met, but you look familiar."

"I came across the desert with Ali and Walid long ago."

"Oh! You're that Hakeem! It's very nice to meet you. I've heard good things about you. And I think I've seen you at some palace events."

"Yes. I've been to several such events, and have seen you, as well."

"You know my dad, then?"

"For a time. We're now friends. I opened a shop recently within sight of your father's store."

"Oh, I didn't know."

"Shapur!" Shamilar's voice suddenly called out from the kitchen.

14

Extended Proprioception

Historians recount that the eighteenth century American military general George Washington fought with extreme bravery in a difficult war for independence against the British. During the time, reports circulated that his uniforms were often marked with holes from musket balls fired at him, sometimes at fairly close range, but that never touched his skin. And this became a thing of legend. The men whispered among themselves that he could not be shot or killed. It was viewed as an ongoing miracle, or power, or something special that had been given this great man, a nearly magical trait that he possessed. And, like many legends, these observations became a matter of pride, reverence, braggadocio, and even humor among his beleaguered soldiers, many of whom seemed to feel, by association, that some of this magic might rub off on them.

The greatness of George Washington was a manifold phenomenon. And its complexity was what made it so interesting. His men actually lost more battles than they won. And this fact makes for a nice life lesson. That's often the way with things we're trying to attain. We fight. We lose. And we bounce back with resilience to fight again. Washington and his men certainly had to bounce back many times. But with his leadership, they fought on and were eventually victorious in their cause. He embodied great nobility and humility together, in a dynamic balance too rarely seen among top military leaders during times of turmoil. He demonstrated in many ways the qualities of Phi.

George Washington may have had a finely developed sense of extended proprioception. He was always exactly where he needed to be to escape the musket fire, cannon balls, and other deadly threats of a determined enemy. The number of times his body was targeted and yet missed amounted to a total that almost everyone concluded was far too great for ascribing to mere coincidence or luck. That historical fact, however, was on the mind of exactly no one at the Wesley Chapel in New York City at a bit past three in the morning, when a German intruder fired his luger pistol right at the chest of the church handyman, Juan Santiago, from a distance of no more than ten or fifteen feet. If he could have seen past his own excruciating pain at the moment, the gunman would have been completely shocked that he missed. The bullet put a small hole in the white shirt of the caretaker, in the fabric under his outstretched right arm, but did not touch his body. The shot was well-aimed, dead center on the caretaker's chest, but after penetrating two layers of woven white cotton shirting, it went harmlessly into the wall behind Santiago. It was as if its target had displayed, on an unconscious level, the same gift from which General Washington may have benefited so many times. But all the man knew who had currently avoided the projectile aimed at his death was that he had turned and moved just as the gun was fired, without even being self-reflectively aware of what he was doing or why. And his serendipitous success had set up what was about to happen next.

But a moment earlier, in the pastor's bedroom, the third intruder into the church had roughly whispered a question to Bob Archdale: "Where are the scrolls?" Before he could respond in any way, the loud gunshot surprised them both. The man spun toward the door, his weapon in position for its own use.

Archdale called out, "Gun in back!"

"Shut up!" The man growled at him and slapped him hard. "Who else is in here?"

"Your friends may be shooting each other," Archdale replied.

"Silence!"

"The police could be here in force. They watch the building at night. You'd better leave or you'll get shot, too." There was a moment of silence and then noises as if from a distance, coming from somewhere else in the building.

"Hans! Jürgen!" The man called these two names into the darkness, but in a loud whisper.

"Hans!" He called out again, and then he listened. "Jürgen!"

There was no response. A few seconds passed with a tense and almost painful pace, as if the sand of a universal hourglass had turned into taffy and was being squeezed through a narrow neck of temporal passage separating the bulb of the unknown coming future from the receptacle of an uncertain present and settled past.

Out of the darkness, a responding sound then split the silence: "Klaus!" The name was also whispered loudly, down the hall or around the corner toward the man who had just been calling out the names of his comrades. Relief and yet concern at the same time flooded into him to hear himself at this instant, and in this way, acknowledged, or sought by his associate.

Then again, the loud whisper: "Klaus!"

"What is it?"

"Quickly!"

The man being summoned held his gun pointed down toward the floor and crept out through the doorway, and at the precise moment he entered the hall, he ceased to have conscious experience in this world. His now limp hand released its grip, and his weapon fell with a loud clatter onto the hardwood floor where his body then collapsed in a sprawl across the hallway.

Reverend Archdale momentarily froze in shock, not knowing what had just happened, or what would transpire in the coming seconds. Then there was another name called out in the dark, this time in a full, though low voice: "Bob! Bob! Are you all right?" Santiago quickly rushed into the room.

"Juan! What happened?"

The handyman quickly began untying the minister as he said, "There were three intruders."

"Where are they now?"

"They're no longer a threat."

"What … did you do?"

"I'm … not quite sure, to tell you the truth. It was all instinct. It was so strange, and a little disturbing, to be honest. But the important thing for us now is that the threat's over. We need to turn on some lights."

Bob got up and walked to the nearest lamp, and lit it. "Was it you just now who whispered the name of Klaus?"

"Yes."

"Was that my captor's name?"

"It must have been."

"But, how did you know it?"

"I have no idea. I just did."

"And you still don't know, for certain, your own name."

"Not yet, and that's extremely odd, to say the least."

"Well, thanks be to the grace of God that you were here, and that somehow you knew what to do to take care of us, to protect our lives, and the church."

"I am the care-taker, after all, in more ways than I realized," Santiago said in reply.

"Yes, and you've been provided here at exactly the time you're needed. But the full how and why still perplex me."

"I'm puzzled as well, about that and many things," Santiago said.

These words were spoken at about the time that Mafulla Adi was finishing up with his quick visit to see his parents, six time zones away to the east. He had just eaten a quick snack with them both, wonderful bread fresh from the oven with jam and coffee, and at the end of it, he said to his father, "Dad, I don't know why, but I somehow feel that the danger I was worried about has passed, at least for now."

"You do?" Shapur said.

"Yes. But I'll ask for a couple of extra men to be posted on duty here anyway, to join the guard escort for you and mom until I feel completely reassured."

"That sounds sensible, if you're certain you need to go to the trouble."

"Yes, and you know, it's never any trouble."

As Mafulla said this, he thought to himself that something strange is going on, something very confusing and odd, and yet he had no idea what. He didn't want to say anything else about it to his parents and upset them any more than recent events had already succeeded in doing. He had learned to be at peace with an inner sense of sudden uncertainty, more than ever before in his life. He wasn't perfect at dealing with this, of course, but better than he ever would have imagined, because of the many lessons of wisdom he had shared with Walid, thanks to King Ali. And as he now sat with his parents, ready to get up and go back out to the palace car that had brought him to visit, he thought back on those conversations, and he experienced what was maybe the oddest sensation of his life.

Some distance away from the Adi home, a single word rang out. "Hey!" It was Jabari's voice and it pulled Set out of a near trancc.

"Oh. Hey. I didn't see you."

"What are you doing sitting on this bench and just staring into space?"

"Waiting for when it's time to go to class."

"Well, it's time. But I meant, you usually have a book out and you're reading whenever you wait for anything."

"Yeah, true."

"But this morning, you're staring instead."

"Thinking, actually—you know, pondering."

"Ah, I see. The staring was all I noticed."

"At its best, staring is just the external manifestation of deep thought, or sometimes of no thought at all, depending on the requirements of the occasion."

"May I ask the subject matter of what's sure to have been deep thought on this occasion, or the pondering?"

"Um. Ok. Ask."

"Who are you? Me? I'm the funny one. I just asked."

"It's girl stuff."

"What is?"

"The object of the pondering."

"You're pondering girl stuff."

"Yeah."

"Like the latest hairstyles and fashions?"

"No. Like figuring them out."

"Girls? Oh. Listen, my friend: There's no such thing as figuring girls out. They're completely unfigurable."

"I don't think that's a word."

"It should be. Because that's what girls are: unfigurable."

"You must mean, unintelligible? Inexplicable? Unfathomable? Impossible to fully understand or completely comprehend?"

"Those are decent near synonyms. But what I mean is unfigurable."

"Ok. But why are you so pessimistic?"

"Let me answer your question with a question. Are you having any luck figuring out the particular girl stuff you're pondering?"

"Well, no, not so far."

"There you go."

"Oh. Ok. How did you get to be such an expert on this?"

"I notice things. I watch. I listen. And I've tried. And I've always reliably failed, miserably, in fact. And now, I know better."

"You do?"

"Yeah. I have a well-honed instinct against engaging in essentially fruitless endeavors. The other gender is beyond our ken, our scope, our horizons of knowledge."

"I just need to figure out one situation, not a whole gender."

"These issues are not as separable as you might imagine, my friend."

"It's pretty specific, though."

"Ok, shoot."

Set hesitated a moment and said, "Don't tell anyone."

"It already sounds like this may be good."

"It's complicated."

"Well, sure it's complicated. It's about a girl. There's no other option. So, what is it?"

"I don't know about this. Maybe I shouldn't talk about it."

"Look. This is why I'm your friend, or it's at least one of the many reasons. You can tell me stuff."

"Ok. I guess you're right."

"So: tell."

Set took a deep breath and let it out, more loudly than he realized. He said, "Well, I've been sort of liking this particular girl in the other class, but just from a distance."

"Ok."

"I've been recently realizing that she's really pretty and smart and nice."

"Who is it?"

"You promise not to repeat this?"

"Yeah."

"No. Do you really, super promise?"

"I promise, on the good health of my dear monkey, Manni, until at least, you release me from said promise."

"Ok, then. It's Khata."

"Oh. All right, then. I can see the really-pretty-and-smart-and-nice business. She's great."

"Yeah, she is. But I think Haji likes her. And maybe she likes Haji."

"Ancient history."

"What?"

"It's old news, ancient history, a thing of the past, if even then."

"I don't understand."

"Haji and Khata: That could have been true for a while, sort of, and at least on his part, maybe. But things have changed."

"What do you mean?"

"Like you, I picked up on the Haji and Khata possibility over the past few weeks, or even a little longer. I notice things. But I'm pretty sure it's different now."

"How?"

"Well, Haji recently walked to school with Khata and Ara."

"Yeah, I know. I heard about it."

"Don't sound so discouraged. You haven't heard the good part yet."

"What's the good part?"

"I happen to have the additional information that, on the walk, he and Ara ended up talking a lot, and by the time they got to school, the emotional landscape had begun to change a bit, to shift a little in a direction that I think you'll like."

"What will I like about this?"

"I suspect, and have come to believe, and don't quote me on this, but maybe Haji sort of hit it off with Ara in a way that surprised him."

"Really?"

"Yeah, and I think she felt the same way."

"And what about Khata?"

"I got the impression that Khata didn't mind at all. She was never thinking girlfriend-boyfriend with Haji, but just friend-friend."

"Where are you getting all this?"

"I'm telling you. I pay attention. I listen to people."

"So, what's your conclusion, you know, about Khata?"

"She's fair game, my friend."

"You think so?"

"Yep. And I could help out."

"How?"

"I could fix you up. Actually, I could 'Set' her up."

"Wordplay. Nice."

"Only the beginning."

"Of what?"

"Watch, and see the master work."

"Ok. But don't do anything that'll embarrass me."

"Worry not, my friend. Just be patient and wait. Soon, young Khata will have a tennis-like victory in her life."

"I'm not sure I want to ask."

"Game. Set. And finally: Match."

Set sighed out loud. "Well."

"I mean it."

"Ok. You're a good man and a good friend. Let's go in now. And if you're right, and you can actually help in this extremely delicate and very, ultra-confidential matter, truly help, I'll sure appreciate it more than I can say, and I'll really owe you, big time."

"Consider it as good as done."

"Ok, then. But ..."

"I know. I know."

In the course of the school day, The New Cupid, otherwise known as Jabari al-Sout, first got Haji off by himself—a task that wasn't very hard—and, after classes, he also did the same with Ara, which took a little more work. The first conversation of the two went like this: "Hey, Haji. Hey. Jeepers. I've got to say, I'm really impressed, super impressed."

"At what?"

"You've got a big admirer, man—I mean, high and lofty among the top echelon of young ladies in town."

"Really? What do you mean?"

"Maybe I shouldn't say anything."

"No, you should. We're buddies."

"Sure we are. But I could get in a lot of trouble."

"No you won't. I won't say anything. Who is it?"

"You promise?"

"Yeah, seriously."

Jabari looked around quickly and whispered. "It's Ara."

"Really?"

"Yeah, big time. That little talk the two of you had on the way to school, I think she's totally over the moon because of it."

"What did you hear?"

"Look, I can't repeat anything. That would just be wrong, but I know she really likes you, man. I just think you should be aware. And she's super cool, so, I'm just saying, don't let this opportunity pass you by."

"Oh. Yeah. Wow. She's really great. I had no idea. I did have an amazing time talking to her when we were walking to school with Khata. And I kept thinking how really good-looking she is, and how nice. And she's smart. And funny."

"Yeah, I know. She thinks those same things about you."

"Really?"

"Yeah, really."

"So, what should I do?"

"I'd cultivate it, man. Don't let this pass. Opportunities are for taking."

"But would it make Khata feel bad?"

"No, not at all."

"How do you know?"

"Look, I know she thinks a lot of you and admires you a whole bunch. But I don't think it's in the girlfriend-boyfriend way."

"Are you sure?"

"Yeah. She totally likes you a lot as a great friend, and she feels the same way about Ara, and she won't be hurt or jealous at all. In fact, I'm pretty sure she'll think it's great. She's a big fan of both you guys and will love seeing you hit it off."

"Wow. So what should I do?"

"Well, to me, it's simple. Take another walk with the young lady. Talk with her. Make her laugh. Share your dreams. Girls love that stuff."

"I will. I will. Look, I really appreciate this, Jabari."

"No problem. But it might be best to act like you never heard this from me. News floats in the air, wafted by the breeze, this time of year. I'm not for a moment suggesting that you should lie about it, but just don't volunteer your source, if asked, which you likely won't be. I don't want to be stepping on any pretty toes. You know how girls are."

"Ok. Got it."

Jabari was able to walk away with a great sense of accomplishment, and half the job done. And then, later, with Ara, it went like this, when the would-be Cupid finally got her off by herself, outside.

"Ara! Hold up a second! I need to talk to you about something."

"Oh! Hi, Jabari! Sure, what is it?"

"Well, I just hope your ears weren't burning earlier, during school."

"Why? Who was talking about me?"

"It was extremely complimentary, actually, and I mean really gushing, but I know I shouldn't say anything."

"No, you should."

"I could get in trouble."

Ara smiled and said, "Let me put it like this: If you turn silent now, I guarantee you'll be in trouble, and really big trouble."

"But this could be a bit of a delicate situation."

"Why?"

"Ok, Ok." He looked around again and whispered, "It was Haji."

"Haji?"

"Yeah."

"Talking about me?"

"Ycp."

"Well, what did he say?"

Jabari looked around again as if to make really sure the coast was clear and said, "He was sort of going on and on about how great you are, you know, in every possible way."

"He was?"

"Yeah, it was almost embarrassing."

"Stop."

"Honest. I mean it."

"Where and why was he saying this?"

"It just sort of came up during a conversation the two of us had, so you don't have to worry. Nobody else overheard us. It's just that he really liked talking to you during that walk to school the other day, and now he can't stop thinking about how great you are, and on and on."

"Are you making this up?"

"No, of course not, I just wanted you to know about it. I thought it was only right. He's as brave as anybody I've ever known, but you know, with girls, we all can get a little shy. So, I thought I'd help you two along a bit by maybe spilling the beans a little. But please, don't say anything about hearing this from me, Ok?"

"Ok. I won't. But thanks for telling me. You're sweet, Jabari."

"Yeah, true. The sweetest. Tell all your friends, especially those who are currently unattached and … drawn to sweets." Then, of course, he did the locally famous double eye-brow jump, which was always well received by his peers, since it was, all at the same time, an appropriated use of, spoof on, and homage to Mafulla's long famous signature move and punctuation device.

Jabari had only one more conversation to go in this initial process for working his magic. But he hadn't seen the next person on his list since the end of school. He considered various possibilities and decided to go look in the library. And that's where she was, but out of sight, off to the far side in the corner, behind tall shelves of books and facing away from the door, reading. So he didn't see her at first. But yet, somehow, the second Jabari walked in, she felt his presence across the room and knew that he had come there to speak with her. Without yet having had any training in it, she was gifted with an unusual degree of natural extended proprioception and something like keen sense of clairvoyance.

Khata also knew in a flash that, because of events that this imminent conversation would represent and set in motion, she would one day live in a house on a hill covered with thick green grass and beautiful old trees, overlooking a field and a lake and a far ridge of other hills beyond, in a place that now waited for her about five thousand, five hundred and fifty five point five miles away from her chair in the library. Destiny had in mind a small town called Bethany in a place known as Connecticut. She somehow understood in the wide moment of that unexpected vision that she should get up and go around the tall bookshelf behind her and greet this friend who was on a mission, and walk outside with him, where she could have the appointed conversation and hear a little about the first steps of the amazing future that now warmly awaited her.

15

The Aftermath

The police had been to the church twice—first of all, in the immediate aftermath of the break-in, as a result of Reverend Archdale's phone call to the station house. Within ten minutes, four policemen were on the scene, hauling off the bound culprits. Two of them were still unconscious, and all were severely injured. Then, a few minutes later, two detectives from the precinct came and interviewed both Archdale and Santiago at length, trying to sort out all that had happened. The second visit was several hours later, after the police had received a frantic call from an early morning visitor to The Wisdom Shop who could see through the door that there had been bad trouble. Arriving at the shop, the officers quickly learned from Ian that there was a connection between the two violent scenes, and since it was now a homicide investigation, they revisited the church to make sure they had all the information from there that they might need.

On the second visit, the detective in charge had started off by stating emphatically that he would have to take the ancient scroll in question as evidence for the ongoing investigation, but Santiago was able to change the man's mind with only a few quiet words. The detective had also been at first deeply suspicious of Santiago's own story, and his alleged amnesia, but, again, Archdale saw him set aside his misgivings in a strangely abrupt and complete manner, right after giving voice to them. It had initially sounded like he was actually going to take Santiago into custody for further questioning. But then, within seconds, he changed his tone and became friendly and sympathetic. He simply dropped the whole idea of any further questions, apologizing instead for all the time he asked of them already, at a point, he said, when the minister and his associate probably just needed to rest.

Learning what had happened at the Wisdom Shop, Reverend Archdale wanted to go visit his friend Ian right away. But the detective told him that the shopkeeper had been taken to the hospital for an examination, and explained that Bob would be able to visit him only after the police could interview the man a second time. They wanted to make sure that there was no communication between the two of them that might compromise the independent details of their respective reports. Archdale understood, as did Santiago.

When the police left the second time, the minister retreated to his room for a nap, and the caretaker went out back to his little cottage where he could lie down for a while to rest and ponder the events of the past several hours. Many exceedingly odd things had happened. And there were no easy explanations. Santiago had found himself intuitively acting in ways he didn't understand in the least. He had seemed to be responding from a level of knowledge and skill that was residing in him somewhere deep beneath the fog and blankness of conscious memory loss that was still so extensive and puzzling.

He had made a truce with the uneasiness that was always a natural result of amnesia. Most people who experienced this mysterious condition feel a flood of both fear and frustration, but Juan had been able to control his emotions and release this one thing that he could not seem to control. The act of letting go allowed for a calmness of spirit that would otherwise have been impossible. His residual inner perplexity shaded more into a keen form of expectant curiosity rather than the troubled knot of anxiety that can otherwise accompany such major uncertainty. He seemed to know intuitively here, as well as in other things, how to deal with what for most people might be an overwhelming challenge. He rested into the difficulty, into the unknowing of it all, and he gave up the natural need for a sense of control that, to some extent, we all have. In this way, he opened himself to whatever deeper insights might come.

For truth to flow, there must be a conduit, and any conduit needs both shape and emptiness to allow for the flow. Santiago had been shaped his entire life to find and receive truth. But it was his ability to empty himself out in the proper ways that at such times made a reception of subtle and otherwise unknowable truth possible.

The police had taken into custody the three badly injured criminals. One was in a coma. Juan felt a deep sadness that the force of resistance he needed to exercise had come up against such a violent opposition that this result was the only one possible, short of a worse alternative. But he reconciled himself to the outcome much as he had made peace with the larger sea of uncertainty in which he was now afloat.

Knowledge is power, the British philosopher Francis Bacon had said in a prior century. And often, that's true. But bits of it can also get in the way of power. Some power comes only from beyond the realm of our ordinary knowledge. And if we can't allow ourselves to venture out with properly open hearts and minds, we can't access that power. Although the church custodian didn't know it at the moment, he had been trained and grounded in the reception of such power. And it was this that he had been using at crucial junctures when nothing else would do. As a result, this distinctive power flowed through his body and soul as it was needed to help him do the work that he was in New York, and at the church, to do.

After an hour or so of rest, feeling now mostly restored from the unusually vigorous activities of the early morning, Juan got up off the bed and left the cottage and walked once more to the back door of the church building. Opening it quietly, he saw Bob already sitting at the kitchen table, reading.

"I thought you'd still be napping," Santiago said.

"Oh, I had some deep and restful sleep," Archdale replied. "I dreamed vividly and woke up feeling quite refreshed, strangely enough, after the night we had."

"It was quite a night," Santiago replied.

"Thanks again for your protection."

"I'm sorry it had to end the way it did for those men."

"I am, too."

"I didn't at any point intend that severe a result. But their degree of determination and violence would not yield to any lesser form of restraint. I couldn't allow you to be harmed and the scroll to be stolen."

"Well, I sure do appreciate it. I could easily have ended up like the poor employees at the Wisdom Shop."

"And there's also a good chance your friend Ian would have been the recipient of another visit that wouldn't have ended well. Such people, sadly, never like to leave witnesses alive."

"It's a terrible thought. But you somehow stopped it from happening."

"I apparently have fairly advanced training in that sort of thing."

"Yes. You must. And, so we know more about you every day.

"I suppose we do, in strange, incomplete bits and pieces."

"It's better than nothing. Now, please, Juan, sit and let me get you some coffee."

"Thanks. That would be nice."

"And we have some breakfast bread and jam and such."

"Great. I could use the replenishment."

"I bet. Oh, and look at this," Archdale reached into his pocket and pulled out something and handed it to Santiago. "It's an item I found in the pocket of your old torn robe, when I recently took it to the neighborhood laundry to see if it could be cleaned and repaired. They said it was too badly ripped up for any decent fix. But I still asked them to clean it. I don't know why. It should be ready tomorrow, in case you'd like to keep it. Regardless, I knew you'd want this ring."

"A ring?" Santiago reached out to receive the item. He looked it over with a sense of perplexity, but also with a strange feeling of familiarity at the same time. "You say that this was in my pocket?"

"Yes. I guess it's another clue."

"Hm. It looks nice, like it might be valuable."

"I had the same thought."

"I wonder if it could be mine. It looks like it might fit." He turned it over and examined it more closely. And then he said, "Until I remember what it is, and whose it could be, I think I should do with it what I apparently did before, and put it in a pocket." He then rubbed it with the edge of his shirtsleeve and stuck it down into the left front pocket of his pants. He said, "Thanks for returning it to me."

"You're welcome."

"I certainly didn't expect anything like this. But, these days, the unexpected has become quite commonplace."

"You've said it there, my friend."

In Egypt, the day was much farther along its course. And there was something in the air. The train from Alexandria arrived at the Cairo station several hours after the morning's paper had run its story about a long lost love and one woman's search for reunion. People were passing the paper around, talking about the romantic tale. The article had ended with the words, "Come back tomorrow for the conclusion of our story." That had everyone speculating about how it would end. Would the man be alive? Would he want to reunite with the lady? Would the separated lovers get back together? What would the passage of so many years have done to their young love?

All the ladies of the city, especially, were chattering with their friends about every aspect of the story and were challenging husbands with questions like, "If we had been separated for over fifty years, would you jump at the chance to be reunited with me?" And, of course, all the men with sense in their heads were jumping to answer that question in a dramatic affirmative: "Of course! It would be the only thing on my mind! How could I do anything else, knowing that you were looking for me?" And yet, the truly wise were more likely to say, "I'm the one who would be looking for you." As you can imagine, such answers generated all sorts of commentary and replies from the wives, from laughter to tears to a chiding about what men could never understand. It was a citywide phenomenon. No story run by the paper in years had generated so much reaction and talk.

Leem and Ibrahim Hadad were both at the train station to meet their client, Bara El-Ari, the former Bara Husani, and her son Ebar. Ibrahim was holding a beautiful bouquet of flowers for her, in honor of the lady's success in her quest, and so as to be more recognizable to her when she stepped off the train. They spotted Bara and Ebar right away, the elegantly attired lady and her dashing son holding her arm as they climbed down the stairs of their passenger compartment. Ibrahim waved, and they both looked surprised, then waved back.

"Welcome to Cairo," Ibrahim said, walking toward them with a big smile.

"Thank you so much! I'm guessing you're Ibrahim?"

"Yes. At your service! It's a pleasure to see you in person. And I'm thinking this is your son, Ebar?"

"Yes, indeed," she said.

"A pleasure," the man offered, extending his hand.

"It's all mine," Ibrahim replied as they shook in greeting. "I'm glad you could come along with your mother for such an occasion."

"I wouldn't have missed it," he commented.

Bara looked into Ibrahim's eyes and said, "I deeply appreciate all your hard work that made this possible."

"The meeting today is of great importance to mother," Ebar said. "Actually, to both of us. As her son, I'm very grateful as well."

"Oh, it was our pleasure," Ibrahim said. "And now it's the talk of the entire town."

"Oh?" Bara said.

"Yes! The newspaper ran a story about your search this morning."

"They did?"

"I hope you don't mind. One of their reporters overheard me talking about the case to a close friend and offered to write a story. This was long before we found your Elam, and it seemed to me at the time that a newspaper article might help us to locate him, so we eagerly agreed. We like to do whatever might benefit our clients."

At this stage, Leem, who had been standing back and allowing Ibrahim this moment with their client, stepped up. "Leem Hadad, at your service," he said with a smile. "I assisted in the search, but Ibrahim here did most of the work. And here's a copy of today's paper with the piece he's told you about. It's the talk of the town, it seems." Leem handed Ebar the paper, folded to display the article.

"Oh, my!" he said. "This does look like major coverage."

"Everyone loves a love story," Leem said. "And, it's a wonderful piece, well written in commemoration of young love and lifelong commitment."

"That's amazing," Bara said.

Leem continued, "And if you don't mind, the paper would like to have their writer at the hotel today to witness the initial meeting and interview the two of you briefly, after you've had some time to yourselves, of course. He's eager to get some personal quotes for a follow up story."

"That would be marvelous," Bara replied with a big smile. "I'm quite honored by all the interest and attention. And perhaps we can get out the message that, in the end, love indeed can prevail."

"Yes!" Ibrahim said.

Then Leem asked, "Do you have luggage?"

"I do, but just a few pieces," she answered.

"I'll get them, Mother," Ebar said.

"May we help?" Ibrahim asked.

"That would be very nice of you. One's a bit heavy. Ladies never travel lightly," he joked.

"We bring with us what we need," Bara explained.

Ibrahim said, "We'll get everything and load up the car we have here, and take you directly to the hotel, where I'm sure you'll both want to freshen up and rest a bit before the big reunion later on today."

"That would be splendid!" Bara gushed.

Leem thought to himself that the lady certainly looks much younger than her years. And then he mused that this is quite unusual for someone who's had a hard life. She must have been blessed in compensating ways. She does seem, by her dress and manor, to have enjoyed at least ample financial resources. And, of course, the joy of the occasion could bring a special glow to nearly anyone.

Within ten minutes, they had the luggage loaded up in a car the palace had provided for them, thanks to Reela's help. And they were soon on their way to the Grand Hotel.

In the palace, the four German Cultural Exchange visitors sat outside Reela's office at that very moment, waiting to be received for their interview. His assistant came out and said, "We've decided the office may be a bit tight for all of you, so please allow me to guide you to a nearby sitting room where Mr. Adi can speak with you."

The lady of the group spoke up. "That will be fine, and is quite considerate of you." They all rose and began to follow the man out of the waiting area. "Do you know what the nature of our meeting might be?" she asked.

"I'm sure the Vice-Regent wants to welcome you officially to our kingdom. And there may be some other matters to be discussed."

"Certainly," she replied. "We're so happy to be here, and look forward to our time with the good people of Egypt."

The man led them down the hall and into a large parlor, where he invited them to sit and be comfortable for only a few more minutes while Mr. Adi wrapped up a prior meeting. And, once they were seated, he left.

"Smile when he comes in," she said to the men. "Look happy to be here. Remember, we're going to be enjoying their art, architecture, urban planning, and other aspects of the city. We'll visit the university, and take in some of the nightlife. And, of course, we'll profit considerably in other ways from our wonderful visit to their kingdom."

The other three nodded their heads quietly. "What if he asks us some questions about specific plans?" One of the men asked.

"Be vague and I'll jump in," she replied. "We're here just to experience the culture, with an eager openness to new things."

"And certain old things," one of the men said. And at that, she shot him a stern glance.

"Oh! Hello, there!" Reela Adi walked into the room with a big smile and his assistant trailing him. The four German visitors all stood to greet him. "Reela Adi, Vice Regent for our ancient kingdom," he said, as he went, in turn, to each of them to shake hands, "Welcome to Egypt! Welcome to Cairo! Welcome to the palace!"

"Thank you," Greta Estand responded with a forced smile. "It's our great pleasure to be with you and an honor to be invited here today."

"Yes," one of the men said. "You have a lovely city."

"It's such an honor," a second chimed in. The third man smiled and nodded.

"Please, sit and be comfortable," Reela said. And as they all arranged themselves on a large sofa and nearby chairs, he sat down with them, but his assistant remained standing, just inside the door with a pleasant expression on his face. Reela said, "I'm sorry for your brief wait, but kingdom business can't always be managed as well and expeditiously as we'd like. There are always unexpected surprises."

"Don't worry. It's not a problem. We've enjoyed simply being in your beautiful palace," Greta answered.

"Good. I'm glad to hear that. Now, if you don't mind, I'd love to ask you a few questions that might help us to welcome you better to our ancient land."

"That would be fine," she said.

"Excellent! Now, I'd be remiss not to inquire first of all into what you do back in your homeland, and what brought you to Cairo."

The tallest man, with light blonde hair and bright blue eyes, spoke up right away, "I'm a political historian at the University of

Munich, and I love to visit the capitals of other nations. So when I heard of this exchange program, I entered my name, right away."

"What's your special focus?"

Dieter Himmel looked confused for a moment. "Um."

"The main area of your research?" Reela clarified.

"Oh, yes, the political history of Germany, with a special emphasis on economic forces."

"I see." Reela looked at Greta and said, "And may I ask the same?"

"Yes, certainly. I'm a landscape designer, specializing in gardens and parks. I've been looking forward to seeing some of your public spaces here in Cairo, and within the palace grounds, if that's at all possible, perhaps even on our visit today."

"We can surely give you a tour. It would be our pleasure."

One of the other men then said, "I'm a clothier. I run a large men's shop in Berlin. I've been eager to see the variety of fashions and styles in such a cosmopolitan city as Cairo, where you have people from so many countries mixing and socializing daily."

"Oh?"

"Yes, and the daily café life especially intrigues me, along with the nightlife."

"Well, then, I heartily recommend The Nile Club and The Foxtrot. You'll see all the latest fashions there, and many traditional outfits as well—really, the entire spectrum of more elegant and formal dress," Reela advised.

"Good, I appreciate your recommendation," the man said. "We've been here only a short time, and we're seeing some of the main tourist sights, but we still have a lot to absorb."

"Yes, I've especially loved the Museum and all the antiquities shops you have. The present-ness of the past is a reality in Cairo," the fourth member of the group said.

Reela noted the mention of antiquities, but decided not to follow up on that topic, saying instead, "Do you have suitable accommodations here in town?"

Dieter looked quickly at Greta, who said, "Oh, yes. The Ambassador has taken good care of us."

"I'd love to know your address," Reela said, adding, "Perhaps I could have some gifts sent to you, to welcome you officially to our kingdom, some things of value representing our past, present, and future."

"That's so kind. But you don't have to go to any trouble," Greta said.

"No, no, I insist! It's no trouble at all."

"Truly, everyone has already been so generous to us, no additional gifts are necessary," she replied.

Reela smiled. "It's just our way of showing you the best of our hospitality."

Greta said, "You're so gracious, but we feel that hospitality already. To receive gifts, well, we'd be afraid we were imposing on you."

"Nonsense," Reela said with a bigger smile. He opened a small box on the table next to him and handed Greta a pen and a piece of paper and said, "Just write your address here and I'll have someone get on it right away. We want your visit to be memorable in all ways and would be poor hosts if we didn't reach out with something special for you. It's not often that we have such cultural exchanges."

Greta was trapped. She thought it important to the integrity of the mission that no one in official power should be aware of where exactly they were based. They liked to work quietly and quickly, with no complications, get what they were after, and get out with as few encumbrances as possible. And here a top official was practically demanding her address. If she delayed further or refused in any way, however politely, it might alert him, raise suspicions, and make things worse. At least, he wasn't the police or in any way connected to the police, as far as she could tell. So, most likely, it would do no harm.

She smiled and said, "You're so kind. We'll be greatly appreciative of anything you might send us. Here, I'll write it down for you." She scribbled for a moment and handed him back the paper. Reela glanced at what she had written and was surprised to see '108 Village Way'—the exact address of the apartment not far from the Cairo Detective Agency where the soldiers dressed as Water Works employees had been told that four Europeans recently moved in with lots of heavy boxes. It was also an address, Reela recalled, that's a mere two blocks or so from Elam al-Buri's home.

The Vice Regent smiled and said, "Good. So now, you can expect something to come your way in the next few days, at least." He stood up and handed the note to his assistant and said, "Take this for me, please, and put it in my office, on the desk, front and center." The man nodded and left the room. And as he sat back down, Reela said, "I hope you'll enjoy what we send."

"Your graciousness to visitors is every bit as welcoming as legend has it," Dieter commented.

"Thank you. But I almost forgot to ask. How long will the four of you be with us?"

"We're not sure," Greta said. "We've been told that we can stay an entire month if we like. But some of us have families and other responsibilities back home. If we can see and do everything we have scheduled, we may be headed back a bit sooner than that."

"Well, please, let me know if I can do anything to be of assistance while you're here," Reela said. "It's especially important to us to maintain good relations with our European friends. We have a long history of welcoming people from your nation, and we benefit in many ways from your countrymen who are in our midst. Which reminds me: Since your arrival, by chance, have you come across any other German citizens who might also be new to our city?"

"No, not at all," one of the men replied.

"We've met a few of our countrymen employed by the embassy since we arrived in town, but they've all been here a while," another said.

Greta then asked, "Are there any of our compatriots, also recently arrived here in Cairo, that you think we should meet during our visit?"

"No, I'm just always on the lookout for newcomers from your country so that we can make sure that our own citizens and officials are responding well to them and their needs."

"That's extremely kind of you," she replied, now anxious to

conclude the meeting. There was something about this man that disturbed her, beneath his friendly demeanor. His eyes seemed able to see more than they should. But she inwardly fought the intrusion.

Just as she was having these thoughts, Reela stood up, and they all did likewise in response as he said, "I've enjoyed our visit today, however brief."

Greta said, "We have as well."

Reela then added, "My assistant will now show you the gardens, a tour that will take only a few minutes, and I think you'll find them of great interest."

"Oh, that's so nice," Dieter said. "But a couple of us do have to get back."

"It won't take long, and we need you all to sign a visitor's book that we'll have for you at the end of the short tour, for our historical record here in the palace."

"Well, it's an honor to be asked. I certainly suppose we could do that, if we don't linger too long in our enjoyment of the tour," he said.

"Good! Then it's settled." Reela's assistant reappeared and the Vice Regent said a quick goodbye to all the guests and walked back toward his office, leaving the staff member to give the brief tour. He then approached a palace guard who had been waiting outside his door and asked, "What have you heard?"

"No one else is there. We're in position, down the street."

"Radio the men and have them enter the apartment for a quick look around. But tell them not to disturb anything. Leave it all as it is. There can be no signs of the entry or the search. They have fifteen minutes, maybe twenty, and then should be gone, without a trace."

16

A Mosaic

The palace school student Bakat Muhammed was having a couple of the other girls over for a fun afternoon. She, Ara, and Cabar were working an art project together that had nothing to do with their class or assignments. They were making a bright, beautiful mosaic just because they wanted to. Bakat's mother, Ita, was an artist, and she had a large studio attached to the house. It was a big, bright room full of light where she could paint, sculpt, and work with tile. Her husband Numan coordinated the activities of Egypt's embassies around the world. He was a graduate of the University of Cairo and the Sorbonne, in Paris. He had also done research at the London School of Economics, and was an expert in international relations.

Her parents often called Bakat beautiful, but whenever she looked in the mirror, she thought that maybe, to the right people, she might seem mildly pretty, but she wasn't like Kissa, Hasina, Kat, or Ara, or, especially her teacher, Hoda. She thought of her face as a little too round and even puffy, as she put it to herself. And she liked good food. She relished big meals and her mom was a great cook, so that a certain rounded softness had begun to characterize her, overall. No one had ever told her that she was overweight in an unhealthy way, but she sometimes worried that she might be, or at least that she could be getting close. And yet, she told herself, it's Ok to be who you are. We can't let other people or the images in our society around us dictate to us in every way what we should be like or look like. The most important beauty is inner beauty, after all, and it will always show through.

Bakat had inner beauty. She was a happy girl, at least most of the time. And she was always doing little kindnesses for others. As a result, her friends all loved her. She sometimes felt a little envious of the more strikingly attractive girls like Kissa and Hasina. But she liked them a lot, anyway. It wasn't their fault that everyone thought they were so great looking. And that can change over time, Bakat reminded herself. Today a funny duckling, tomorrow a swan—that was a mantra she often repeated to herself. Her mother, Ita, was certainly attractive. And her parents were very affectionate with each other. Her dad obviously thought her mom was beautiful. She hoped that maybe her own baby fat would go away in a year or two and she could also mature into the sort of look she admired in her mother.

But Bakat didn't typically dwell on these things. She was a very positive young lady and could be extremely funny. In fact, on this particular afternoon, laughter often punctuated the conversations around the studio, as the girls did their work.

"I don't think boys often do art together," she said at one point to Cabar.

"I don't think they can," Cabar answered.

"Why not? Is it because there's no fine art that involves kicking a ball or knocking someone to the ground?"

"Ha! Funny," Cabar said, and added, "Boys are just too competitive, and the sort of art we're doing takes cooperation, even real collaboration."

Ara commented, "Yeah, I think if there were boys doing this, they'd be keeping count of how many tiles each of them had done, and thinking things like 'So far the mosaic has 327 pieces, and my 93 are really the most important to the pattern.' That's just boys."

"True," Bakat said, as she was now placing a small tile into position. "But, let me ask something. Cabar, you just said that the art we're doing takes cooperation rather than competition, and you said, even collaboration?"

"Yeah?"

"What's the difference between cooperation and collaboration? I thought they were basically the same thing."

"Well, sometimes, but most often, cooperation means going along, not competing or fighting, just not resisting. When you say to your little brother, 'Please cooperate,' you're not usually asking for much, only that he drop any active resistance to whatever's going on, or whatever you're trying to do."

"Ok. I get that. And collaboration?"

"My mom explained it to me once when we were cooking together. Collaboration is more like partnering up and bringing the best of what you can contribute to a joint enterprise, a unified effort. Collaboration is really about working together well, anticipating what you can do to help or inspire or even push the other person, and also to contribute your own personal best to whatever the project is. It sort of goes a lot deeper than just cooperation. It's much more active and involved."

"Oh! Well, then, here's to collaboration!"

"Yeah," Ara said, "and to the girls who can do it!"

"Oh, I almost forgot to ask," Cabar said to Ara.

"What's that?" Ara replied.

"Is there a little something going on with a certain Mr. Afah—a new form of ... collaboration in the air?"

Ara blushed and felt her stomach do a flip. "Why do you ask?"

"Um, I saw you and Haji talking right before we left the palace to come over here."

"We were just talking."

"Oh?"

"What?"

"It looked like more than just normal talk."

"What do you mean?"

"Body language, my friend. Laughs. Leaning in. A touch on the arm, even. You know what I'm talking about."

Ara let out a huge breath and said, "Ok, Ok, I can't pretend."

"What?" Bakat now said.

"I sort of, maybe, like Haji," Ara admitted.

"We all like him," Bakat said. "He's very likable."

"I mean, you know, in a … special way, if you're going to make me spell it out in all its embarrassing detail."

"Spell it out slowly," Bakat said, and made Cabar laugh.

"You two!"

"This is juicy news!" Bakat said. "We want all the details!"

"Well, there aren't many details. It's just that I thought Haji liked Khata, you know, in a special way, and it turns out that he really likes me."

"Well. Good. And?"

"Yeah and, well Ok, I really sort of like him, too."

"In that special way," Bakat said, slowly.

"Yeah, maybe," she replied.

"Ara Masoon has a nice ring to it," Cabar said.

"A nice ring would be good," Bakat said, "eventually," and they all laughed.

Ara said, "It's too soon to even think about that!"

"Too soon for a Ma-soon?" Bakat said.

"Funny."

"And, remember, Haji's name itself means one who's on a quest, so maybe this quest will lead to popping the big quest-ion," Cabar pointed out.

"You two are just too clever."

"And that big question may lead to a big ring," Bakat said.

"Right now, it's just leading to big embarrassment, so let's stop talking about it," Ara pleaded playfully with her friends.

"Ok, but keep us posted," Bakat said, as she began to fit another tile into the mosaic that now sat, maybe a third done, in front of them. And then she added, "Come on now, collaborate with me here."

At the church in New York City, Santiago was clipping some bushes in front of the building. There had been lots of rain recently, and everything was growing lush and full. The larger shrubs were getting a little uneven and he was spending some time to rectify the situation.

"Hi." A small voice came from behind him, and he turned around.

"Oh, hello again." Santiago smiled to see the little boy who had spoken to him so enigmatically on one recent occasion before, while he was working inside the church. The boy was at the moment a couple of feet away from Juan, just outside the church entry door, which was cracked open. He could hear the boy's mother inside, talking with Reverend Archdale. The two of them had apparently been in the building and were now about to leave, and the boy had come out ahead of his mother.

Santiago added, "How are you today, my friend?"

The child replied, "I'm good."

"That's nice to hear."

"I know a boy named Alim."

"You do?"

"Yes. He lives far away."

"How then do you know him?"

"He visits with me when I'm asleep, sometimes, in dreams."

"Oh?"

"Yes."

"Alim, you say?"

"Yeah. He's small like me. He knows you."

"I don't recall him right now, but I'm sure he's a fine boy."

"He is. He told me you have a special ring."

"He did?"

"Yes, and you'll have to use it soon."

"How does he know this?"

"He didn't tell me that."

"What will I use it to do?"

"He didn't say. But he's really nice."

At that moment, the boy's mother came out the door and said, "Clark, are you disturbing the nice man while he's trying to work?"

"Oh, I thank you, but he's no bother at all," Santiago said and smiled.

"Well, I appreciate your being so kind to him."

"It's my pleasure. I enjoy talking with him."

"He told me he's spoken with you before."

"Yes, we exchanged pleasantries here one day. He's a fine boy."

"Thank you. I'm very proud of him."

"I can imagine."

"I'm Martha, by the way."

"It's good to meet you, Martha. They call me Juan."

"It's nice to meet you, as well, Juan. We need to be off, now."

"Well, it was pleasant to speak with you."

"And you. Goodbye for now."

"Goodbye." As the boy walked away, holding his mother's hand, he turned around, smiled, and waved. Santiago waved back and wondered to himself what in the world was going on with this child and his mysterious remarks. And, in that instant, he recalled what the previous odd conversation had been, at their first meeting. The boy had suddenly said something like: "You'll have to do your work soon." And Juan had said, yes, he needed to fix the door whose lock didn't function properly, and the boy had replied, "No, your other work," without any further explanation. And that was just hours before the break-in had happened, and Juan had been moved to leap into a form of action whose contours and possibilities he didn't really understand.

And now, the boy seemed to know about the ring that Reverend Archdale had retrieved from the torn robe and given him. Had it come up in conversation between Bob and Martha? That was quite unlikely. So, how did the boy know? It was all strange, very strange. He referred to it as a special ring. What could that signify? And what did Clark mean about using the ring soon? Plus, who in the world is this dream friend, named Alim? It was certainly a mosaic of weird, or of the exceedingly strange that was being expanded anew each time they spoke. And it kept getting a bit more mystifying.

The great reunion of old loves at the Grand Hotel had taken place in the midst of photographers, a reporter, and various interested observers who had read the story in the paper and had somehow learned or guessed the place and time of the long awaited meeting. Bara El-Ari simply glowed in her long, deep purple gown, and Elam al-Buri beamed his approval, standing taller than he had in years as he basked in the warmth of this lovely lady's successful effort to find him. His son Asham had closed the antiquities shop for a time this afternoon to be able to attend the great event. And his grandson Nappi was also there for the occasion. There was celebration and hoopla aplenty at first, and then Leem and Ibrahim managed to arrange some quiet time alone for the happy couple so that they could talk privately during their late afternoon meal together. Even the hotel staff had clustered around the dining room to see these two and chat about their story. It was one of those universal fairy tales of love lost and rediscovered that nearly everyone enjoys.

But, unknown to the crowd, it was actually a tale of avarice, greed, desperate hope, and deception. No one was aware of this side of the story that was currently unfolding, except for the beaming Bara El-Ari, herself and her adult son Ebar, who was at this moment across town, "occupying himself," in her words, or, in more precise terms, quietly breaking into Elam al-Buri's home while everyone was at the reunion now taking place at the hotel. And so, as planned, there was no one around the house to stop him, question him, or get in his way at the last known likely long term home of the scrolls.

As to appearances, on the outside, Bara had aged very well, indeed. In fact, most people would say that she looked at least twenty years younger than the date on her birth certificate and some quick math would indicate, and perhaps even more. But, as she would be just as quick to say, "Numbers lie," and yet again, in another sense, they never do, unless they're forced to deceive. Bara, however, was prepared to use whatever force was necessary. She had not even begun to reconcile herself to the numbers in her life that chronicled the passage of time. Of course, this always-flowing cosmic river had brought all sorts of things to her, both good and bad. It had allowed her to accomplish much and to enjoy many things, but not enough, not nearly enough, given the price it had made her pay for the years she'd lived, so far.

In her youth, she loved the large gilded mirror in her home. It brought her delight and endless promise for the future whenever she gazed into it. And this friendship continued to flourish, year after year. But, gradually, in her adulthood, there came a period of time when she started to suspect that the mirror had begun to betray their friendship and lie to her—not with any obvious, big distortions, but rather small deceptions, perhaps to take her down a notch and to make her a bit humbler. She even entertained the whimsical possibility that there was a spirit of the mirror who had become envious of her beauty and so was altering her reflection in an attempt to subdue her ongoing, natural celebration of herself, her form, and her countenance.

For all the years of her life, she had felt the same dreamy exuberance inside as she had experienced in her youth. And yet, the mirror no longer showed her that youth. It presented her with skin that wasn't as flawless, and with subtly different shapes that had not appeared previously. This newly untrustworthy surface of reflective glass had at first begun to confuse her with fine lines on her face that were never there before, and then much later, it showed strange, deeper creases where there had been only smoothness. Many years further on, it presented her the appearance of a slight looseness in her skin, rather than the taut healthy resilience she had long admired and come to assume would always grace her presentation to the world. It was perplexing, and then agitating, and finally, one day, even frightening.

As time passed, it was then as if the initially deceptive mirror had been able to exercise real power and actually make things happen to her body—surprising things that she had, of course, seen in other people, but had never expected in her own image. It was as if this deeply magical reflective surface framed in gold was now creating in her the lines and the wrinkles it had already deceptively claimed to be hers. She went to other mirrors, but found quickly that they were all in league against her. She would have taken every one of them down and banished them from her presence, but she needed to inspect her choice of clothing before she ever left the house. She learned to now use the mirrors selectively, averting her gaze from what they insisted on saying about her own body and accepting now only their judgments on fashion and style.

It was all too clear that the mirror's initial lies and insulting illusions were now becoming true, which was obviously even worse, and the lady who was still admired by all could no longer resist the natural conclusion about what was happening to her beauty. She had always thought of herself as different, as truly exceptional, and perhaps even as one of a kind. It had never occurred to her that anything like this might eventually transpire. Her entire identity and self-image were tied to what she thought of as her admirable, spectacular beauty. And now she faced what was for her an ultimate crisis.

To her own direct sight and touch, as the years now passed, her skin grew thinner, and it clearly wanted to become nearly translucent on her hands and arms, as if it had a mind of its own, or had been stricken by a curse to make unexpected revelations of realities that had long lurked beneath surface appearances. Veins emerged, as if they were tired of doing their intimately vital work unnoticed for so many years, and now were demanding finally some attention and respect and even appreciation. But respect and appreciation were the last things they were going to get from their owner as they arose to make their claims. She also now saw small bumps, rough spots, and discolorations on her skin, all things that had never been there before. It was not her body any more. It was not her properly flawless beauty. It no longer reflected what she thought of as her soul. It was instead something alien that was overtaking her.

The arranged marriage she had suffered through had altered her life too soon. Her difficult and demanding husband had made her daily existence a misery in many ways, but he had also earned money, and lots of it. She had come to take refuge in that money and what it could buy. Her values changed. She became materialistic in more than one way. Her focus was not just on her face and form, but her lavish adornment and domicile, her travel, and her experiences of food and music and exotic hobbies. And yet, no matter how much money there was, it was never enough for her felt needs and desires. Greed and panic began to take over her soul as age was conquering her, bit by bit. As a result, no problems on the outside could rival at all the ugliness encroaching on the inside. And yet, she learned to hide those inner problems as she was busily seeking to mask the outer ones, as well.

The handsome young soldier she had loved and lost had written her long ago recounting his adventures in nearby lands, and telling her of the antiquities he was rescuing for their native Egypt. In one letter, he described the scrolls he had been given, and intimated what had been said about their potentially great future value. He even passed on to her what his supervising officer had told him, almost in jest, it seemed, but nonetheless, it was a rumor that the scrolls now in his possession had something to do with stories about conquering age, defying death, and living forever. That's what he had written.

The casual words in his note had struck deep in her heart. And they planted a seed. Even at that young age, she had been able to imagine what it would be like to have everlasting life, eternal beauty, and the equally endless resources to fulfill all of her dreams, whatever they might be. The vision his letter inspired eventually became intoxicating and overwhelming, and even life changing. Her aspiration and urge to be with Elam had then, over time, subtly shifted from one of romantic young love and affection to a fevered dream of ambition and endless desire, and even greed. But of course, her dream had been blocked by the harsh reality of parental demands and an unwanted marriage that was forced on her for the sake of business needs. By most standards, she was already, as a result, extremely wealthy, but her own demands required more.

As the years went by and her unhappiness grew, she began to hatch a plot. If she could just outlive her difficult husband, she would set events into motion that would help her to realize her dreams. She would find Elam again and gain everything he had to offer her, one way or another. No one could stand in her way. She served her husband extravagantly rich foods and fed his natural worries with new anxieties. She urged him to make dangerous trips for financial gain. She flaunted her beauty around men she suspected might then seek to take her away from her husband by doing him harm. She was a master at creating stress and unhealthiness for the tyrant who dominated her life. She would outlive him. She was determined. She would prevail and execute a plan to gain everything that she had come to believe was rightfully hers. She would take action.

And she did. The plan seemed to be unfolding beautifully. She was sitting today in the Grand Hotel as a result of that plan, and as a part of it. Her old love Elam was apparently as innocent now as he had been decades ago. He was a good man. She could indeed use him easily in one way or another for her crucial purposes, thanks to a private detective agency in Cairo and to her only child, her son and conspirator, whom she had raised quite successfully to share her values and dreams.

The scrolls that Ebar was now seeking, she had told him, had to do with a secret to everlasting life. Elam hadn't known much about this in the time of their youth, and hadn't been able to tell her much. But his commanding officer had shared some of the legend with him. And he had subsequently heard more of the whispered secrets that might pertain to these scrolls. He didn't actually believe these tales at all, at least, at that point in his life, not really. He'd learned that wild fantasies and outrageous promises usually signal mere myth and legend, and no more than that. They populate the land of wishful thinking. But, in any case, Elam personally had no desire to live forever in this world, preferring the traditional religious promise of life everlasting in another and better form of existence. So, for this, as well as other reasons, he had never sought to have the scrolls translated or read. He had only hidden them away, trusting the promise that one day they could be financially valuable to have.

And when, in recent days, he had told his adult son Asham the story of the scrolls, the younger man had only laughed and said, "Father, your officer was duped by a silly old tale, and as a young man, so, perhaps, were you. There are no magical scrolls, or documents from antiquity with secrets of immortal life. These are just false rumors and base deceptions. That's all. If anyone had such a secret, it's he who would be ancient and present among us, not some scrolls passed down by him. And that's simple logic, not fantasy."

Elam had immediately felt that this made sense, but still hoped for some financial relief from a sale of the scrolls. And after further discussion, his son, who was now one of the top antiquities dealers in Cairo, had accepted them from his father for sale, but had explained that they were likely worth only a modest price. Not many buyers sought scrolls these days, and he would have to take whatever he could get for them. Accordingly, they sold to Shapur Adi for what, in the mind of Elam, was a terribly disappointing pittance. But even a little cash was helpful to the old man in his current financial need.

The lady who was the love of his youth, of course, knew none of this. She had come to think of his scrolls as nearly supernatural objects, and of immense value, from the little he had told her long ago. With the information they must contain, she was convinced that she would be able to deny both age and death their terrifying power. She would take back control over her body and return to the glory of her youth, to maintain it then forever. And that belief had ignited a fire in her soul that could not be quenched by anything other than its ultimate fulfillment. She would live eternally, in unending beauty and, after learning and using the secrets of the scrolls, she would then sell them for such a fortune that even she, in her new and endless life, could never spend it all. The plan was almost too perfect for words. And it was now, she believed, within her reach. But what she was soon to discover would reveal a mosaic of events already in play that she could never have anticipated.

At that moment, not many miles away, the four cultural exchange guests from Germany walked up to their front door at 108 Village Way. But at the threshold, Greta Estand stopped and whispered to her colleague Dieter Himmel, who stood right behind her, "Someone has been here. Someone has been in the apartment."

"How do you know?"

"I just know. We must enter normally. We're likely being watched."

Dieter dropped his head and said in a low voice to the other two, "Act naturally. Don't look around. I'm going to laugh now and you both do the same in response." He then held up his head and laughed loudly, and so did the other two men. And with a big smile, he said, "We'll go inside for a few minutes and then decide what to do." And then he laughed again and patted one of his colleagues on the back.

They entered the apartment, and two of the men sat quietly for a minute in the front room. Dieter leaned against the wall. Greta paced the floor, and then spoke. "In thirty minutes, we'll go out for dinner. Then, we'll spend tonight at the embassy, going directly there from the restaurant. Tomorrow, we'll find another place. We have to leave all our things here aside from the clothing we need."

"Are you sure?" One of the men asked.

"Yes, I am. Someone is somehow on to us, in whatever manner. I don't like it a bit. It could compromise everything. Tomorrow, we'll need to do something drastic to attain our ends quickly. There's no time for anything less."

"What can we do?"

"I have a plan. We'll be cagey. We'll be shrewd. We'll act decisively, and there will be truly catastrophic results for anyone who seeks to get in our way."

17

Breakfast Talk

It was the next morning.

"Ugh." Walid said, as he suddenly appeared in the doorway. He looked and felt terrible.

"Oh! And a hearty hello to you as well, Your Royal Majesty." Mafulla's eyebrows were raised nearly a fourth of the way to his hairline as he viewed his friend's uncharacteristic entrance. Walid had opened the door and slid almost sideways into the breakfast room, but had then stood motionless as he uttered his morning groan.

"This kingly stuff is getting to me," he said.

"Up too late?"

"Yeah. I had a lot to read, some things to sign, and I just couldn't get to sleep, due to the drama that's going on around us right now."

"It's a strange time," Mafulla said.

"The strangest ever," Walid agreed.

"Well, would you like me to bring some coffee and breakfast over to you so that you could eat while continuing to sort of stand, leaning against the door frame, or will you complete your interrupted journey and join me here at the table, my regnant friend?"

"I'm coming. Don't get up." Walid shuffled over to the coffee and poured a cup. Then he picked up a plate and began to load it with breads and fruit. The boys had a deal. When they were alone, none of the details of royal etiquette applied. Mafulla didn't have to stand when Walid came in, or engage in any of the other decorum normally operative in the presence of the king. It was Walid's idea that it was better for the two of them to just be normal, whenever they could get away with it, and Mafulla heartily concurred.

The current king then sat down, looking exhausted, half asleep still, and mostly out of it. "Double ugh. Maybe triple."

"Somebody should write a book about our lives," Mafulla said, out of the blue, as he reached for some grapes. "They could choose to omit this scene, of course. You're not at your best. But, still. And there should be a movie, or maybe, several movies. I see a series."

"I don't know," Walid replied.

"I wonder who'll play me?" Mafulla looked thoughtful. "Hollywood's full of handsome leading men, but will they be able to find one with the right amount of … élan vital?"

"Ok. It's too early for this. But what's élan vital?"

"Life force, high spirits—and of course he'd need penetrating wit."

"Not to mention elastic eyebrows," Walid said.

"I prefer the term vivacious."

"What?"

"Vivacious eyebrows, energetic, full of the joy of life, like their owner."

"Oh. Ok."

"But you're right. For sure, they'll have a hard time finding an actor with the right eyebrows and the requisite control over them."

"Maybe you could play yourself."

"No, you see, that wouldn't work, despite what I suspect might be truly astonishing natural acting abilities."

"Why not?"

"Isn't it obvious?"

"Not to me."

"Well, clearly, because the story has to start when we first met, or maybe a little before that, so that readers and viewers will appreciate the drama of my arrival into the storyline, or the overall narrative—the sheer impact of when you met me in The Kidnapper's Hotel. You remember. It was a scene made for the movies."

"Yeah, I do remember. But I'm the one who made the dramatic arrival. You were already there."

Mafulla ignored this point and went on, saying, "And of course, I'm older and bigger and stronger now than I was then. They'll need a smaller, younger boy to play me in the opening scenes—someone suitably thin and wiry. But then, he'll have to grow tall and extremely muscular during the time of the filming, or else he'd never get the current me right. And, the question is: how's that even possible? It's going to be a difficult casting search, I can tell you that."

"I'm sure."

"You, by contrast, will be relatively easy to cast."

"I'm almost afraid to ask, but why?"

"I mean no offense, of course, but the standard tall dark and handsome young actor could nail your part, practically in his sleep. What's difficult? As long as he has a certain verbal facility and doesn't have a tendency to hog the scenes, any promising star could do it."

"Why can't he hog the scenes?"

"You're not kidding?"

"I'm too sleepy to kid."

"But it's not obvious?"

"No. It's not obvious at all why the actor playing me couldn't hog the scenes. He would be the prince, after all, and then the temporary king. And the royalty stuff is sort of central."

"No, no, no. I understand your confusion, but you fail to grasp the basic reality here."

"What's that?"

"Ok. It sort of pains me to have to actually point this out, but, the movie audience will want to focus on me, naturally, the human dynamo, the wise and yet flamboyant side-kick who's really the spice in the stew."

"Oh?"

"Yes. And the actor playing you will have to learn to be the straight man, and, you know, take a back seat now and then, despite all the obvious, princely, and now, for at least a time, kingly stuff. And even under ideal conditions, the straight man can be a bit hard to play."

"I see. Could I interrupt all this for a moment and ask the human dynamo to dynamically pass me some of the jam you have there?"

"Yes, as always, I'm happy to help you out in the case of any jam."

"He wittily, wisely, and flamboyantly retorts," Walid said.

"Thank you for noticing," Mafulla replied. "I'll be really hard to cast."

At the Grand Hotel, plans had changed. Toward the end of their long reunion luncheon and talk the previous day, Elam al-Buri had asked the lovely Bara if they could meet a second time, for breakfast the next morning, right back in the dining room of the hotel where she was staying. She was now extremely glad she had agreed, because there had been an unexpected twist. After the long-planned initial meeting had taken place under such public scrutiny and they had talked for hours over their meal together, she could not have been more surprised, when she returned to her hotel suite, to hear what her son Ebar had to report. He had been waiting for her in a state of immense frustration and concern. Their golden plan had not worked. He told her that he had been entirely unsuccessful in his best efforts to find the scrolls. He had gone through Elam's home with great care during the ample time provided for the search. He had looked in every nook and cranny, through drawers, in closets, and everywhere. He had even checked for loose floorboards or secret compartments in the walls and under furniture. And he found no sign of the scrolls.

He had also been considerably perplexed as to why Elam was living so simply and humbly if he owned ancient artifacts of such great value. Surely, he could have been exploiting them in some way. When the man had then finished going through Elam's home earlier than he expected, he decided to break into the house of the man's son, Asham, just next door, because he had discovered papers in Elam's desk identifying the son and his address. A search there also turned up nothing. It was a good thing everyone was at the Grand Hotel for the reunion. Ebar had then also gone to the son's shop, intending a third stealthy break-in, on the assumption that it was closed up for the reunion. After all, it might be an ideal hiding place for such scrolls, especially given the nature of the business. But as he approached the shop from the street, he saw what must have been the proprietor himself, newly back from the hotel, putting up the "Open" sign in his doorway, to snag any late day business off the streets.

So Ebar took a big chance and entered through the front door, as if he were a customer. He hadn't met Elam's son at this point, and had managed to stay out of any photographs of his mother and her lost love. This was still a risky move, but it was the only one available to him at present. A small bell rang as he opened the door.

"Oh, hello," Asham had said.

"Hello there."

"May I help you?"

"I'm scouting today for some antiquities, and depending on what I find, perhaps buying tomorrow."

"Very good. What are you hoping to find?"

"Three things: pottery from the time of the pharaohs, small statuary from the same period, and ancient scrolls, from nearly any period."

"Well," Asham had replied, "we have some pottery from that time, and a few statues, small ones, but no scrolls at present."

"Oh, that's fine," Ebar said, and hid his true feelings. He then asked, "Do you ever get in scrolls?"

"Yes, now and then," Asham said. "But there's no regularity. Why do you ask?"

"Oh, no reason, really. I just like to collect such things."

"You could always check back in a few weeks. Sometimes we get them. I just never know in advance."

Ebar nodded and looked around casually for a few minutes,

and then promised to return. Later on, throughout the subsequent evening talk with his mother, he had reported all this in detail. So Bara's major plan had failed. She couldn't go back to Alexandria right away as she had intended in possession of the scrolls, unless she could in some way still gain access to whatever hiding place Elam was now using. The last she had been told, the scrolls were being kept safe in his home. But now, obviously, they must be elsewhere. At breakfast, she would attempt to find out where that is, and if she had success, she would seek to give Ebar one more chance to take them. The only alternative was the much more lengthy process of trying to get Elam to offer them to her as a token of love or esteem. But that could be difficult. And she would prefer for no one to know that the scrolls were in her possession for her own use, and later, for the acquisition of the fortune she would need. Otherwise, she might have to deal with problems that she strongly preferred to avoid. The entire scenario kept her from getting the sleep she had wanted, and now she had to act decisively. She pondered through all this as she took the elevator down to the main floor where, within seconds, she would once again see her old flame, and the only man now who could help her to realize her dreams.

"Oh there you are, you beautiful lady!" Elam said, as the door of the elevator opened.

"My Goodness, here you are as well, you handsome man!" Bara exclaimed. "At the elevator itself to meet me!"

"I didn't want you to have to walk all the way to the dining room unescorted, when I was already here and eagerly available for the pleasure of sharing your company at every possible moment!"

"Oh, you're just the most wonderful thing!" she gushed. "And a real gentleman," she added.

"At least we can meet in peace this morning without photographers and reporters and crowds." He offered her his arm.

Taking that arm eagerly, she said, "Yes! I was delighted by all the goodwill shown to us yesterday, but it's also nice to be alone for a bit, just the two of us."

"I agree. Even when Leem convinced everyone to let us have

some space and time, they were still standing around and watching us from a distance. You would have thought we were movie stars."

"Indeed. Now, it's just me and my man," she replied, and he smiled.

They were shown to a private table and sat down to enjoy each other once again. First, there was some small talk, and then after coffee, tea, fruit, and breads were put out on the table, they began to speak more intimately about their lives, touching on topics from the previous day, but this morning they could get into more details. Bara was completely charming, and Elam was floating on air as she alternately complimented him, gushed over his achievements, and mentioned again and again how much better her life would have been with him in it for all these years. She had such kindness in her voice, and such goodness. He was lured more and more deeply into her web, exactly as she intended.

It must have been about forty-five minutes later in the total charm offensive when she first broached the topic of the scrolls, bringing up the subject in the most casual way, almost like an afterthought. He had mentioned some hobbies of his and how his interest in antiques and antiquities had inspired his son to open a shop by that name.

Bara then said, "Oh, I remember when we were young and you came into possession of your first ancient scrolls. Do you recall writing me about them? They sounded so fascinating."

"Oh, I do. I vividly remember the letter in which I told you the whole tale."

She laughed and almost whispered, "I recall vividly that you said you were going to keep them close to you and that, wherever you lived, you'd find them a good hiding place not far from your bed."

"I did say that. I remember. And I stayed true to my word. When I came back to Cairo, I created a special hiding place in the house where those treasures lay for decades."

"Whatever became of the old scrolls? Do you still have them squirrelled away somewhere?"

"No, no, not at all, I'm afraid. I gave them to my son to sell in his shop, just a short time ago."

"Oh?" She tried to seem merely curious and to hide the complete panic that had suddenly risen up inside her.

"Yes, I was tired of owning them for no real purpose any more."

"But you had said they would one day be so valuable."

"That's what I had been told by, apparently, a very gullible man. Of course, as it ended up, I was every bit as gullible as he—at least, when I was at such a young age." Elam laughed and she did, in response, as well. He added, "It was easy to fall prey to a legend that promised so much to anyone blinded by ambitions and hopes."

"What in the world do you mean? I recall your being a very sensible soul." She smiled and fanned herself to keep from flushing with heat and perhaps changing her skin tone in such a way as to reveal the ardent interest she had in the subject.

"I was young and naïve. There were all sorts of rumors about legends and myths and nonsense concerning the scrolls, and I almost believed them all."

"Do you mean … about what the scrolls contained?"

"Yes. A secret for everlasting life and youth. Can you imagine that?"

She laughed and said, "I can, actually. And people would pay you a king's ransom for that secret."

"Well, as my son Asham said to me, quite reasonably, not long ago, if someone in the distant past had possessed such a secret, then we would have among us a truly ancient person, and not just an ancient scroll." He laughed again, and so did she.

"But you know," she nearly whispered, "We may indeed have both."

He looked amused and puzzled at the same time and said, "What do you mean?"

"If there is a secret to everlasting life and to holding off the more cosmetic depredations of age, there could be a man, or woman, hundreds or thousands of years old among us, and we'd never know. He, or she, could perhaps appear to be of any age."

"How so?"

"If a man used the secret in his youth, he might still appear youthful. If he used it in his middle years, he might appear to be of that age. Or it could even be a secret that turned back the hands of time to some extent, and we'd never know what to look for. Such a person could be among us anywhere. He could be a schoolboy, or our young waiter this morning."

"Well, my goodness, I had never thought of that. And what you're saying is so simple, yet, at the same time, profound."

"I thank you for your kind words."

"They're deserved."

"You're just being generous."

"I mean it. What you've said is so logical. Asham and I were foolishly assuming that if an ancient person lived among us, he or she would certainly look very old, or would be vocal about their age, allowing all the world to know of it. But that likely makes no sense at all."

"You're right. Such a person would be mobbed, and besieged ten thousand times more than we were yesterday, set upon constantly by well-wishers and curiosity seekers and even by dangerous people desperately wanting to know the secret. Everyone would crave what that person had—or I'm sure most people would, at the very least. And can you imagine what some individuals might try to do to get that secret for themselves?"

"You're absolutely right. This had never occurred to me."

"Has your son actually sold the scrolls?"

"Yes, he did, not long ago."

"For a king's ransom, I would imagine?"

"No, not at all," he laughed, and added, "unfortunately."

"Did you ever have them translated or read them to see for yourself what they contained?"

"No, I didn't."

"Really? You weren't curious?"

"Well, I glanced at them. One was in a very old, archaic dialect of Arabic. The other was in a different language I couldn't identify."

"But you worked for an archeologist."

"Yes, on mostly discoveries of decorative pottery and weapons, with some work excavating monuments. But it wasn't my job to translate anything, especially documents."

"So, for all you know—for all we both know—those scrolls could indeed contain exactly what the legends and rumors said they held."

Elam said, "Well, I suppose. It's highly unlikely, but indeed possible."

"Ah. Our having breakfast today after all these decades would have been thought highly unlikely as well, though, wouldn't it?"

"Yes, you're right again."

"The highly unlikely happens every day."

"I suppose that's true."

"And even miracles occur now and then."

"You make a very good point."

"And behind every miracle is some secret."

"So, you think the scrolls could actually contain miraculous secrets?"

"It's possible."

Elam nodded his head and said, "Maybe that explains what's been going on."

"What do you mean?" she asked.

"Some people have been trying to find and take the scrolls in any way they can."

She felt herself tense up inside and said, "Wait. What's that again?"

"Some men have recently been trying to steal the scrolls."

"How do you know this? What happened?"

"Men came to the shop and attacked my son and tied him up."

"No!"

"It's true. They threatened him with a gun, demanding that he hand over two scrolls they believed were in his possession."

"Really? Who were these people?"

"Germans. Violent men."

"But you said he had sold the scrolls."

"He had. He had already sold them to a local collector before the thieves visited him with all their unpleasantness."

"Do you know the name of the buyer?"

"Yes, it's Adi. Shapur Adi. He has a shop in the main marketplace and a home in a neighborhood not far away."

"Did these violent men then go after the collector?"

"They did, or to be more precise, they went after the scrolls in his possession. They raided his shop when he wasn't there. They knocked out a guard. And the man was lucky not to have died."

"Did they get the scrolls?"

"No, the items weren't in his shop, but apparently at his home."

"What do you know about this man, this Adi who has acquired your precious antiquities?"

"He has a good reputation as a shopkeeper and as a human being. He has a family, with a wife and three children. They're quite active in the community. His eldest child, a son, lives in the palace and works with the king."

"Oh, is that so?"

"Yes. I met him the other day when the king visited my home."

"I was so impressed to hear that you had met the king."

"Well, I'm honored to know him."

"And you said that he visited to ask you some questions about an important matter, but that you couldn't be very helpful to him."

"Yes."

"Was it about this?"

"It was."

"And you met the Adi boy who lives at the palace?"

"I did. He came by to visit with the king."

"So I suppose he has … special protection. I mean, the son, and then, most likely, the father as well? Any close friend of the king would have protection, I could imagine."

"I think he does. I think they both do."

"Good. That's good. So then, the scrolls should be safe."

"I imagine so. They're being guarded, with access provided

to only Mr. Adi and a few other men. And they're looking for a translator."

"They are?"

"Yes, that's what I've been told. They want to know what's in the scrolls so they can better understand the nature of the threat that these violent men pose, and why they're in such pursuit of the items."

"Have they found anyone yet who can translate?"

"There's one man at the university, a professor, who could likely do it, but he's apparently away for some research work in Paris."

"What exactly do they need?"

"Someone who can read an ancient Arabic dialect and also Aramaic, and perhaps either Akkadian or Sumerian."

"My son Ebar can do all that."

"Your son?"

"Yes. His education focused on ancient middle-eastern and near eastern languages. He teaches them at the university in Alexandria."

"Really? I didn't know that. I mean, you told me, of course, that he was a professor, but you hadn't mentioned the subject"

"Yes, ancient languages, and he's very good at his job."

"Do you think he could translate the scrolls?"

"I would be surprised if he couldn't."

"Where is he now?"

"Having breakfast at a nearby café, I believe. If you could give me the Adi address, perhaps he could go over and introduce himself to those who need his skills."

"I believe that Leem Hadad, whose office is not far away, is actually in charge of finding the translator."

"The Leem Hadad who found you for me?"

"Yes. One and the same."

"Oh! Well, then, I should get the two of them together, right away. After breakfast, they should have a talk."

"I bet Leem would appreciate that a great deal."

"Good. I'll make it happen. I'd love to be of help."

18

A Conflagration

The Germans had spent the morning locating Shapur Adi's home and going by to observe it. Two of them were disguised as locals just passing through the neighborhood, with two others actually going door-to-door at nearby homes under the guise of soliciting repair or maintenance work for hire on a project basis, or at a day-labor rate. They had done free external inspections at some of the homes, under the pretense of discovering anything that might need to be fixed. In the process, they had seen the armed guards at the Adi home and were aware of how difficult it would be to get in through any normal means.

They had also watched a truck and two cars pull up in front of the house at various times, stay a bit, and then drive off. There was too much activity at the place. And they realized by now that if they ventured any sort of direct approach to the house, under any conceivable false pretenses, their accents would likely give them away. As Germans, they would be under immediate suspicion. They had left too many witnesses alive in their earlier failed attempts to get the scrolls. But the Black Widow had formulated a plan. And if it worked, they would have the scrolls on this day, within hours, and could leave Cairo before the authorities had a chance to close in on them and discover or interfere with their mission. There might be many deaths as a result of the plan, but that didn't concern her in the least.

In New York City before dawn, and twelve city blocks from the Wesleyan Chapel, another Widow was up early, spinning a web of her own quite similar plan. Violent things were soon to happen in two widely separated parts of the world, and they would show a common style of proceeding.

At the back of the Chapel, the new caretaker quietly unlocked the door and slipped in. To his surprise, Reverend Archdale was already having his coffee, earlier than usual. As the man sat and read the morning paper, he heard the key in the lock and saw Santiago enter, and then greeted him with the words, "Good morning, my friend."

"Good morning. I didn't know you'd be up this early," Santiago said in a tone of surprise.

"The telephone woke me."

"Before dawn?"

"Yes. There's news from the police."

"Oh?"

"The head detective called. One of the men escaped."

"How?"

"It was a man who left here unconscious. They took him to the hospital instead of the jail, and when he awoke, he apparently pretended to still be out until he spotted an opportunity and got away before anyone even knew he was conscious."

"That's not good."

"I know. Ian will be worried."

"Yes, and with good reason."

"Do you think the man will come back?"

"You mean here?"

"Yes. Do you suppose he'll come to visit us again and try once more to get the scroll?"

"I have a feeling he will. And it may be more difficult for us this time."

"How can that be? Two of his friends are in jail for good."

"I suspect that he has more resources than just those two."

"Oh?'

"Yes. I imagine that they won't give up easily. And last time, we had an element of surprise on our side, to match and neutralize their own surprises."

"But I just don't understand why all this is happening. Have you had a chance to read any more of the scroll?"

"Yes, I have. Last night, I stayed up a bit with it, actually for a few hours."

"Did you learn anything that might explain what's going on?"

"I did." Santiago now turned to get coffee.

"Fix yourself an egg or some toast if you'd like," Archdale said.

"Buttered toast and jam should do it for me right now," he replied. And then he added, "Thanks, as always."

Archdale smiled. "There's one piece of bread already in the toaster. I put in two and decided I just wanted one. That'll get you started."

"You're having only one piece of toast?"

"My belt has been complaining to my belly. I need to do something about it. But I do worry that my best effort will only switch where the complaints are originating."

Santiago laughed and said, "I see. Ok, then. I'll take the temptation away from you." He got out a small plate and put the abandoned piece of toast on it, opened a jar of jam, and then spread some of it, along with butter, on the still crunchy bread. He dropped two more pieces into the toaster and brought his plate to the table, saying, "I tell you my friend, we've stumbled onto quite a document."

"Really?"

"Yes, it's indeed ancient and it promises to be important."

"So, what exactly is it?"

"Well, after some preliminaries and warnings to anyone who is not a part of a particular secret society that they should put the scroll away and not attempt to read it, there's a long poem or poem fragment that makes no sense to me."

"What's the poem about?"

"Well, that's the problem. It appears not to be about anything, really. Its lines never seem intended to flow, one to the other, like a normal poem."

"I don't understand."

"It was quite disorienting at first. To start, I was reading an ancient and archaic dialect of Arabic. And then, as if that was not challenging enough by itself, there's no continuity to its lines and sentences. It took me a while to puzzle it out, but it started looking like there must be another poem, somewhere else, or an apparent poem that, like this one, is only a partial work, and that will interlock somehow with ours and then together provide something that could be sensible."

"That's very odd."

"Yes, it is. Someone has gone to a lot of trouble to create this. And here's the bad part."

"I can't imagine."

"After I had spent far too much time working over the lines and finally concluding that this is something like one half of a poem, rather than the entirety of one—and further, one half in a most unusual sense—I unrolled more of the scroll and came to the end of the long, confusing construction, and then was able to read something beyond it that said exactly what I had hypothesized."

"Really?"

"Yes. It said that any member of Phi—that was the name, just the single Greek letter, in a sea of Arabic—who is level four and above, whatever that means, should find a second, companion document that looks much like this one, and is the other half of a key that these two works of perplexing literary art together will provide for reading and interpreting a third scroll, which is apparently something like a master document." He took a big bite of toast and said, "I've paraphrased a bit."

"This is all very complicated."

"I thought so at first, too. But apparently, it's all simpler than it initially seems."

"Ok. Please explain it to me then in the simple version."

"There's apparently a very ancient document whose contents are vitally important, and crucial to protect from people who are not qualified to read it and use its ideas properly."

"I see."

"And so it was written in some sort of code, at least in part. And then a key to that code was created in the form of a long poem, split into two parts, by lines, and even parts of lines, and written onto two different scrolls that would be hidden and protected, separate from each other. Anyone who wants or needs to read the most ancient scroll of the three, the one whose main secrets are in code, will need to find and piece together properly, and then fully translate, the other two key documents, one of which we have on this scroll. Does that make sense?"

"Yes, for all its complexity, I think it does. So what the Germans were trying to steal from us is a part of a key to decoding and reading another document."

"Correct."

"I wonder whether they know that."

"They could already hold the other half of the key, and if it has a comparable explanatory passage somewhere on it and they have read and understood it, then they'll know they need ours as well."

"Or," Archdale mused, "perhaps they know nothing of codes and keys and think that we have the primary scroll they're after. They could believe that we have the ultimate prize."

"That could also be true."

"I wonder how they tracked down this one."

"Well, it was hidden away in the chest that Ian gave us. And so they must have learned about that, somehow. And probably they knew or had found the previous owner of the chest, and in that way discovered that it had migrated into Ian's custody. And then, of course, through the questioning and unpleasantness they inflicted on him, they learned that it most recently came to us."

"What could be so important that people presumably from another country far away from us are here in New York trying to steal it, and callously torturing and killing people along the way?"

"Perhaps, if we could come to understand that, we'll know how best to deal with these individuals."

"I don't know why," Archdale now said, "but I have a strange feeling that we're supposed to have this scroll in our possession right now, and that it's our job to protect it and also to do something with it, but I don't know what."

Santiago sat quietly for a few seconds, holding his piece of toast, and then said, "I feel the same way." Then, the toaster popped up the other two pieces of bread. But the two men were focused on the topic at hand.

Archdale sighed and said, "It would be nice to have some idea of what we're meant to do. Without that, it's hard to plan for whatever might be coming next."

"You have a good point. And yet, as with much in life, it seems that we simply have to be open and ready for whatever sense of calling or direction we may receive along the way." As Santiago said this, he felt a slight itch on his upper thigh, and when he instinctively moved to scratch it, his hand brushed against the ring in his pocket, and feeling it then made him pause for a moment and think, but not of anything in particular. He just had an inkling of something important that was on the way.

Upstairs in the palace in Cairo, Mafulla walked into Walid's office, where the monarch was engrossed in a report on his desk. "Hey."

'Hey, back. What's going on?" Walid replied and looked up.

"Well, you know, there's no school all day long, and I think we should go do something that's hard to do on a class day."

"What do you have in mind?"

"Viper and Storm Patrol."

"Really?"

"Yep. After that talk with Masoon, we haven't really done anything."

"We had the masks on when we ran into your dad's shop and found Badar on the floor."

"True. But that wasn't actually the result of a patrol."

"Viper and Storm stuff doesn't have to depend on random patrols."

"You're right. And that's always a good reminder. We've talked about this before. But still, the random patrol, better known as the innocent wandering around town, is the classic scenario for Viper and Storm action."

"I agree wholeheartedly to your precise point," Walid said. "And I can actually take a break now."

"Good."

"So what do you want to do? Where exactly do you want to do this sort of innocent wandering that you have in mind?"

"I don't know. Let me think." Mafulla took a breath. "Ok, here's an idea. Let's walk to Mom and Dad's house. We never have a chance to take long strolls any more, since this temporary king stuff started. And going there, we'll take all the standard retail and residential streets along the way. And who knows? We might be able to do some good for somebody."

"That sounds reasonable. But will your parents be there at this time of day?"

"Well, dad will likely be at the shop for a little longer, and Sammi's normally at his best friend's house, a few blocks away from home, when there's no school, but mom and Sasha should be at home."

"Good. So, what do we take with us for the patrol?"

"The full deal?"

"I don't know." Walid made a bit of a face.

"Ok."

"Unless you have a feeling we should."

"No, not really."

"Then, let's go light and natural."

"Fine with me."

"Get the masks for us both, Ok? And the wrist bands, which we basically forgot about at the shop."

"Oh, yeah, you're right. But that was sort of a rush job and we weren't in full stealth mode."

"True. So, you get that stuff and I'll meet you for a snack first in just a minute."

"Where are your mask and wristband?"

"Top drawer, right side. Same as always."

"Ok." Mafulla whipped around and walked at a quick pace down the hall in the direction of their rooms.

Five minutes later, with snacks quickly eaten and fruit juice enjoyed, they headed for the big front staircase. Mafulla said in a low voice, "So, how do we best get out of here?"

"Good question. The guys at the gate will not want to see us leave without a palace guard escort."

"You're the king. You can do what you want."

"Well, within reason, but that might create a serious bout of consternation.

"Consternation. I like that word."

"Yeah, but we wouldn't like the situation it names."

"No, you're right."

"Let's check into the guardroom and see if Paki or Omari, or Amon might be around. One or two of them could get us out of the grounds with no questions asked and, I don't know, we could send them off to enjoy an hour at a café or something while we go on the prowl."

"That sounds like a plan."

And the plan worked. Paki and Amon were both in the guardroom taking a break when Walid and Mafulla got there. The boys explained that they had a simple need to get "off campus," as they put it, and take a walk and that they'd be wearing sand masks for anonymity and that, if the two Phi would escort them out, they could take a well deserved break at The Blue Camel or any other café of their choosing, as the monarchy's treat. The older guys agreed right away, or rather, after having asked the obligatory "Are you sure you don't want extra protection?" question and gotten the answer they expected. Then, as soon as the two guards changed into their civilian clothes, the adventure began. Out the side gate, down the street, a few blocks over, and the official escorts were happy to be left behind at The Blue Camel to sit and enjoy the strong coffee, the great pastries, and the pleasant light breeze that was blowing through the city today. The Viper and the Storm were equally happy to be free to enjoy the city and the sense of excitement a possible adventure easily brought them.

But before the guards entered the busy establishment, Paki looked at Walid and said, "YM, let us know if you need anything," and he touched the side of his head twice with his right index finger.

Walid replied, "I'm not sure I can do that yet."

And Paki responded, "You'll be able to if you really need to. Just focus on us completely and hard. Remember, it's us. A strong radio receiver with a big antenna can pick up even a weak signal."

"Yeah, I get it. You're right, of course," Walid smiled, and with a final word to the guards, went on with his friend. The next ten minutes of their walk were relatively uneventful, except for a cat on a second floor window ledge and a distraught little girl begging him, or her, to come down. Who ever heard of a tiny cat named Pharaoh? Nevertheless, with the regal feline safely in the girl's arms, the famous superheroes of the city ventured on down the road in search of their next major challenge.

"Well, so far, this is not quite like the old days," Mafulla said.

"Well, we're not old enough to have anything we can truly call 'the old days,' and hey, remember—early on, we rescued Yippers."

"True. And then we had to rescue him again."

"Yeah. Really. So, it's not always about kingpins of crime and international megalomaniacs."

"Still, I like a challenge."

"You could have slipped on the window ledge."

"Yeah, and why did it have to be me doing the high wire act?"

"You're always boasting about how limber you are."

"Remind me to boast less."

At that moment, they heard a car motor nearby, slowing down and pulling up behind them as they walked. Walid turned slightly, as did Mafulla. It was a dark sedan of some sort. The window closest to them rolled down and a voice said, "Isn't there some law against monarchs just walking around, out and about, in the middle of the day and with little or no entourage?"

"Hasina?" Mafulla said.

"Do you gentlemen need a ride?"

"What is this?" he said, gesturing to the glistening automobile, whose coat of wax was shined to a high polish that practically blinded them as they looked at it.

"A new car," she said with a big smile.

"Whose?"

"Ours! Get in and take a ride with us!"

Mafulla looked at Walid, and he said, "Ok. Sure. Let's do it." So the Windstorm opened the back door and held it for the king, who got in and slid across the burgundy leather rear seat.

Mafulla said, "Wow. This is nice. And it's got the new car smell."

"Yea, isn't it great? Hi there, Your Majesty and Mafulla," Layla said from the driver's seat.

"Layla? You're driving?" Walid said.

"Yes. Modern women do modern things," she replied.

"This is awesome," Mafulla said as he took his seat and closed the door and looked around.

"Thank you," Layla replied.

"It's super nice, isn't it?" Hasina gushed. "We just got it, and we're going to go show it to Kissa after we've taken our initial drive in it."

"Amazing."

"Where can we drop you two men of mystery?" Layla asked.

"Oh, yeah, the sand masks," Walid said and laughed, tugging his down.

"We were just going to visit my family, at the house," Mafulla said, "if you could take us by there."

"Sure, it's not far."

"Were you doing a little Viper and Storm stuff?" Hasina asked.

Walid's eyes grew big and he grimaced and nodded toward Layla.

"Oh, that. Mom knows," Hasina said.

"Yep." The confirming remark came from the driver.

"What?" Mafulla said, in shock.

"I've known for a while," Layla clarified. "I figured it out. Don't worry. Hasina didn't spill the beans."

"Oh." Walid said, and added, "So, then, at least you know what kind of crazy riff-raff your daughter is mixed up with."

"Yes, but we're hoping the riff will eventually overwhelm the raff and all will be well," she replied, as she accelerated down the street.

The boys actually felt a little relieved about this news. They would have one more powerful supporter for their adventures around town. And within seconds, their talk returned to the car. They both gushed about it as they explored the details of the interior and enjoyed the solid, quiet ride. Hasina spent most of the short trip twisted around in her seat so that she could see her friends as they talked. And, in seemingly no time, they pulled up to the front of the Adi house and Layla parked the car.

Before the boys could say thanks and open the door, there was a huge explosion nearby that shook the ground and the car. Debris and fire shot from a house only a short distance down the street. Not more than three seconds later, that terrible sound was followed by another explosion that was even louder. BOOM! Five doors down, another dwelling was mostly demolished and instantly, in a deafening conflagration of fire and smoke. Not three seconds after that, the front wall of a house across the street and up the block a bit suddenly blew outward and its roof flew off in sections and pieces. The occupants of the car had instinctively flattened themselves against their seats at the sound and shock wave of the first bomb blast, and had covered their ears with the second and third. Fortunately, none of the debris had hit the new car. It was far enough away to miss them, up until now. But smoke was already swirling around them and filling the air.

Mafulla suddenly said, "Mom and Sasha!" and opened his car door, leaping out, and running toward the front door of his house. Walid followed him close behind, and within about two seconds, Layla and Hasina were also in pursuit.

"We've got to get them out and away from here," Walid yelled back to Layla and Hasina as new clouds of black smoke now billowed through the air and engulfed that part of the neighborhood. The guards at the Adi house had been stunned by the series of loud explosions so near them, and immediately took defensive positions, as if for a gun battle.

"Get my family out of the house!" Mafulla shouted at the first guard he saw, who was in a crouched position, with his rifle pointing toward the source of the latest explosion.

"What?" the man said. He didn't recognize Mafulla right away in the confusion of the situation, and almost pointed his gun at him.

"Mom and my sister Sasha! We need to get them out of the house and to safety!" he repeated.

BOOM! A fourth explosion from somewhere nearby shook the house and the ground underneath them. It was like a war zone. Fires were already raging throughout the neighborhood. Mafulla ran through the front room and into a hallway.

"Mom! Sasha!" he called out. And there was no answer. He walked a few more steps toward the back rooms.

"Mom!

"Sasha!"

19

The Plan Unfolds

"So, what do you think?" Jabari asked his friend as he walked up to him. "How's my plan working so far?"

"Magic, it's just magic," Set answered. "I mean, I really have to hand it to you. I'm shocked at what you've been able to accomplish in such a short time."

"I'm a guy you can count on," Jabari said.

"That's for sure," Set replied. "Now Haji and Ara are suddenly a couple, and Khata feels good about it, and she and I are hitting it off, big time. And Haji has no hard feelings at all about the two of us."

Jabari was smiling. "Yeah. I told you. It's pretty awesome."

"Are you a real-life wizard or something?"

"Just a humble student of psychology with genius overtones, to be completely honest," he replied.

"You'll get no argument from me."

"I'm a careful observer, and I know how best to use what I've learned."

"Well, you may have to be the best man one day."

"Yes! That sounds perfect. The Best Man … Ever—Jabari al-Sout!"

Set laughed and said, "Who knew?"

"Ah! I have many skills," Jabari said. "Just ask if you need anything else as the plan continues to unfold."

"Wait. There's more? There's more to the plan?"

"Of course. I do nothing halfway."

"Wow. Ok. I can't imagine, but I really appreciate it."

It was still early morning in New York. The sky looked like it was going to be a clear blue later on, but at present there was some haze. Traffic was starting to pick up throughout the city. A few people were already coming through the front door of The Wesleyan Chapel for an early morning choir rehearsal. A volunteer had just put out coffee and pastries for the first arrivals. Three ladies who made up the entire membership of the church's Hospitality and Bereavement Committee were also already milling around in a small parlor off the sanctuary. They were meeting to plan their cooking and casserole deliveries for the upcoming week to several newcomers, shut-ins, and a large neighborhood family who had just suffered a sad loss.

Santiago had mentioned to Reverend Archdale that he thought it was strange to have one small group of people serving the church with such an unexpected name, whose terms juxtaposed such divergent matters as hospitality and bereavement. Bob had said that he liked to think of it as the "Glad to See Them Come and Sorry to See Them Go" Committee—or the "Hello and Goodbye People," for short. He explained to Juan that both welcoming newcomers and sympathizing with a loss often involved visitation, as well as preparing and sharing meals, and that people who were good in one of those situations were usually good in the other as well.

Bob at the moment was in his office preparing his sermon for the next morning. He was planning to talk on the nature of faith and how it's more about perception and values and commitment than just belief. He had decided to use as his biblical text the famous meeting at night between Jesus and the Jewish Rabbinical leader Nicodemus, as reported in the Gospel of John, chapter three. At a time when most of the religious establishment either disliked or feared Jesus, this prominent teacher had gone to see him at night, when, presumably his visit would not be public knowledge. He approached the controversial figure and actually said, "Teacher, some of us know that you were sent by God, because no one could do the things you do without divine support." And then Jesus, rather than acknowledging the scholar's rare open-minded reasoning and remarkable belief, says something instead that can be very puzzling on more than one level. His words in response were: "Truly, truly, I say to you, unless a man is born again, he cannot see the kingdom of God." Nicodemus is of course perplexed and says, "How can anyone return to the womb and be born a second time?" And then Jesus answers in such a way as to indicate that his entire ministry and mission aren't primarily about reasoning and belief, but personal transformation into what's really a new life—with new perceptions, values, and commitments.

Bob knew that, at almost any time, many of the people in his church were showing up, week-to-week, to make a deal with God. They would believe whatever they needed to believe and do whatever they needed to do in order to gain divine favor and everlasting life. Some were likely just hedging their bets and maybe living out the famous Agnostic's Prayer: "Oh God, if there is a God, please save my soul, if there is a soul." They were there in an effort to perhaps improve their lot and maybe defeat death. But God wanted them there to defeat spiritual blindness and deafness and idolatry and selfishness. He wanted to see them born anew, raised from the death of alienation and separation and selfishness to a new life of union with him and each other. He wanted an eternal life for them now, which was more about quality than it was about quantity.

Bob really wanted to get this point across to everyone who showed up for the service. The faith they were being called to embrace is about new life, new values, and new commitments lived all day, every day. He wanted them to understand that when the insistent felt needs of the untutored ego can be released, its real needs can be met. And then, we can experience the genuine power of humility, compassion, and deep faith. The reverend was hoping to get all this across in a persuasive and illuminating way, so that at least many of the members of his congregation could perhaps see the issues of faith in a new and richer light.

When people approach religion for what they can get out of it, they ironically make it nearly impossible to get the most out of it. It becomes a tool, an instrument the ego is merely using to enhance its own interests, whether those interests are healthy or not. That's why we've had so much war and violence and oppression in the name of religion throughout history. These things have nothing to do with true spirituality, but are perversions or deformations of what faith and the quest of the spirit are supposed to be all about. We often come across people pursuing their own greed, with their own ambitions, and superstitiously seeking to assuage their worst fears under a false patina of religious language, ritual, and sentiment. And this wasn't just a danger for other times and places, Archdale knew, but it's a temptation for any of us unless we can come to a true understanding of spiritual things.

Right now, with all these thoughts in his mind, he was looking for some more verses he could quote to make his points. He was flipping the pages of his Bible, and had a big Bible Dictionary open in front of him. Santiago was out front of the building, sweeping the sidewalk, and examining the short, old wrought iron fence that ran across the church grounds beside the walk. It needed new black paint in a few places, and he was trying to figure out how much paint he should buy. Neither he nor Archdale had any clue as to what the next few moments would hold in store for them.

Facing the church from the street, there was a fairly large yard to its right, bordered by an alleyway, and a smaller area of yard to the left. In each open space, there were outdoor benches and meandering sandy walkways, lined with bricks. Beyond the alley to the right was an abandoned shop. It had once been a shoe store and leather goods repair place. But the man who ran it for many years had recently retired and no one wanted to take it over from him. So the space had sat empty for several months.

Behind the church's back grounds and garden area was an old brick building that housed a restaurant and bar that were popular, but open only in the evenings. It was a source of much local humor that the church and the bar were back to back. You can easily imagine the witty remarks that this generated. The main doors of the bar and restaurant faced the next street over. And the building they were in was separated from church grounds by a high fence that was covered in ivy and nearly hidden by additional tall shrubs and thick, leafy, short trees. Santiago paused for a moment in his movements, in response to the sound of a dog's loud, aggravated barking somewhere not far away. Then, it happened.

There was a mind-numbing explosion at the empty shoe shop, as if a gas line had ruptured catastrophically and dynamite had set it off. Santiago instinctively dropped into a defensive crouch. The blast was at least momentarily deafening. Flames shot from the front of the building, shattering the large glass windows into millions of shards that were instantly propelled across the street and toward the facing structures there. Fortunately, there was no one on the sidewalk outside the building at the moment, or they would surely have been killed. Black smoke poured from the now open front of the structure.

Then, before Juan could stand back up, there was an equally loud concussive blast in the restaurant building behind the church. Whatever it was, it actually punched a whole in the rear brick wall. The shock waves shook the church and the sound, like the earlier explosion, was easily heard inside the sanctuary by all the choir members, the ladies in their meeting, and Reverend Archdale. There were many sudden exclamations of shock and concern throughout the groups. People who had been sitting stood up, frightened and perplexed. And many who had been standing now bent down, or moved quickly in any direction they thought might be safer, away from windows and into inner hallways.

Then a moment later, there was a lesser, secondary explosion from the restaurant. At this point, no one had any idea what might happen next. And as this very thought crossed Santiago's mind, a parked car that was a block down the street beyond the shoe shop suddenly blew up. This was too much. Juan ran to the front door of the church and dashed in, urging everyone to evacuate the building. He had in mind to lead them quickly out the front and in the one direction where there had not yet been any explosions. But they had to get out now, in case the church was in danger of being next.

"Bob!" Santiago yelled out toward the pastor's office. Then he turned to one of the men in the choir who was standing nearby and said, "Please, help me get everyone out and down the street to the right as you leave the door. There's safety in that direction, it seems. And we need to go now!"

Suddenly, the small boy Clark caught his eye. He was with his mother, who sang in the choir. Juan looked at the startled lady and said, "Everything will be fine. There's a problem with some of the buildings in the neighborhood. You need to get your son outside quickly. Please follow this man who will lead the way to a safe area."

Archdale had jumped up from his desk, stunned and confused as to what in the world could be going on. He started to leave the study and head out toward the sanctuary where he thought he had just heard Juan's voice, but something held him back. He shouldn't leave without something. He needed to get something, to save something. What? Oh! He reached down and grabbed his sermon notes and turned and headed for the door. But as he passed through the doorway of the room, Santiago practically ran into him.

"The scroll!" he said. "Do you have the scroll?"

Archdale looked shocked at the sudden realization that these words brought and said, "No!"

"I'll get it!" Santiago didn't hesitate. He ran by Bob and jerked open the chest and picked up the inner box. Glancing around, he saw a burlap sack lying on the floor in the corner, grabbed it, shoved the small box into it and made for the door like the building was already on fire. As he now followed Archdale into the sanctuary and through it toward the door, he coughed hard from the black smoke that was already creeping in through the opening as people were leaving. A charred, burnt, ugly smell was in the air, as of gasoline mixed with oil and wood and rubber, and other things melting and giving off fumes.

"Bob!" He called out, and Archdale turned around. "Here, take the bag and go, so I can help more of the people get out!"

Archdale reached forward and grabbed the sack from Santiago, and they continued to walk quickly to the entrance, as Juan took hold of two panicked people, frozen in place, and steered them to the door. They could already hear distant sirens as they got into the street out front and urged people to keep going, farther down the block, away from the sites of the recent explosions and from the noxious billowing smoke that was already causing so much respiratory distress at this point, and nearly blinding their vision.

This was all a massively destructive diversionary tactic, identical to the one being used, oddly enough, around a particular house in Cairo. The idea in each case was to frighten people away from a specific building, and then get into the place by stealth and retrieve a wanted item or, in the case of the home in Cairo, a pair of items. In both of these locations, bombs and incendiary devices of various kinds had been employed to this end without any concern for property or any people who might get in the way.

In the neighborhood of the Egyptian conflagration, Mafulla Adi had just rushed into his home and called out for his mother and shouted the name of his little sister. He had heard nothing in response. He yelled out again, "Mom! Sasha!" He could hear another explosion outside somewhere. "We need to get you out of the house!"

"My son! We're here!" Shamilar responded from the back.

Mafulla heard her and instantly ran toward the main bedroom. Walid was right behind him, and so were Layla and Hasina.

"Are you Ok?"

"Yes! Yes! We hid in the closet as soon as we heard the first explosion, not knowing what had happened." Sasha was already crying, tears streaming down her face.

"Everything's going to be fine," Mafulla said to reassure them.

"We'll get the two of you out of the house now and to greater safety," Layla emphasized. Just then, another small explosion could be heard at a distance.

"What's going on around us? Are we under attack? Is there a war?"

"We don't know yet, but, so far, our house is fine," Walid said.

"What should we do?"

"We just have to get out as quickly as we can!" Mafulla put his arm around his mother and Walid scooped up Sasha, and they headed for the front door.

"How many guards are there?" Mafulla now asked Walid.

"Two here. Two left earlier when the shift changed. There are two more on the way from down the street."

"They need to stay with us, now," Mafulla said, "not with the house."

"You're right," Walid responded.

"Oh!" Mafulla looked at his mother and said, "We should grab the scrolls!"

"They're not here."

"What?"

"Soldiers were sent to get them more than thirty minutes ago, before all this started," Shamilar said, as they began to leave the house.

"Quickly. We need to get to the car," Layla directed, and held open the door.

"Why did soldiers come for the scrolls?" Walid asked Shamilar, as they walked.

"They have a translator," she said quickly, "and wanted the work of translation to take place at a more secure location."

"Oh, good," Walid replied as he looked around, distracted by the smoke and noise. "Here, please, get in the car, you and Sasha."

"What will you do?"

"We'll jump in the backseat."

"Good."

"And we'll have the guards follow us in the truck they have here." Popping sounds came loudly from one of the fires nearby.

Walid turned around and shouted something at the closest guard, and he sort of waved and nodded. Smoke was pouring toward the house at this point from three directions.

Walid slipped into the back of the car. "Let's go!" he said to Layla, and she gunned the engine, turning the wheel dramatically and whipping them around, back in the direction of the palace. He turned to Mafulla and said, "The two guards here will follow us, and won't wait for the others from down the street. Those guys will be checking houses as they approach and won't be here for a few minutes, at least. We can't wait for them. We just need to get everyone to safety."

"You're right," Mafulla said.

"What a shock!" Hasina exclaimed in a low voice.

"Yeah, we had no idea such a thing would happen," Mafulla replied. "We wouldn't have been here so quickly to help without you two ladies picking us up."

"Yeah. I'm glad we saw you."

Shamilar said, "I don't know what we would have done without the rescue you've all provided us, and your kind words of reassurance." She held Sasha close.

Walid said, "I hope the car's Ok."

Layla answered, "It looks completely undamaged, I'm glad to say, just totally covered with ash."

By that time, they had cleared the thick smoke and had it in the rear view mirror of the car. Approaching them were two fire trucks, heading toward the houses that had exploded so suddenly.

"I hope no one's hurt, and that no one gets hurt," Mafulla said.

His mother replied, "Most are not home this time of day. I pray for everyone's safety."

Walid turned to her then and said, "Where did you say they're taking the scrolls for translation?"

"No one told me," She replied. "Just somewhere more secure is all they said."

"Oh. Ok. Who came for them?"

"I hadn't seen the men before. There were two of them. They

said they had been sent on orders from the palace, and the head guard seemed to know one of them."

"The palace? I wonder who they meant?" Walid looked over at Mafulla.

"Most likely, Uncle Reela," Mafulla guessed.

"Is he even in today?" Walid asked. And then he said, "I thought he had something he had to do, some place elsewhere in town."

"No, I actually think he's just working from home today. And, if it's not him, then who would have given the order?"

"I don't know," Walid said. "Maybe Masoon? He could be at the palace and working today. But I don't know why he wouldn't have sent … friends for an important transport mission like this."

"I hope the guys who came to pick up the scrolls were actually there on proper authority."

"Yeah," Walid said and looked concerned. "Really."

"What do you mean?" Shamilar asked.

"Well, we just don't have any idea what the Germans might try, at this point. They're pretty determined."

In New York, as everyone had left the front of the church in a great rush, two people slipped into the rear door—a man, and a woman. They immediately launched into a systematic search of the pastor's bedroom, the kitchen, and the study. In the study, the woman saw the trunk with its top open.

"In here!" She yelled out.

"Where?"

"In here, in the book room, in the office!"

The man ran to her and she pointed to the empty open trunk.

"It was here," she said. "It was here. This is the trunk."

"They took it with them?"

"Yes! They must have!"

"So, someone on the street has the scroll."

"We have to get it!" The woman strode toward the back door, the man following close behind. "No failures this time!" she said with authority. They left through the rear entrance, heading around the building to jump the short fence over to the side so they could get to the group of church members and others who were now farther down the street.

Two fire trucks suddenly appeared in view and one ambulance followed them. Other sirens could be heard on the street a block away where the front entrance of the restaurant was located. One fireman jumped down from the back end of the first truck that arrived near the church and started waving people to get even farther away from the sources of all the flames and smoke.

"The smoke alone can kill!" He shouted as he gestured. "You need to get as far back as you can! Get away from the source of the smoke, please, quickly! Go! Go! Go!"

Young Clark was nearby and was coughing loudly. His mother looked up at the fireman and shouted back, "You say the smoke itself is dangerous?"

"It can be deadly!" he replied loudly. "So, please, everyone continue quickly to get farther away! Keep going!" There was no real wind to dissipate the smoke, but there was a light breeze keeping the worst of it from them. They heard wood sizzling and cracking in the distance, with even more loud pops now and then, and they could hear the roar of the fires burning, at this point, out of control.

Neighbors had been flooding out of their homes and businesses with shocked looks on their faces. "What in the world has happened?"

"What's going on?"

"Some buildings exploded!"

"Are we being attacked?"

"It sounded like bombs blowing up!"

"I can't find my wife!"

"Who's bombing the neighborhood?"

"Come this way!"

"Where are the fires?"

"Watch out for the trucks!"

Neighbors shouted comments, questions, and warnings like these, back and forth. The smoke was impeding visibility a good bit and it was burning people's throats and eyes. Two police cars came roaring up with their sirens now piercing everyone's ears as well. The policemen who emerged from the cars immediately ran toward the buildings that had exploded into flames. And in all this commotion, no one really noticed or paid any particular attention to the woman and the man who were not a part of the neighborhood or the church congregation, as they jogged toward the main group that had left the church together. Scanning the other people as well as they could see them in all the smoke, they saw lots of lady's handbags, some small and others larger, but nothing to alert them, until two big men got out of their way and the woman could suddenly see Reverend Archdale with the burlap sack.

"There!" she hissed at her companion.

"Where?"

"Over there, beyond the two big men, near the mother and son!"

"The man with the sack?"

"Yes! He could be carrying the item."

"I think he's the minister! I've seen him!"

"Then he's the one! We can't let him escape our sight."

The man reached around and felt his gun tucked under his belt in the small of his back.

"Is everyone Ok?" a fireman was asking as he made his way through the crowd. "Is the boy Ok?" he asked, pointing at Clark.

"Yes, I think he is," Clark's mother said. "But his eyes have been tearing badly," she added, as her son coughed again.

"We may have to get him some fresh water to flush out the smoke and debris," he replied, looking around.

Right away, the fireman noticed The Black Widow and the man with her, and she saw him at the same moment. She nodded twice and looked toward Archdale, pointing discreetly.

20

Something Bad

It was quiet in the park. The two young men would have the space to themselves, as they converged from two different directions. "Hey."

"Hey back. So, what's been going on?" Malik asked, as he walked up with a soccer ball and tossed it to his friend. Haji dropped it to the ground and gently kicked it back to its owner.

"Nothing too much," he said, as Malik stuck his toe under the oncoming ball and lifted it, launching it back, in a low arc through the air to his friend. Haji caught this one on the top of his left foot and flipped it back.

"Well, that's not what I hear," Malik replied.

"What do you mean? Who've you been talking to?"

"Our favorite monkey man."

"Oh. What did he say?"

"He told me that you and Ara have been hanging out."

"Yeah. You've been really busy doing stuff for your dad."

"Hey, it's not a problem. I'm just asking. I'm curious. And the project I've been helping with is about done. So what's up, really?"

"Ok. Yeah. Well, Jabari told me that Ara was recently talking about me and he said that she sort of likes me."

"I thought you and Khata had been hitting it off. Last I heard, she was the golden girl of interest. I thought you liked her."

"Sure, yeah, as super good friends."

"That's it?"

"I think she's great. And I had a little twinge for a while."

"A twinge?"

"Yeah, you know, a little feeling of something maybe special between us. But when I went by her house the other day to walk her to school, Ara was there, and we all walked together and, you know, I started noticing stuff I hadn't really appreciated before."

"What stuff?" The ball arced into the air again.

"Just stuff."

"Hey, this is your best friend asking you."

"Ok, Ok." He stopped the ball and popped it back up into the air, bounced it with his knee and passed it back.

"We got to talking and she's really smart and super nice."

"Where have you been that you didn't know that before?"

"No, I mean, I knew it, but I didn't really pay attention enough or appreciate it or something until that day."

"Oh."

"And she's really nice looking—pretty, even maybe sort of beautiful."

"Again, news to no one but you, I suppose."

"Well, I don't know. I mean, sure, you see things, but you might not really see them or notice them well enough or, I have no idea how to say it. I sort of just have a new level of appreciation for lots of stuff about her."

"Like you sort of woke up and, boom, there it was."

"Yeah, sort of like that."

"And, so?"

"So, I think Set and Khata have sort of gotten together now."

"Oh, Ok. I saw them walking down the street together earlier, and they were both laughing. It looked like they were having fun."

"Really?"

"Yeah."

"That's great."

"Great?"

"Yep."

"Ok, good. I was worried that you'd think it was a bad thing."

"No, no, no. It's good. In fact, I'm relieved."

"Why?"

"Well, you know, I did sort of like Khata, and I think she suspected it."

"You went to her house to walk her to school. That might have given it away a little bit."

"True. But I think she had even caught me looking at her a couple of times before that."

"Oh. That's not good."

"Except when it is."

"I guess."

"So, anyway, yeah, well, I had gone over to walk Khata to school and then ended up with Khata and Ara, and Ara is actually the one who started talking to me a bunch, and I was answering, and we got into this great conversation. And I thought, wow."

"How did Khata feel about it?"

"Well, I'm not an idiot, you know, so I was always trying to bring her into it with the 'What-do-you-think, Khata?' kind of questions, and all that. I felt really self-conscious that, you know, here I was coming to her house to ask her to walk to school together and then I'm actually walking with her and yet jabbering on with her best friend. And as I started feeling really attracted to Ara, I felt guilty at first, super guilty."

"I bet," Malik said, adding, "And that's not a bad thing."

"No, no, it's not. It's like my mind sort of split into two parts and while one part was talking to Ara and getting really interested, another part was saying, 'Wait a minute here. What's going on?' And that was the part that felt guilty, while the other part was feeling good."

"I get that. I've felt the same sort of thing about other stuff."

"And then, a bit later, when I was thinking about it and getting pretty confused over it all, I had this unexpected talk with Jabari, and he told me that Ara was feeling the same way about me. And then he told me that he thought Khata and Set were sort of hitting it off. And, man, that was a huge relief because, you know, I didn't want Khata to feel like I had been doing the old bait-and-switch and had dumped her or abandoned her, or anything. That would have been bad."

"Yeah."

"But when Jabari told me what he did, it was like, wow, I'm liberated from all the inner worry and conflict and sense of disloyalty and stuff."

"That's good," Malik said. "You know, things don't always work out as easily as this."

"Yeah, I know."

"You should be very glad and even grateful."

"I am. I'm really super glad things did work out so well this time. And I feel good about Set and Khata."

"You do, really?"

"Yeah. I think he's actually liked her for some time, but he thought the two of us were special friends, so he kept his distance. He's just a good guy like that, you know?"

"Yeah, he is."

"He's sort of noble," Haji said.

"Yeah. High-minded, concerned about other people, able to do the right thing and let go of what he wants and, instead, do what he thinks is best for everybody else."

"True, and that's in stark contrast to all the small-minded people in the world who go around celebrating their selfishness and actually feeling proud of being jerks."

"You got that right. He's so the opposite of those people."

"And there are always too many of those people."

"Yeah. Crowds. Multitudes."

"So I'm really glad that my new feelings for Ara have sort of cleared a path for him to do what he may have really wanted to do for some time. And, you know, in addition, to me at least, he's a hero for showing up to take care of Khata. And she's super and deserves it, and I bet he's really happy about it all."

"Yeah, it's great to see nice things happen to good guys," Malik said. "And, as a couple, they're sort of like Khalid and Hoda."

"What do you mean?"

"A philosopher and a Phi."

"Oh, yeah, I hadn't thought of that."

Malik passed the ball back to Haji and said, "So, then, what's next?"

"You're the best man, I guess," Haji said.

"Ha! Gee! It's way too soon for that, my friend. Way too soon!"

Haji grinned and said, "Oh! Good one. Mafoolery. Ha and Gee—my name. That's not bad."

"Thanks for noticing. I'm practicing for the best man thing. I'll likely have to say a few words."

"I'm just kidding."

"Uh, huh."

A couple of miles away, Kissa had walked her dogs down the street and back. Shibby, these days, was helping a lot to keep the puppies in line. Walking them all at the same time used to be impossible. But it had gotten manageable, if not exactly easy. Hoda came out the front door, shading the sun from her eyes and looking for her daughter.

"Mom! Hey!"

"How were they?"

"Better! Much better!" Kissa walked up closer to the house, leashes in hand, with the dogs preceding her and sniffing the ground for whatever dogs tend to sniff.

"Let's put them inside for now. There's something I need to tell you," Hoda said.

"Ok. Is everything all right?" Kissa asked, looking concerned.

As she led the dogs into the door that Hoda was holding open, her mother said, "I hope so, but I think that, possibly, something bad has just happened, or is about to happen."

"Who's involved?"

"Our friends, Layla and Hasina, along with Mafulla, and Walid."

"Oh, no! Are they Ok?"

"I think they're all Ok, but that they were nearby to great danger when something bad took place a little while ago, or they're nearby now."

"Where?"

"Somewhere here in town, but not the palace—out somewhere, maybe near the marketplace, or it could be near the Adi home."

"Should we go?"

"I'm not sure, for the first time ever. That's why I wanted to talk with you about it, quickly."

"Well, I didn't even know anything was going on," Kissa said.

"Yes, but you have good intuitions, good instincts."

"Ok."

"And there may be something else, something far away."

"What do you mean?"

"I just have this vague sense of something bad happening far away, and very much like whatever's going on here. There's a strange parallel, in a multiple way. And what's distant is somehow even more troubling than what's near."

"How do you know?"

"It strikes my heart deeply with concern."

"How far away?"

"It could be in America."

"The United States?"

"Yes."

"Why are you feeling this?"

"I don't know. I think we should go see Masoon or Hamid, and right away."

"Ok, let's go. Where are they?"

"I think Masoon's working in the palace today. Hamid may be there, too." The two Phi went into the house to tell Khalid where they were going and then, with him coming along to get a book from the school library, they began the short walk to the palace.

Layla's car was on its way toward the palace as well, but from a different direction. Mafulla turned to Walid and said, "I have a strange feeling."

"What about?" Walid asked him.

"This whole situation."

"What do you mean?"

"Well, why were there all those explosions in the neighborhood, all of a sudden? It's a residential area. No one stores dangerous, combustible chemicals. And especially not in different houses."

"Yeah, the explosions happened in several separate places," Walid said and looked puzzled.

Layla spoke up and offered, "All of them were near the house but not too close, and they left an avenue of escape, almost as if to force someone to evacuate Shamilar and Sasha."

"You think somebody did all that on purpose?" Hasina asked her mother.

"Well, like Mafulla said, it just doesn't make sense that it would spontaneously happen in such a place by accident, in many different, dispersed, but nearby locations. The question would be: How? And I can't fathom an answer other than intentional arson for a purpose."

"Multiple arsonists," Mafulla said.

"Most likely," Walid answered.

"And not just fires—big, loud, dramatic explosions and fires."

"Like bombs."

"Yeah, like bombs."

"For what reason?"

"To create a diversion and an alarm and a keen desire to protect whoever was in the house that didn't explode and get them out to another, safer location."

"So, if someone did it, they likely knew the house was guarded."

"Yes."

"It's got to be the Germans, trying to get the scrolls."

"Yeah. We need to go back, now," Walid said. "We know where they are. We can find them and stop them."

And Layla, anticipating what he would say, was already turning the car. The following truck, with the soldiers who had been guarding the house, continued to stick with them, and also made the turn right behind them.

"But the scrolls are gone," Mafulla said.

Walid said, "Then, why's someone blowing up the neighborhood? They must not know the scrolls are gone. Or is this just a shrewd effort at diversion? Are they trying to make us think they don't know the scrolls are gone? Do they, in fact, already have the scrolls?"

"But what about mom and Sasha?" Mafulla said. "This could get bad."

"We can split forces. Layla and I go after the Germans. You and Hasina stay in the car with your mom and sister."

Wearing stolen Egyptian military uniforms at this point, the adversaries they were discussing had made entry into the house a few minutes earlier. They had emerged from hiding places near the burning homes from two directions as soon as they saw everyone drive off. The guards had left so fast that the front door to the Adi home was never locked. One of the support guards who had been moving toward the home had seen everyone leave with their escort, and so he and his partner were allowing themselves a few minutes extra to help a family nearby. The Germans were in the house quickly and they were searching frantically in each room, moving as swiftly as they could.

Dieter Himmel came out of the back bedroom. "Nothing!" he shouted.

Greta Estand had just finished overturning everything in the living room. "Nothing!" she said in a loud voice.

The two other men were in the kitchen and a second bedroom at this point. Greta dashed into the kitchen to help there. They were going through cabinets and storage containers, looking in, under, around, and behind everything. Their pace was frenetic, but systematic.

"It's not in here!" she shouted, and ran into the second bedroom.

"Nothing!" the man in there yelled in a disgusted voice.

Dieter was already in what would be called the study, Shapur's special room where he had in fact kept the scrolls. He opened cabinet after cabinet, and rummaged around and suddenly shouted out, "Here they are! I found them!"

"What?" she called back to him.

"I found the scrolls!"

"You found them?" She came dashing into the room.

"Yes!"

The two other men joined them. But she looked up at them and said, "No! You must be on lookout at this point! Make sure no one disturbs us! Go to the front door!" One of the men appeared angry at her words, but he joined his colleague and did what she said.

Their timing was perfect. As they reached the front door and opened it, they saw two men approach the house in civilian clothing, but with guns. "Everything's under control!" One of the Germans waved and shouted, in his best effort at an Egyptian accent. He was the only one who could conceivably have pulled it off. It had been a part of his training.

"What's going on?" One of the approaching men yelled back.

"We don't know yet! We need you to go search the surrounding houses on that side that are untouched! We have everything secured here!"

"Where did the Adis go?"

"An official car took them to shelter! We need you to go into those homes and check for suspects immediately!"

"Ok! Will do!" The two men turned and ran toward the nearest house that wasn't on fire. And just at that moment, two fire trucks pulled up in front of three burning homes in the neighborhood.

The German who had been speaking looked back into the house and said, "We just turned away two armed men who were coming toward the house! We need to get out of here before there are more!"

The Black Widow replied, "In a minute!"

Dieter lifted the beautiful leather box from the cabinet where it had been kept and sat it on a table and, while opening it up, said, "I was afraid our diversion wouldn't work, and that they would take the scrolls with them. But you were right. The suddenness and extreme violence of the attack made them forget about these and just act to save themselves."

Greta produced a bag that she had been carrying and scooped the four scrolls out of the box where they had been stored.

Dieter then said, "But we're looking for two, not four."

She put all four into the bag and said, "We don't have time to examine them now and pick the right two. We need to get out of here, so we'll take them all! Let's go!"

"Ok. Let's go!" he shouted, in turn, to the other men. And they all moved toward the front door.

As they were doing this, Layla's car was getting closer, and was now less than a mile away, traveling at a high rate of speed.

Outside the Wesleyan Church in New York City, amid all the chaos and black smoke and shouting, there was a lone fireman who was not currently occupied with the trucks, hoses, and burning buildings, but was walking amid all the people who had fled from the church and nearby structures, apparently to check on them. And he now approached Bob Archdale.

"Are you with the church?" he shouted above the roar of fires and other noise.

"What did you say?"

"Are you with the church?"

"Yes! Yes, I am!" Bob answered. "I'm the minister."

"Then please come with me!" the fireman instructed.

"Wait! This is my handyman who works with me," Archdale said, pointing at Santiago, who was right beside him. "We have to stay together."

"Ok, then! We need both of you!" the man directed, and motioned for them to follow him as he walked back in the direction of the church building.

"What's going on?" Santiago shouted to the man, as he followed behind Archdale in the direction they were being led.

"I need you to help with something," the fireman replied. And he added, "Please, we have to hurry!" He stopped for a moment, and turned around and said, "I'm sorry, I almost forgot." And he handed them both wet cloths that had been in his large coat pocket. "Breathe through these!" He put a third one up to his own nose and mouth. And he led them on toward the building next to the church that was also not on fire, and was as far away from all the other people as they could quickly get, at the moment. He then stopped and turned around, and, reaching into a coat pocket once more, but a different one, he pulled out something else.

"I have here some blank paper," he said. "I need you to sketch quickly for me the layout of the church, so we can make sure that everything is protected that needs to be kept safe."

"Well, there are two floors, and a back building," Archdale said.

The fireman instantly ripped the long sheet of paper he was unrolling and handed one piece to Santiago and the other to Archdale. "I need one of you to sketch the first floor, the other to do the second and any out buildings," he said handing each of them a fat pencil with soft lead. "We have to move fast to protect the church."

Reverend Archdale was of course still holding the burlap bag with the scroll, and he tried to tuck it under his arm as he reached for the paper and marker he was being handed. The fireman said, "Here, let me hold your bag for you while you draw, quickly."

Archdale reflexively held it out toward him but, in the same moment, Santiago suddenly touched his arm and said to his friend, "No." Then he turned to the fireman and said, "I'm sorry, no. I can take it."

The man said, "What do you mean, no?"

"We have to keep this bag with us at all times."

Then, another voice, one with an icy tone, coming from behind them, said, "No you don't. Give it to the man, now."

Both Archdale and Santiago turned and saw two guns pointed at them. And Juan felt something like physical power or focused energy emitted toward him from this woman, but he didn't exactly know what it could be that he was feeling. Yet, it instantly concerned him. He didn't remember ever feeling anything quite like this before. But still, it triggered a sudden concern, as if he did. The force of it alarmed him, and he knew that this situation of danger would be different from the others he had recently faced. And yet, he could not possibly know what was about to happen. No one could.

21

A Translator

Before the explosions took place in the Adi neighborhood, some other things relating to the scrolls had been happening across town. Bara El-Ari had gotten word to Leem Hadad that her son Ebar could read in most ancient near eastern languages and that he would be keen to help out, in case his translation skills might be needed by the palace. She explained that her old friend Elam had told her about the scrolls his son had sold to Shapur Adi, and that there was now an urgent need to have them translated.

Leem was relieved to hear this and said he'd come by the hotel to pick up Ebar and take him to the palace, where he could get to work right away. Meanwhile, he'd phone in to let Reela or Masoon know that they finally had a translator.

It turned out that Masoon was on the way to work and wasn't yet in his office, but when Leem arrived with Ebar, he was able to talk with Naqid and introduce the two of them. The head of palace guards then agreed right away to set up a room for the translations to be done. He also sent men to get the scrolls from the Adi house. The plan from the beginning had been that, when a translator was available, the work would proceed at the palace for the sake of enhanced security.

When Leem and Ebar had first arrived and been escorted to

Naqid's office, Ebar told them both that he would need a typist to make a copy of whatever he translated, as he was doing it. He explained that this would allow him to leave the original translation in the palace along with the scrolls but take the copy with him to ruminate on, later at the hotel, regarding nuances of meanings and context. And he could in that way perhaps do some editing of his first pass. He explained that rendering ancient languages into modern form was not often easy when detail and precise accuracy were important. Both Naqid and Leem understood and agreed with his proposal. So the head of the palace guards got to work right away on finding a typist who could join Ebar in what would be the translation room.

Naqid set them up in a small conference room on the second floor of the palace not far from Masoon's office, and gave instructions to the typist who had now joined them on how to work with the translator. The two men spoke for a few minutes about how their efforts together could most efficiently proceed, and Leem, meanwhile, brought some coffee and snacks into the room for their convenience.

When Ebar was asked about how long the translation of two standard size scrolls might take, he cautiously answered that it all depends on the quirks of the document. The nature of the dialect used, the quality of the penmanship, and matters of aging could all make a difference, in addition to variations and challenges that he might encounter due to the specific nature of whatever subject matter was on the scrolls. After he inquired about what was already known concerning the nature of the documents and he was told that one was in an ancient dialect of Arabic, whereas the other seemed to be in, perhaps, Aramaic, he nodded and reported with confidence that he could probably have the work done within a couple of days, at the most.

The men sat and talked a bit more while waiting for the scrolls to arrive, and finally Naqid got up and said, "This is taking much longer than it should. Let me see if the men have checked in downstairs yet with the scrolls."

He walked out of the room and down the hall for a phone, and was gone for maybe five minutes, but it seemed a lot longer to Leem and Ebar and the typist. When he finally came back into the room, Naqid looked concerned and said, "They're still not here, and there's no report of a delay, so I've sent some additional men along the route to check for them."

"You don't think there's been trouble, do you?" Leem asked.

"Well, with what's been going on, you never know," Naqid said. "It's best to be cautious."

"Did you initially send very reliable men?"

"Yes, of course, but I could have sent even more senior guards. And now I wish I had," Naqid replied.

A very long ten more minutes passed, and the concern of the group grew. Then, suddenly, the door opened and one of the two men who had been sent to retrieve the scrolls walked in and said, "I'm so sorry, Naqid! We had a flat tire on the way back."

"We were beginning to worry about you. Where are the items?"

"Here, they're here. Iban will be right in with them. I dashed up the stairs quickly to let you know that we've finally made it back. I knew you'd be concerned."

"Good," Naqid said. Then he added, "We need much better communication procedures for such situations."

At that moment, the palace guard carrying the scrolls came through the door. "Naqid, we're so sorry for the delay."

"That's quite all right, Iban. I'm just glad you're here now. We need to turn the scrolls over to this gentleman and let him begin his work of translation.

"Certainly," the guard said. He took them out of the box in which they had been transported and placed them gently onto the table.

Ebar then took up the one closest to him and said, "Well, I suppose we'll begin. I'll take a moment to look at each of them and decide which one to start translating first."

"Good, good," Naqid said. "Leem and I will be nearby if you need anything. I'm posting Iban right outside the door for extra security."

"Oh. Ok," Ebar replied. He had his plan already in place, and it seemed to be working well, so he was perfectly fine with the presence of a guard. His mother would be absolutely thrilled with how things were finally coming together. They would get exactly what they needed and in a way they had never expected.

"All right, then. We'll let you get on with it," Naqid said. "And I'll make sure Masoon knows we're underway. He's coming in to his office shortly, and should be here very soon."

"Thank you. I'll begin now," Ebar replied, and got down to work.

Less than twenty minutes later, Hoda and Kissa had arrived at a reception area outside Masoon's office. They now sat and waited. They had been told that the general was in an important meeting, but that it was almost over and he could see them momentarily. Then, not two minutes after that, the door to the office opened and Sab Maayuf stepped out.

"Sab!" Hoda said. "You're back from your travels."

"Yes," he answered with a smile and hugged her, then Kissa. "I knew I was needed here."

"You're always needed."

"You're kind."

"We should catch up," Hoda said.

"We'll do that very soon," he replied.

"I want to hear what you've learned."

"There's much."

"Where's Meskhenet?"

"She's at our new guest cottage with old Gimpy, thanks to Hamid."

"Good. I look forward to speaking with her again soon. We're here right now to see Masoon because I've just had a bad feeling that something has happened, or is about to happen. It seems to involve our good friends Layla, Hasina, Walid, and Mafulla—and, possibly, there's also something else at a great distance. But whatever that might be, it seems a bit mysterious."

"Yes," he said. "There were explosions a little while ago around the Adi home, in their neighborhood, but not touching their house itself."

"Was anyone injured?"

"Miraculously, no. And the friends you mentioned were there, but suffered no harm."

"Good. I'm relieved. But what's going on? What caused the explosions?"

"There are some ancient scrolls that dangerous people apparently have come to Cairo to steal."

"Yes, I know of them. Do you have any insight about all this?"

"Indeed. There may be some secrets hidden among their contents, some information that the powerful leader of the Germans wants, in his endless quest to become even more powerful."

"Who's the leader you have in mind?"

"Adolf Hitler, the new Chancellor in Germany."

"You think these people work directly for Hitler?"

"Yes, I do. He's a man who lusts for worldly political power in much the way that our antagonist Santiago lusted for spiritual power."

"And the scrolls contain secrets that will help in this quest?"

"He clearly thinks so. And he will do anything to get them."

"I see. And you say that our friends, nonetheless, are safe."

"For now, yes. I'm sure of it."

"What do you mean, for now?"

But then, Masoon emerged and said, "Oh! Hoda and Kissa!"

"Hi, Masoon. We need a moment with you," Hoda replied while Kissa said hello as well.

"That's fine," he answered. "If don't mind, please go inside and have a seat in the office. Sab and I have to do something that should take less than three or four minutes. And then I'll be right back."

"No problem," Hoda said. "We just had a brief conversation with our friend here that's removed some of the most immediate urgency from our concerns. But we still would like to talk as soon as it's possible."

"Absolutely," Masoon said, and gestured toward the inner office.

As she walked in, Hoda paused and turned around and said,

"Sab, please greet Meskhenet for us, and tell her we're glad you're both back." And he smiled and nodded, as Masoon began to direct him to the conference room.

The two men walked down the hallway toward Iban, who stood up from his chair by the door as soon as he saw them coming and, when they got near, he saluted the general. Masoon nodded back and opened the door and walked into the room.

"Yes?" Ebar said, as he looked up from the text before him.

"I'm General Masoon Afah, Egyptian chief military commander and Vice Regent of the kingdom," Masoon offered, by way of introduction

"Oh."

"I'm in charge of this endeavor with the scrolls. And my friend here will be helping me."

"I see. It's an honor to meet you," Ebar said and stood.

Masoon nodded. "I'd like to look at what you've translated so far."

"Well, I've been at work for only a short time, really just a matter of minutes now, and so there's not much yet to see," he replied.

"That's fine. Just show me what you have."

"It's only an opening paragraph from the ancient non-Arabic document."

"What's the language?"

"Aramaic, as suspected, but a very old form," he answered. And he turned around the page on which he had been writing and slid it down the table toward Masoon.

The general picked it up. He read aloud. "This is the confidential work of Gilgamesh, King of Uruk, who knew the nations of the world. He was wise and saw mysteries and uncovered secrets. In these notes are the most important deep things he learned from Utnapishtim, The Faraway, and other matters hidden from the world, things that must be kept by the wise and not revealed to those who are unprepared to respond properly."

Sab, who was standing behind him, said, simply, "That's it." Then he turned to Ebar and said, "Is that the other scroll, beside you, the one you were not yet translating?"

"Yes, it is, right here," Ebar replied.

"May I see it?"

"Certainly." He reached across the table, picked up the second scroll and handed it to Sab. The older man began to unroll it and saw at the top the Greek letter, and quickly rolled it back up and said to Masoon, "We can take over now."

Masoon then smiled and said to Ebar, "I want to thank you, sir, for your generosity with us and your start on the work. I'm sorry we can't give you any more time on it. We won't need your services any further on the project. We'll have to take over now."

"What's that?"

"I'll have our man outside the door show you the way out."

"But."

"We do appreciate your gracious offer to be of assistance on the project and thank you for this beginning of a translation. But we won't need to proceed any further with your kind help, at present."

"I don't understand." Ebar was floored by this development.

"The contents of the document, we now know, are not to be translated in this way."

"But, what do you mean? How will you translate it?"

"We have our oldest expert here, Mr. Maayuf, just back from … out of town." Masoon turned and gestured toward Sab. "He'll be in charge."

"But, I just got started."

"Yes, and we're very grateful for your time and good work. We didn't know we were going to have the help of our old friend here until about twenty minutes ago, when he arrived back from a journey quite unexpectedly and came to see me, probably no more than moments after you started your work. We know enough now to realize there will be some security issues involved with the translation, and that's why our senior colleague will have to be the one who continues on with it. I'm very sorry for the inconvenience. And, again, we greatly value your willingness to help us. It won't be forgotten."

Ebar was by now inwardly frantic, and his mind nearly went blank, but somehow he thought to say, "Well, certainly, I understand. But I was going to have your typist make a copy, so that I could take it with me to the hotel while leaving my original here, and perhaps go over my renderings later tonight, and edit. I also meant to rethink my initial interpretive readings. If you'd still like to make a copy, you could delete any sensitive information, and I'd be glad to see the remainder and offer my own perspectives, which you might find helpful." If they would just agree to this, he realized, he could still perhaps get his hands on what he and his mother so desperately wanted. A copy of an edited translation wouldn't be quite the same as the ancient original, but it was really the unique content that she craved, and that would bring a distinctive and glorious fortune. And, surely, nothing relevant to their concerns could impinge on national security.

"Thank you so much for that quite useful offer," Masoon said.

"Oh. It's my pleasure." Ebar felt a moment of relief.

Masoon then continued, "But it won't be necessary." He turned to the guard. "Iban, will you escort our friend out of the palace and get him back to his lodgings at the Grand Hotel?"

The man was utterly stunned by this turn of events and, at the moment, had been stricken speechless. His insides seemed to have frozen, and a hole had opened up in his gut, where all his hopes and dreams were swirling away like water down a drain. He found himself standing up, and then he stepped forward around the table without any further conscious thought. He allowed himself to be led out the door, through the hallway, down the stairs, and eventually out the main entry to the palace. He could still hardly think at all as he now blinked in the sun. He and his mother would need yet another plan, a third possible way to get these scrolls. And it would not be easy at this point. But he wasn't yet even trying to conjure up such a thing in his current condition. He was simply in a state of shock and inner panic, as he instinctively and almost automatically did everything he could to hide his feelings and pretend to be fine.

Across town, the Germans had gotten away with their four scrolls no more than a minute before Layla pulled up outside the

Adi home and everyone except for Layla, Shamilar, and Sasha got out of the car. Their plan had changed. The senior Phi would guard Mafulla's family, while the three younger people went in search of the Germans.

The thieves were weaving their way through neighborhood homes, and using the stolen military uniforms they were wearing to their continuous advantage. They barked orders at crowds of shocked onlookers and bluffed their way through all the people who would have otherwise easily recognized strangers in their midst and been suspicious. They moved quickly and yet with an air of authority.

Mafulla led Walid and Hasina into the house and straight to where he knew his dad kept the scrolls. The beautiful leather-covered box was on the top of his desk. Mafulla walked over to it and opened it. "It's empty," he said. "All the scrolls are gone."

"All of them?" Walid asked.

"Yes. There were six."

"But if someone from the palace came for the two important scrolls, they wouldn't have taken all of them, would they?"

"No. Why would they? There would be no reason," Mafulla said.

"Maybe to keep all of them safe?" Hasina suggested.

"No, I don't think so. The others aren't really valuable, except to my dad. There'd be no reason to transport them to the palace, especially right before all the explosions started happening."

"I see," Walid said. "But it's still possible that they didn't know which scrolls to take, and so to make sure they got the right ones, they just took them all."

"That's … possible," Mafulla replied.

"Maybe someone else has been here," Hasina suggested. "I even have a sense of that, I think."

"You think someone came for the scrolls after the explosions, and didn't know that the vital ones were gone already?" Mafulla said.

"If they were gone," Walid muttered.

"That's possible," she answered. "That would make sense of what we're seeing. And it wouldn't make any sense for the palace to have taken them all. I understand your suggestion, Walid, but I think the two important scrolls would surely have been separate from the others at this point, and well marked for the guards to identify. Nobody would have allowed the situation to be confusing now."

"Ok. I get that," Walid said. "You're right."

Mafulla jumped in. "And, if the important scrolls were separate and well marked, and the guys saying they were from the palace accordingly got the correct two, then if someone else took the other four, it must have been the Germans. And if that's right, then, it likely wasn't them who came earlier for the two important scrolls."

"So, either it was indeed someone at the palace who sent for them, or someone else is after them, too, " Walid remarked.

"I'll go with the palace," Mafulla said. "Who else could be involved in this mess?"

"You never know," Hasina commented.

Walid said, "Ok, but in any case, there's a good chance at this point that the Germans are out there now with four scrolls, thinking that they've got what they want. But when they figure out they don't, then we'll still have to deal with them."

"Yeah, and look at what they're capable of doing," Mafulla said.

"Let's get back to our moms," Hasina said to Mafulla. "I think we then should go straight to the palace. And someone has to tell your dad what's happened, and that Shamilar and Sasha are fine."

Across town, it was a normal day at the largest of the city's big public parks. At this point, people were out with their dogs, kids were playing, and old men were sitting on benches, talking with friends and feeding birds. Young couples were having picnics spread out on blankets. Someone was flying a kite. Set and Khata were on a bench off by themselves, taking a break from the walk they had been enjoying together. They were now quite animated and talking about all sorts of things.

Set had been really nervous about inviting Khata on the walk at first, but then, once they got going, it felt very comfortable and easy to be around her like this. Khata had experienced the very same evolution of feeling. She was a little shy at first, but quickly warmed up to the conversation and to being with Set in this sort of way. He was really smart, and a lot funnier than she had realized. He had the quick wit of Mafulla and Jabari, but was too serious to joke around like they did in most school related contexts where she normally saw him. But on the walk, within minutes, he had her laughing about all sorts of things.

As they sat on the bench and talked about various things, a time came when they grew quiet for a moment and Khata said, "There's something I haven't told you."

"What?" Set replied. She hesitated for a few seconds. He said, "You can tell me anything."

"Ok. You remember the class trip to Memphis and Giza, when you and Jabari got kidnapped by mistake?"

"Yeah, that's a hard thing to forget," he said. "It's still pretty vivid to me. I remember almost all the details."

"Yeah, memory and emotion go together."

"Really? I didn't know that."

"When something is having a big emotional impact, you tend to remember it long afterwards, unless it's far too traumatic, and then your mind sort of goes in the other direction and suppresses it. But normally, emotional impact and memory go together."

"Interesting," he said. "I didn't realize that."

"I read about it recently," Khata explained. "I know how emotionally powerful it was for you to go through that awful mess. I actually knew what you were going through while you were going through it."

"What do you mean?"

"Well, it's not like I could see everything, but I had flashes come into my mind, and I could feel a lot of what you and Jabari were feeling, and especially at the worst times during all that happened."

"Really? How?"

"Hoda had us all going through a meditation thing, and I hadn't ever done that before. But as soon as I tried it, I started feeling what you were going through, and it was pretty powerful. I sort of came apart and was crying like crazy. I didn't want you to be scared or get hurt or suffer. I was pretty much a mess for a few minutes, until Hoda came over, and some of the other girls, and they helped me through it."

"Wow, I had no clue."

"Yeah, and I have no idea how it all works, but now and then, I get a feeling about something, or know that something's happening, and there's no way I should know it by any normal channels or methods, I mean. I guess I'm just sort of really intuitive or something."

"That's amazing," Set said.

"Yeah. It amazes me pretty often."

"You can really know things and feel things, at a distance?"

"Sometimes, not often, but sometimes. And when it happens, it can be pretty vivid."

"Wow, that's great."

"Maybe, but then lots of other times, it's not so great."

"What do you mean?"

"I mean, like, when you guys were fighting the kidnappers, it was pretty hard to feel some of what you were feeling, especially when I was so far away from you and completely helpless, and just sitting on the sand, knowing it, and I couldn't do anything about it."

"Oh. Ok. I understand. That must have been hard," Set said and put his hand on her arm.

"Yeah."

"Thanks for feeling bad for us, or, with us," he said.

"You're welcome," she replied. "But Hoda actually helped a huge amount."

"How?"

"Well, first, she realized I was really upset. Like I said, I was crying as I felt what you guys were feeling. And she gently asked what was going on, and I told her as well as I could. And she guided me to ask for a shield of protection for you and Jabari. And so I was sort of praying for you, and that made me feel better, like I was not just completely passive and helpless in the situation."

"Wow. I'm saying that a lot, I know, but still, wow. I'm sure it made a big difference for us. I mean it's totally amazing we weren't killed or injured really badly in that whole situation. And, at a certain point, after feeling completely panicked about whatever was going on, we sort of got calm and I experienced an almost brave assurance, and I bet that was due, at least in part, to what you were doing for us."

"I hope so," she said.

"It's just, well, I don't really have any words for it, but thank you so much. I had no idea."

"I felt connected to you," she said. "I still do, even now."

"I've felt somehow deeply connected to you for a long time," he replied, and he felt almost scared that he was saying it.

She reached down and took his hand briefly and squeezed it.

"That's really nice," she said. And then she added, "Me, too."

"Tell me the next time you get one of your intuitions or feelings. Ok?" He looked into her eyes as he spoke the words.

"Ok. I will," she replied.

"Good."

Khata hesitated for a second and said, "I got a little bit of a feeling earlier today about Mafulla and Walid and Hasina and Layla."

"What sort of a feeling?"

"That they were in danger, and then the feeling passed. And I think the danger, whatever it was, went away for now. But I didn't get anything really vivid, and so I made myself stop thinking about it."

"Should we go check on them?"

"I don't know." She hesitated for a moment, and then said, "And there was something else."

"What?"

"Something super strange, as if someone really powerful was facing something very important, and there was danger and something was going to happen. And maybe it did happen, or maybe it was about to happen, and I don't know, I just got all confused, because I had no idea what exactly I was feeling or sensing. I mean, I couldn't even tell who I was having the feelings or intuitions about. And then you came by a few minutes later, and I sort of distracted myself and closed off my awareness about all of it, and we started off on our walk."

"Have you sensed anything more about this mysterious event?"

"No, I haven't. But I feel like something's coming our way soon."

"Something bad?"

"That's what really bothers me."

"What?"

"Maybe it's something really bad. Maybe it's something really good. That's just another thing I can't tell. Maybe a situation is on the way that involves both good and bad, and in an unusual way, and in a new sort of measure. I just think that, whatever it is, it's going to be really big."

"Well, it sounds pretty complicated. But let me know as soon as you sense anything else about it all," Set said.

"I will. And thanks."

"For what?"

"For not thinking I'm weird or crazy or something."

"I think you're great."

"Awww."

"And a little spooky."

"Ha!"

"But good spooky, and with the emphasis emphatically on good."

22

Something Unexpected

"What's going on?" Bob Archdale said in a tone of shock and total perplexity. The two guns pointed at him could not have been more of a surprise.

Santiago said, "Did you?"

"Yes. We set the explosions to scare everyone out of the church, but you took what we needed before we could get to it. And now you can give it to us," the woman said to them both. Santiago suddenly noticed that the fireman, or fake fireman, had gone around the corner of the building they were standing next to, and that he was now out of their sight, apparently having completed his part of the mission.

"Put the bag down on the ground," she said.

"No," Santiago urged his friend. "These people cannot take the scroll."

"We'll shoot you where you stand," she said, "both of you."

"Bob: Galatians, chapter four. Give it to me," Santiago said.

The biblical reference puzzled the woman and stopped her for just a second. It took Archdale a moment to realize what Santiago was saying. The time had fully come for something—but what? He didn't know. And yet, as Saint Anselm the medieval theologian and philosopher had pointed out long ago, faith often precedes understanding. So, without hesitation, he gently tossed the bag to Santiago, who easily caught it and cradled it in his arms.

The two Germans then turned their guns from Archdale to Santiago, following the path of the bag. "I'll kill your friend here," the woman said to Juan. "If you don't put that bag down on the ground in front of you in less than ten seconds, he's dead. I promise you that."

Santiago hadn't at first even realized what he was doing or why he was doing it. But before he had mentioned the book of Galatians, while the two adversaries were looking at Archdale and the bag, he had slowly put his left hand into the left front pocket of his trousers and slipped his finger into the old ring that was in there, the ring that had been discovered in the pocket of his torn robe. These actions were purely instinctive. Then, when Archdale tossed the bag to him, he grabbed it with both hands, and the minister caught a glimpse of the ring on his finger. He was then struck by a new moment of surprise and a wave of relief that he didn't understand at all.

"He knows nothing about the scroll, and shooting him will accomplish nothing for you except to draw the police here." Santiago spoke with a voice of authority. And as he did, he used the thumb of his left hand to fiddle with the ring. Again, he didn't know why, but he felt a strong impulse to do so, and it was an urge he naturally obeyed.

The next moment could not possibly have been more confusing for everyone present. The two criminals and the minister all had something like an inner experience of a loud pop or a bang, or some sort of modest explosive sound that seemed very close by, and yet somehow inside their minds rather than out in the air. And it was sudden enough and loud enough, at least in their heads—if that makes any sense at all—that the woman and the man holding the guns both flinched, as did Archdale. They all momentarily shut their eyes by reflex and ducked their heads in a bit of a defensive crouch, with arms or hands over their faces. And in that fraction of a second that their attention was distracted and their visual gaze was broken, Santiago and the bag had simply vanished.

They all immediately looked back up, tense and ready to react, but the man wasn't to be seen where he had been standing in front of them just a thin sliver of a moment before. "What?" The woman shouted and looked left and right.

"My goodness!" Archdale said. "Where?"

"Where is he?" The woman yelled. "Where did the man go?"

"How?" The other man with a gun said while looking utterly stunned.

"Where is he?" She yelled the same words again, as much at her armed companion as at Archdale, and even at the smoke in the air.

She immediately forgot her threat to shoot the minister. And that, of course was pointless now, anyway. She ran toward the edge of the building where the individual in the uniform of a fireman had earlier disappeared, and she again shouted into the space around her the very same words, as if she couldn't think of anything else. "Where is he?" Her head swiveled in all directions as she desperately looked about for the man with the bag. "Where did he go?"

The other gunman followed her, and she said, "No, you fool! The other way! You go the other way!" And he turned and nearly ran in the opposite direction, into the smoke, bent over, and searching frantically behind every bush and shrub and trash can. Archdale was suddenly alone. Both gunmen had abandoned him now that he was without the item they sought, the thing that had just somehow disappeared, along with his friend.

He didn't have to be told that he should get out of there as quickly as he could and find a policeman, which wasn't hard, since there were now several of them not far away, questioning people as to what had happened and what they had seen before or during the time of the explosions. He approached the first officer he saw, and it was one of the policemen who had visited the church after the earlier nighttime break-in they had experienced.

"The Germans are back!" he shouted as he approached.

"What?" The policeman said.

Archdale ran up to him and said, "The Germans, the people who broke into the church and killed that older couple at the Wisdom Shop, they did this!"

"What do you mean? We took them to jail! Only one of them got away later!"

"I know, but it was the man who escaped, he's the one who did this, and he was with a woman, another German. She seemed to be in charge. They both just had guns pulled on me, demanding some item they're seeking to steal. And they're still around here somewhere, armed with guns."

"Are you sure?"

"Yes! They set the explosions! They told me. They almost bragged about it. They said they were going to kill me! I just now got away as they ran off chasing someone else. They're somewhere near!"

The policeman blew loudly into his metal whistle, sending a shrill, nearly ear-piercing call out to his colleagues, and three other officers came running in his direction.

"Armed felons in the area!" he shouted to them. "A man and a woman, Germans! Armed and dangerous! They're the arsonists!"

"Where did you last see them?" He asked Archdale, as he scanned the area.

"I was over there!" Archdale pointed toward the one building next to the church that was not billowing smoke. "We were to the side, this side, almost behind the building, and they ran off in two directions, one toward the church, one that way," and he gestured to indicate exactly where he meant.

The policemen immediately split into two groups and gave chase, hoping to find the culprits before they could do anything else. Bob Archdale stood there in the street, for the moment now totally alone, apart from the dozens of people who were all around watching the other firefighters try to control the blazes from the various buildings on the block. A shiver ran through his entire body as he thought of what had just happened, whatever it was and however it came to be.

What indeed had happened? He couldn't even begin to say. One second, his new friend was standing beside him, holding the burlap bag with the ancient scroll. The next second, he was completely gone. How? Where? What in the world had just taken place? Was it something like a miracle? What else could it be? The man who had come so mysteriously had now just vanished even more strangely.

Bob was having a hard time even forming thoughts about it. He turned left and right and peered into the still thick smoke. His body now had a moment to cough again. And there was no sight at all of Santiago or of the Germans. He saw more policemen at this point, and most of them were running. But he had no idea what he was supposed to do. Was he still vulnerable? Could danger even now be at his heels? Would one of the Germans sneak up on him again at any second? He was starting to have such questions come clearly into his heart and mind, and each one brought with it a stab of uncertainty and a tingle of fear. Faith, he thought to himself. Faith. Eyes wide open and with faith.

And yet, despite a measure of inner struggle, something seemed strangely right. And there had been a sense of relief. The time had fully come … for something. But he had no idea what. One of his favorite biblical concepts had just come into play at what may have been the scariest moment of his life, and he didn't know exactly, or even approximately, how. Where did Juan go? And how did it happen, whatever had just happened? The ring. He thought of the ring. He had seen it in a flash, he had noticed it, as if it had drawn and demanded his attention, and he felt a moment of comfort. And then, within seconds, there was nothing. His friend was gone. Was it the ring? But how in the world could that be? He had no answers, and began to walk slowly back down the street toward the church.

After no more than a few steps, he sensed something, and stopped for a moment and looked back. The little boy, Clark, had walked away from his mother without her noticing, while she was talking with another of the choir members over near one of the fire trucks. He had now come up to Archdale and stood, looking at him, while holding a wet cloth over his mouth.

"Clark!" Archdale said, "You should go back to your mother."

The boy pulled the cloth away from his face and said, simply, "Your friend is gone."

Archdale had a very odd feeling come over him. He bent over and asked the child, "Where did he go?"

"Far away. He had to go."

"He did?"

"Yes. He has a job to do."

"Are you … sure?"

"Yes."

In that moment, so much flooded into Reverend Archdale's mind. There were countless stories of Hindu holy men who were said to have simply appeared, or disappeared, in ways that seemed to make no physical sense. He had always discounted such tales of the apparently miraculous outside of a Biblical framework, but now, suddenly, he wasn't so sure. There were, of course, also many similar stories in the west. On rare occasions, people had been said to appear to friends or family members hundreds, or thousands, of miles from where they were known to be located—or at least, from where they had been located just moments before. They had come, and perhaps greeted loved ones, or passed on a message, and then they had gone and just vanished. Some of these appearances were after the death of the person involved, but others were said to have happened during life. And, yes, some of these sightings were surely dreams, or hallucinations, but others reportedly seemed different. An elderly religious woman he knew well and trusted had actually told him confidentially of one such instance she had witnessed herself.

Of course, Archdale knew of passages in the holy scriptures of his own tradition where angels appeared and spoke with people and then disappeared. In the Gospel accounts of the resurrection of Jesus, the executed itinerant preacher and Son of God had reportedly departed from the physical plane of existence and simply disappeared, leaving his burial tomb empty. And yet, on several occasions after that, he had also suddenly reappeared to a single person, or to a group of people, and he walked with them and spoke with them, and even ate with them. And then, as Luke the physician wrote in his Gospel account, after one such meal with two followers, "he vanished from their sight." So there was some sort of precedent for such a thing.

But Santiago was certainly not Jesus, Archdale thought to himself. And he seemed nothing at all like a biblical angel or a mystical Hindu holy man. And yet, there was something clearly different about him. He did in fact arrive at the church suddenly and mysteriously. And now, he seems to have just vanished, instantly and shockingly, and at the precise moment when he needed to get away in order to protect the strange item that was in their possession. But, how in the world does such a thing happen? It was a problem to process such an event mentally, even for a man of strong faith. It was somehow easier for him to believe miracle accounts from long ago than the evidence of his own eyes now. And where did Juan go? The question kept reasserting itself. Where is he now?

It was all, on one level, as confusing as anything could possibly be, to the point that the plain-speaking southern minister could barely believe what he had just experienced. His head was swimming with confusion. And yet, at the same time, it somehow oddly felt right, like whatever he had witnessed had happened for a crucial reason, and that it might fit perfectly into a broader natural order of things beyond what we understand, or think of, as possible. Didn't Jesus himself once say to his closest followers that those who believe in him would do the things they had seen him do and, according to the Gospel of John, chapter fourteen, "even greater things"?

As all these musings ran through his mind and heart, Archdale took the hand of young Clark and led him back to his mother, who had just that moment, in a panic, noticed that he was no longer standing beside her. And in that act of returning the boy to where he belonged, Bob realized that Santiago, in his own way, could be doing something similar with the ancient scroll, and returning it to where it belongs. But of course, he had no real idea what exactly that meant.

The four Germans in Cairo had just arrived back at the second apartment across town that had been provided for them by their

Ambassador since their first residence had been discovered and searched, presumably by either police or agents of the monarchy. They parked their car down the block and quickly got the four scrolls now in their possession into the new place for a thorough examination, initially to pick out the two they had been sent to retrieve. Once Greta had scanned the street once more for anyone who may have been following them and had locked the door securely, their work could commence.

Dieter was the one among them who had some training in ancient languages. It was now his job to go over the scrolls and identify what was on each one. He asked that they be put on the kitchen table in the apartment so that he could sit and do his examination. Unrolling the scroll closest to him, it took him only a few seconds to say, "This one looks like a merchant's log of sales. Unless it's a ruse, here at the outset, this is not our document." He unrolled more of it, and saw more of the same.

"Faster," Greta urged him.

"No, I can't go faster," he replied. These scrolls are delicate and fragile. If I tear one and it's the one the leader wants, would you like to have to explain personally that the destruction was a result of your impatience and orders?"

She glared back at him and said, "Well then, proceed as quickly as you safely can, of course." And she turned away to look out the front window.

"It's all the same to the end," he reported. "Things bought and sold."

"So, carry on and get to the next one," she said.

He set the first scroll aside and selected a second to examine. "Let's see about this one." He began to unroll it and read.

"The same thing," he said, agitated. "A merchant's log, an account of purchases and sales."

"To the end," she instructed.

"Of course." Thirty seconds to a minute passed as he worked. "No," he concluded. "This is not it."

"Who would collect things like this?" She said in exasperation.

"Well, he's a merchant himself. It could be that he enjoys the history of what he does."

"Examine the third. Quickly."

Dieter gently rolled up the scroll he had been scrutinizing.

"You don't need to be quite so careful with that one," she nearly barked at him.

"Respect for antiquity demands it," he replied.

"We don't have time for that," she said.

"We have seconds to protect centuries of painstaking storage." He was standing up to her on principle here.

"Don't take your eyes off our goal," she said.

"Arguing about this is wasting more time than the careful handling itself," he pointed out.

"Fine. Just work."

He picked up a third scroll and began to unroll it and read. "This may be something," he said.

"What is it?"

"According to the first few lines, it's historical, from a time when some of the pyramids were built and, as it says here, men of great knowledge and power roamed the earth."

"That could be it."

"Ok. I need to keep reading."

The Black Widow stared at the back of his head for a few seconds and then walked away. She was going to check on the other two men who, when they first arrived, had gone into another room to change out of their Egyptian army uniforms and back into their own clothing.

She talked with the others briefly and then went back to the table where Dieter was working. "Well?"

"Still reading. This is a long one and densely written. The language isn't easy."

"Does it say anything about secrets?"

"Not yet, but give me time. I can't talk and concentrate on this, and it's not an easy translation. Let me do my job," he said.

"Watch your tone. It's been too long since I killed with my hands."

"Greta, when you threaten me, you threaten the mission. Without my expertise, you'd be taking some merchant logs back to Berlin, and I don't think that would go over too well."

She took a deep breath and regained control of herself—or, at least, some measure of control. It was her nature to feel cold fury toward anyone who did not treat her with the greatest respect and deference, and show actual fear in her presence. Dieter was always standing up to her in small ways that frustrated her immensely. But he knew how to play a strong hand, and she realized that she had no good options if she were to strike at him as her nature might insist.

"Read then," was all she said in response. And she became quiet, walked across the room, and sat down in a chair from which she could still keep him in view.

Minutes passed. "I'm about a third of the way, and so far, there's nothing about secrets. There's no hint at all of what we're looking for here."

"What's it about?" She sounded gravely concerned.

"The building of one of the pyramids, so far, with some names of officials and details about their family history. But there are sentences here and there where, on a first reading, I can't quite make out what's being said. It's a little bit confusing. But there's nothing I can spot that is at all about secrets or life or the topic we're seeking."

She replied more cordially, "It might be prudent then to stop where you are, and look at the fourth scroll. There are two that we're here to retrieve, as you know—one, the main document, and the other that's said to be something like a key to coded passages in the first."

"You already think this is one of them?"

"Well, there were four scrolls at the Adi home. The other two are worthless. That leaves the one you've been reading, and the next one."

"Yes. True."

"This one may be a code breaker, somehow. It could be that whoever wrote the sentences that are more difficult to read may have intended precisely those sentences not to be read in isolation, but rather to be used as deciphering keys to the main document whose secrets we seek. In order to evaluate this possibility in connection to what you've been reading, we need you to get a taste of the other, last scroll."

"Ok, that's a good idea. Your reasoning is compelling, I have to admit," he said, and began to roll back up the scroll he had been reading. And when that small job was finished, he reached for the fourth scroll across the table.

Greta commented, "This one could be the master scroll, the main quarry of our quest."

Dieter began to unroll it very carefully. And after only a few seconds, he said, "I can't believe it!"

"What?"

"This is impossible!"

"What is it?" She stood up from her chair and began to walk toward him and bend over as if she'd be able to read what he had just seen.

He looked up at her and said, "I don't understand this at all."

23

The Pool

Masoon was getting everyone together for a meeting that would be of tremendous importance. By now, Layla, Hasina, Walid, and Mafulla were all at the palace with Shamilar and Sasha. Walid had no idea yet that Sab Maayuf was in the building as well. And he had no clue as to what Masoon had just learned from a conversation with Sab.

Bancom had radioed the Sakat brothers and told them to go over to the Adi Shop and tell Shapur what had just happened in the area around his home, and that his wife and daughter were now safe at the palace, while his house was, mercifully, undamaged. Two guards were being sent to get him and Sammi, who had been at a friend's house more than a mile from their home, and to bring them over to the palace for a gathering of the family and a full discussion of the situation as it now stood.

Reela Adi had also come in to work, and Hamid had now arrived as well. Leem was there, and Ibrahim had gotten his friend Ahira to spend a few hours with Ben at home so that he could also be present. Masoon had taken over a large conference room in the palace that was not often used, anticipating that nearly twenty people would be in the session. He wanted to have plenty of space for the pool of talent and wisdom that would need to be represented on this occasion.

Hoda and Kissa were already in the room. Omari, Paki, and Amon had been asked to find everyone else and direct them in to the right location, which had long been known as the Sphinx Room, due to the prominent presence of a large sculptured replica of that ancient wonder at one end of the room. A guard had also been sent out to look for Haji and Malik and bring them to the session, if possible. And a car had even been dispatched for Khata, so she could be included in the meeting and get there both quickly and easily. Meskhenet Maayuf was also on the way in, and was being escorted by a guard who was deeply trusted by Masoon and Hamid.

Across the Egyptian desert, there was a very different gathering about to happen as well. At the edge of a widely used oasis, two men were working on a fence within sight of each other, but a good distance apart. A young boy came running from the central area of trees not far away and approached one of them and spoke with him for a moment. The man asked him to remain where he was while he ran over toward his companion, waving and shouting out to him.

"Bamur! Bamur!" Shaz got his friend's attention.

"Yes?"

"Hamish has come with a very strange report."

"What is it?"

"He says that there was a great booming wind a few minutes ago on the other side of the oasis, while many were still having their mid day rest inside."

"Yes?"

"A short funnel spout of sand came roaring toward the pool where he had just been playing, and for moments he couldn't see because of the stinging of the sand. And then, suddenly, there was another sound that was different and very strange. And when it stopped, there was a man on the ground next to the pool where no one had been just seconds earlier."

"What?"

"The man who suddenly appeared is face down in the sand, without movement, and we need to go see if he's hurt, and who it is."

"That's very odd. I heard nothing." Bamur put down his tools.

"I didn't, either."

"Hamish says he didn't recognize the man?"

"He told me he saw him only from the back and at a distance. He didn't touch him or even approach him. He just ran to get us because he was afraid! He wondered if the man dropped from the sky. We need to go see."

"Yes. I agree!" The two men turned and walked, and soon increased their pace and jogged toward the boy, and he began to repeat his tale and ran with them to guide their steps to this unexpected sight. In the couple of minutes it took them to get to the place in question, a small group of people had gathered—two ladies and three young children were standing not far from the man's body, and two elderly men had just walked up behind them. The figure on the ground was still face down and motionless in the sand.

"What happened?" someone asked.

"Who is this?"

"Is he all right?"

"Don't move him!" Bamur shouted from a distance as they approached. "Don't touch him, in case he's badly injured!" A few people present then took a step backwards. Others spoke to one another, airing their perplexity at what may have happened.

"Who is the man?" Someone called out to Bamur as he approached, asking again the question he had just posed to those around him.

"Is he dead?" Those gathered were also asking each other about the wind and the noise as well as about this figure on the ground.

Shaz was the first to arrive beside the man, as Bamur had paused briefly to speak to someone, and he got down on one knee to look more closely at the individual who was lying flat, face down, on the ground. It was a little bit unusual to see anyone dressed like he was here at the oasis. It happened now and then, but not often. And no one had seen him around before a few minutes ago. He had on what seemed to be a pure white western shirt that had been stained or darkened by something, and he was wearing light trousers. A more familiar item of attire was that leather sandals were on his feet.

"My friend, are you all right? Are you still with us?" Shaz spoke to the back of his head and in a gentle voice. The man's face was truly buried in the warm sand.

Bamur then bent down on the other side of the body and said, "We should move him slightly so he can breathe—if he's alive." And with those words, he carefully took hold of the man's shoulders and shifted him over just a bit, so that his nose and mouth would be out of the sand.

"Oh, my!" Shaz said. And then turning to the people standing nearby, he said, "Get the lady, please, and quickly!" But even as he was saying this, Mrs. Golan was already halfway to them, coming from her place of work.

"My goodness!" She said, as she came closer. "Bamur, fetch some water from the pool!"

"Oh!" The man groaned and then coughed loudly three times and tried to spit sand out of his mouth. His hand was now out on the sand, seeking to support his body, but he was still prone and facing down. "Ooooh. What just happened?" He gasped and mumbled in a groggy, surprised tone.

"You poor man!" The lady exclaimed. Bamur handed her a small jar that had been sitting beside the pool. He had filled it with water, and she poured out some on the back of the man's head and neck, just a bit. And then she spoke what sounded like a prayer or incantation of some sort. "May the sand of the earth, the air of the sky, the fire of the desert, and the water of the pool bring you strength and healing from whatever you have suffered," she muttered in a low voice, as she poured out further small amounts of cool water on him.

"Thank you," he croaked out from beneath a hand that was now shielding his face. And he sputtered and then turned and looked up and said, "Please. Where am I?"

"My stars!" she exclaimed, as she experienced the greatest

surprise and most sudden mental confusion of her life. "I had no idea! No idea at all!" There was now suddenly a gasp from several others who were close by.

Far across the desert in Cairo, inside Bara El-Ari's room at the Grand Hotel, Ebar had just updated his mother about everything that had happened at the palace. She was at first livid, and then distraught.

"I thought we had our solution!"

"I did, too!"

"We were so close!"

"Yes, we were."

"The whole plan is ruined. I'm ruined," she said. "We're both ruined."

"I did my best. I had convinced them completely to let me translate the scrolls and get a copy of each. I was actually doing the work. We were so close." Ebar couldn't believe their terrible luck, either.

"I've never in my life!"

Ebar had been pacing, and now he just sat down, almost throwing himself into a chair, in nearly complete despair. "It's the worst thing that could happen. All our dreams are now impossible."

"Wait," Bara said. "Just wait."

"What do you mean?"

"We have to calm ourselves and think. There's always a way. A goal of infinite worth beats any obstacle of finite size. Problems that stop some merely redirect others. We just have to find a new way forward. We are not here for nothing. The path is somehow still awaiting us. We simply have to find it. Do you hear me? We have to think more and find the right path that's here waiting for us. It's here. I know it is. We are already at the brink of what we have dreamed of for so long."

"You're right, mother. You must be right, but what can we do? They have the scrolls in the palace and now we have no access at all."

"There are others seeking to take the scrolls," she said.

"Yes, which makes our plight even worse," he replied.

"Does it?"

"What do you mean?"

"Well, I can think of two scenarios, right away. On one way forward, we join forces with the others who are after the scrolls and through our combined schemes, perhaps we can still get them."

"But what then?"

"We agree on a mutual use of the secrets and we split the eventual sale, which is surely what they're after, as well."

"But what if they refuse, or they don't intend a sale?"

"Why would they refuse us if we can help them?"

"How can we help them now? What can we do? We're helpless ourselves."

"No. We're never helpless. We have leverage still."

"What do we have?"

"We have Elam's trust. And the palace values Elam. He's the original owner of the scrolls, the source. Surely, we can use this fact."

"But what if the others are able to be convinced that we can help them, but they don't want to sell the secrets and split the profits?"

"Why in the world would anyone steal such secrets, certainly the most valuable in human history, without intending to sell them?"

"They could just want to use the secrets."

"Well, so do we. But then, anyone who uses them and achieves the dream must somehow have funds to support the dream."

"Yes. That's true."

"And I have no idea how you'd get such funds without selling the scrolls. They probably have no idea, either. So they'd need what we need, the vast amount of money that would surely come from such a sale to the right person. We can surely convince any partners to join us in a use of the secrets, and then to sell them as well!"

"Ok. You're right, I imagine. But what if they betray us?"

"We could betray them first."

"You said there were two scenarios."

"Yes. One is that we partner up with the would-be thieves. The second possibility is that we somehow simply exploit their efforts for our own gain."

"How?"

"We lie in wait for their move and when the palace is fighting them or trying to stop them, we move in and snatch the scrolls unsuspected."

"But the devil is in the details."

"Yes, and yet still, where there's life, there's hope. We're smart. We're resilient. I've lived and hoped for this opportunity for many years. And now we're here. We've found our man, and he's pliable to our will. We were meant to have these scrolls and their secrets."

"I'm amazed at how you can turn things around, mother. Just a minute ago, I was nearly in total despair because of external events that are beyond our control. And now, so quickly, you've helped me to rethink it all. So much of life is in how we think and act, and react."

"Yes. That's right. You're a good son. You're very smart. You're just sensitive. And that can be a good thing. You'll learn such quick rethinking for yourself, as you confront more of life. But now, we should get out a pen and some paper and try out different ideas as to how we can pursue our two broad options."

"Excellent. And in doing so, we're taking action already," Ebar said, as he rose to walk over to the desk in the room.

"And in taking action, we can begin to turn circumstances in our favor," Bara added.

There was a lot of activity going on in the palace. The Adi family had just met in the king's private sitting room with hugs and tears and many affirmations of love and concern. Walid had briefed them on what was known and what was being done to protect them from any further threats. They were going to be guests for at least one night in the residential area of the palace while police and a unit of the military secured their neighborhood and pursued the arsonists.

Shamilar and Shapur both asked about their neighbors and were reassured that, miraculously, no one had been badly harmed. The houses chosen for explosive charges had been picked precisely because there was no one at home in any of them to interfere with or complicate the mission the Germans were carrying out. Even one neighbor who didn't work outside the home had been away for a shopping trip at the time of the explosions and, although her home had not been destroyed, it was badly damaged while she was gone. The palace was dedicated to rebuilding and repairing all the awful destruction and damage as quickly as possible. And soldiers were even now on site assuring their neighbors that no such thing would happen again. After explaining all this and comforting the family for a few more minutes, Walid and Mafulla had left them in the living area and in the company of a couple of their favorite palace guards, as well as Kular, to look after them.

The large conference room was abuzz with many lively overlapping conversations, as everyone waited for whatever was to come. Khata El-Noor had just walked in and looked a little confused. Haji saw her and stood up and walked over to greet here.

"Hey."

"Hey back. What's this all about?" Khata asked.

"I don't know. Dad should be here any minute and explain it to us."

"I've never been in this room before."

"I haven't either," Haji said, and then he added, "Why don't you come sit with me and Malik over there?" He pointed to where he had been seated for the past few minutes.

"Oh, Ok, thanks. I didn't know what I was supposed to do. I don't even know why I'm here." She looked around the room.

"You're Phi. Some meetings seem to include all of the Phi in the city, or at least all of us who are in some way involved in palace life. And sometimes, there are others who know us well or work with us who are also included."

"Oh."

He explained, "We're just waiting and talking until the meeting starts." Khata looked down for a second and took a deep breath. Haji anticipated what might be on her mind and said in a low voice, "I feel like I need to tell you something."

"What?"

"Set's one of my favorite people in the world."

"Really?"

"Yeah. He's a super good guy."

"You are, too."

"Thanks. But I think you guys are great together, really. I feel good about your … special friendship."

"Thanks. I feel the same way about you and Ara."

"Good. That's great. Let's go sit down. Everything's fine."

"Ok. Ok, good."

They walked farther across the room together and Khata was greeted a few times by friends like Layla, and Hoda, and Kissa, and Hasina, and then Walid. And as soon as she and Haji had sat down, Masoon walked through the door to the room, with Sab and Meskhenet Maayuf close behind him. He offered Meskhenet a chair near the door and she slowly settled into it. Sab continued to stand, slightly behind Masoon. The conversations around the room dwindled.

When there was finally silence and everyone was looking at him attentively, Masoon said, "First, I want to thank you all for making your way here so quickly today. I thought it would be important to update you as soon as possible on what's been happening, and on some major, new, and surprising revelations we have."

Hoda turned to Layla and said, in a low voice, "I wonder if it has to do with Ali? I've been having some very strange feelings."

"I know that some of you are probably wondering whether this has anything to do with our beloved Ali," Masoon said, not a second later. "I wish I had news on that topic, but I'm afraid I don't." There was a murmur around the room of brief and disappointed comments in response to this remark. "But you can be assured that if anything comes to light on that vital topic, I will let you all know immediately."

"Ok, but I'm surprised," Hoda whispered to her friend. She then added, "There's something going on."

Masoon paused and looked around. "The reason for this meeting today is that we have new information about the two ancient scrolls that are now in protective custody in the palace. As most of you know, these two items long ago came into the possession of one of our local citizens, a Mr. Elam al-Buri, when he was a young soldier working in service to the kingdom. He was told that they could be very valuable one day and that, because of this, he should keep them and protectively hide them away. Strange legends abounded concerning the contents of the scrolls, and at least one death occurred long ago in connection with knowledge of them. Elam's son Asham recently sold the scrolls at the request of his father, and to our friend Shapur Adi, who is a collector of such artifacts as a hobby. Shapur had no idea what was in these particular scrolls or that there might be problems associated with them." Masoon paused for a moment.

"Meanwhile, there are some German citizens in town who have been seeking to acquire the scrolls, using violence, threats, and now arson in pursuit of their purposes. They've stolen four scrolls from the Adi home on this day in the belief that they have, among those four, the two they've been pursuing. But they don't. And we're in close pursuit of these people. We hope to have them in custody soon. The Adi family is safe and unharmed and now here in the palace for their protection until we make a bit more progress in our investigation."

He then paused again, and continued. "I thought it was important to make sure that all of you were up to date on these details. But the much more important aspect of our gathering has to do with the content of the two scrolls. I would like for our friend Sab Maayuf to share with you what he told me just a bit earlier. But first, I have to ask each of you to make a solemn promise—that nothing you hear from him in this session will be shared with anyone else without our explicit permission, his or mine. If you're not prepared to make and keep this promise, I'll understand, and

I'll ask you to leave the room now, before we continue. No one should feel forced into this position of confidential knowledge that you've not asked to receive. But I think it's strongly in your interest to hear it. It carries no known danger, but great illumination. And yet, it should stay just among us." With those words, Masoon stopped once more, for longer this time, and waited and glanced around the room.

All eyes were on him, and everyone was totally quiet. No one even moved. "No one will mind if you leave. Every person here should feel completely free to rise and exit the room." He continued to look around and examine the faces that were all turned his way.

"Good. So, by remaining with me now, from this moment forward, you are agreeing to keep confidential anything that Sab will say to you." He paused again for maybe three seconds. Heads nodded around the room. He turned to his old friend and said, "Please," as he stepped aside and invited Sab to come forward.

"I have for you some big news, very big news," Sab said. And there was a strange look on his face. Then, however, he smiled. "What I must now say to you will be quite surprising, I'm sure, even to those of you who have known me for a long time. Perhaps it will even be shocking. But I will make you a promise just as solemn as the one that you have now made to Masoon and me. I pledge to you that everything I tell you today will be completely true, however unlikely or far-fetched, or even impossible it might sound. I never thought I'd be sharing this with anyone, ever. But I think that now is a time to do so, and that you are the friends to hear it."

In a small and dingy apartment across town, Greta Estand stood over Dieter Himmel, looking at the scroll he had just begun to unroll.

"I don't get this at all," he said, nearly repeating his previous words.

"What? What is it?" She asked, with an insistent and almost harsh tone.

"This is another merchant scroll. It's not what we've come to get."

"What do you mean?"

He gestured around him. "There are three simple bookkeeping scrolls here, and one historical document that seems to have nothing to do with what we're seeking."

"Are you sure?"

"Yes."

"Unroll it all the way. Sometimes, a ruse is used in such scrolls at the beginning and for quite a stretch, as a misdirection."

"Yes, of course. You're right." His mouth was dry. His stomach churned. He knew that failure here wasn't an option. And the clock was ticking. He unrolled the scroll as rapidly as he could, while still being careful with it. There were more numbers and prices, more inventories, and more purchases and sales. Camels. Saddles. Donkeys. Feed. He became almost dizzy with a growing panic as he skimmed the contents of the scroll. "No, no, no, no," he intoned.

"Is it more worthless record keeping?"

"Yes. That's all it is."

"Could it really be a secret code?"

"No. I've seen many such documents just like this. It's an old ledger."

"How can this be? We got all the scrolls that were there!"

"There must be more."

"Where? We searched the house completely."

"Maybe not at the house."

"Not at the store. Not at the house? Then, where?"

"How should I know?"

"We have to get Adi himself. We'll make him tell us. That's the only thing we can do."

"But he has heavy security and there are just four of us."

"I'll radio Berlin for backup."

"How?"

"From the Embassy."

"What sort of backup?"

"Some of my group."

"What do you mean?"

"We have a big problem. So we need more problem solvers. I have a powerful web of contacts available to me at any time through the Thule. And now is the time to use it."

"What's the Thule?"

"You don't need to know, if you don't already. I shouldn't have mentioned it."

"What about the rest of us? You won't kill us, will you?"

"I make no promises. But you may be still be useful."

The other two men had been listening in on all this from the next room. One of them feared for his life, and that fear so overcame any other thought of consequences that he made a fateful choice and quickly but quietly stepped into the doorway of the room with a gun aimed at Greta's back.

Dieter saw him instantly and was shocked at the sight, but much more so at what happened next. As he instinctively jumped out of his chair and dove toward the floor, he lost sight of the others for a second and the loud gunshot assaulted his ears and filled his mind as he hit the tile flooring. From the position that he now occupied, when he opened his eyes a split second later, he could see only the body collapse and the pool of blood begin growing around it.

24

Stranger Than Fiction

At the desert oasis pool, Mrs. Golan looked up at Bamur and said in a voice of shock and great surprise, "It's … Ali!"

"What?"

"It's our Ali! Ali Shabeezar! King Ali!"

"How could it be?"

"I don't know! Something's happened. And he's here."

She turned back to the struggling figure. "Ali! Are you all right?"

"Ohhhhhhh." The man gave out another long groan, almost a moan. Bamur came closer and took hold of his arm to help him straighten up. He rolled over, blinking his now open eyes. There was something underneath him where he had been lying. From the corner of the item that they could see, it looked like an old burlap sack.

"What's happened to you? How did you get here?"

"What?"

"There was a sudden violent small storm and then you were here!"

"Where am I? Who are you?"

"Ali! I'm Amita Golan, The lady of the pool, and you are in the oasis where I live. Ali! You know me!"

"What? No. No. I'm sorry. I have no memory."

"Either you are the exact twin to our king, or you are my old and good friend, Ali Shabeezar!"

"Where did you say I am?"

"The desert, in the kingdom of Egypt. You're at an oasis that you've visited many times before."

"Oh." He then coughed four times, violently.

"Here, rinse your mouth and spit the sand out," she said, handing him a small jar of water. "Then you can drink, once you've cleared out the grit."

He did as she suggested, twice, and then a third time. He cleared his throat and spoke again. "How? How did I get here?"

"Well, that's the question I just asked you," she replied. "There was a small but intense storm here, and when the air cleared from all the tremendous dust and flying sand, you were on the ground. And we had not seen you arrive before that. It's all very mysterious."

"You say you know me?"

"Yes."

"You call me Ali."

"Yes. That's your name."

"I'm so sorry. I remember very little. I've experienced recently some strange things. I have extensive amnesia about my own identity, and this is so confusing that I'm finding it hard to think straight."

"You can't remember who you are?"

"That's correct, I'm afraid."

"I see."

He was silent for a few seconds as he began to brush himself off. "May I speak freely?" he asked.

She looked into his eyes for a moment and said, "We can go into my shop, into the back room where it's private, and you can tell me anything you want to say."

"I appreciate it. You may be able to help me."

Bamur and Shaz gently lifted him up from the sand and brushed him off thoroughly. "This seems to be yours," Bamur said, showing him the sack that had been in the sand under him. "I'll carry it for you."

"Oh, yes, thank you," he replied, and then added, to both men, "I'm still a bit dizzy and disoriented. My legs feel weak."

"You're a man of great strength and power," Shaz said. "You must have been through something very difficult and terribly taxing on your body. We'll help you walk over to the lady's shop. Come."

"Thank you," he replied. And as they supported him, he walked at first with a bit of a limp. And then he began to straighten up, but he still moved slowly all the way to the small store under the trees. The men got him inside and into a back room and settled onto a chair. Bamur put the sack at his feet. Someone brought him another jar of water.

"Do you need anything else?" Bamur asked.

"Something to eat. Something small. Anything."

"Just a second," Shaz said and disappeared. And then he came back with a bowl of figs and bread. He handed it to the visitor and said, "Here, this should help."

"Thank you."

"It's my honor. Can we get you anything else at all?"

"No, not at the moment. You're most kind."

"Then we'll leave you alone with the lady and be just outside in case you need our assistance for anything."

He took a deep breath and looked around. "I do feel like I've been here before, somehow." At that moment, a cool breeze blew through the window.

"You have," the lady said. "You've been to this oasis many times in the past, but on every other occasion you arrived by camel with friends, not by a sudden storm and alone."

"Oh, I see."

"Now, what would you tell me, old friend?"

He gazed into her eyes for a couple of seconds and said, "I woke up not long ago on a bench in a church building in New York City, in America, and I didn't know who I was or what I was doing there."

"That's very strange. Has it ever happened to you before?"

He laughed. And then he said, "Well, I wish I could tell you. But my entire history is shrouded in what seems to be a nearly impenetrable fog. My memory is mostly blank."

"You remembered nothing?"

"Well, none of the normal things like my name, my identity, place of origin, job, family, friends, history."

"That sounds fairly inclusive."

"Yes. But now and then, there would be a clue. Something would break through, some small fact."

"What sort of clues have you had?"

"I knew one name—Santiago."

"Oh. Really?"

"Yes."

"Santiago."

"The minister of the church started calling me that since it had suddenly, spontaneously, come to mind when I was taking a bath at the church on the night I mysteriously arrived there. Then a friend of his was intrigued by my amnesia and especially by the fact that I needed a name, a full name, in his mind. So he tried out various given names on me, and only one sounded at all familiar to me."

"What was it?"

"Juan."

"Remarkable. It's quite remarkable. What else did you recall?"

"That I was an avid reader, and could read several languages. And, that I'm in some way a religious man, even deeply spiritual. I'm naturally philosophical. And I seem to have many unusual physical skills, as an elite warrior or top military man would. I have highly advanced and developed abilities that I can use without a prior awareness of them or of how to employ them. It seems to be just natural in a situation of danger, or when I have to protect a friend."

"You had occasion, in New York City, in America, to use those skills?"

"Yes. I'll say more about that in a minute."

"Ok. Certainly. Go on."

"I'm intuitive in other ways, as well. I know what I'm supposed to do at any given moment, but only enough to do it."

"Can you give me an example of what you mean?"

"Yes." He took a deep breath again, and now began to relate the story of his time in New York, but just recounting the more dramatic aspects of what developed and how he reacted. He spoke of the Wisdom Shop and the thief with a gun and what he did, and the old chest and the scroll that was found in it. He talked of the night the Germans broke into the church where he was then working and living, and what he did to stop them. Then he related to the lady the explosions and the fires, and taking the scroll from the church. He told about being accosted at gunpoint, and the credible threat to kill Reverend Archdale, and the ring that Archdale had found in his robe and given to him. He explained that he had then put it on his finger and twisted it at the most crucial moment without knowing why, and that the very instant he had done so was the last thing he could remember until waking up face down in the sand just now, confused and aching mightily all over his body.

The lady listened intently and pondered all these things in her heart. She had her own strange story to tell, but waited at present, until the time should fully come. And yet, she knew she would not have to wait very long.

In Cairo, inside the large palace meeting room, all eyes were on Sab Maayuf. He looked around at everyone there, paused for a moment, and then began to speak once more. He said, "Long ago, I met a remarkable man. He was the monarch of a small but advanced kingdom far from where I lived. He was physically impressive and intellectually keen. And there was something else about him that I had not experienced for a very long time. But when I first saw him, he was completely exhausted from a long and arduous journey. He had come to me to talk, in search of an answer to a question that was plaguing him. He had heard that I possessed a rare quality connected with the object of his quest, and he came to me, he said, to learn my secrets. I didn't trust him at first, and I started to send him away, but my good wife here with us today prevailed on me to give him a chance to show me who he really was."

Sab looked around the room. "This man who had come to see me was struggling with certain issues about life and death. He couldn't reconcile himself to creaturely mortality. He had lost his best friend in the world, and at the time perhaps his only real friend. And he was despondent with grief and determined to learn what he could in order to defeat what he then had come to consider the main enemy of man, mortality itself. Once I understood his sincerity, his anguish, and his need, we talked. And when I came to appreciate his unusual talents and gifts, I talked more freely. I saw that I had a chance, possibly, to make a major difference in his life and, through him, in the lives of many others for a long time to come."

Sab reached over to a glass of water sitting on a small table near him and took a sip. He put the glass back down and said, "I told the man what I knew of the world and its wonders. I explained to him what I had learned about life and death. I shared my own peculiar story. And he said he would one day write down all that I was recounting to him, and would do so in such a way as to preserve and protect the many secrets I was sharing."

Sab then again looked around the room, making eye contact with several people, and then he said, "The man's name was Gilgamesh, King of Uruk." And, with these words, he paused.

A sudden, thick perplexity enveloped the room. Mouths fell open. A couple of people could be heard to whisper, "What?" A hand then shot up, as if they were all in a big academic lecture hall. It was, of course, Mafulla.

Sab saw the upraised arm waving about and said, "Yes?"

Mafulla put down his hand and said, "But we've been told that a king named Gilgamesh lived and ruled Uruk over four thousand and six hundred years ago, around twenty-seven-hundred BC."

"Yes. That's correct."

"But who is the Gilgamesh of Uruk that you're talking about?"

"It's one and the same."

"What?"

"That's the man, the one you indicate."

"But … how is that possible?"

Sab smiled and then looked almost wistful. He said, "Well, I'll soon come to that."

"Oh, Ok. Sorry."

"No, no. Don't be sorry. It's a natural question that probably occurred to many in the room just now, and you had the spirit to give it voice. I appreciate that and applaud it. I commend you."

Mafulla looked at Walid with his eyebrows up high on his face. Sab then gazed around the room again and said, "But, to continue: This keenly intelligent man and I spoke of many subjects. I told him things that no one today knows, but that you may have suspected. And all these things he remembered. When he returned to his kingdom, he decided to share a bit of his life story, or what he considered the most important parts of it, to a scribe. Actually, he relayed it all to a lady, a priestess who knew him well and could add her own interpretations to his words and write it all down for him as he spun the tale. It's this piece of writing that's come down to the present day and is known to us as the Epic of Gilgamesh. In it, toward the end, he relates some of the things I told him, but filtered through his own experiences and beliefs. And yet, my friend was true to his word and left out all the secrets that he promised me he would both protect and preserve."

Sab raised his right index finger into the air as he said, "Gilgamesh kept his promise. And it's that promise I must explain to you today. It will be hard for you to believe some of what I say, and yet easy to believe other aspects. I ask you to consider the source, and treat all that I will tell you with equal consideration. There's great power in the truth, no matter how far-fetched it might sound. In fact, it's some of the most esoteric and hidden truths, and thus the hardest to believe, that are the most revelatory and vital in life."

Sab paused once more, as if gathering his thoughts. And then he continued. "You may know the part of the story about Utnapishtim, The Faraway, and his wife who is unnamed in the Epic of Gilgamesh. It's a main part of the narrative toward the end of the story. The king, Gilgamesh, had heard of this man who lived far away from cities or other men, who was said to have the attribute of everlasting life, in defeat of physical death. There had been a major, devastating flood on the earth, and the man and his wife had been spared, as an act of divine grace. They had been told to build a boat and take on it all the animals they could, and when all else was lost in the deluge that followed, they survived. This was, of course, long before the man came to be known as Utnapishtin, or The Faraway. He went by another name, also recorded to history. He had been prompted to do certain things, and with his wife had obeyed the promptings faithfully. And, at least in part to acknowledge their faithful and careful action in carrying out their duties, the two of them were given a remarkable gift, a precious object. A benefit of this gift was at first to protect them from harm, to heal their infirmities and any injuries they had sustained up to that point, and to give their bodies and minds renewed energy and resilience. But in time, living with, or very near to this rare object conferred even more benefit than they had suspected. It made its owners increasingly youthful and vigorous in many ways. And the longer it had its effects, the more enduring those effects would be."

Mafulla turned to Walid and whispered, "I wonder."

Walid said, "Shh."

Sab continued. "As the epic recounts, Utnapishtim gave his visitor Gilgamesh a gift that reflected in some small way the one he and his wife had been divinely provided. The visiting king received this gift to take back with him to Uruk, but as the story also relates, the item in his possession was subsequently lost on his way home. Only The Faraway and his good wife retained an object, the original gift given to them, that would continue to strengthen and lengthen the life of anyone in possession of it."

He stopped again at this point and studied a few more of the faces around the room. He suddenly smiled. "But you may be asking yourself: why is our old friend from the village of Dromeda telling us all this? Well, there is a simple reason. And I tell it to you with complete sincerity and soundness of mind." He paused for a moment again and smiled. "I'm sure this will surprise you. I am the man once known as Utnapishtim. And my wife does have a name, though it was not recorded in the famous epic. It is, as you already know, Meskhenet. We are the couple who advised and counseled the great Gilgamesh, King of Uruk, in his time of need."

Those words evoked a hushed gasp from throughout the room, and a murmur. "The gift we were given so long ago was a beautiful stone that had been hidden away from perhaps the beginning of the world under the sea, at the base of a lovely plant that, as a result of its proximity to this remarkable stone, had taken on and replicated much of its power without reducing at all the potency of the original source. That thorny plant is what Gilgamesh received and lost. The original gift to us that had nourished the plant under the sea was a beautiful green emerald, the jewel that you now know as The Stone of Giza."

Another murmur enveloped the room. Everyone present knew of the stone. It was in the palace. It had healed Kular and several others. The butler, who had possessed it for many weeks, had been saved from a serious poisoning by its action, and then given new youth and creativity and strength, just from that relatively short period of contact.

Sab continued. "Once we had owned the stone for a thousand years, its results seemed to have become permanent, or so we thought. At that point, I took it and hid it. I buried it deep under the ground at a special place, a wondrous spot at the feet of the Sphinx, in Giza." A hand was once more raised in the air.

"Yes?"

Mafulla said, "So, I sort of have to ask: How old are you now?"

Sab nodded and answered, "Nearly six-thousand years old."

Again, an immediate reaction could be heard throughout the room. Mafulla then spontaneously said, with a very serious expression, "Wow. You look amazing for your age." And nearly everyone laughed.

"I thank you, Mafulla. I exercise and eat well." That brought more laughter. "Plus, my wife keeps me young. And part of that comes from chasing her around the house for a kiss. She's a good runner." He paused and chuckled at his own remark and shot a glance over at Meskhenet, who was smiling. And then he looked back at the group and said, "But you may be wondering, if you've grasped all that I've said here, why I don't look like a man of twenty or thirty. And that's the next piece of news. The power of the stone is not everlasting unless your possession of it is. Its effects begin to wear off over time, if they are not continually replenished by bodily contact or fairly intimate proximity. When we relinquished the stone and buried it for safekeeping, we allowed an extended process of aging gradually to begin once more within us. It didn't start immediately, or even for a very long time, by normal standards. But we now show the signs of age that would usually be expected at a healthy stage of eighty-nine or perhaps ninety-some years into a normal journey on this earth. And yet still, those results have been mitigated and modulated by an inner joy that always energizes us and keeps us resilient and eager and ready for a new day." Sab looked around the room, studying the faces that were all fully attentive to his words.

"Now, if you're still with me, and can allow yourself to believe this admittedly amazing tale, it's time to arrive at our more immediate concerns. There are two ancient scrolls that have come to our attention recently. Their existence has long been rumored throughout several parts of the world. And they are real. But I had never actually seen them before now. They are currently here in the palace and it's my hope that they'll be fully translated soon. I've already looked them over. My old friend Gilgamesh, it seems, wrote both of them himself, with no amanuensis or scribal assistant, I would suspect, because of the sensitivity of their contents. He wanted to keep them private, so that they would be shared only with certain people. One of the scrolls is the primary document, the longer of the two, and in it are many passages that he cleverly encrypted in code. The other scroll is part of a key to those coded passages in the major scroll. But it's only a piece of the key. There's apparently another element of the key, and we do not at present possess that second part, which is presumably on a third scroll. The two parts of the key were separated for extra safety, the primary scroll tells us. And to translate the entirety of the main document, we need both components of the key. There are, however, some passages that are not coded, and they indicate to some extent, in a very general way, what's to come in the scroll. And, if my hunch is correct, the information the coded passages contain relates, at least in part, to the many secret revelations that I entrusted to my friend, and that provide explanations for several mysteries and wonders that have long been sought by wise and inquisitive souls in various cultures. There are revelations in the main scroll whose details I do not myself at present fully recall, due to the aging that has occurred since we hid away the stone for safekeeping long ago. Otherwise, I wouldn't now be so elusive, or mysterious about those contents."

Sab reached over and took another sip of water. He paused and drank a bit more. And then he went on. "There are some people who are in violent pursuit of the scrolls because they desperately want access to one of the secrets it contains. They have no idea how many more valuable disclosures are to be found in it, if it contains all that I suspect is there. And, consequently, it's of the utmost importance that these people not acquire the scrolls. I believe that they've been sent by their supreme national leader to obtain these items. And if I should be right about this, then in his hands they would be used to do terrible harm on a nearly unimaginable scale. It's our job to prevent such a thing from happening. And that's why I've chosen to tell you all of this at the present time. The potential consequences of any failure on our part are so great that you must know what we're up against, as well as what we're protecting. And you are the people in the world I trust the most, due to our deep connections, our history, and thanks to our precious friend, Ali, who even now, I believe, is somewhere and somehow working for us, to help us in this great challenge."

Sab nodded his head silently and then said, "I'm sure you have many questions about what I've just told you. I'll try to answer them all at the proper time. But now, Masoon wants to divide you up into small groups to plan and strategize what we need to do most immediately for the safety of the scrolls, their secrets, and our greater world."

With those words, Sab bowed slightly to Walid and to the others in the room, and turned and walked a few steps back to where Meskhenet was sitting, to join her in an empty chair next to hers. He looked at his wife, and she smiled at him while patting his hand. She then whispered in his ear and he nodded with his own smile.

Masoon took his place in the front of the room and, after a few remarks commenting on the revelations just shared with them all, and also reminding them once more about the importance of their promise not to reveal to anyone else beyond those in the room what they had just heard, he began to ask various combinations of people present to rearrange their chairs and gather in smaller groups throughout different parts of the room.

It's often been said that truth is stranger than fiction. But when truth meshes with what's long been thought of as fiction, some of the strangest things of all can result. Everyone present was still stunned by the revelations Sab had brought to them, but there was still much yet to be revealed.

25

The Biggest Surprise of All

The reunion of Mafulla's family at the palace before the big meeting had been a joyous and tearful experience of great relief. As Shapur came in the door with Sammi, he called out, "Shamilar! Sasha!" The little girl ran to him as Sammi also dashed over to his mother. Both parents embraced their young ones and then each other. "I'm so happy you're both safe!" Shapur said.

"Yes, it was terribly frightening, with bombs and explosions and fire all around us," Shamilar said.

"I had no idea that my simple hobby could ever lead to such things. I'm so very sorry that the scrolls put you in such danger."

"It's not your fault," Shamilar said. "It's just a hobby. Who could have imagined that you would unknowingly purchase items sought by such awful people?"

"I just feel so helpless."

"Mafulla was here to check on us earlier. He had to go to a meeting."

"Good. Is he Ok?"

"Yes. He's fine. And Hamid came in also while he was with us and assured me that everything would be done to stop these people and that we would be safe from now on."

"Good. I wish I could have done more to prevent all this."

"I know you do."

"It's just been one thing after another recently."

"It has. I'm sure things will calm down soon."

"It was the biggest surprise of all to hear that our own neighborhood, our entire neighborhood, had been blown up and set on fire. And, for all this to happen while I was at work—it was simply astonishing."

"Our house is fine. And many of the others are, too. It was just a few. And Hamid explained to us that the explosions were staged for maximum drama, rather than extensive destruction. It was all about diversionary tactics, he told me. It was meant to get us and our guards out of the house so that it could be searched for your scrolls."

"By the Germans?"

"Yes."

"And the culprits took the scrolls?"

"Four of them. But the two most important scrolls, the ones they actually wanted, had already been transported here to the palace for translation."

"Good. Good. That's a relief."

"Those people should know by now that there are no more scrolls at our home or at our shop."

"Finally. This is good." Shapur hugged his wife again.

"Hamid is confident the palace guards will be able to recover what was stolen from you and return the scrolls. He also said that we will be amply compensated for the ones that have to remain here."

"Oh, that's so good of him, and of the king."

The happy Adi family reunion went on, and wonderful snacks were brought into the room for the two children and their parents to enjoy. Walid had sent them all a reassuring message. And Mafulla included in the message a quick note that he was planning to stop in to see them as soon as he could. He wrote how glad he was that they were all safe, and promised that this would all be over soon.

It was now a few hours later. The meeting where Sab spoke

with such unexpected and stunning revelations had broken up. Everyone was off to wherever they had to be next. Mafulla and Walid had visited Shapur, Shamilar, and the kids and were now back in a hallway, walking alone.

"So, what do you think of the big session?" Mafulla asked his best friend. He and Walid were on their way to Ali's sitting room.

"I don't think I could have been more surprised by anything that anyone might say," Walid replied.

"What if Jabari told you that he was secretly the strongest person in the world?"

"Nope."

"Or that his monkey Manni can recite Shakespeare?"

"Not even that. To me, this is much bigger, by far. I mean: I've known Sab and Meskhenet since I can remember, since I was a little kid. They were my totally normal and really nice old neighbors."

"You didn't realize they were, roughly, six-thousand years old?"

"No, nothing gave it away."

"Not even the number of candles on any given birthday cake?"

"Very funny."

"It would have been a blaze you could see for miles around."

"We didn't really do birthday cakes in Dromeda."

"Oh. Then, how about wedding anniversary yard signs? 'Happy Five-Thousand-Nine-Hundred-and-Seventy-Ninth!' That I know would have given it away."

"Sorry. No yard signs in Dromeda."

"I forget what a small and quiet place it is."

"Yeah."

"I'm confident you were festive in other ways. But, you're sure you never heard Sab say anything to his wife like, 'As I explained to you clearly just three-thousand years ago,' or any such thing at all?"

"I promise," Walid replied.

"Ok. So I see how this could come as a shock. But I, by contrast, am not fazed."

"Why not?"

"He always seemed a bit old-fashioned to me."

"You're very funny."

"I'm totally historical, though not quite like Sab. So, why aren't you actually laughing?"

"I was using irony."

"Oh. That's new."

"For me, maybe, but it could be as old as he is."

"Well, you got me there."

Walid was silent for a moment and then said, "Did you notice his reference to Uncle Ali?"

"Yeah, sure I did. Do you think he knows something he's not saying?"

"No, not really. I think he would say if he knew more."

"You're likely right. Still, it was pretty promising to hear, and sort of hopeful."

"Yeah, but I can't imagine what would be going on."

"Since when does that create a problem for positive outcomes?"

"Good point."

As they turned a corner, Mafulla said in a low voice, "I have a strange feeling that something's going to happen soon, related to all that."

"You do?"

"Yeah."

"What?"

"Hey, like Sab, if I knew, I'd tell you. It's just a vague, general feeling, an inkling, an intuition that's sort of leaning forward, an intimation that maybe a resolution or revelation is on the way."

"Ok. Let me know if you get more specifics."

"Will do."

As they approached Kular's office, the head butler happened to come out, looking as if he was on his way somewhere. But then he saw the boys. "Oh, Your Majesty! Mafulla!"

"Hi Kular!" they both said.

He stopped where he was and asked, "Would you two like something to eat? An early dinner, perhaps?"

"Well, actually, Kissa and Hasina are coming by in a few

minutes, and it would be great if we could have something put out in the dining room," Walid replied.

"I'll get on it right away," Kular said and bowed, and then he walked quickly down the hall.

Walid said, "He does move around with the stride of a young man."

"Yes, he does. The good old Stone of Giza works wonders."

"It sure does. Let's go into the sitting room."

"After you. Age before beauty."

"Ok. But that's a big stretch." The king led the way and they both collapsed on sofas in the big room.

Mafulla let out a long breath and remarked, "I've got to say, though, that what Masoon told us after our small group sessions was almost as surprising as what Sab had said earlier."

"Yeah, in a sense, absolutely," Walid responded.

"I mean, who knew that Sab was the first Phi ever? The father of it all, the original, the paradigm, the archetype."

"Yeah. I sure had no clue."

"But, of course, as soon as Masoon said it, I though it was interesting that Sab spoke up and made clear right away that there could have been many people before him with some or all of the talents, but that he seemed to be the first who recognized them as such and worked to develop them in himself and other people, and then began to build a network of like-minded, trained people. And, that it was all after the big flood and his time with Gilgamesh that this happened."

"Which may be part of the reason he was spared."

"Yeah. True. I hadn't thought of that."

"He had important work to do."

"Yeah. For a long time."

"And then, it was pretty amazing to hear that various Phi had been responsible for all Seven Wonders of the Ancient World."

"Also true. And it was totally wild to hear that Phi members have been responsible for all that other stuff, too, all those big breakthroughs and discoveries that Masoon mentioned. But it really makes sense, I guess. Those who are tuned in to more can create and accomplish more. Their vision wasn't limited to the ordinary."

"Yeah, they were way out of the box and brought what they saw back into our normal reality. And in a sense, by doing so, they expanded the size of the box."

"True. It's all pretty astonishing."

"Yep."

"It was especially good to find out where The Stone of Giza came from and why it works the way it does, to some extent at least, and all that stuff it can do."

"Yeah, I had no idea, although there's still a lot we don't know."

"Also true."

"And it was just as wild to hear the surprising story behind The Ring of Phi, and also The Book of Phi."

"Really. It's like when you thought nothing could get stranger, it did, and over and over." Just as Mafulla said this, the door across the room opened.

In a small apartment across town, Dieter Himmel had just dived down to the floor when he saw his colleague enter with a gun pointed at Greta Estand's back. And as he hit the floor and there was a single gunshot, he looked up and saw the victim's body fall and a pool of blood instantly begin to grow large next to it. In shock, he gasped out the words, "What? What just happened?" And he tried to think what he should do in response.

The answer was hissed back, "Idiots do idiotic things and they pay the price!" But before he could even form a coherent thought in response, he saw her move and heard footsteps and realized that he was now alone in the room. Then, there was another single shot from close by. At that point, he was almost overcome with panic and confusion and, as he slowly stood up, holding on to the table, she reappeared in the doorway. "Come. We need to go."

"But."

"No questions. Follow me." She turned and walked toward the outer door and held it open for him as she passed through it. He caught the door as she continued on, and as he crossed the threshold, he glanced back quickly and saw the other man's body slumped inert on the floor behind them. People peered out of two or three windows across the street.

"What did you do?" he whispered.

"What had to be done," she replied. "But you may still prove useful."

"But … what about their bodies?"

"They're not your concern."

"Where are we going?"

"Stop asking questions. We'll go to the hotel now, to a room that's always available for visiting dignitaries. No one's supposed to be there at the moment. We'll stay until we have a plan and our backup arrives." The two of them walked the rest of the way down the street and to their car, and got in and drove off.

Across the vast desert, the lady of the pool, Amita Golan, now sat looking at her unexpected guest. They were still in the back of her shop at the oasis far west of Cairo. After hearing his story, she sat quietly for several seconds, nodding her head. And then Ali said, "What do you make of this?" She took a breath.

"I think there's something very strange going on, perhaps stranger than anything I've ever experienced or even imagined. There is someone I want you to meet. It's another visitor to our oasis, a man who came wandering up out of the desert on foot several days back. He was dehydrated and exhausted and seemed feverish. He could remember nothing prior to waking up in the sand, face down like you were a short time ago. And, from what you've just told me, it sounds like his appearance here among us was not too long after the time that you awoke on that church bench in America."

"Really? This is far too strange."

"Yes. I tell you the truth."

"I can feel it. But who is this man?"

"He was like you in many ways, and seemed in some sense to be fresh to the world, reborn with few explicit memories."

"That's amazing."

"Yes it is. And after a day of talking, he could recall only one name that seemed at all familiar to him. And you may find it interesting that the name was Ali."

Her guest listened intently to her words and did not at this point respond. He was simply perplexed. He had no idea what any of it meant. After a few more seconds, he did manage to get out the words, "But that's the name you called me."

"Yes."

"I don't understand."

She then said, "If you can excuse me for a minute and wait right here, I want to go get the man to come in and meet you. I think the two of you are supposed to see each other now." And when the time had fully come. And when the time had fully come. These words ran through his head twice and then again, slowly. He sat still with an expectant curiosity as to what was going on and what it all meant. He instinctively trusted this lady. She seemed wise and knowing. She was gone from the room for less than five minutes, but the time seemed to slow to the pace at which an old camel might meander across the sand. A light breeze blew into the room. He twisted his neck to look out the window and then turned back and saw her enter the room again. And behind her, there was another person. He stood slowly from his chair as they entered and turned just a bit so that he could fully face the two of them. The man who had now come into the room stopped as well and stood motionless. The first thought or feeling that each of them experienced was a keen sense that the other had a vaguely familiar face, and a deeply resonant overall appearance and presence. There was something, something here. The time, perhaps, had indeed fully come, a proper time for something where the past and future would meet powerfully.

The lady said, "I would like very much for each of you to say the first name that you have remembered. Please. Say it out loud."

The visitor to this oasis who had most recently arrived, the one who had been sitting in the room awaiting the lady and her other guest spoke first. He said, "Santiago."

The man who had just walked into the room said, "Ali."

And in that moment, everything changed. Mrs. Golan could feel something almost like electricity in the air. And it somehow affected her so deeply that a momentary dizziness passed over her mind and she had to focus hard to cut through it. She placed her hand on the top of the chair in front of her and looked with a new perspective from one of her guests to the other.

The man who had just said the name of Ali took a step forward, and then another, and the two men suddenly embraced with tears in their eyes as if they were the best of friends, or even brothers, long separated by fate. And the next words astonished the lady.

"My dear Ali."

"My brother, Juan."

"It's you."

"Yes."

"I know everything now."

"I do, as well."

"It's all come back in a flood."

"Yes, it has."

"I hardly have words.

"Nor do I."

Santiago, the real Juan Osvaldo Santiago, gently extended his arms and achieved some small distance from the embrace, to hold his new brother of the spirit, Ali Shabeezar, at arm's length and look now into his eyes. "I'm so sorry."

"I know," Ali replied from his heart. "I know."

"Please forgive me."

"I already have. You're a new man."

"Yes. I just had to say it here."

"I understand."

"I couldn't have been more wrong. It was terrible, what had me in its iron grip."

"But you finally saw your path for what it was and turned and chose a better way."

"Yes."

"And you now apparently have an extremely rare opportunity.

You have a second chance, here, to do as you should, and to accomplish something that, perhaps, only you can and should do."

"You saved me. You turned me around."

"Well. You were turned around by a power vastly greater than anything I command." Ali smiled.

"But it was through you."

"Yes. It was through me."

"And no one but you could have done what you did."

"Perhaps. In the situation, at least, it was my calling. It was my task. And so, it was my great joy."

"And yet, I know it was tremendously painful and very hard for you."

"Yes. And it was also painful and terribly difficult for you as well."

"I had to be broken down to be built back up as the man I was meant to be. I had to be nearly destroyed so that I could be delivered. Decades of accumulated falsehood and greed, misery and arrogance had to be stripped out of me. And it was all so entwined with my soul that it was crushingly hard for me to shed and lose all that and still survive. I was laid low. It was devastating. There was a time when I was unsure I would survive at all."

"Yes. The farther we wander astray, the more immersed we are in counterfeit goods, the more utterly wrenching and arduous any possible return will be. And for some, it tragically never happens. They find it impossible. But you were able to choose anew."

Santiago then gripped Ali back into a fierce hug again and said, "Thank you. Thank you."

"Yes. It was an unexpected turn of events, to be sure, and a deep honor. And the result was, without a doubt, even for me, the most wonderful and biggest surprise of all."

"I remembered only your name."

"And I remembered only yours."

Juan released Ali and stepped back, while still holding on to one of his arms. He said, "I'm once again here in this amazing and challenging realm of existence where I failed so miserably the first time, and I know that it's for some immeasurably important reason. I'm absolutely confident of that, while yet totally unaware of what the reason might be. Do you know what it is?"

"We are to do something together."

"What is it? Can you tell me?"

26

Life and Death

Two days had passed since the big meeting in the palace. Everyone present was still absorbing what had been said. Mafulla and Walid had talked about Sab's revelations long into the night. Kissa and Hasina had enjoyed a great early dinner with the boys and had aired their own views about what Sab had said and what it might mean for the challenge they were all now facing with the scrolls and their protection. All four of them were astonished at the story their old friend had told, and it expanded their collective sense of what's possible in the world. Sometimes, truth pushes the imagination beyond where it would ever have thought to go on its own. And the influence can work in the opposite direction as well. The reality in which we live is much stranger and full of wonder than our ordinary experience would typically ever hint, at least, on most days.

In Khalid's class on this new morning, Haji brought up an aspect of what he had been thinking about since the palace session, but without mentioning why it was on his mind. Khalid had just made some offhand remark about how much the great English author William Shakespeare was able to accomplish in his life. And then he noted that some famous people had lived very short lives and still had brought exceptionally great things to the world. He mentioned, in particular, the French scientist and creative mathematician, Blaise Pascal, who accomplished so much before his death at the age of thirty-nine, bequeathing to posterity several important advances in thought and, even outside of science, leaving us his notes on faith and reason that have been read and interpreted throughout the centuries since his short time on earth in the seventeenth century.

"Khalid," Haji said, his hand up in the air.

"Yes?"

"Are there many people like Pascal who have accomplished a lot in a relatively short life?"

"There seem to be a great many such people."

"And I'm guessing that, because their lives were cut short, they had their period of intense creativity or accomplishment in their younger years, or at least starting then?"

"Many did experience that, in fact."

"Has anyone ever had a burst of original activity in their later years?"

"Yes, there are prominent examples."

"Could you give one?"

"Certainly. The great British philosopher John Locke published his best and most influential work in his late fifties or early sixties. Some of the great modern French painters like Monet and Cezanne were the same. They became innovative and especially important in their later years. Michelangelo did immensely significant work in his seventies and eighties. But why do you ask?"

"I've just been thinking about life and time and accomplishment lately. Some people seem to do so much in a short time. And others seem to accomplish very little in a much longer time."

Khalid nodded his agreement and commented, "The first century Roman philosopher Seneca once said that, despite the common complaint that life is too short, he saw it as fully ample in its normal provision for the greatest of achievements, if only it's used well. And he even employed the concept of investment. It's all a matter of how we invest the time we have. People seek to live longer. We should seek to live better or more fully each day. Ultimately, the important thing is not adding days to our life, but adding life to our days."

Set spoke up. "Wow. That's an interesting idea. We all have various, different amounts of time, but I guess that some who've had relatively little on earth have invested it well in activities that have benefited the world greatly. They were people who added life to their days."

"This is true," Khalid replied. "But we must remember that investing time well isn't just about hard work and productivity. It can also be about creating great relationships and having deeper and richer personal experience, with good growth and inner peace."

"So, a life that looks like it hasn't accomplished much on the outside, could be really rich and full on the inside?" Jabari spoke now with a questioning inflection in his tone.

"Yes. Most definitely," Khalid answered. "Lives are not to be judged by external standards alone. In fact, it could be the internal standards that are always the most important."

"So, what we call a quiet life could actually be a full life that's very well-lived," Set ventured.

"Absolutely," Khalid replied. "Remember the philosophical adage we're always coming back to that things are not often what they seem. An outwardly busy life, and one of massive external worldly accomplishment, can appear so important. A quiet life can seem the opposite. But the reality may be quite different."

Mafulla spoke up. "We live in a world where people seem to assume that more is always better, at least for all those things that can be good to have or experience in some degree."

"That's true," Khalid agreed. "And yet more of one thing may prevent a good measure of something else that's of equal or greater value. More worldly accomplishments may displace any time for inner personal growth, or for a rich and fulfilling family life."

"Can I ask a question about the 'more is better' idea?" Haji said.

"Sure."

"Most people seem to assume that about life itself, that more is always better. Almost everyone seems to want to stay a little longer, or a lot longer to be in this life. And if the bad parts of aging weren't a factor, they'd want to keep on living and living. I've never met anyone who said they'd want to leave the earth at a particular age and go on to whatever's next."

"My experience is the same. I think you're right about that, at least for the people I've known over the years."

"When we were reading Mary Shelly's book *Frankenstein*, it got me to thinking. What if scientists in the future could figure out how to stop all the bad stuff associated with aging—the aches and pains, the wrinkles, the weaknesses, the memory problems, all of that. And what if they could repair anything that got damaged. Like, for example, if you lost an arm or an eye, they could build you a new one just like the old one, or better, if you wanted. So, in this advanced state of science, nothing could kill us anymore. Even if you got blown up by a bomb, they'd be able to rebuild your body and brain from basic chemicals and stuff, just the way you were before the explosion, or better, if that's what you wanted."

"Wow, what an idea!" Jabari exclaimed, and some of the other boys made similar comments as well.

"Ok. I follow you," Khalid said, looking very thoughtful. "It is, indeed, a dramatic idea."

"Well then, science would have given people everlasting life on the earth, living forever into the future, like what Sab was talking about, but for everyone."

"As long as the earth continued to exist," Khalid qualified the conclusion.

"Yeah, as long as the earth continued to exist," Haji said.

Set spoke up and said, "But then, if science was that advanced, at some point, they'd know what to do if the earth itself was threatened, or if the sun was in danger. And they could maybe get these newly everlasting people out to another planet or solar system or something and keep it going even longer for them."

Jabari said, "That's a wild idea, for sure. But what if the whole physical universe has a lifespan and one day just conks out, and totally stops working, and won't support life anywhere?"

"Well, the scientists would likely have had a really long time to figure that one out, too," Set concluded, adding, "And maybe they'd have come up with a workable solution for even that problem by then."

"Ok, so suppose science could extend human life literally forever, for each of us," Haji said. "Would this be the ultimate More-is-Better, or not? I mean: then there would be time for everything, right? You could devote decades or centuries to outer accomplishment, and then still have endless time for inner growth and stuff like that."

'Well, let's think about that for a minute," Khalid said. "The great western religions, at least the traditional monotheistic religions, have promised eternal life to the faithful, and this has been seen as an ultimately good thing."

"But that's in heaven, right? Not on earth," Bafur said. "I mean, it's in a paradise where everything is good, not in Cairo or the desert where there can be good days and bad days."

"You make an important point," Khalid said. "In the main western religious traditions, when eternal life is promised and praised, what's being presented is a qualitatively different and better form of existence, not just a quantitatively more extensive one. It's supposed to be fully wonderful, and not just long. Eternal life is about, primarily, spiritual experience, love, and meaning. Second, it's about duration."

"What's interesting to me here," Set said, "Is the idea that, suppose Haji's future science became a reality and everyone was given an earthly everlasting life. I would guess that, in this scenario, longevity would not just be the norm, in the sense of being the ordinary typical thing, it would become the norm in the other sense of the expected, the normal, the healthy-minded, the thing that should be done, and maybe even the thing that must be done."

"What do you mean?" Jabari asked.

"If this had gone on for a while, I could imagine that people would start thinking that anyone who didn't want it for themselves was abnormal in a psychological sense, unhealthy in their thoughts, even deeply sick and needing intervention—just like people who feel suicidal now, in our current world."

"Ok."

"So, if someone actually wanted out, wanted to die and go on to a next phase or dimension, they wouldn't be allowed to. They would be rebuilt if they tried anything and, you know, kept alive and treated with therapy or whatever to cure their deviance, their sick sensibility."

"Wow, I see what you're saying," Jabari commented.

"I mean, imagine that some guy wants out. He really wants to move to the next dimension, or whatever. So he tries to get killed or even kill himself, and they keep bringing him back and treating him as mentally ill and in need of rehabilitation. And he just wants to say 'Enough of this!' He's ready for the next adventure, a different phase of spiritual existence. So, then, rather than this sort of scientific everlasting life being anything like the wonderful promise of the religions, it would be more like a form of endless imprisonment. He's imprisoned forever in this world."

"So, heaven turns into hell," Mafulla concluded.

"Yeah. Maybe, for that person," Set said. "Maybe so."

Khalid said, "That just highlights the difference between eternal life as a spiritual concept and everlasting life as a scientific goal. The scientific counterfeit could be truly worthy of Frankenstein, after all. But remember," he added, "The Greeks always said that hardly anything is, in itself, intrinsically good or intrinsically bad, but that rather it's up to us how we use it, what we do with it, and how we feel about it. A very long life here could be joy to some and a torture to others. It's all in how the hours and days and decades are used."

"There's an old image that sort of relates to this," Set said.

"What is it?" Jabari asked.

"There are two horses pulling different carts to market: One has to be whipped and prodded the whole way, at every step, and is irritated and angry and miserable. The other just trots merrily along and is happy. Both go the same distance, to the same place, but they go very differently."

"I like that," Malik said. He had been quietly listening up until now. "It makes sense. It's all about how we choose to feel."

"It's a good image," Khalid said. "And it's often used, in various forms, throughout history, by our wisest advisors. Attitude is almost everything in life. Live with love. Work with passion and joy. Choose happiness. It's up to you, and each of us. Ultimately, the quality of our experience is an inner game, to be played with joy."

"So, if a guy lived a very long time," Haji said, "that in itself wouldn't guarantee anything. He could be bored or fulfilled, blissful or agonized in his feeling. In the end, it's up to him whether each day along the way, or the sum total, is a blessing or a curse."

Khalid then said, "That's correct. And it's something most people never seem to realize. Plus, it's very relevant to something else that was mentioned earlier—suicide. Those who seek to end their lives because of emotionally difficult situations see death as a release. But the only genuine release is a matter of inner attitude. The premature ending of a life on this earth, some could argue, might be acceptable for truly extraordinary situations of extreme and torturous physical pain that will not otherwise ever abate. But as a way of dealing with even the most extreme personal problems of other sorts, it's never rational: first, because it confuses the issue of where emotional release is truly to be found; and second, because it conflates the imaginable with the possible."

"What do you mean?" Set asked.

Khalid nodded, and said, "Even the worst seeming situations can have possible resolutions that go far beyond anything you might imagine when you're in the midst of them. Your imagination might not be able to stretch that far, but reality can, as things play out. Life is unpredictable, and there are infinitely many paths forward that are possible. Good can prevail over anything, given the time."

"Ok, that makes sense."

Khalid paused for a second and said, "But that could get us onto a whole different discussion, and I think it's a little past time for lunch. Good food needs to prevail over my current hunger." And with those words, he looked around at the boys and said, "So, for now, let's go outside."

There were various comments from the boys and, as they got up to go, their teacher added, "From the classroom, you now have a fully rational, yet temporary form of release."

Bara El-Ari and her son Ebar were just finishing their lunch in the Grand Hotel's main dining room. At another table a short distance from them, a man and a woman had recently been seated and were now speaking to each other in low voices. Nonetheless, Bara could overhear their distinctive German accents. After saying something to her son, she got up and walked over to where they now sat. "I'm sorry to interrupt, but I couldn't help but overhear your wonderful accents. I think we may have something important in common. May I join you for a moment?" she smiled sweetly as she said this.

Greta Estand and Dieter Himmel could not have been more surprised. They had each altered their appearance so that they could still go out and about in Cairo without being recognized by the authorities, and were now dining in the famous hotel because it was so far away from any neighborhood in the city where they might have been spotted in the past. They were very confident they would not be identified by anyone who might have seen them at the palace or in their old apartment. So they did not respond to this interruption with any real concern. Greta actually smiled in a forced way and said "It's so nice of you to approach us like this, but as it happens, we're in the middle of an important conversation right this moment, and I'm afraid that, if we break our concentration at all, something urgent will not get done. But I do thank you for your kindness."

"I see," Bara replied, still smiling, but now even more broadly. "What I have in mind is as urgent as anything can be, and is nothing less than a matter of life and death, and perhaps of greatly extended life, rather than death."

This was exceedingly odd, Greta thought, and she quickly glanced around the spacious room as she considered a proper response. "You see," the lady continued, her desperation making her bold, "I have reason to believe that some of your countrymen are in town and in pursuit of something I'm also eager to possess. And if you happen to know them or know of them, I was hoping that you could get them a message that I have … unusual access to the object, or objects, that are being sought, and could be of great help, although I myself also need a bit of help of a different kind."

Greta replied, "Please, take a seat." The brash initiative was working. Dieter got up instantly and pulled out a chair for Bara. She smiled and gracefully sat. "You must know the people to whom I allude," she said. "And that's good."

"There are not many of our countrymen in Cairo at the present time. We're a small community," Greta said.

"Yes, that's also my understanding and the reason for my being so forward in approaching you as I have," Bara responded.

"Do tell me more," Greta requested.

"Yes. Well. Long ago, I met a young man and fell in love with him. And before we were separated by a cruel twist of fate, he came into possession of two ancient artifacts that he has kept safe, hidden away, for all these decades, until quite recently. He and I were just in the past few days reunited, and I can tell that the old feelings are being rekindled already in his heart."

"I may have read about this in the paper—the two young lovers reunited at a more advanced age."

"Yes, that big article was mostly accurate and was about us."

"You say the man had two ancient artifacts?"

"Indeed. But that wasn't reported in the paper. However, you see, he sold the two immensely valuable objects a short time ago to someone who may be altogether unaware of their full value."

"Oh?"

"Yes, but he knows the current owner and, even more importantly, he knows the exact location of the items. He's also on excellent terms with those in whose possession they're being kept safe. My adult son has just recently seen and held them in his hands."

"Is that so?"

"I assure you that it is. He even had the rare opportunity to begin a translation of the contents of these items."

"Oh?"

"And he confirmed that they are indeed the items we seek."

"So, you say these are objects you are interested in acquiring?"

"Yes. And I, of course, also have reason to believe that others are just as intent. But since they have not yet been successful in their efforts, I'm thinking they might be open to a partnership, of sorts."

"In what way?"

"If I can provide access and they can provide the means of extraction, then we can obtain the treasures of our mutual pursuit."

"How soon could such a thing happen?"

"Very soon."

"I would need more exactness."

"Within a few days, at most."

"And how would a joint endeavor benefit either party?"

"That's an important question." Bara knew she had them.

Greta said, "Just because there are two items, it doesn't follow that they could be split up to the satisfaction of anyone."

"No, no, not at all. But I happen to know that the items being sought by us both are old documents. And I suspect that, in the case of the other party, as in my own case, it's the content of the documents, their secret, rather than the artifacts themselves, that constitutes the main and perhaps only real subject of interest."

"That could be so."

"And, if it is so, then a possession of the items would allow the content to be shared. In my own case, it's definitely the information contained in the documents, rather than the documents themselves, that would of interest."

"I see."

"Once the documents are in hand, their contents can be translated and duplicated easily and quickly, for both parties to use and enjoy. My son is a top expert in such translation."

"Is that so?"

"Yes. And I would be perfectly happy not to retain the originals."

Dieter was sitting quietly, listening to all this. But now, he spoke. "Do you know the nature of the documents?" Greta looked over at him, cautiously, but not with any negative feelings.

Bara replied, "They're ancient scrolls, one in an old form of the Egyptian language and the other in Aramaic. The one in Aramaic begins with a preamble ascribing the document to an ancient king."

"Ah," he said. "I see. You know much, it seems."

"Yes," Bara answered.

"How so?"

"My son was asked to look over them at their present location and begin a translation. But then, as soon as he got underway, he was taken off the job, in favor of an older man, a friend of the monarchy. The form of access that would have made transcribing the documents easy was taken away."

"Why was that?"

"My son's initial translation revealed things the kingdom said were matters of top security. They then wanted to have their own people translate. And their expert, who had been traveling, just came back to town."

"But you still have some form of access to the items?" Greta asked.

"Yes, more indirect at the moment, to be sure, but it can be turned into an effective form of access, for those who know how to exploit it," Bara answered.

"This sounds very interesting."

"I hope it's interesting enough to launch a collaboration."

"Yes. It just might be. But how would another party know that you're to be trusted?"

"I've hoped my entire life one day to acquire these items just for the knowledge they will convey about life and death and," she now whispered, "everlasting youth."

"And?"

"And I will certainly honor anyone who helps my dream come true. I have tried my own plans and have failed. The Germans I seek have tried their own plans and have failed. From what I've heard, and from what I infer, we have ways of augmenting each other's strengths at this point and making the desired state of affairs come about. I have no reason to want to betray any collaborator. I have no reason to keep the physical items, once they're retrieved. My partners can have those. I want only a complete knowledge of the secrets they surely contain, for myself, and my use. Whatever my partners might want to do with the documents and their contents is their business, not mine. Nothing they do will adversely affect what I seek. So I have no motive to betray them in any way, or to seek exclusive possession of these most valuable scrolls."

"I see."

"And if my partners wanted to copy the secretes for their own use, and then sell the ancient artifacts to a third party for what would likely be a vast fortune, I'd be happy to take a half share and wish them well with their new bounty and the additional power it would convey."

Greta took all this in, and it made sense to her. She couldn't fathom any hidden reason or motivation that this woman might have that could cause any trouble. And, despite the fact that help was already on the way, access would be vital for keeping the scrolls safe and intact. They would be no good to anyone if they were inadvertently destroyed in a violent conflict over them. So, if such violence could be avoided, the success of the mission might be more guaranteed. Force would still be available, but perhaps finesse might win the day.

"I think that what you say sounds reasonable," Greta replied. She looked into Bara's eyes and said, "We are the Germans you seek, the two of us, and we would be happy to be your partners in this quest."

"But I had been given to believe that there were at least two men involved."

"I often disguise myself," Greta said. "But I can assure you that we are the two you seek."

"You are strong enough, the two of you, to provide what's often called the muscle for such an operation?"

"Yes. And much more muscle, as you call it, is on the way, scheduled to arrive very soon."

"What do you mean?"

"You literally cannot imagine what I mean, but it will all be in service to our now joint operation. Irresistible power will be brought to bear, if and as we need it." Greta looked deeply and searchingly into Bara's eyes, and Bara had a chill extend throughout her soul and into her flesh as she had a thought occur to her: She was making a deal with the devil.

"Good." That's all she said, in the face of evil. And then she turned and waved at Ebar to come over and join them.

27

Visitors From Afar

"I like it out here." Reela Adi had just sat down with Masoon and Hamid on the palace grounds back near the stables and the royal garage in a large attractive open area where a few tables and chairs had been placed for staff enjoyment. Bright flowers were in colorful pots arranged all around the area. A small fountain gurgled near them. Darwishi, the head driver whose office was close by, had provided coffee and pastries that were laid out on the table.

"Yes, I like it, too," Masoon said. "We started coming here first thing in the morning just recently. It's a nice way to get some fresh air and maybe some fresh ideas along with it."

Hamid looked at Reela and, pointing his thumb toward Masoon, said, "He's never been one for indoor offices and desk work."

Reela laughed and said, "No, I suppose not."

At that moment, Darwishi came out of his office again walking toward them and, getting closer, called out, "Gentlemen! Is everything all right? Do you have what you need?"

"Yes, Dar, thanks," Masoon answered with a smile and a small wave of his hand. "We're good."

"I could use an attractive masseuse," Reela turned and said to his companions, with a completely serious look on his face.

"Ha! The Adi wit," Hamid laughed.

Reela smiled and said, "Actually, I have to admit that I'm painfully serious. I just started a new exercise routine the day before yesterday and I'm as sore as I've ever been in my life. I'd forgotten how many locations for pain receptors there can be in the human body. They're all speaking up to remind me."

"There are indeed many," Masoon commented.

"I think I've discovered them all."

"Where's it the worst?" Hamid asked.

"Arms and legs, but the lower back is pretty bad as well."

Masoon said, "I could probably take care of that for you, fairly quickly."

"Thank you, my friend, but you're forgetting a couple of the therapeutic qualities I had in mind—womanliness, and a measure of feminine beauty," Reela replied. "The charm helps the healing."

"I see." Masoon shrugged and sipped his coffee. "No way, then."

"You could be thought, in the proper light—suitably dim—to have a certain rugged charm," Hamid said, appraising his friend.

"So, those are officially your famous last words?" At that, Reela and Hamid both laughed.

"Not to change the subject," Hamid said in order to do precisely that, "But Reela, my friend, before the aches and pains of renewed fitness become too severe for you to be able to speak at all, would you please tell us, what's this new information that's come to you?"

"Yes. Indeed. Thanks for reminding me of why we're here right now. It was yesterday. An old friend from my time in the intelligence world got in touch. He said he was worried for me."

"Why?" Masoon wondered.

"He's been in Austria for some time now and heard rumors from friends that a secret group scattered about Europe has just been ordered to Cairo."

"What's the group?" Masoon asked.

"He said they're called the Black Widows."

"Never heard of them," Hamid commented and took a bite of pastry. "Who are they?"

"He says they're an elite group of 'problem solvers' for the new leadership in Germany, most likely spies and expert assassins, and are all women, interestingly, with exceptional training and with origins, he thinks, in the esoteric Thule Society."

"Thule? I haven't heard of that, either."

"They're a group of people in Germany who are fascinated by the hidden, the occult, the dark side of the spirit—a bit like the obsession of our former adversary, Juan Santiago."

"How many of them are there?" Hamid asked.

"No one knows. But there are rumors that the society supplied the beginnings of the Nazi Party that's brought Hitler the core of support he enjoys at present in his nation, as well as providing some of his top advisors, especially the ones whose names are never in the papers."

"Interesting."

"Yes. He's surrounded himself with people who claim to have accessed darker powers, and the Black Widows are a part of all that. At least, this is the story I've been told."

"So, these Black Widows are coming to Cairo?"

"Yes, apparently so. That's the rumor."

"Do we know anything more about them and how many to expect?"

"Not much more than I've already said. But my friend thinks there may be a dozen of them headed this way, perhaps more."

"For what purpose?"

"To get the scrolls."

"Your friend said this?"

"Well, he heard only that they're in search of some ancient artifacts, and with what we know, those would surely be the two scrolls."

Hamid said, "I agree, since the scrolls have been pursued so vigorously of late by the countrymen of theirs who are already here, and who seem by their methods also to be trained operatives."

Masoon added, "From the start, I've suspected that these were not just average German criminals. And now that we know what's on those documents, at least in part, it's obvious to me that it's most likely Hitler himself behind all this. And he's after nothing short of invulnerability, immortality, and any sources of occult power he can discover." He took another sip of his coffee and added, "I don't hesitate to say that, from all we know of him, it would be as Sab said, disastrous beyond imagining if he were to get what he wants."

"Those are my thoughts exactly," Reela commented. "This is why I wanted to share the information with you as soon as I could. We need to plan for some new and extremely unpleasant visitors from afar."

"And we now have no idea where to expect them to gather, since we raided the apartment the others had been using and found all the radio equipment they had." Hamid looked concerned.

"In addition, there was no information that would help us at this point. The place had been kept clean of evidence." Masoon said.

Reela added, "And, since even their car has now been found, abandoned, we have no clue for how to locate them in the city."

"We're starting afresh," Hamid said.

Reela nodded. "Yes. And I have a suspicion that there must be a Widow here already, since so many others are apparently on the way. She would be the one who has helped her associates to stay so elusive, up until now."

In New York City, Detective Antonio Sardo knocked lightly on the doorframe of Bob Archdale's study door. "Oh, Detective!" Archdale said, looking up from his work. "Please, come in."

"Thank you, Pastor. I'm sorry to stop by unscheduled, but I was a few blocks away and thought I should drop in for a minute."

"You're always welcome here, and especially around the time of choir practice. Actually, we're in desperate need of a good baritone."

"I'm flattered, but you know, I'm Catholic."

"That's Ok. As I said, we're desperate."

Sardo laughed and said, "You're too funny to be a man of the cloth. My priest never cracks a smile or a joke."

"Life is wonderful, and tragic, and often funny."

"I'll give you that, for sure. Look, I really don't want to get in the way of your work, and I won't be but a minute today, Father—I mean, Pastor—but I just wanted to come by and check in on you."

"That's good of you, Detective. Please, have a seat."

The big man squeezed in to the chair he was being offered and said, "So. How've you been doing?"

"I'm all right, I suppose," Archdale answered. "Of course, the deaths at the Wisdom Shop, along with the recent injuries here in the neighborhood and the terrible loss of property have concerned me greatly. But, all in all, everything considered, I'm personally Ok."

"That's good."

"I have to confess that all this has enhanced my prayer life greatly. I'm blessed to have made it through such a harrowing time."

"Still no word from your friend, Santiago?"

"No word at all."

"And I know you've told us this at least maybe six times before—me, three—but to your best recollection, he just suddenly disappeared with a burlap sack containing an ancient scroll of some sort?"

"Yes. He vanished."

"Right in front of your eyes."

"Yes. Well, in the moment or two that my eyes were closed."

"He was there. And a second later, he wasn't."

"That's how it looked to me."

"There was no sign of him running away, or jumping, or hiding, or anything."

"No. There was nothing like that at all. I was as close to him as I am to you. He was there one second and completely gone the next."

"There were no sounds to indicate what he might have done?"

"None."

Sardo scratched at the side of his head. "Sorry, Reverend. I got itchy skin this time of year."

"I have a few allergies, myself," Archdale replied sympathetically.

"I gotta tell you, Pastor, the story is the talk of the station house. Nobody knows what to think of it. Everybody believes that you're a good guy and an honest man and that you're being as straight as you can be here, but still and all, as I guess you can imagine, we've never quite heard a tale like this before. Ever."

"Yes, I can certainly imagine that."

"I mean, people sometimes have stories in their families, you know, about strange things happening, and what you might call miracles, but we don't often come across such stuff in the course of our particular work."

"I'm sure this is a unique situation," Archdale said. "And I've done all I can to remember anything that might be helpful. But I have to tell you that the situation I experienced that day surprised me then every bit as much as it surprises you now, and probably a good deal more, because as you know, seeing is believing. And suddenly not seeing is not knowing what exactly to believe."

"That pretty much says it all," Sardo replied. He scratched at the same side of his head again and said, "So, in your personal and professional opinion, do you think we're dealing with something like a miracle here?"

"Well, my friend, I have to be completely candid and tell you that I really have no idea what to think. Santiago's original appearance, as you know, was almost as mysterious as his disappearance. He could be an angel."

"A what?"

"An angel, a special messenger of God. When you read the Bible, it's part of the package, however odd. And then, by contrast, Juan could just be an ordinary man on a special mission, or rather, a pretty exceptional man. I don't know what to think, except that I know he's a good soul, and that he was as unusual and as skilled as he was considerate and helpful. I miss him a lot. He was a hard worker and a kind friend, despite his short time here."

Sardo nodded his head. He said, "I'm just glad we found the Germans. It was a shame it all had to end the way it did, with a long gunfight."

"I was very sorry to hear that."

"It was bad. We've never had so many cops firing their weapons at the same time, in the history of the department. But those people were determined not to let us capture them alive."

"It's such a shame."

"Yeah, it is. We couldn't talk to them and get any answers."

"The dead carry their secrets into the next life, I suppose, and the living are left with questions."

"That's for sure. And for that phony fireman to have pulled a gun and tried to shoot a couple of the beat cops, well, he got what he deserved, too."

"I'm sorry there had a be such a loss of life like that," Archdale said.

"Yeah. Where there's life, there's hope," Sardo replied. "That's what we always say. But maybe the way it ended was in some sense for the best. I mean, those were really vicious people, violent people, and I couldn't ever see them surrendering, especially that woman. Jeez, was she a case! It took seven slugs in her to bring her down. I never saw such a thing. Some of the guys ended up with a bunch of weird injuries we'd never seen before. And then the coroner's report said the woman had a tattoo of a black widow spider on her arm with that red hourglass shape, and in another place, a bunch of numbers. It's all just too creepy."

Archdale said, "Yes. It is very strange and a little unsettling. I suppose we're immensely fortunate, truly blessed, that there weren't even more deaths on that day."

"We are," Sardo replied. "And to think, it was all over some old scroll. It's just way too weird for me."

"It's very far off the beaten path, all right. I hope never to go through anything remotely like the bad parts of it again."

"I hope your friend Santiago is somehow Ok, you know, whatever it was that happened."

"Thank you. He was, or is, and I fervently hope I can use the present tense accurately here, a good, kind, and intelligent man."

"Yeah. So it seems. We need more like him."

"Indeed."

"I think I've bothered you enough. I should let you get back to work." The detective stood up as he said this, scratching again, and Archdale rose as well in response, and with a smile.

"Remember, if you have any desire at all to participate in a wonderful music ministry here at the church, to raise up your robust voice and sing, just let me know and I'll introduce you to our choir director."

Sardo laughed, and said, "Well, Pastor Bob, don't hold your breath on that one. I got a deep voice, but I can't carry a tune worth anything. And I don't think either you or your choir director could fix that. We're likely out of local miracles for now. But I thank you for the invitation. Although, after one rehearsal with the choir, maybe even halfway through the first tune, I bet the director would make me vanish about as quick as your friend did." Archdale laughed.

In Cairo, Kissa, Hasina, and Khata were walking together to Kissa's house. The school day had just ended, and they were going to get together with Hoda and Layla for a time of conversation about Sab's revelations in the palace conference room. Hoda had anticipated that the girls might have a lot of questions about it all. And so she had invited Layla to come over, with the idea in mind that it might be a good time for them all to share their thoughts and feelings about these huge surprises. Khalid had work to do at the palace and would be home later than usual, so they could have the house to themselves.

Ara and her friend Cabar were also walking home together today, headed for Ara's house. Cabar wanted to get the whole scoop about Ara and Haji and what was going on. For a while, she had secretly admired Haji's best friend, Malik, but she had never said a word about it to anyone. She was truly interested in her friend's new relationship, but she also thought that Ara might be able to give her more insight now into Malik and what he was like, since he and Haji were so close and did so much together. Surely, Ara had heard her new boyfriend talk about Malik, and could likely share some things that Cabar didn't know.

They were at this point only a few blocks from palace grounds. It was a nice temperature, with a light breeze out of the north. And they were, at the moment, walking by a row of retail shops. "Class was interesting today," Cabar said.

"Yeah, really," Ara replied.

"Hoda seemed extra enthusiastic."

"I thought the same thing."

"That stuff about existentially writing our own biographies, through our choices every day—that was pretty interesting."

"Yeah, for sure. The whole view of life as art that she was talking about was new to me. But I looked over at Bakat a couple of times when Hoda was explaining it, and she was nodding her head like she'd already believed it for a long time."

"Well, she is super arty," Cabar said, "like her mom."

"That's for sure," Ara said, then added, "I really liked the analogies Hoda used, you know, like: Every action we perform is a stroke of paint on the canvas, a chip out of the marble, a movement in the dance."

"Yeah, that was all pretty vivid. I like the painting analogy the best."

"Why's that?"

"Because, if you paint some lines that don't work, something wrong, something, you know, that was a mistake and ends up sort of ugly, you can always come to realize that and then paint over it something that's much better. Great art often has corrective layers."

"Good point."

"And what's sort of deep about the analogy is that the wrong stuff doesn't really go away. It's still there. But it teaches you something when you recognize that its wrong, and then it forms the underlying base for the good that you put over it."

"Yeah, that is deep. It's a lot like our mess-ups in life."

"Yeah. Mistakes are bad, but we all make mistakes. And, at least most of the time, they're not fatal. We learn from what we do wrong and we move on, doing something better because of the experience."

"Absolutely."

"And the mistakes sort of become a part of us, and provide a foundation over which we can make the corrections and create the better painting that we really have in us."

"Yeah. True."

"Oh, look!" Cabar suddenly stopped and pointed. She had noticed something in the storefront next to them. It was a bright display of beautiful scarves. "Another form of art!"

Ara stopped, too. "Wow," she said. "Very nice. Super nice, in fact."

"Yeah, the colors really jump out."

"Do you have time for us to go in for a minute?"

"Sure, let's go look! Come on," Cabar said, and opened the door, holding it for her friend.

It was a small shop, full of stylish ladies' clothing and accessories, along with beautiful textiles that could be used for custom made items. The owner was sitting in the back with a newspaper. "Welcome," he said as he heard the door open, and then settled back into his reading.

"Thanks. We'd just like to browse for a few minutes, if that's Ok," Ara said.

"Sure, help yourself, look around. And take your time. Just let me know if I can be of any assistance," the man said.

"Ok," Ara answered. She turned to Cabar and said, "Look at these other scarves."

Right after the girls had walked into the store, two other visitors followed them in. A lady and a man, dressed in western clothing were right behind them. The lady had looked up and down the street before she entered the shop. On such a warm day, these new arrivals were the only customers to have come in wearing long sleeves over their arms. And when the second of the two had gotten through the doorway, she reached to grab the door and close it behind her. As she stretched out her arm, her sleeve moved ever so slightly up from her wrist and, if the girls had been looking at her, they might have been able to see the ends of two darkly inked spider legs barely emerge from below the cloth. Someone was about to be caught in an unexpected web.

28

Two Pieces of Paper

"Your Majesty," Kular had just poked his head in the door, "Bancom has given me a message for you."

"Sure, Kular. Come on in. What's it about?"

The head butler walked toward the table. "I haven't looked. It's in a sealed envelope." He handed it to Walid and asked, "Is there anything else that you and Mafulla would like?"

"Maffie? You want anything?"

"No, I'm good."

"I think we're both fine, thanks. But please tell the kitchen that, once again, it was a great early dinner, really amazing."

"I'll do that, Your Majesty," Kular replied and smiled, and then he quietly left.

"I wonder what this is?" Walid said to his friend as he turned the envelope over in his hands.

"Open it, and let's see. Or, you could just put it down on the table and we could stare at it and try to guess."

"Ha. I like that idea the best," Walid said with a smile, and placed the unopened envelope on the tablecloth between them.

"Now we stare and think really hard," Mafulla said, pretending to focus on the rectangular form in front of him.

"Ok, Ok. Who's it from?" Walid asked.

"Hmm. I'd be tempted to say a secret admirer, but it was addressed to you, not to me, and so that sort of rules that out."

"Very funny."

"Is it your mom?"

"Well, she is out of town with her best lady friend, doing that research, that fact-finding thing about some of the spiritual sites south of here. Maybe it's a message from her."

"No, I don't think so," Mafulla said.

"How do you know?"

"If you have to ask, your memory's going and I'm worried about you. I do have certain skills, however limited and episodic they might be."

"Oh. Right. Ok. So who else could have sent it?"

"The Sakat brothers?"

"They'd just call with any message."

"Yeah, but to Bancom, and he could write it down and give it to a guard to bring here."

"But why the sealed envelope? And if it was the Sakats, Bancom would have said something to Kular, don't you think?"

"Yeah. Maybe."

Walid let out a breath and said, "Leem? Or maybe Ibrahim?"

"Could be. But I don't feel it."

"Your parents?"

"Addressed to you? Why? Wait. Maybe to ask you to give me a raise, something long overdue, I might add."

"Your parents have already raised you as high as you're likely going."

"Ok. Decent riposte. Despite the crack about my height."

"No, I meant ..."

"I'm plenty tall and still have years to grow."

"Never mind."

"And I can't think of any reason that mom or dad would send me a note or a message with your name on it. Except the real issue of a raise, of course, and not the topic of your lamely deflected effort."

"Hey, a guy's gotta try."

"So, what are you thinking?"

"I'm thinking … it's from far away."

"Really?" Ok, that's interesting. You've got my attention," Mafulla replied.

"That's a first," Walid said.

"Hardee. Har."

Then Walid turned serious and said, "We're not doing this right. We're goofing around. We should totally concentrate. I mean, really concentrate. Make your mind a complete blank and focus. Use the envelope as a vehicle, not just to see what's in it, but what's beyond it, all the way to where its message originated. It's a link in a chain of events. So what events led to this thing before us now? Be open. Allow the truth to come to you."

Mafulla nodded and refocused, staring at the stark white paper. He took a deep breath. They sat in silence a good thirty seconds, and it seemed like a lot longer. The silence in their minds grew fertile, like rich soil ready to receive a seed.

"It's military," Mafulla said.

"Yeah, I didn't know that until you said it, but I'm somehow sure you're right," Walid replied, a bit mysteriously.

"It's about something that's going to happen soon."

"Well, you could have guessed that, in any case," Walid said, adding, "It's the sort of thing a carnival psychic would say, for a small fee. Should I leave your payment on the table or would you prefer to levitate it out of my pocket?"

"Shh. Quit messing with me," Mafulla said. "We're not goofing now. Remember? I almost had something."

"Sorry."

"We're getting visitors."

"Who?"

"I don't know."

"When?"

"Nothing there, either. Just soon."

"For what purpose?"

"We need them."

"Ok, good enough. Should I open it now?"

"Yeah, open it."

Walid hesitated for another moment. Then he slowly picked up the envelope and held it for a second more, as if considering it one last time and inviting any of its hidden secrets to manifest themselves. But there was nothing more, so he carefully tore open one end, and slid out the paper that was inside it. He read. "Well."

"What?"

"It's a message from that military outpost we visited when we were going to Dromeda, and also coming back."

"Ok, I was right. It's military. I've still got it. So, what do they say?"

"Your Majesty: Please prepare for the arrival of two guests who will be staying in the palace. One is an old friend. The other is a new friend. They're bringing something you need. Sincerely, the camp commander's name, and today's date."

"That's all?"

"That's it."

"An old friend and a new friend. This is what sounds like the carnival psychic," Mafulla said. "And they're bringing something we need."

"Yeah, I wonder why the vagueness? Why the mystery?"

"I have no idea. Who could it be that would fit such a description and be coming here, and passing through there on the way?"

"Somebody from the village, maybe?"

"Ok. But who do you know well enough that they would expect to stay at the palace?"

"I don't know. Aleph and Zet Noni?"

"The message said one old friend."

"Oh, yeah, so maybe one of them?"

"It could be. But I don't think so," Mafulla said.

"Do you know something you aren't saying?" Walid asked.

"No, no, not at all. That just didn't feel right."

"And who's a new friend? Who have we just met?"

"I have no idea."

"Well, I'm …"

Before Walid could finish his sentence, Bancom came through the door with a very serious expression, saying, "Sorry, Your Majesty, Mafulla, but there's something extremely urgent." He handed a piece of paper to Walid, who then stared at it. And his face fell, and then his expression turned hard.

"No." He said this in a low voice, to no one in particular.

Mafulla, completely surprised by the look on Walid's face, glanced up at Bancom and then back at the king and said, "What is it? What's happened?"

"Call Masoon," Walid said to Bancom.

"I already have, Your Majesty. He's on the way."

"And Hamid."

"He's coming, too."

"What?" Mafulla asked. "What's going on?"

Things were happening across town in what was now a seedy neighborhood. It was an old commercial building, long out of use. Some windows were boarded up. The previous owner had surrounded the property with a high chain-link fence, brought in from Norwich, England. At this point, the fencing looked old and discolored. Vagrants and vandals had deformed it in several places. One section in the back was completely missing, presumably stolen at some point. But in this part of the city, that wasn't unusual. Under the previous regime, corruption had taken down many businesses whose owners would not cooperate with the criminal elements in power. As a result, many buildings still stood empty where vigorous and productive activity had once taken place.

Inside this building, by the light of several lanterns, a meeting was about to get underway. Nine figures stood around a table in the large, otherwise dark interior area. They were clothed in various forms of traditional Egyptian garb, both male and female. Shadows played across their faces and there were low, murmured conversations between and among several of them.

A door creaked loudly and two more people walked in. One

was Dieter Himmel. The other was Greta Estand. They both moved straight to the table and Greta looked around at the visitors, nodding at several, and then spoke. "I want to thank you for your quick travel. I know you've all come from great distances and have journeyed here in different ways. We have temporary housing for you right here, and will be providing for your needs of food and drink. We've located the two scrolls we've been pursuing. And we've lost all contact with the group in New York City. So, they should be presumed dead at this point. But why, I wouldn't know. They had firmly believed they were on the trail of a scroll and were very close to acquiring it but, as I said, the two we know of for sure are here in Cairo."

One woman in the group spoke up in a raspy voice that was nearly as deep as a man's. "Then, why don't you have them already?"

"We've been one step behind the scrolls, as they unexpectedly changed locations throughout the area. It was like moving heaven and earth to track them down initially and, when we went to where they were supposed to be, our men discovered that they had just been sold and taken away. We quickly visited the location where they would most likely have been moved, but they weren't there. At a third place, where we were then sure we'd find them, we located only four worthless scrolls, mostly of a mercantile nature, and one of a more broadly historical record, but irrelevant to our quest."

"What happened that you failed so many times?" The voice asked.

"Failure is never an option," another added, and there were affirmative murmurs around the room.

"There has been no failure at all. We've simply experienced a natural sequence, consisting in several steps of pursuit as we've closed in on the items while they were being transferred from one place to another, and then again. Such a quest is a process, as you know. And successful progress has been made, to the point that we are now poised for complete success."

"It was quite dangerous to ask for our help so suddenly and bring us all to the same location in such a short period of time," another voice said, most likely female, but also a bit masculine in tone. "Why do you think you require assistance from so many of us at once?"

"We now know that the scrolls we need are being protected in the palace here in Cairo, surrounded by the might of the Egyptian army and the palace guard. Two of us could not do this alone."

"There were four of you."

"Two of the men performed unacceptably. I had to relieve them of duty and breath."

"Good. That shows decisiveness."

"What would you have us do?" Another voice now asked.

Greta looked for a moment at the one who had asked and said, "We have a plan in place that may not require much of you."

"Then, again, why are we all here?" Another voice demanded.

"You still might all be needed. And if you are, then you'll be needed quickly and in force. It's a risky plan we have now, but it's simple and straightforward. And yet if it doesn't work, the backup alternative we've charted out is an extremely demanding path that will require all of you at your best. There's no time at this point for any more delays. Our leader needs what he needs. Our orders are strict."

"Is our presence here official?"

"You wouldn't be here if he didn't want you here. Nothing will work the way it's intended to work in his long-term plan if we fail here. So that means …"

"Failure is not an option, as I said before," a familiar voice finished the thought.

"Indeed."

"Why is this man with you?" Another voice was raised to ask this.

"He's a member of the original team who has performed well. He's our translator for the scrolls. His presence is vitally important."

"Can we trust him?"

"Of course you can or I wouldn't have him here. I'd never tolerate anything else."

"You've not been showing a mastery of the situation in other ways."

"That's not accurate. I must suggest that you're speaking out of supposition rather than knowledge. There's been all required mastery, but within an unpredictable and fluid situation."

"And yet, here we are."

"Yes. We've succeeded in learning that you're needed. And those not now here among us are the ones who didn't show mastery."

"I can grant you that."

"You can trust me, and you can trust the situation."

"For the greater good, we will."

"For the greater good." Greta looked around the group, focusing on each face and reading their level of commitment, to assure herself that she could speak freely. And then, she went on. "We've just made the first move in our new plan and need you to operate in a support capacity. I'll explain now what the plan is, and everything that needs to be done. When we finish here, a team will have to go to New York and complete the required work there. But first, we have to implement our plan for success here."

In the king's private suite in the palace, Walid turned to Mafulla. He had just read the urgent message. His insides felt like ice. "Two of our good friends have just been kidnapped."

"What? Who?"

"Ara and Cabar."

"Oh, no! Why?"

"This note says that they will be traded for the two scrolls we have, and that if we don't follow all the directions here, both of them will be killed in a slow and painful way."

"That's terrible."

"Yeah. I need a second." Walid closed his eyes and took a deep, cleansing breath.

"I guess it's the Germans," his best friend said.

"It has to be."

Mafulla suddenly made a fist, and with his hand lightly pounding on the table, he said in a voice of exasperation, "Why can't things ever be normal around here? There's always some new disaster!"

Walid sighed and looked at him and said, "Maybe that's just part of what normal is for us these days."

At that instant, Masoon and Hamid walked in through the door together. "Majesty. Bancom told us about the situation," Masoon said.

"I'm so sorry," Hamid added, and then said, "We both are."

"Have you seen the demands?" Walid asked Masoon.

"No. May I?" Walid handed him the piece of paper, and he read. "I see."

"Their timetable is short."

"Yes, it is."

"They sound deadly serious."

"I doubt very much that this is a bluff, considering what they've done already."

"We need a plan."

"I have some ideas. We should sit and talk."

"Please, take a chair," Walid said. "Both of you." Then he looked around and said, "Maffie, would you go tell Kular to bring Naqid in on this?"

"Sure thing," Mafulla said, and he walked toward the door.

"And Bancom, would you get word to Hoda and Layla and their daughters that they might be needed here?"

"Yes, Your Majesty, right away."

"Oh, and send a message to Haji and Malik that I want them here, as soon as possible, but maybe you shouldn't tell them what's going on yet. Let me do that."

"I understand," Bancom said and walked toward the door.

Masoon then reminded everyone present, "Under no circumstances can these people be given the scrolls or any form of access to them."

"Of course. You're absolutely right," Walid agreed.

"Yeah," Mafulla said.

And then the king felt a sudden sickness churn deep in his stomach, with a sharp wave of fear for his friends. He said, "What do you think we should do?"

And just as he asked Masoon this question, the thought ran through his mind that if only his uncle Ali were here, he would definitely know what to do. He reminded himself in the next instant that he certainly trusted Masoon and Hamid as much as anyone could possibly trust anyone else, and he knew they both had great wisdom about such things. But no one was quite the same as Ali. And Walid knew that Masoon and Hamid would be the first to agree with this simple assessment. Yet, it made no sense to spend any time or mental energy at this point wishing for what he and everyone would most want, rather than focusing all his mind on what they had to deal with in this actual situation, and with the considerable resources they did have available. He remembered then that his uncle used to say about any challenging circumstance: "We use what we have and move quickly, with confidence."

But, in actuality, the current king, Walid, along with his most trusted advisors, had no idea what the full magnitude of the situation would soon be found to involve, or what their own resources would quickly come to include.

There were many things yet to be revealed.

29

A Hole In The Floor

Ara and Cabar didn't realize that they were in any danger until the moment they were confronted. When a foreign looking man and woman entered the women's shop just seconds after them, they hardly noticed. It was a busy afternoon up and down the street, although this store itself was otherwise empty, apart from these four customers and the proprietor sitting in the back, absorbed in what was most likely *The Kingdom Daily News.*

The man who had just entered scanned the shop and walked to the back to exchange a few words with the gentleman who, as it turned out, was just watching over the shop on this afternoon for his wife while she was out having tea with an old friend in a nearby café. The foreigner then rejoined his companion not far from where their intended targets were standing. The woman was feeling the fabric of something folded on a table in front of her. If the girls had looked over again toward the back corner at this point, they would have seen the poor man who had been reading now slumped down in his chair, the paper on his lap and a section of it sliding down onto the floor. The time had finally come when no witnesses would be left.

"Oh, I like this one," Ara said to Cabar as she held up the edge of a particularly colorful scarf for her friend to see.

"I do, too," Cabar replied. "It's so bright. I love the geometric pattern of yellow and orange on that blue background."

"I wonder what mom would think of it?" Ara said, as the lady turned and silently approached her.

"Hello," the lady said in a low voice.

"Oh, hi," Ara responded.

The woman said, "You both need to come with me."

"What? What do you mean?" Ara said, as Cabar just seemed confused.

"I need you to help me with something," the woman said.

"I'm sorry," Ara replied, but before she could say any more, the stranger had put a hand on her arm.

"No, I'm the one who is sorry, because if you don't come with me quietly at this moment, I'll have to kill your friend here and her entire family."

"What?"

"No more questions. And the same goes for you," she said to Cabar. Come silently or your friend dies right now, and her loved ones."

The girls both felt a slight dizziness and a plummeting sensation in their stomachs. Cabar's throat seemed to close on her. She could hardly think. "What have we done?" Ara whispered.

"Nothing, and you should keep it that way."

The man opened the door of the shop as the woman showed the girls a curved knife with a serrated blade that was tucked tight into her belt. "I'm serious about what I said. You must both come with me now and quietly. If you speak to anyone or even look at anyone else between here and our car, I'll have to kill you and that person on the spot and then visit both your homes to kill your families."

Ara had a metallic taste in her mouth, as a chill of fear coursed through her entire body. Cabar was frozen in a panic that would not allow her to respond. "Now," the woman hissed, and jerked on Ara's arm. For a split second, Ara studied her face and could see in it nothing but focus and a fierce determination. She thought to herself that this woman's features even look cruel. But the thought was interrupted as she found herself walking beside her toward the door and out of it and down the sidewalk, moving forward in a blur of partial consciousness, almost as if she was in a strange dream, a terrible nightmare here in the middle of the afternoon.

There was a car parked less than a block away. The man opened the door on the passenger side and tilted forward the seatback so the girls could get into the rear seat. There were tears in the eyes of both Ara and Cabar at this point, even though they couldn't begin to know how to process what was happening, largely because they had no idea what might be going on. But clearly, these were violent people. And the suddenness of the whole thing was enough to rattle anyone, even beyond the horribly severe threats that had been made.

The girls had no clue about what was going on or why. Their consciousness floated almost above the situation as they complied with everything they were being told or shown to do. And they remained silent, as they had been commanded. The man pushed the seatback into its regular position and the woman got in. Then he briskly walked around to the driver's side and opened the door, slipped into the seat, and quickly closed the door. He started up the engine, put the car into gear, and pulled forward. Everything outside the vehicle was a blur as they began to move.

And then it suddenly occurred to Ara that she should pay attention to where they were going. This might be their only hope. Didn't people get blindfolded at times like this? And they weren't. They were being allowed to see where they were being taken. Was that a good sign, or a very, very bad one? She had to fight to suppress her panic and clear her head to think and see. She started to breathe slowly and deeply to calm herself and to take it all in, as much as she could. Hoda had taught them to meditate. Now was a time to use that technique to calm down and focus.

Far away, across a vast stretch of seemingly endless sand, something very different was going on. In some obvious ways, the two older companions who were crossing the desert together could not have been more different, and to the extreme. One had spent his entire life in service to others, and preparing to do great good on the broadest possible scale. The other had lived an existence dominated by selfish concerns and blind to anything like a normal sense of moral considerations. One had saved many people from harm and death. The other had injured many and killed nearly an equal number. One had been thought of as great and honorable. The other had been considered terribly powerful and frightening. One's soul had been elevated by compassion and love. The other's had been torn and deformed by greed and hate.

And yet, a wondrous and immensely improbable turn of events, a rare twist of destiny, had brought them together. In fact, it was the twist of a ring. And that turning motion had launched a series of events that neither of them could have predicted or even imagined. They had found themselves, in an instant, spiritually and bodily transported to somewhere vastly different. It was a realm or domain or dimension, or a form of existence that, from the first, felt deeply familiar to one of them and terribly alien to the other. They had been taken to a place, in the broadest possible sense of the term, where they each had a job to do, if they would both accept and attempt the task.

There was no question about it in the mind of one, and initially nothing but confusion and rebellion and fear in the mind of the other. And the man who was initially alienated and panicked by his new surroundings and assigned task had much indeed to fear. We have a concept of creative destruction. And that aptly captures what was to happen. At least, it had to happen first. The refining fire of ultimate love, the intensely searing creative and refining heat of the source of all had to do its work, and this would call for responsive actions on the part of both these men that would stretch each of them, but in different ways. One would be a conduit of power and then be called on to act almost like a potter. The other would be the clay. And this one would be dug out, twisted, pounded, molded, and formed, then fired in a blazing kiln of unimaginable power.

The process went on and the work was done. Then, something just as radical had to happen. Neither had any idea how he then made the transition from one world to another, from a far different land and back into this world. The trauma of the passage had erased all awareness and remembrance of these events for at least a time, as well as much else, besides. But meeting again as they had in the desert, at the oasis, and in the presence of the lady of the pool had sparked sharp fragments of recollection from both men. There was no way that their normally embodied minds could retain all that they had experienced in the ring of fire beyond our world, where the deep transformation had taken place. But at that moment, they instantly recalled enough to evoke in both their hearts the most complete humility and gratitude and joy that can be experienced in this world. One soul had been changed and moved from the darkest frozen night to the most brilliant and healing warmth of a day that never ends. The other had been recognized and honored and employed in a special collaboration to help prompt and elicit and then guide that change. It was the hardest work that either had ever done, but the most thoroughgoing and the best.

This arduous labor of the spirit could have been refused by either of them. But both ultimately embraced it with full free choice. One saw it as his wonderful opportunity and merciful duty. The other at first fiercely resisted and fought and held firm, but then wavered and considered and rethought it all. He had initially perceived the new path ahead that was now being offered as a confusingly difficult challenge, full of options and possibilities that he had never considered or even understood in the past. And this man had indeed created scars in his soul that could never be removed, even within the overall transformation that he then eventually accepted and sought when he was confronted with the full and radiant light that alone brings life to the dead. He would bear within himself always some marks that he had imposed on his own spirit. But, despite those scarred wounds that would remain as reminders, in every other way for the present and future, all things otherwise were now made new. There were deep reasons for him to enter his new life still bearing those scars, because they were to be a strange part of his distinctive power and calling. The terrible knowledge and spiritual effects that his wrongful and awful way of life had produced could now, in a completely unexpected twist, position him for a distinctive role in the dangerous and transformative things that were to come.

There are ways we could seek to capture what had happened, but all are so woefully inadequate, and each would be more misleading than illuminating. We could say that these men had been through hell together, or that they had been given a glimpse of heaven. What they had experienced had certainly combined elements of purgatory and paradise, but in the end, it had been all about purpose. And the process could never be put into words that would give anyone else an adequate sense of what had transpired.

And at the end of their initial work together, well after the culmination of those labors that had taken place in a land far beyond, these men now remembered in flashes, but all were fleeting or vague. They each had a sense of having been in a huge magnificent hall, as you might see in a palace, but vastly bigger and more ornate in décor than anything on earth. And there had been an interview, or else a conversation, or a ceremony of some sort, it seemed, though neither of them could picture it fully now. But they had also seen something like a large opening, or a hole, in the floor of this spacious hall, and they had approached it, knowing that in it was their destiny. And the sides of the hole were made of gold, it seemed, and there were jewels embedded in the gold, and they sparkled and glimmered from a light that somehow appeared to be everywhere. And there was a magnificent staircase lining this opening in the floor that descended down through other levels and areas and dimensions.

And they knew it was time. So they walked down these stairs, one in the lead, the other right behind. They slowly descended the steps, as they were invited and destined to do. And then, at one stage of the process, one of them experienced something like being on top of a high bridge and looking down, while reclining on something solid beneath him. And the other one had an experience that was a bit like this, but his perch was on the top of a high desert dune. And yet, they could not think or speak of this transitional thing, not in words. And then one awoke on a church pew, as if from the deepest sleep of his life, and the other came to consciousness, face down, in warm desert sand. And now, after one of them went through another unexpected transition and also came to land in nearby sand, thanks to the same legendary ring, they were back together again.

And they were now in the last stage of their initial journey together back into this world, across the land of Egypt, to a place where the two of them would be needed. They had met and remembered, and then had talked extensively all day and through the night. And they knew they had to depart together on the fastest camels they could find. A purpose was calling them.

All they carried with them from the oasis were light garments and sandals, simple food and water, two powerful rings, and one ancient scroll. But some time later, at this moment, in fact, after stopping at a remote military post and sending a cryptic message to the palace, they were seated in the back of a truck, headed down the final stretch of their unexpected journey to the capital city.

In the palace in Cairo, Hoda was walking down a hallway with Kissa, Hasina, and Khata. And up ahead, from an adjoining hall, Haji and Malik suddenly appeared, walking fast.

"Hoda!" Malik called out. "Hey! What's this all about? Do you know?" The two guards behind the boys slowed down, to give them a bit more space and some degree of privacy as they approached the ladies.

Khata walked faster up toward the boys, and put her hands to her mouth for a moment, and then spontaneously blurted out, "Haji, I'm so sorry!"

"What?"

Hoda looked over at Khata and said, "I think the king wanted to be the one to speak with Haji and Malik."

"Oh," Khata said, looking surprised and scared that she had just done something very wrong.

"It's Ok," Hoda reassured her.

"What's Khata sorry about? And what's Ok?" Haji asked.

"I think the king wants to talk to you."

"What's going on? Has something happened to my dad?"

"No, no, your dad's fine, and he's in the king's sitting room now, I think, waiting for us to arrive."

"Then what does Khata know that I don't, and that she's sorry about?"

"Come," Hoda said, taking Haji's arm and quickening her pace, as Malik just looked puzzled and followed them.

Two palace guards opened the door outside Kular's office for them, and another guard inside opened the inner door to the king's sitting room as they all walked quickly forward—Khata, Kissa, and Hasina now following Hoda and the boys. This is not normal, Haji thought. Why are so many guards here? They entered the big sitting room. Masoon and Hamid were on chairs over toward the right side of the room, talking in low voices. There were many others there as well.

"Hoda, please, what's going on?" Haji said in a low voice as soon as he saw his father across the room.

Walid had seen them come in and immediately made his way across the room to intercept his friends. "Haji!"

Haji turned and said, "Walid! I mean, Your Majesty, what's all this?"

Walid drew closer to him and put a hand on his arm. "There's a little bit of trouble. I don't want you to worry or panic or take action to do anything about it right now. We're taking steps to solve the problem."

"Please, you just have to tell me."

"Yes, but promise me first that you'll stay right here with me, regardless of what I report to you."

"What?"

"I need you to stay here after I tell you what's going on. I mean it."

Haji looked around at the people already in the room and said, "Ok."

"You promise?"

"Yeah, I promise. So, what is it?"

"Ok, take a cleansing and calming breath," Walid replied.

"Ok." Haji shot a glance at his father again, but the doctor was in an intense conversation with Masoon. Then, he did as he was asked.

Walid took his own deep breath and said, "Our friends Ara and Cabar were walking home from school and were kidnapped."

"What?"

"Ara and Cabar have been kidnapped."

"Are they Ok?"

"Yes, we think so. They haven't been harmed at all, so far as we can tell, and they're being kept safe to use in a trade."

"But why? What trade? Who did this?"

"Some Germans are responsible, the people who've been after the scrolls. They've demanded that we give them the items by noon tomorrow in exchange for our friends."

"Or what?"

"They've made the classic, extreme threats."

"What about the palace guards that were following them?"

"The guards were apparently giving them some distance, as we've instructed all of them to do, and it was obviously a little too much."

"Do they have any information about exactly what happened, and about where the girls are now?"

"Unfortunately, the guards' bodies were found some time ago."

"Oh, no. This is really bad. What can we do?"

"That's why we're all here. We're going to plan out how we can best rescue the girls."

"I should be doing something." Haji looked toward the door.

"Well remember, you've promised that you'll stay here with the rest of us and not go do something on your own. We need you to be a part of the plan, not a lone hero."

Haji just stared at Walid for a moment, and then said, "Ok, Ok." He let out a big breath of frustration and resignation.

Walid glanced down at his Reverso to check the time. He then looked back up and said, to the room generally, "I think everyone's here. So, let's go ahead and start." Naqid closed the door and took a seat.

The acting king nodded toward Reela Adi, who now stood and said to everyone assembled, "Thank you all for coming together on such short notice. I have some new information that's important to share and that will help us understand our current crisis, and what we're up against." He paused for a moment and began his report by saying, "There's a secret society of German women who are highly skilled sharpshooters and assassins with elite military training and who, together, are known as the Black Widows."

Hoda spoke up. "Reela, a number of us recently had dreams of real black widow spiders. And we had no idea why, or what the dreams meant."

"Oh, indeed? Well, it may have been something like a precognitive awareness or intuition that these individuals were on their way. I say this because, from some old sources of mine, I've learned that there's a widespread belief among various intelligence agents working in Europe and the Middle East that small teams of these 'problem solvers,' as they're often called, have recently left their homes in various countries. And there's a rumor they've all been headed here."

"Why?" Layla asked. "And what else do we know about them?"

Reela said, "We think they were originally recruited and groomed by a shadowy group in Germany called the Thule Society, a clandestine organization comprised of people interested in psychic phenomena and other esoteric and occult matters. Some of the top advisors to the government in Germany at present are members or former members of this group." He looked around the room and said, "These Black Widows, we think, work in direct service to Adolf Hitler, the new and very troubled Chancellor of Germany."

"But why exactly are they here, or on their way here?" Layla repeated a part of her question.

"Well, the people who have been seeking to acquire or steal my brother's scrolls are German. And if these women are here, or are coming here, it's probably in connection with that effort which, as you all know, has been, up until now, unsuccessful."

"When I saw what was going on at the Antiquities Shop, there were a couple of men who were looking for the scrolls," Haji pointed out.

"Yes, originally. But because they failed, it may be that the Widows have been sent in to finish the job."

"Sent in by … Hitler?" Hoda asked.

"Most likely, or by his top people," Reela answered.

"Why would the leader of Germany want my dad's scrolls?" Mafulla asked from the back of the room.

"Because it's apparently his fervent wish to live and rule the world forever," Reela answered. "It's as simple as that."

"Are these Widows the people who have Ara and Cabar?" Haji asked.

"Most likely, yes," Reela said. "And they will be formidable opponents. Their power and effectiveness in making things happen is already legendary." He paused for a second and then said, "In addition, we've just received word out of The United States, from the police in New York City who've sent telegrams to German authorities and the governments of several Arabic nations reporting that a German woman has been killed there in a major gun battle while she was apparently attempting to steal an Arabic antiquity from someone. And they say that on her forearm was a tattoo of a black widow spider."

"Why was she killed?" Hamid asked.

"The report said that she had planted fire bombs in a neighborhood around a church."

"Fire bombs?" Mafulla said.

"Yes."

"Just like around my house."

"Exactly. And it was for a similar purpose, apparently. Then, when she was found and the police sought to apprehend her, she reacted with great violence. She had been attempting to steal a scroll."

"Another scroll?" Haji said and looked around, as a murmur of voices swirled around the room.

"Yes."

Hamid jumped in and said, "First of all, that's indeed what just happened around the Adi home. And similar actions often come from coordinated plans or planners similarly trained." He then turned toward Sab and asked, "Could this other scroll be the missing piece of our puzzle?"

Sab replied, "Yes, it could be. It may be the missing part of the key to reading all of the master scroll, the one component of the decryption key that we don't yet have in our possession."

"Why would this third scroll have been in New York City, of all places?"

"Actually, I have no idea," Sab said. "Remember, the existence of the master scroll itself was, to me, merely rumor. I had never actually seen it before now. And the second scroll we have in our possession is a part of the key to reading it. Of course, I never knew at all about that one. I had just heard that there were scrolls, in the plural. But I've learned from reading passages that aren't encrypted on the scrolls we have that there is another part of the key, without which we can't have full access to the master scroll's contents. All we've learned so far is that it exists, or at least that at one time there was such a thing out in the world somewhere, and that it had been hidden away. Perhaps this New York scroll is indeed it. We don't yet know. But our adversaries apparently think it's important."

"Where's the New York scroll now?" Hamid asked Reela.

"The report was unclear, except to say that it had apparently disappeared at about the time of the gun battle."

"But the woman with the spider tattoo is dead?"

"Yes, one such woman is dead."

"One?"

"If it was a German Black Widow, they often operate in pairs, so there could have been another."

"And she could have the scroll?"

"It's possible."

"And if that's true, then, if they were to get their hands on our scrolls here, they would have the master and the full interpretive key."

"Yes. It's entirely possible."

"I see."

Hoda spoke up and, addressing Walid, said, "Your Majesty, something just occurred to me. Is there anything in The Book of Phi about any of this, about these scrolls?"

"I don't know. That's an interesting question," Walid replied.

"We should look into that."

"I agree." Walid turned to Mafulla and said, "Would you go into king's bedchamber and get it out for us to consult?"

"Sure, Your Majesty, right away. It's in that same place?"

"Yes. Thanks."

Mafulla then stood up and walked toward a back inner door that led from the sitting room to the private sleeping area. Haji asked again about Ara and Cabar and, in response, Reela retrieved and read aloud the note they had received. Haji had just started to ask about their plan for rescuing the girls when Mafulla rushed back into the room without the book. Only a few feet back through the door, he just stopped, completely still, with a totally surprised and puzzled look on his face.

"Excuse me, Your Majesty?"

Reela stopped what he was saying, mid sentence, and Walid said, "Yes?"

"There's … a big hole in the floor."

"What?" Walid stood up and took a step in his direction. As he saw everyone else begin to rise, he motioned them to stay seated.

Mafulla looked straight at his friend and said, "I went to get the book, and near where it's kept, I happened to see what looked like the edge of a hidden door panel on the wall that I had never noticed before. There was a thin seam along it, something you wouldn't detect unless light hit it at exactly the right angle and you were really staring at it."

"That's strange."

"Yeah. And I pushed at it, and then again, and a third time, and it opened up. The panel opened up a little bit at first, and then all the way. And in a large dark open space behind the wall, there was this area, maybe five or six feet wide, maybe seven, and I could see in the floor, right in front of me, a big hole about four feet across. And I went over and bent down to look at it, and there's a ladder going down a circular, walled passage. I couldn't see a bottom."

"A hole and a ladder?" Walid said.

Everyone was silent as Mafulla repeated, "There's a ladder." And then he said, "A narrow ladder is built into the side of the hole in the floor behind the king's closet wall. And it goes down, somewhere, but I couldn't tell where it goes or for how far. It seems to go on for a long way. And I had a sudden, strange feeling come over me."

Walid quickly walked toward Mafulla and the door from which he had emerged. Masoon instinctively looked over at Hamid and the muscles in his legs tensed. Hoda glanced at Layla. No one knew what to think about this very odd piece of news.

30

The Most Stunning Moment

As Walid crossed the room toward the door to the private bedchamber, Masoon stood up and called out, "Majesty, I'd like to come with you."

"Oh, Ok," Walid answered, as he paused and looked back. Masoon then walked over to join him. The room was now abuzz with conversations as everyone speculated or wondered aloud at what this secret hidden hole in the floor could be and whether it might be in any way connected to their current problem. Walid, Mafulla, and Masoon disappeared through the door as nearly everyone talked.

Reela suddenly spoke over the chaos of crosstalk and said, "Excuse me, everyone. Excuse me, please. Your attention, if I could." The chatter died down and then stopped, and he said, "Thank you. Let's remember why we're here. Whatever is learned about Mafulla's odd discovery just now, we need to get right to work on planning the rescue of our friends. The clock is ticking. Time is limited. I think Hamid has some initial ideas."

"Yes, thanks, Reela." As Reela sat down, Hamid stood up, and all who were present shifted their attention to him. He looked around at everyone and said, "As we await the likely imminent return of the king and our other colleagues, I should begin at least to provide an overview of the likely possibilities for action, as we see them now."

He then summarized what was known about the range of abandoned buildings in town and other possible hiding places where Ara and Cabar might be held. But just then, Mafulla suddenly ran, or almost dove, stumbling back into the room, and as soon as he was again in view of all who had been listening to Hamid, he stopped and said in a loud, frantic, astonished and excited voice, "The king!"

Everyone turned to look at him and he repeated himself, looking more excited and stunned and agitated than anyone had ever seen him. "The king! The king's here! The king is back! He's back! King Ali!"

And, at that instant, Ali Shabeezar walked through the door from the inner bedroom and into their view. There was a loud collective gasp, mingled with various exclamations of surprise, wonder, and relief, and then a stunned moment later, everyone rose to their feet. Masoon and Walid quickly reappeared right behind the king.

"Where?" Hoda spoke one word. A chill of excitement ran through the room, almost like static electricity dancing across everyone's skin. There was a sudden wave of energy and even giddiness in the shock that each person felt at that moment. Nothing could have been more incredibly welcome, or more utterly surprising than this.

Ali stopped and held up his arms and said, "Greetings, dear friends. It's a great blessing to see you again and to be back with you. I regret any distress my absence may have caused."

Now, it was Hamid's turn. "Your Majesty! What happened?"

"In due time," he replied with a smile, and he walked over to the group and reached out to shake hands and touch shoulders. The ladies were all crying in their relief and gladness to see him alive and apparently healthy. Tears were running down many cheeks. And several of the men wiped at an eye or two as well, as they were all exclaiming and greeting him, and expressing their great thankfulness to see him, as well as showing the tremendous emotional burden that had just been lifted from each of them. A thrill of wonder was passing through all their hearts as they almost had to shake themselves and reaffirm in their minds that what they were seeing and hearing in this unexpected but desperately hoped-for moment was indeed real, after weeks of worry and deep dread that the king was dead and gone forever from their lives on this earth.

Walid and Mafulla were beaming and crying at the same time. But they were hanging back at this point to allow everyone else to have the chance to speak to the king and touch his hand or arm or back. It was the wide and wonderful moment that had been long awaited, and yet it was somehow at the same time experienced by all the others present in a fog of mixed perplexity and awe. A full realization of who was in front of them was perhaps still breaking through a dense mist of confusion, helped along by a fast rising joy. And the decorum of the court had simply vanished from everyone's minds, so they spontaneously reached out to him physically as a friend and man they both loved and revered.

Walid and Mafulla had already shared with him the most intense embraces ever, moments earlier inside his private chamber, right after they had received the shock of their lives in seeing him climb up the ladder that had just been discovered. First, the top of his head had appeared as they approached the hole in the wall and Masoon had grabbed both of the young men to hold them back, not knowing who would appear in this way, entering as if by stealth. And it was the most unexpected, most stunning experience of all that then played out in an instant. It was Ali! Masoon practically dove toward him to help him up and then grabbed him into a nearly crushing hug. And the king said, "My good friend." And then, just as quickly, the great warrior fell to one knee with head bowed while Walid brushed by him to throw his arms around his uncle and squeeze him and exclaim in a voice he could barely muster above a whisper, "Uncle! Uncle Ali! You're alive! You're alive!"

"Yes, yes, dear boy." That was all he said, initially.

And Mafulla came up to them and hugged them both, putting his arms around his best friend and even the king, also forgetting in that tremendous moment all royal propriety. And he suddenly felt himself sob uncontrollably and said, "I can't believe it! I can't believe it!" And that's when he made himself let go and run back into the room to announce what had happened, and who had just appeared.

In the happy chaos of it all, the king then asked everyone to sit, and they did, while still stunned beyond words. He said, "I think we have a lot to catch up on," and that made many of them laugh as a great tension was released from their souls. He then found a chair and sat down and began to talk briefly about all that had happened, from the confrontation with Juan Osvaldo Santiago in the palace, to the remarkable events that had transpired next, as well as he could recall and describe them, through the amazing story of Santiago's deep struggle and transformation. Even as they listened intently to his words about their former adversary, those present could barely understand what they were hearing.

Ali then spoke briefly of his own awakening in New York City and the events that transpired there and how, through the use of The Ring of Phi, he had in some way wound up back in Egypt, face down in the sand in the big desert oasis between Dromeda and Cairo. He paced himself well with the entire narrative, knowing instinctively that there was some sort of an urgent need that had to be met very soon here, back in Cairo, although he was as yet unaware of its nature. And he was preparing to ask about it as soon as he had accomplished all that needed to happen in this moment. But he first had to tell them what he could about the recent meeting in the oasis with the man who had been so dramatically changed.

If this particular tale of spiritual metamorphosis had come from anyone else, there's not a person in the room who would have believed it for a second. But this was Ali, the man they knew they could trust above all others. And even though they were all shocked beyond words at what he was telling them about Santiago, it was in reality no more impossible than so many other spectacular and miraculous bits of his story, including the very fact of his being, now and here, suddenly again with them. And, yet, apart from Ali's unimpeachable authority, this one part of the narrative would have strained credulity far past any remote possibility of acceptance.

"The man who was our terrible enemy is now, by the power of the greatest mystery, our friend." That's the way Ali summed up his story about Santiago and his hard-won spiritual turnaround. Then he said, "I will ask you all to remain seated now, as a great favor to me." And there was a new bit of puzzlement in all of their hearts at hearing these words. "Please," he said again, and looked from face to face, ending with Hamid and Masoon. "I ask you, out of your gracious love for me, and from the depths of the trust we have developed, please stay exactly where you are, no matter what you see or feel in the next moment." Then he turned around in his chair and looked back toward the door from which he had emerged into the room, and said in a loud voice, "Oz! The time has come!"

And, as if they could not be more surprised than they already had been, each person in the room was once again shocked almost beyond the point of grasping what they were seeing when the man himself then emerged from the doorway and slowly walked into the room. Even those who had never seen him before knew in an instant that this was Juan Osvaldo Santiago. A visceral alarm jolted many hearts in that moment, and a surge of wariness and readiness coursed through their veins, despite what they had just been told and asked. The unlikely visitor, then just a few steps into the room, suddenly dropped down to his knees and stared at the floor, and then look up once more at them.

"I beg your forgiveness, each of you," he said to them all, with his right hand over his heart. "I'm not worthy to be here, or to be your servant, but this is what I seek to become."

"You killed my father," Walid said in a trembling and perplexed voice, feeling a wave of fury and confusion as he began to stand up from where he had been sitting, and then remembered and sat back down.

"You tried to kill mine!" Mafulla said, still in his chair.

"And both my parents," Kissa said, in a low voice. Then, she added, "And others in this room."

Santiago, remaining on his knees, said, "Yes. Yes, you're right. Tragically, I did all that. I did it when my soul was twisted and blind and mired in a fury of need and desperation that I didn't understand, and that I couldn't understand. But, thanks be given to the grace and goodness of God, and to your Ali, our Ali, my eyes were opened and my heart was remade. I now feel the deepest remorse you can imagine, and even more. I'm so sorry for all that I did, totally and abjectly sorry."

"But, my dad's gone forever," Walid protested, with a mixture of hopelessness and offense, and agitation and anger, and deep sadness all mixed together in his voice.

"No, not forever, if I may say," the man explained. "And he's close, so close even now. And one great and glorious day, you'll be reunited, the two of you, not here, but where he is. I've seen him. I've been with him, and I've talked with him. I've laid myself open to him and asked for his justice."

"What?"

"It was a crucial part of what happened, of my transformation. I had to confront the spirits of those I had harmed and that … I had … killed."

"Where? How?"

"It can't be fully explained. Our words that we have from this world are made primarily for this world. There's so much they can't say. But, in the other place where I was with Ali, I met your father for the first time, your wonderful Rumi, and I opened myself to him for whatever justice and punishment he would wish on me, however severe. And instead of that, he accepted me and forgave me, and wanted for me only healing and love."

"How can that be?"

"He was able to understand. It's the nature of love."

"But."

"He loves you even more than you can know, here and now, in this life." Santiago let out a deep breath and said, "We know so little here. We understand so little. I felt the love from him, and at the same time the searing rejection of my actions, of what I had done to separate him from you and your mother, and all of you. And I also experienced the inexpressible compassion that he had toward me in his heart, and the complete forgiveness that was offered to me freely. It flooded into me and through me, and was the completion of my transformation. And he gave me a job to do here with you."

"What do you mean?"

"I'm here because of your father's wishes. He knew that I have knowledge and power that will be needed soon to help you."

"You shouldn't be here with us at all. And I don't want your help. We don't want it." Walid felt only hard disgust and a wave of hot resentment.

"Yes, in this moment, and perhaps for a time. I understand. But you do want your father's wishes to be honored and respected. I know that. He's a great man, full of love. And you love him deeply."

"You shouldn't even speak of him—you, of all people! You have no right!"

"He … gave me the grace of that right, and it's now my duty. I stood before him, guilty and without defense. But when I met him, I had shed the evil, the wrong, and all the massive misunderstandings of my life. And it was your father, it was Rumi, who brought me to the highest peak of the transformative love that's enabled me to come back here to serve you and your good friends."

"I … can't."

"In your heart, I know you want what he most wants for you, with all the knowledge he now has, and all the love in his soul overflowing forever for you and your mother and Ali and these others." He paused for a moment and then said, "When we face him again, it will mean everything to hear him say that we've done well.

We need to honor him. You can honor him in this way. Please. I humbly beg you. Let go of your abundantly justified anger. Put it down. Release it. Take me in as the fully and deeply changed man that I am."

Walid was silent and shaking with emotion. A tear ran down his face, and then another. He was inwardly trembling all over and felt cold, and he was filled with rage and confusion and all the pent up emotions that he didn't know until now he still harbored within him, from what had been done. Mafulla had a similar tempest of feelings assaulting his mind and heart as he also listened to the man's words, despite his own desire not to feel such things.

Ali stood up, motioning for all the others to stay in their seats, and he walked over to Walid and bent down and put his arms around him and whispered something into his ear and held him, and everyone took it all in. And the man on his knees was still and silent, as if awaiting something. Then Walid started sobbing, with loud spasms of grief that bent him over. He shook and convulsed with the immensity of it all. And Ali continued to hold him. Then a warm and powerful inner sensation passed from the older man into him and through him. And there was something else, something healing.

And Kissa then jumped up and rushed to him and put her arms around him as well, to weep with and beside him. And after a couple of seconds, Mafulla hesitantly got up from his chair and walked over, with hardly a thought in his head, but with his own eyes full of tears, several running down his cheeks. And he bent down and put his hands on his friend and on Ali. And Hasina soon joined him and her Kissa, and Walid. Then, something welled up within these four young people, conveyed to each of them through Ali, and yet from somewhere, at once, far away, and at the same time so close as to be almost within them, but still beyond them and connected to them.

Time then seemed to stop to respect the moment and the fullness of all that was happening in it. The others in the room could hardly breathe.

At that point, Ali spoke again to Walid in a low and loving tone. And the Prince of Egypt nodded his head. The king looked at Mafulla and at Kissa and Hasina, and they each showed their agreement. And he then helped them all up and led them over to the man now still on the floor, and put his hand on this man's shoulder, and looked at him with a new, sudden rush of compassion and kindness and even a sort of strange pride in what this soul had now managed to do and allow and become.

Walid took a deep breath and let it out and then slowly and hesitantly put a hand on the man's other shoulder. "Oh!" The soul of the prince almost shouted in release. Mafulla moved around behind him and touched the man's head. Kissa did the same. And then, Hasina did. And they took a few moments in those positions, as the infinite significance of these small but great actions rippled around the room. Tears ran down their faces in streams. And everyone present felt what was happening.

Then Ali raised his face back to his friends seated across the room and said, "This is a man who has died to his ways and renounced his murderous flaws and has been reborn, brought back to us as the soul of strength and caring that he was originally intended to be." He paused and took a deep gathering of breath and said to them all, "The four of us are utterly overwhelmed and deeply gratified to present to you … our newest brother of the spirit who will soon be known as a friend, the man I now call … Oz."

There were plenty of tears throughout the room. This was uncharted country for them all. And it was in one way almost completely disorienting to everyone present. And yet, at the same time it was showing them things they knew and believed and had built their lives around, drawing on these truths and putting them front and center in a way and to a degree they had never experienced before.

These people of the warm sand were, in a sense, as surprised as they would be if they suddenly had blinked their eyes and found themselves at the frozen center of the South Pole, standing on slick ice and trying to walk, as painfully cold air began to crystalize their hair and skin. This was, in a sense, every bit as strange. But yet, it was also and at the same time deeply right. A murmur of comments could gradually be heard from various of them, with words and phrases like "unbelievable," and "I never imagined," and "I wouldn't have thought it possible," and "inconceivable," and "truly a miracle," and other such expressions of marvel and awe.

There were then several seconds of thick and profound, though still fragile, silence. And then Masoon was bold to look across the room at the man's face until he also looked up and their eyes met. And he addressed this former adversary directly in a statement that was really a question. "You … can be trusted now."

Oz nodded slowly and said, "Yes, my friend, if you will allow me to be presumptuous enough to call you that, in anticipation of the future."

"I hear your words. And I hear also and feel what's now behind them and within them." Masoon paused and said, "As unanticipated as all this is, and as hard to grasp fully, I will tell you that I trust what I feel. I trust the king and the prince. I trust in the deepest forces that we do not see. I believe in what's been at work in you and that's now touching us, all of us."

As Masoon said these words, every single person in the room could recognize that they had been feeling something deep in just the past few seconds, a sense of reassurance and an impulse to let go and accept this new thing, despite all that had happened before. It was a strange and powerful sensation, with a stirring that seemed to be opening each heart in order to convey the love behind all things to this formerly unholy and unworthy fellow, who was now apparently born anew. And so, in a new way, he was deserving of their regard, respect, and esteem.

Masoon slowly stood up and looked at the king, who had glanced his way, and he said, "If I may?" And as the king nodded, he walked quickly over to the man and offered him his hand and helped lift him slowly back to his feet.

Masoon then paused, as if in recognition of what was happening in each soul in the room, and then he said to the man, "I accept you and I welcome you as a fellow servant of the good, who will become our friend. And I will now know you by the name of Oz Ali. You are new."

Oz looked at Masoon and said, "Thank you, my brother. I am honored by what you call me." He turned and bowed to Walid and said, "Thank you from the innermost recesses of my fully changed heart." Then he made eye contact with Mafulla. "Thank you, deeply, my friend." And with Kissa: "Thank you, so much. Your great goodness assures me." And then, Hasina: "May you be richly blessed for your kindness, in this world and forever more."

Masoon then put his hand on the man's arm and said, "We all welcome you into the fellowship of the mind and heart that we enjoy together. You'll be a new brother of the spirit to us all."

"You won't regret your compassion," he said to Masoon. And then to all the others he said, "I promise you this: I'll seek in all ways to protect and support each one of you, and everything of value to you."

Mafulla then looked down at the man's left hand and said, "Is that the Ring of Gyges?"

"Yes, yes it is."

"And it can still make you invisible?"

"Yes. But now, it will not, without a truly good cause and purpose. By contrast, as a man, I want to be completely transparent in my motives and intentions, but never invisible to those who trust me, unless it's in the mutually desired service of our efforts together."

"You've truly changed," Mafulla said, and he then looked over at Ali.

The rightful King nodded and Oz replied, "Transformed by the alchemy of love, from the ultimate source of all."

"That's a good answer," Mafulla said, with no expression on his face or in his voice, and the happy incongruity of his tone evoked a few nodding heads and some odd smiles around the room, however suppressed they might be.

"Your Majesty," Masoon took a deep breath to clear his mind and interrupted at this point. "We have an urgent situation on our hands, with two of our young friends in captivity by violent people."

"Oh. I see."

"We need to fill you in on what's happened."

The king gestured toward the open chairs and said, "Please do so right away and we can get straight to work. My new companion will join us. I'm sure this is, at least initially, why he's here."

No one had really noticed Walid slip out of the room less than a minute earlier, or else had thought anything of it until he now reappeared and approached the king. "Your Majesty, I have something for you. Here's your watch that I've wound for you every morning since you've been away. So it's perfectly on time, as I think you are. You may need it for what's to come."

Ali smiled and said, "Thank you, Your Majesty."

"Wait. How did you know?"

"I knew that things would be done properly in my absence."

"I didn't feel right about it, but I had to say yes. And I've tried my best. But I've had a lot of help."

"I'm sure you have, and that you all have done a brave and marvelous job in a massively confusing and difficult situation."

Walid said, "We've all worked to honor you. But now, I suppose the one remaining part of my job that I need to do is to officially, in the presence of these witnesses, return the throne, the monarchy, and all duties and privileges of office to you, my dear Uncle Ali Shabeezar, the once, and now again, rightful King of Egypt." The prince bowed.

Ali smiled and said, "I thank you, and I gratefully accept your kind conveyance of role, duty, and right, in the presence of these witnesses. May the kingdom long flourish."

Many voices in the room joined in a second later, saying the same words, "May the kingdom long flourish!"

"Long live the king," Masoon said.

"Long live the king," everyone repeated. And there was muted applause.

And then the king said, "Thank you. And now, the time has fully come. Let us begin."

31

Time For Action

About an hour had passed, and maybe a little more. The meeting had broken up. A plan had been sketched out. Naqid had left to speak with Bancom and set in motion the gathering of a team. But otherwise, many of those present were just standing around, still talking in clusters across the room and in the hallway outside Kular's office.

Walid and Mafulla remained in the sitting room, in their chairs, talking intently with Oz Ali, who was patiently and gladly answering their questions the best he could. Hamid and Layla were standing nearby, just barely within earshot, as they spoke with each other and also continued to take the measure of this man whose mere presence among them was one of the more unlikely events in all of kingdom history, and perhaps in the overall human adventure. Haji and Malik were also close by and were listening intently to everything that was being said, both to and by Oz.

Kissa, Hasina, and Khata were with Hoda outside in the hallway where Hoda had been talking to Sab Maayuf for several minutes. Kissa and Hasina were at this point just a few feet away from them, speaking in hushed voices to each other while Khata stayed next to Hoda, listening to her conversation with the older man.

Then Khata, after several seconds of silently staring at the floor, spoke up. At first, the words felt like they were coming out on their own, apart from any conscious intent. They were just whispered, slowly, as if a surprised inner thought was making itself audible out in the world, but just barely. "I … know … where they are." Then, she turned to the older woman beside her and said, louder, but still not in a full voice, "Hoda! I know where they are!"

"What?"

"I know where Ara and Cabar are right now."

"You do?"

"Yes. I know where they're being held!"

"You can see it?"

"Yes, I can."

"Masoon!" Hoda called out, and then said to Khata, "We need to tell him right away." They walked the short distance down the hall to where the general was standing in conversation with King Ali.

"I'm sorry, Your Majesty. You both need to hear this."

The king looked at her and said, "What is it?"

Masoon also spoke up and asked, "What do you have for us?"

"Khata has just now seen where the girls are being held."

Ali looked at the young lady intently and asked her, "Can you describe the place?"

"Yes, Your Majesty. It's a plain looking building, pretty big, with lots of windows, but they're covered over with something from the inside. There's a door in the front and one in the back."

"Can you tell where this building is located?"

"Over not far from the river, where there are some old factories and warehouses. It's an otherwise empty one. There's an old metal fence around it, and in the back, there's a section of fence missing. The girls are in a room in the building, like an old office or something in the back, and they're tied to chairs, and they're scared."

"Do you see others?"

"Yes."

"How many?"

"I could see … five, I think, and maybe more, maybe two more. I'm not sure."

"Are they armed?"

"Yes. They have pistols and rifles."

"Where are they positioned?"

"There's one in the front, a second close to the front, one in back, and the rest are moving around. It's like I could see inside the building. I don't know how."

"You can trust your vision. Can you direct us there, to the building?"

"I think so. I think I can."

"Would that be safe?" Hoda asked him.

"If she could take us close enough, to make sure we had the right place, she could be escorted away before any action was taken."

Hoda looked at her and said, "Do you feel Ok about that?"

"Yeah. I do. I want to help my friends."

"Still, there could be some danger," Hoda said.

"It's all right. I guess I have to get used to that."

"Ok, then." Hoda said and turned to Masoon. "What now?"

"We go as soon as we can. Hoda, if you could take Khata down to the back entrance, I'll get the team together within ten to fifteen minutes, tops."

In the building Khata had seen, Ara and Cabar were sitting on wooden chairs, tied down by their arms and legs. They were also tied around their waists, exactly like Khata had seen. It was extremely uncomfortable. And they were both really frightened.

A woman had just come in to see them. She stood in front of them and said, "Here's what's going to happen, if you stay quiet and cooperative. Someone from your palace will bring us two items that we need and we'll exchange you for these things. It will happen tomorrow at noon. Until then, you'll remain here. You'll be fed soon and brought water to drink. We don't plan to harm you, but we'll be forced to if you try to resist, yell out, or escape."

"Don't hurt our families, please," Ara said.

The woman looked into her eyes and said, "They'll remain untouched and even unvisited, as long as you both cooperate. It would be a shame for you to be personally responsible for the death of your mother, or your cute little brother."

"How do you know about my brother?"

"We know more than you think. And we're prepared to kill everyone dear to you if you don't follow our orders."

An icy chill ran through Ara's heart. She had a vivid mental picture of her mom and dad, and of young Alim, her sweet and smart brother.

"We'll do anything you want us to do," Cabar said while Ara was envisioning the family she needed to protect.

"Good," the woman replied and walked out of the room.

The girls were silent for a few seconds and then Cabar whispered, "Did you see her arm?"

"What? No." Ara whispered back.

"She had a drawing or something of a black spider. I think it was the kind that Hoda talked to us about."

"I didn't see it."

"Her sleeves were rolled up a little and I saw it on her left forearm. It creeped me out."

"I was looking at her face. I didn't notice. She really scares me."

"We need to get out of here."

"They'll kill our families! You heard her," Ara whispered back.

"It could just be a threat. She could be lying to intimidate us. Maybe they don't have anyone near our houses."

"But then how would she know about Alim?"

"Maybe she saw him one day with you. Who knows? But she and her friends or helpers, or whatever they are, may all be here right now, with no one near our homes to carry out the threats. Maybe the threats are just empty and meant to control us."

"We can't take the chance."

"Silence!" A voice outside the room boomed out and another woman stuck her head into the doorway. "Be quiet in here! No speaking!" she barked, momentarily glaring at the girls, and then she disappeared.

Across town, Bara El-Ari was sitting on the sofa in her suite at the Grand Hotel. Her son Ebar was in a chair near her, reading the paper. A slight sound announced a note that was being slid under their door. Ebar stood and walked over to retrieve it. Unfolding it, he read it aloud. "The guests have arrived and we expect the party to begin tomorrow at lunch time. We'll be in touch."

"Oh, marvelous."

"Mother, I wonder, should we be more involved at this point?"

"Why do you ask?"

"I just worry."

"What's the concern?"

"I'm afraid that if they get the items with this first plan, they'll simply disappear and leave us with nothing. What reason would they have to include us?"

"Well, we do have a deal."

"Yes. But what will that mean to them if they haven't had to use our form of access? They won't feel like they owe us anything. These aren't the most honorable and generous people. They're bound by nothing but their mission. I don't think we can trust them at all."

"I see your point," she said. "And it's a good one. Perhaps we should indeed involve ourselves now, before the potential culmination of it all. We need to be there for the delivery."

"But we don't know where they are."

"They gave us a contact."

"The lady at the embassy?"

"Yes, the one they described as a short, red haired woman who works there. They said that if we needed to get in touch, we should make contact with her and she'd get a message through to them."

"That must mean she knows where they are."

"I'd assume so."

"But if we asked their whereabouts, I'd be almost sure she'd dodge the question or just flat out refuse to tell us, saying they need privacy or stealth."

"Well, suppose we don't ask so nicely as to give her a way to refuse."

"You mean?"

"Yes. We have to bear down in pursuit of our dreams."

Ebar looked impressed. "I think you're right, mother. When should we visit her?"

"When she leaves work this afternoon."

"It's getting late."

"Well then, we'd better get over there."

"But, wait. Isn't Elam coming by?

"Oh, yes, yes he is."

"Should you cancel that?"

"He has no telephone."

"You're right. When's he supposed to arrive?"

She glanced at her small, elegant wristwatch and said, "Oh! He should be here in just a few minutes. I'd completely forgotten. He's just coming over for a time of talk. We set it up on his last visit. I'm still working to prepare him to do whatever we might need him to do."

"Yes, and that's good. But if we're going to the embassy now, should I quickly get downstairs and meet him and tell him you're not feeling well? We could reschedule for this time tomorrow."

Bara thought for a moment. "No, actually, let's take him along."

"What?"

"I think that now may be the time. I've woven my web. And the honey I've put on it has succeeded in attracting the fly. I have something in mind that should get him to go along with whatever we have to do, and he may be of help."

"Are you sure about this?"

"Quite sure. Sometimes, you have to trust your instincts."

"Well, I trust yours."

"Good boy. You'll be duly rewarded."

Upstairs at the palace, Masoon walked back into the king's sitting room. He saw the men he sought standing over to the side, talking. "Paki! Omari! Amon! I need you now. I want you to go down to the guardroom, arm yourselves heavily but quickly, and meet me in ten minutes at the rear door. A truck will be waiting."

"Right away, boss," Paki said, and the three of them headed for the door.

Walid looked up from where he was sitting. "What's going on?"

"We have new information. Khata has seen where the girls are being held captive and she's offered to guide us there."

"Who's going?"

"Hamid and I will lead a team of the three who just left, plus you and Mafulla, if you'd like to go."

"Yeah, of course. I know Haji and Malik will want to go, as well."

"Haji's too involved emotionally. He and Malik need to stay here to help guard the scrolls with the king and Sab."

"How can I help?" Oz Ali spoke up from several feet away.

Masoon looked at him intently. "How strong and skilled are you now?"

"In your terms, I think, level five, and perhaps beyond."

"How do you know?"

"Ali."

Masoon hesitated for just a second and pulled out a knife so quickly that no one could even get a good look at it before he threw it at full speed toward the man's left shoulder, handle first, so that it could badly bruise him if what he had said was false, but not wound him.

Before anyone else could react at all, Oz had caught it in mid-air by the handle, while twisting away from it. He actually smiled at Masoon and said, "Nice test. Nonlethal, but serious."

"Good reaction. Impressive, in fact," Masoon replied and asked, "How strong are you in hand-to-hand?"

"As strong as you need me to be. Probably less than you, but good enough for any purpose I can easily imagine."

"Level five, also?"

"I think so."

"You can handle all standard military weapons effectively?"

"Yes."

"Would you like to join us under my command?"

"I would relish the chance to begin to make a difference."

"We'll be trusting you with our lives."

"I'll be worthy of your trust." Oz took a few steps and handed the knife back to Masoon.

Masoon took it and said, "All right. We'll clear it with the king, if it's acceptable to the prince." He looked over at Walid.

This was all happening so fast. Walid took a deep breath, and said, "Well, everything else is otherwise just words at this point, isn't it? What we do shows what we think." He looked over at Mafulla and made eye contact with his friend. Something passed between them, and the prince looked back at Masoon and said, "Ok. It's time to take action and make a difference together. Let's go."

32

Feelings

When the old gentleman, Elam al-Buri, arrived a short time later at the Grand Hotel, Ebar was downstairs to meet him in the lobby and take him up to their suite.

"Elam! Greetings! I know Mother's excited to see you today. Let's go up to the rooms."

"Oh, thank you, Ebar! It's good to see you again. And it's always a joy to be around your mother," Elam smiled and said. "I can't believe how long it's been in our lives since we first knew each other, and yet in other ways it seems like no time at all since we were young." He followed the younger man to the elevator as they continued to talk.

"She's a remarkable lady, and still so young in so many ways," Ebar said.

"Yes, she is. She's truly remarkable."

"She says you make her feel like a school girl again." He smiled.

"Good! But are you sure this is all right? I mean, are you fine with it?" Elam asked. "I would never want to make you uncomfortable, or try to take the place of your late father."

"No, no, I approve wholeheartedly. My father was a difficult man. He was absent a lot and there was great stress in the house when he was around. He was not a happy man, I'm afraid. It's finally time that my mother can have some joy come back into her life." They had now arrived at their floor. They walked a few steps down the hall and at the door to the suite, Ebar took his key, unlocked the door, and pushed it open for the older man, gesturing for him to enter first.

Bara had fixed herself just so and was awaiting Elam, armed with all the charm and beauty she could muster.

"Oh, there's my man!" she exclaimed as he walked through the door.

"My wonderful dear friend, you're so kind to me," he replied. "And you look marvelous, as always. I love that dress!"

"You're so nice. Come, give me a hug," she said, and moved slightly toward him with the bracelets jingling on her now open arms.

"Gladly! That's an invitation no one could refuse," he said, as he spread his own arms and embraced her in as gentlemanly a way as he could in the presence of her son. And as he drew close, her perfume awakened all his senses and transported him to a new place in his heart.

"Now," she said, pushing him only slightly back so she could look in his eyes. "Let's sit. I have something important to share with you."

"I'm eager to hear whatever you would tell me."

"Ebar? Would you bring us some tea?"

"Yes, mother, right away." The younger man turned and walked across the large sitting room, as Bara and Elam relaxed together on the elegant sofa. Within a moment, he had delivered two cups of tea on elegant saucers, placed them down, and excused himself into his bedroom to finish a letter he said he was writing. He wanted to leave the two of them alone. And his mother approved.

She took Elam's hand into hers. A large diamond ring caught the light and sparkled brightly on her finger. She tilted her head ever so slightly and spoke in the voice of an angel. "I hope you know how much you mean to me."

"I'm overwhelmed to say that I think I do. And I can assure you the feelings are mutual and deep."

She let her gaze linger on his eyes and through them and said, "I never want this feeling to end."

"I don't, either."

"I mean it, literally."

"I feel the same way, dear one."

"Well, then, there's something we can do about that."

"What is it?"

She lifted one of her hands up to push back her cascading long hair, and primarily to call attention to it. It was one of her features of which she was extremely proud. Even at her current age, her hair was thick and lustrous, and almost glowed in the light. The rings and the many bracelets she was wearing sparkled with her movement and directed Elam's eyes to that hair, as she now tossed it back and smiled. And it had precisely the effect that she intended. His heart was hers at even a new level, and he was even deeper in thrall to her charms.

"I've met the people who desperately want your scrolls."

"You have? How?"

"It was largely by chance, or perhaps the intent of a greater purpose. You know, I believe that love will have its way in the world."

"I do, too, and we're living proof of that."

She smiled even broader, and in a way that was dazzling. That was another of her powers that she knew and was using to the full, as she often did. She could almost hypnotize with her smile.

"Aren't those people extremely dangerous?" Elam asked.

"Well, I met them right here in the hotel, down in the dining room. Ebar and I were having something to eat, and they were sitting close to us. I overheard a part of their conversation and noticed right away their German accents, so I went over and had to introduce myself."

"Oh my, you are brave, indeed," he said.

"Something told me it was the right thing to do. There were two of them, a man and a woman. They looked normal, European, and in age, I'd say mid-forties, at the most."

"What did you say to these people?"

"I just struck up a conversation and hinted that I knew there were some things in town that some Germans would very much like to have in their possession, and that I might be able to help."

"Really?"

She laughed and said, "I was quite persuasive, and they identified themselves as the people who were in pursuit of an item or two. I think they realized they might need help."

"And you could help?"

"Yes! Because of you, dear man."

"Me? But, you know I don't have the scrolls now."

"Well, since you owned them for so long and you know the current owners, I reasoned that we had connections that might be able to help them get closer to, or perhaps even access, the artifacts without any more inappropriate violence or roughness."

"Do you think that's a good idea?"

"Oh, yes! And I can explain it fully."

"What did you have in mind in your approach to them?"

She laughed and said, "I didn't really know! But I was acting on instinct at that point. Something deep inside me told me that you and I need the secrets of those scrolls so that we can stay together forever and grow deeper into our love for each other."

"That would be wonderful," he said. "If they contain such secrets, it would be everything I want."

"I'm sure they do."

"But how?"

"The presence and methods of such people here confirms it, don't you think?"

"Well, perhaps you're right."

"Serious people don't go chasing around the world for silly nonsense."

"You have a good point."

"And since these people are in such fervent pursuit of the scrolls, it occurred to me that it would be better to have them as friends than as enemies."

"I see. That's very shrewd."

"I told them that I was interested in personally viewing the documents they sought, and learning their contents. So, I proposed an alliance. They were at first skeptical, but I told the woman, who seemed to be the one in charge, that I had special access in a way that couldn't be replicated and that, together, we might be able to attain our distinct goals. I told her about you and I even mentioned that, because of you, my son had recently held the scrolls in his hands, while sitting in the midst of the building where they're now being protected."

"Oh, my. You were indeed persuasive. You know just what to say."

"Yes, thank you. Always. And I assured her quite specifically that I didn't need to possess the items themselves, only to know their content, and that she could have the original artifacts to do with as she chose. You and I could simply copy and use the secrets in them, regain our youth, and then sell the unique information to others for the fortune we'd need in order to be able to support ourselves in suitable comfort and opulence for all our additional days of love and wonderful living."

Elam looked pleased. He said, "That's brilliant! What did they say?"

"I was a bit surprised. They quickly agreed. They had tried so many other things already, and I presented them with a new option that really had no downside. So they accepted my proposal."

"What does it mean for us? How can we actually help them, to help us, of course?"

"Well, they had a plan already underway that they said might work. They wanted to play it out first, before using our contacts in the palace."

"I see. And we then become partners after that?"

"No, actually, we became partners at their table in the dining room, at that moment. Part of the deal was that, after our conversation, whoever managed to access the scrolls would share with the other party in the ways promised."

"But if they get what they want, and by their own plan, what will you or we have provided that they will value enough to think of us as deserving our part of the prize, even though we'd not be taking anything away from them but the time to copy the secrets in the important parts of the scrolls?"

"We will have provided them with a solid backup plan and so a sort of insurance that they didn't have on their own, and a plan so good that they will consider it to have been a guarantee, based on what I told them. Of course, I built up my access far beyond any thought of how we might be able to make that work. And without questioning me, they bought it. I think it was my confidence. That always works. People like confidence."

"I'm not at all surprised by your success. You have a way. But do you think they'll keep their word and hold up their end of the bargain, especially if their own previously launched strategy works?"

"No, actually, I don't."

Now, he laughed. "You don't?"

"No. I think that if their current plan gets them the scrolls, we'll never see them again."

"Is there anything we can do?"

"That's what I've just realized, only a few minutes ago, before you arrived. We can leave right now and go to where these people are and make ourselves part of the action before the scrolls come into their possession. If their original plan were to work, then we'll be there when it happens. And so they won't be able to avoid us and simply cut us out of the deal. But to do that, we have to act right away."

"When will they get the scrolls, if their plan does work?"

"Soon, I think, before the end of the day tomorrow. So we'd have to join them as soon as we can."

"It could be dangerous. They might indeed still want to betray us."

"We'll be prepared for that."

"Really?"

"Yes. I'm always prepared." She answered with that confidence that had so often led people to believe her without any hesitation.

"So, do you know what they're doing now in their present effort to get the scrolls?"

"No. I didn't ask."

"But at least you know where these people are to be found?"

"Actually, I don't. Not yet. But a woman at the German Embassy knows, and we know how to find her."

"Will she tell you or lead you to them?"

"I think we can make it happen. We need to. It's our only hope, or we'll certainly lose the chance we have for a love together, forever."

"We can't lose that."

"No, we can't. And, dear Elam, remember, if the secret is what we think it is, it won't just give us the opportunity for endless love, but we'll be returned to our youthful vigor. Can you imagine how wonderful that will be?" She tilted her head and intimated in a lower voice, "In those days, I had the heart of a tigress, and an endless exuberance for all the good things of life. And now, if we do this right, we'll be young together again, and this time, forever."

He squeezed her hand and said, "I truly want that!"

"If the three of us go to the Embassy now and arrive before they close for the day, we can find the contact, a red haired woman, before she leaves and get from her the information we need. And I'm afraid that if we don't act now, right now, it will simply be too late."

"What will we do?"

"You and I can wait outside the embassy and when we see her, we'll approach her with friendliness. No one will fear a couple our age, dressed as nicely as we are, out in public. We'll engage her in conversation, and Ebar will be nearby to help us persuade her to answer our questions. This can make our dreams happen."

"Yes, yes. But I have a remaining question."

"Certainly, darling."

"If we find the Germans, and their current plan for obtaining the scrolls doesn't work, how do you think we can help to get them?"

"I have ideas on that, certainly, some good ideas, but let's take one thing at a time. If we don't leave now, we'll miss our chance at any options whatsoever. I'm completely sure of that. Our destiny now calls and we need to answer!"

"Yes. I agree. Let's answer the call."

In the palace, King Ali had approved Masoon's plan, and the men who were going off to follow Khata's lead were already downstairs and ready to leave. They thought it best to stage the rescue with only a small number of expert operatives involved.

Sab had given the king a brief account of the large meeting where he had revealed his big secret, and to say that Ali was surprised would be a tremendous understatement. But the unexpected revelations resonated deeply and made sense of so much that he had long felt about his old friend and neighbor. He instantly saw the many details of their long relationship in a new light, and he laughed heartily at a few jokes that Sab was making about his age and accumulated wisdom. The much older man now also speculated that, as close as the stone had been to Ali since shortly after he took office, its natural anti-aging effects on him were probably already well underway. In addition, he suggested that these effects to some extent might be felt by Walid and Mafulla as well, though not by reversing age at their early stage of life, but in terms of protecting them, to some extent, against harm, while enhancing their vigor and keeping their bodies and minds healthy in all ways.

Ali's first thought on hearing this was that if his brother Rumi had just been exposed to the stone and its effects more and for a bit longer, a great tragedy could possibly have been avoided for the entire family. But, as his wisdom would have it, his very next thought was that, in ways we can't now fully understand, things must indeed happen as they need to, and often, despite our desires and hurts. There was an old saying relevant to this that came to him. We do our best and release the rest. Ultimately, the unfortunate events that enter our lives need not, in the end, keep from us the ultimate goods that we aspire to experience. It's the role of faith to stay strong amid all the "might-have-been scenarios" that we can conjure and otherwise regret not having had the chance to enjoy. Faith and hope can indeed be as important in life as love.

Sab also reassured Ali that he and Meskhenet still felt the effects of the stone in their own lives, in terms of health, physical strength, and other forms of power, and to the extent, he said, that he could indeed be of help in watching the scrolls and protecting them from any attempt at violent theft. The two men then had even more laughs together as they joked on about this and shared their keen sense of humor over it all, as only two deeply kindred spirits can.

Hoda and Layla were staying at the palace for a simple, light and informal dinner with Kissa and Hasina, the king and Sab. Hoda had sent a note to Khalid, briefly explaining what was going on and letting him know that the two of them would be part of a special guard detail for a while, and perhaps even all evening. A palace messenger had taken him the news.

Some distance away, at a private family home, there was a knock at the door, but at first no one heard it. Then, there was another knock, and another, louder and more insistent. Ama al-Sout called out, "Jabari! There's someone at the door! Could you answer it?"

"Sure, mom!" Jabari called back to her, jumped up from the floor, and walked quickly from his room, closing the door behind him on his way to the front door. He opened it and was surprised to see Set and Bafur standing there.

"Hey, guys, what's up?" Jabari said, a big smile on his face, as soon as he saw them. But he noticed instantly that they weren't smiling.

"Hey, can we come in and talk?" Set said.

"Sure. Is something wrong?"

"Maybe," Bafur offered.

"Oh? Ok, Come on in."

The boys entered and Jabari said, "You want to go to my room?"

"Yeah," Set said.

Ama called out from somewhere, "Jabari, who is it?"

"Just Set and Bafur! We're going to my room!"

"Ok, good. Say hi to them."

"Mom says hi."

"Yeah, thanks," Bafur replied. Then he looked in her direction and said louder, "Hi Back, Mrs. Al-Sout," as they followed Jabari.

"Come on in," he said and opened his bedroom door. Manni

was on the other side of the room, quietly playing with a ball. But as soon as he saw the boys, he jabbered in monkey language and gave them a single screech, which they supposed was a sort of jungle shout-out of friendly greeting.

"Hey, Manny," Set said. "Good monkey."

"Yeah, hey, monkey man," Bafur added. "How's everything in Banana-land?"

"E, E, E," was all that Manny said in reply.

Then Bafur got serious again and said, "I saw something and I'm worried about it."

"What?"

"I was out for a walk a couple of hours ago. You know, I'm trying to maybe lose a few pounds and get healthier."

"Yeah, I know. How's it going?"

"Not bad. But when I was walking, a car went by and I happened to look up and there was Ara, and maybe Cabar in the back seat, but I couldn't be sure it was Cabar. She was sort of blocked partially. But I think so. And I saw Ara clearly, and she looked really scared or strange or something, and in the front seat of the car was some woman I've never seen and maybe a man driving, and I got a weird feeling right away. Something seemed wrong."

"Really?"

"Yeah."

"So what happened?"

"Well, Ara saw me, and put her hand against the glass of the window, spread out, with her fingers on the glass."

"Ok."

"It was like she was asking for help or something."

"Seriously? Oh, man."

"Yeah," Set spoke up and said. "And Bafur came over to my house to tell me about it, and we thought we'd better go tell Khalid. But then it came to me that maybe we should stop here first and get you."

"Why me?"

"I don't know, you and Manny are sort of a super-team in times of trouble, and you were on the way to Khalid's."

"Oh, Ok. But Manny's the super guy. I'm just me," Jabari said.

"Well, you want to go with us?" Set asked.

"Sure, but you know what?"

"What?"

"Manny was acting strange a little earlier, maybe about the time you saw Ara, and maybe also Cabar," he said.

"What do you mean, strange?"

"He suddenly started yelling and twirling around."

"Really?"

"Yeah, like there was something going on he didn't like, but he was just here in the room and nothing had happened to set him off, or I mean, nothing here."

"Wow, you think, maybe he somehow knew?"

"With Manny, it's possible. Who knows?"

"You want to come with us, then?"

"Sure. And Manny, too?"

"Of course," Set said. "We always need the super-simian."

"Yeah," Bafur echoed. "And I think the sooner we get there, the better. I'm really worried."

"Me, too," Set said. "I've got a bad feeling about this that I don't understand."

"Now, I've got a strange feeling, too," Jabari said, with a look of concern on his face. "I'll tell mom we're going over to Khalid's for a few minutes. She'll be fine with it." He grabbed his backpack and Manny jumped in. "Let's go."

33

Into the Web

They stood on the sidewalk near the German Embassy and talked. "There she is," Bara whispered to Elam when she saw the woman of interest leave the building. Then, a few seconds later, she said aloud, "Excuse me! Madam? Excuse me, please!"

The lady stopped and turned. "Yes? How can I help you?"

"My husband and I are in need of a word with you."

"Is it about embassy business?"

"Well."

"If so, our office will reopen at ten o'clock in the morning."

"No, no, it's of a more personal nature."

"I'm sorry?"

"No, it's I who am sorry," Bara said with her most gracious smile. "I hate to bother you like this after your hard day at work, but I have an urgent message that I've been told you would want to hear."

The lady looked wary but said, "What's the message?"

"There's something I'm supposed to give you. It's from some of your countrymen who are here in Egypt on a special assignment. I've been assured that you'll know what the item means, however puzzling it might be to me. My son has it around the corner in our car."

"In your car?"

"I couldn't carry it. But I can show it to you quickly, if you have just a moment." As Bara said this, Elam, standing behind her, just smiled.

The lady from the embassy said, "I don't understand."

"It's a puzzle to me, as well. But the Germans who approached me insisted I come here with it for you. I'll have to ask you what to do with it." Bara smiled and shrugged. "They said it was an urgent matter."

The still surprised administrator said, "Well, all right, I suppose."

Then Bara touched her arm and, beaming, made a joke and completely disarmed the women with some instant and charming small talk as she led her around the corner and on to the side street where indeed there was a car parked. It was one they had obtained for hire through the hotel. Ebar was sitting in it, and as soon as he saw the three of them approach, he got out and waved and smiled, as his mother had. Then he jogged around to the passenger side and opened the door as if there was something inside that he was going to get out for the lady. She looked at Bara quizzically, but trusted her pleasant face and walked over toward the spot where Ebar was now holding the door and bending into the car. Then, just as she drew near, he pulled a loaded revolver from his belt and pointed it at her, holding it low so that no one else who might appear on the street could see.

"Get into the car, now," he said in a low voice.

"What? What is this?"

"Your last moment on earth unless you do as he says," Bara answered, with a strong tone of conviction that persuaded the lady to comply with the threat, against all her instincts to the contrary. She slowly climbed into the automobile and to the back seat, as directed, while desperately trying to think what to do to get out of this situation, whatever it might be.

"I'll have no hesitation to shoot you right here," Ebar said in a low voice. "It isn't even my car, so someone else will have to clean up the mess."

"But."

"You need to be quiet and just answer our questions, to escape any harm."

The woman was sitting in the back at this point, as she had been told, and was further surprised that the older man, Elam, now joined her, coming in from the other side and pushing at her a bit with the words, "Slide over a touch, if you don't mind."

"Why are you doing this?"

"I'm so sorry for the inconvenience, and of course for any upset that this is causing you," he replied. "But our need is great, and I'm afraid we have no time for normal pleasantries."

"Who are you and what do you want?" she asked.

"In a moment."

At that instant, Bara got into the front seat of the car and Ebar went back around to the driver's side and slid in while closing his door. Bara turned and said, "We need to know right now where your recently arrived German friends are, the ones who are in pursuit of the scrolls."

"I have no idea what you're talking about."

"Well then, you're no good to me, so we'll make it clean and get you to the edge of town to kill you and leave your body. Start the car, son."

Ebar started it up and the lady said, "No, wait. I know nothing about any scrolls, but I do know there's a team of operatives here from my homeland, and they're on a sensitive mission. They're likely the ones you're talking about."

"Do you know where they are?"

"I know how to get a message through to them."

"I need you to take us to them."

"I'm afraid I can't do that."

"Well then, you should be afraid of much more." She looked at Ebar and said, "Drive us to the edge of town, to that remote place."

The lady said in a tone of desperation, "No, wait. I have strict orders."

"We don't care about that. We need to see our partners right now."

"Your partners?"

"Yes. We've entered into a partnership with them, but they were keeping their current location secret, even from us, until a plan they're enacting has a chance to play out today. And yet now, something's come up and we need to get word to them in person, right away, and with no delays. They'll want to see us, once we get there and they hear what I have to tell them. I can assure you of that. You won't be in trouble at all for leading us to them."

"You're sure of this?"

"Of course I am."

"They've mentioned a lady who might need to be in touch with them."

"I'm the lady."

"But they didn't say anything about being taken to where they are. That wasn't a part of my job."

"Well, jobs can change, and yours has, today. Unfortunately, you already know the alternative."

"Ok, all right, there's no need of further threats. I can see that you're serious, and you wouldn't likely know about me unless you were the person they mentioned to me, so I suppose this can be acceptable. I'll cooperate with you. I'm sure they'll understand when they hear all the circumstances."

"Good. Take us to them right now." Bara spoke with decisiveness in her voice. "Direct my driver."

"Ok, turn the car around and get back on the main avenue. I'll give you the directions you want. Those you seek are in a building recently purchased by the embassy for storage. But I can simply tell you how to get there. You don't need me to guide you all the way. I can get out as soon as I've written down the directions and drawn you a map."

"No, the directions could be false and the map fake, and you'd be home free. You'll stay with us until we see our partners in person."

Not far from where this conversation was taking place, there was a far different and much more benevolent gathering underway, however serious it still was. "So, what do you girls think?" Hoda asked, as the four of them sat at the king's table alone for a quick, early dinner.

"Well, it's a lot to get our heads around," Kissa said.

"That's for sure," Hasina added. "I was just telling mom that I can hardly process all that's happened in just the past couple of days. First, Sab's big wild revelation, then the kidnapping happens, King Ali's back, and now a changed Santiago appears."

"Oz Ali," Kissa said to her friend.

"What?"

"Oz Ali, remember? He's not called Santiago any more."

"Right. Ok, yes. Oz Ali. It's just all too much."

"It is a lot," Layla said. "In fact, I can't recall a point when there were more big developments in such a short time."

"We've all been through a lot since the wonderful day the king came to power," Hoda reflected. "Along with so much good, there have been all the adversaries in various guises that we've had to face, from ordinary criminals to legendary monsters. But this series of developments is indeed the biggest ever."

"For sure," Hasina said.

Kissa said, "Some of the stuff, like about Sab and Meskhenet, is clearly great, even though it was so totally unexpected, and it really sounded almost crazy at first—like, is this a gigantic joke?"

"Yeah, really. I'm just glad to have some much older friends, for a change," Hasina remarked, as she took another fork full of stew.

Kissa laughed and said, "Yeah, older."

"There's a wise saying," Layla offered. "Older friends show us the way forward, younger friends give us the energy to get there."

"I've always liked that," Hoda commented. And then she looked back at Kissa and said, "But really, and I mean it: How are you girls doing, emotionally, at this point?"

"Pretty worried about Ara and Cabar," she answered.

"Worried?" Hoda asked.

"Um. Concerned."

"That's better."

"And Santi … I mean, Oz Ali, is going along on the rescue mission?" Hasina said.

"Yes, he is," Hoda answered. "The king confirmed it to me."

"Well, the king has always known what he's doing before, so I guess his choice about that deserves our wholehearted trust right now, even though it's maybe a little quick for my spirit to adjust to," Hasina said.

"Yeah, we had no chance to get used to this whole transformed man thing and, boom, they were off," Kissa said.

"Well, let's hope there's no boom," Hasina commented.

"True."

"And, poor Haji. He must be feeling so helpless in all this," Hasina said.

"Although, I have to say, Masoon made the right call on that, as usual," Hoda remarked. "Haji's just too close to Ara right now to be included in this mission. Serious mistakes could result."

"But, I bet he would have been brave and done something decisive if he had been present when the kidnap first happened," Kissa said.

"Well, yes, we have to be prepared at all times to defend our loved ones and ourselves in any threatening situation. We make the most of what we have and who we are. But in a strategic or tactical situation where there's time to plan an assault and you have plenty of options, it's always good if a young man Haji's age can be put onto another task, supposing that some other activity of importance, or even perceived importance, is available. It would have been bad to just ask him to go home and wait, or even to stay here and wait. But putting him on the immediate scroll protection team in the palace was a good idea. He has a job to keep him focused and occupied. And Masoon's group can operate without any concern in the backs of their minds about anyone's emotions getting in the way."

"Yeah, Ok, that makes sense. I understand," Kissa said.

"Me, too," Hasina added.

"Mom, why aren't you and Layla, or at least one of you, on the rescue team?"

"We had to stay here to guard the scrolls."

"But couldn't the king do that just fine by himself?"

"Yes. But I'm supposed to be here, for whatever reason," Hoda said.

"I feel the same way," Layla agreed.

"Ok, that's good enough for me," Kissa replied.

"Before we go on our stretch of guard duty, I think we need to take some time together in meditation and prayer for the girls and their rescuers," Hoda said. "We want everyone back safe."

"I've already been praying for them," Kissa said.

"Good," Layla commented. "The girls have been on my heart and mind since we heard the news. I've been asking for their ability to stay calm, deep down, below any surface fright, and for them to have clear heads so they can make wise decisions in big or small ways during this terribly stressful time."

"Yeah, I guess it's really different when there's a mission to rescue a Phi," Hasina said. "We know what to do when an assault starts. We can mostly see it coming and join in the flow, but Ara and Cabar ..."

"Well, remember how Masoon led a team to rescue Mafulla's family that time, and none of them had any training, either. They were all fine in the end—a little shook up, but fine," Kissa said.

"True."

"I'm just concerned that these aren't normal adversaries, you know, like your ordinary local thieves and political bad guys," Layla said. "These Black Widows have lots of training, apparently, and could give our guys some fierce resistance."

"Yeah, but remember, our team has a new member, formerly known as The Monster of Legend, no less. And he may be able to provide a new kind of edge," Kissa said.

"Life is strange," Hoda commented.

"It sure is," Hasina replied.

"And sometimes, I suspect that it's even much stranger by far than we could ever imagine or realize," Layla added.

"You said it, sister," Hoda responded. "You said it there."

The rented car pulled up outside the abandoned factory building. "This is it?" Bara said. "This is the place?"

"Yes," the lady with red hair answered.

"You're sure?"

"I'm sure. Now, will you let me go?"

"No, I'm afraid not."

"What will you do with me?"

"You'll go in with us."

"Why?"

"We still don't know that you've guided us accurately. Until we see our partners in person, you're on probation, and you're life's still on the line."

"And what then?"

"Well, in principle, you'll be free to go. But, how, I'm not yet sure."

"What do you mean?"

"You can't have the car. And we don't have time to take you back. And who knows if there's any other transportation around? So it looks like you'll have to be patient, at a minimum."

"I've done my part. I've done as you asked."

"So you say."

"You should have your driver take me home. He can find his way back here just fine at this point."

"Save your voice. We'll do what's right for us. And you're coming in with us now." Bara turned to her son and said, "Cut off the motor. We're going in."

"All of us?"

"What do you mean?"

"Shouldn't someone stay with the car?"

"Why?"

"I don't know. Maybe you're right. We should all go in. I'll lock the doors."

They all got out. Elam looked a little stiff and was moving a bit more slowly than normal. Bara noticed but didn't say anything. He might have been cramped in the back seat, and it had taken them a lot longer to get here than she had expected.

One of the Black Widows saw the car pull up and watched

everyone get out. It looked like two couples, and one of them an older pair, although the age of that woman couldn't be determined from a distance. She seemed to dress in a youthful way and with a degree of extravagant elegance, at least for someone alighting from a car outside a long abandoned building in the industrial part of town. And there were two others, a man and a woman, it appeared, who could possibly be their family. This was very odd, and unexpected.

"Greta!" The guard called toward the back of the building.

"What is it?"

"Someone's here."

"What do you mean?"

"Someone has pulled up in front and gotten out of a car."

"Who is it?"

"I don't know. There are two older people, a man and a woman, and a younger couple with them, it seems."

"Two couples?" Greta began to walk toward the front of the building.

"From appearances."

"Let me see."

"There."

"Oh. No, no, no."

"What?"

"The staff member at the embassy we trusted—that's her—the younger one, the red head. And she's with that woman from the hotel, the person who wanted to partner up with us to get the scrolls."

"What are they doing here?"

"I have no idea. No one was supposed to be brought here."

"What should I do?"

"Well, at this point, I suppose, just let them in. They're no obvious threat. We'll see what they want. But be prepared to eliminate them all if I give the signal, or I move in that direction myself."

"Kill them?"

"Of course. She only thinks she's a partner. And the younger man is her son."

"Who is the older one?"

"I have no idea. Wait. He may be the original owner of the scrolls we're seeking."

"Really?"

"Yes. She told me about him, a man about her age, but he'll likely look yet older. That's what she said."

"Then that could be the man."

"Ok, this might be more interesting than I at first thought. Let them in and send them back to me." Greta turned and walked back toward the rear of the building, near the office where the girls were being held hostage.

The visitors began to walk from their car toward the front gate in the surrounding fence. It had been left unlocked. Ebar swung it open, and gestured for the others to go through. He then followed, to keep his eye on the woman with red hair and not let her get far from where he could reach her.

As they walked up to the front door of the building, it opened, and a guard stood before them in western garb, holding a military issue rifle of some sort. Bara spoke. "I'm looking for my friend Greta."

The guard replied, "She's inside and is expecting you."

Bara turned to look at Elam and then Ebar with a puzzled expression, and then she said, "Good."

"Please come in."

"Thank you," she responded, and they all entered the building, with no idea of what was about to happen.

34

The Assault

Khata's guidance was accurate. Her natural Phi skills were unusually acute. She directed the men down streets she had never physically seen and through turns that, from a normal point of view, she would have no way of knowing, Finally, she told the driver to stop and pull over. From where the truck parked, they could see the old factory building up ahead a short distance. And it was surrounded by fence. A single car was sitting out front.

"That's where the girls are," Khata said, as she pointed. "They're in a room in the back, on the left side, from our point of view. It's an old office. They're against the left wall in the room, tied to wooden chairs. There are seven women and one man I can see who are involved in this. They've been there for a while. Two other men and two women have just gotten out of that car a couple of minutes ago, at most, and joined the rest of them inside. The door was opened to them and they were invited in. The new arrivals are inside voluntarily and aren't afraid. They must somehow also be a part of this."

Masoon said, "Thank you, Khata. Is there anything else we should know?"

"I can't think of anything. That's all I've seen and felt."

"It's all we need. I'll have the guards in the truck behind us take you back home. Your mother knows you're helping us with something. We told her that you're safe and well protected. But still, she may want to hear from you soon."

"Ok, thanks, but can I go back to the palace, instead of straight home?"

"Why do you ask?"

"I want to be around to find out what happens, you know, with this."

"You're sure?"

"Yeah. I feel something like a sense of duty, or responsibility, and that maybe, in some way, my part isn't quite over."

"Ok, if that's how you feel. Just have the driver take you back to the palace. You can join Hoda and Layla upstairs with Kissa and Hasina. And you can call your mother from there or send a message."

"I will. Thanks, again, Masoon. I'm glad to be helping."

"You've been a big help. It could have taken us hours and even into tomorrow before we would have located this place, if we could have found it at all. No one else is having these visions you've been given. We're glad you're here."

"I appreciate it. Be safe. I'll see you later." Khata opened the door slowly and quietly, even though they were at least a couple of blocks away and partly shielded by a building between them and the factory. She wanted to be as careful as possible. She felt good about what she had been able to do to help her friends. And then a new feeling came into her heart the moment her feet both touched the ground outside the truck, when it flashed into her mind that these friends would be going into a very dangerous situation where not everyone might come out alive.

She felt a wave of something wash through her soul, but she continued to walk back to what would be her ride to safety. She was supposed to go now. She could feel that, clearly. She just had to hope her friends would be successful and safe.

Khata then got into the second truck and Masoon watched them turn around and drive away. The vehicles were both unmarked.

Neither looked at all military. They could have been normal commercial or delivery trucks of any sort and wouldn't attract undue attention in this part of town. However, there weren't many other people around, since it was slightly after normal business or factory hours, except for a few places in the area that had a late shift and, of course, those who were in the area for criminal purposes.

Masoon then got out of the truck and went to the back. He opened the rear doors and briefed the men inside on what Khata had told him. Within a minute, a full plan was drawn up and roles were assigned. The overall assault would involve Masoon, Hamid, Walid, Mafulla, Paki, Amon, Omari, and their new companion, Oz—seven Phi and one reformed monster of untested capabilities. They knew they had at least eight trained adversaries inside, and possibly more, and that many or most of them would be armed. They would have to get to Ara and Cabar without doing anything that could cause their harm. That was always the greatest difficulty of any rescue mission in the face of armed opponents. And these were not normal opponents.

This was a fact that had again just crossed Walid's mind, along with the accompanying thought, "Why didn't we bring Hoda?" He had seen what Hoda could do, on one recent and quite memorable occasion, and it was apparently supernatural to an extent that no one else had ever displayed—except, of course, the king. That thought was then followed by the question, "Why didn't the king come?" But the king didn't normally go on simple rescue missions. So, he must consider this simple; otherwise, surely, he would have come along. But he was just back from a big adventure. Maybe he's tired. Maybe that's the only reason he didn't come along. But, he has to think it's Ok. And he knows better than anyone else how to assess situations like this. Such thoughts cascaded through Walid's mind.

"Hey, I agree," Mafulla whispered, as they climbed out of the truck.

"What?"

"I heard you and I agree."

"You heard me?"

"Yeah, you were thinking pretty loud."

"Oh, man. I didn't know you were already at that point."

"Just now and then, and mostly with family and you."

"Oh, Ok. I'll be careful what I think."

"A fine policy in any case."

"Good point."

The guard driving the truck was one of the top military guys who worked directly with Masoon. Walid had seen him many times on important missions. His role would be to take the truck down the street by the front of the factory. Paki and Amon were going to be in the back, and they would roll a large explosive under the parked car when they passed it, one that wouldn't go off right away, but when it did, the explosion would serve two purposes. It would destroy the one clear means of mechanized transportation available to the Germans, and it would help to create a big diversion in front of the building. But it was timed so as not to go off until after another explosion happened that Paki and Amon would set up in a building on the far side of the factory that sat closer to it than any other structure. Again, the explosion would be at the front of the adjacent building, which was apparently abandoned and sitting empty. The two bombs would be crucial for what was then to take place.

Everyone else had assigned tasks as well. They were to wait as long as possible to engage the enemy in gunfire, because once that line was crossed, the nature of what was going on would be clear to all their adversaries and access to the girls would be vastly more difficult. There had to be as much deception and stealth as possible, in order to make success possible here.

Everyone got fully armed and then scattered in the directions and toward the hiding places that Masoon had assigned them. The driver waited until he could see or reasonably infer that they were all in place, and then he put the truck into drive and began to move forward as slowly as he could without calling any undue attention to the vehicle. Only a minute before, another truck had rumbled down the street, and before it, in the other direction, two others, and a car. So, as a consequence, their vehicle and its movements wouldn't be unusually conspicuous in the immediate context. That was a stroke of good fortune, or serendipity, that would help to mask their actions. Context affects perception and belief more than we typically realize.

From where Walid was hiding, he could see the truck now rolling down the street like any other delivery vehicle in this part of town, and as it passed by the parked car, he saw Paki toss the device underneath it with near perfect placement. The truck then continued on toward the building on the other side of the old factory.

Walid's mouth got a little dry with nervous anticipation, and his stomach felt odd. But he had experienced the sensation before and realized that it just meant he was primed and poised for action. He also knew that he should take charge with his mind and use his imagination well to get his emotions under more control. And of course, next to him, Mafulla was doing pretty much the same thing. Omari touched both of them on their shoulders from behind and said, "Let's get a bit closer." They followed him farther down the side of the building that was being used to hide their presence, and they all crouched low at the end of the wall. They were to be the exit support team. When the girls were in friendly hands and were being brought out, Omari, Mafulla, and Walid would be acting to suppress any hostile fire or other interference that might arise. But for the moment, they were to watch and wait.

Masoon, Hamid, and Oz were the primary hostage rescue team. Paki and Amon would create a secondary diversion after the explosions they set, and seek entrance at the front of the factory under the guise of being blast victims from the building next door. The diversionary tactics would be concentrated in the front of the structure, and that's when the rescue team would enter from the rear and secure the hostages. This was the plan in its main outline. And as the primary rescue team then moved to free the girls, the exit team would come in to provide support and cover, guns blazing as needed. At least, that's how it was supposed to go.

The seconds now seemed to expand beyond all reasonable measure. Time did what it almost always does in such circumstances and began to slow in such a way as to make ample opportunity for any needed action to take place in full cognizance of whatever else was occurring, now fluidly, within each of the large and stretched moments currently being made available. Once Walid broke through the initial agitation of his nerves, he began to feel a sense of flow in his soul. Like the grain in a piece of wood, there was a grain in this situation and in this stretch of time, a way forward that the rescuers were all respecting and following with a sense of honor that allowed their actions to carve out with minimal resistance exactly what needed to be done.

The first explosion, the one from the front of the nearby building, was bigger than Walid had expected. It brought a jolt to his whole system, shocking him out of the thoughts that had been floating across his consciousness and preparing him for action.

"Oh, man," Mafulla whispered. "Look!"

Walid peered toward the scene and saw Paki running forward with black soot all over his face and his clothing torn. It even looked like his coat was on fire. There was smoke around him. He was yelling, "Help me! Help me!" and running straight toward the door of the building where Ara and Cabar were being held.

Amon was behind him, shouting "Stop! Stop!" and holding what looked like a bucket, as he ran after his friend. Was this a part of the ruse, or was Paki really in trouble? Walid temporarily forgot, if only just for a second or two, what exactly was supposed to play out, because it was so realistic. His throat tightened up as he fought the natural urge to jump up and run to help his friend.

"Help me!"

A woman appeared at the door of the building, stepping across the threshold and out a couple of feet into the sand, shading her eyes and looking to see what had just happened. She was holding a military rifle. A second woman, also armed, was right behind her.

"Help me!" Paki nearly screamed as he ran toward them. "Fire!" Black smoke seemed to be coming out of his clothing.

Amon yelled, "Call the fire brigade!" And as they approached the women, he threw a bucket-load of water onto his friend's back, and Paki instantly cried out and fell to the ground. The women both momentarily froze in shocked surprise at what they were seeing. Beyond the fallen man, who still seemed that he might be on fire, and his companion, who was now bent over and scooping sand toward his friend's smoldering back, and fully within the sweep of the scene, the building behind the men was pouring out thick black smoke.

Suddenly, the bomb under the car went off in a huge, thunderous explosion that shook the ground and nearly tore their eardrums with its impact. And it then created, moments later, a secondary explosion in the car's shattered gas tank. Several windows were broken out by the impact of it all. Both women crouched protectively and looked up as they raised their weapons toward the car. And both were taken down that very moment by silent knives thrown with deadly force and precision. They had been caught completely by surprise, and now slumped down without a sound, dropping their weapons to the sand as they fell. Paki quickly grabbed both knives and threw them aside as he slid out of his still smoking coat and entered the doorway, his friend behind him, with their primary weapons still hidden.

They saw others inside, but at a distance, some moving toward the door they had just entered, and Paki instantly continued his charade. "Help me! It just … exploded!" He fell once more, this time to his knees, in order to stay in a position of vision and power. "Help! I've been burned! Badly!"

"Call the fire brigade! Please!" Amon shouted from behind him, bending down, apparently to help his friend. "We need help!" The women now moved quickly toward them, unsure as to what was happening. The security of their building couldn't be compromised and they had to know what was going on here.

Outside the building, Omari threw out an explosive device that Walid didn't even know he was carrying and, within seconds, it went off halfway between them and the factory building. He then directed the prince and Mafulla to follow him in a flanking maneuver, while any adversarial attention was probably at this moment split between Paki and Amon, right inside the building, and this new big explosion, outside and also in front, but to the side.

Omari's bomb, in addition to being another diversionary device, was also a planned signal to the rescue team, now positioned near the back of the building, but out of sight.

Inside the otherwise empty office where they were being held, Ara and Cabar had heard the explosions and the sound of a male voice shouting in the front of the building. "It's something big," Ara said to her friend. "It may be a rescue. We've got to get loose!" She pulled and twisted and struggled. So did Cabar. The Black Widows were, fortunately, not accustomed to tying up young teenage girls, and so the ropes were either a bit looser in places than they should have been, or else the girls were more limber than normal adult victims. They worked at their ropes with complete concentration, intensity and persistence, hoping to wiggle loose and take advantage of whatever was going on. If they could just get to the back door—they thought there was a rear entrance they had heard someone use, and from there they might be able to escape. The threats that had been made earlier against their families weren't even coming to mind in this moment of chaos and confusion. A survival instinct had taken over and they were just desperate to get free and out of there.

The guard at the back door had been completely distracted by all the commotion up front, and had stepped away from her post to peer forward in an effort to see what was happening. At that second, the back door burst open inwardly, as if someone had broken the lock and flung it hard, and she instantly spun around, gun up and ready to react. But no one was there to be seen.

Omari was leading Walid and Mafulla around the edge of the building now and toward the back. They all ran forward in as low a crouch as they could, heading for the area behind the structure. There was a high metal fence, and they would have to either go over it—which was dangerous—or enter the grounds through the front gate, which was just as bad, or at the very rear, where a section of the fence was missing. As they chose to go toward the back, but could still see the front, Omari noticed one of the front guards who had been taken down earlier. She was stirring and beginning to get up. If she weren't stopped, she could enter the door behind Paki and Amon and they would then have enemy combatants on two sides of them, front and back, which would not be good. With a single shot and a sound that he instantly regretted, he put her down. And now, without hesitation, they moved on toward the back of the building. But the crack of the gun was easily heard inside, and that was the moment when it became clear to all exactly what was going on.

Paki and Amon had no choice but to open fire on everyone they saw and then dive sideways to take cover behind a large desk that was maybe twenty feet inside the door they had entered, and off to the left. The guard at the rear then suddenly dropped to the floor, at least unconscious and perhaps dead, but for no apparent reason.

Paki had shot, in his initial burst of gunfire, one of the Black Widows, who was now down and wounded, and his rapid fire had caused two others to take cover. Amon had shot at one of them the split second before she dove down, and the bullet from his gun had then taken out another woman who had been standing behind her, unseen. It was the lady with red hair from the embassy. Her official complicity in this whole ugly situation had put her here in the line of fire and had, as a result, ended her life in an instant. Of course, she didn't want to be in the building. But she was. And because of it, she paid a price that really would seem more justly extracted from others, higher up in the embassy and in the government. And yet, it was her body now that was on the floor, unmoving.

Walid and Mafulla had gotten to where they could see the back of the building, and they watched as Masoon and Hamid rushed through that door. They couldn't see Oz anywhere at that point, but hardly thought about it. They had their own jobs to do.

Inside the main area of the building, Elam al-Buri had pulled

Bara down to the floor for protection as quickly but as gently as he could. He also stretched himself over her to shield her from the gunfire, putting his own life in jeopardy. "What's happening?" She asked.

"I don't know. Stay down to be safe!" he said.

"You hurt me!"

"I'm trying to keep you alive! We need to be quiet!"

"But!"

"Stay quiet!"

There was a lot more shooting, all directed at this stage toward the front of the building, and return fire from the large industrial desk and a pile of boxes and some crates next to it where Paki and Amon were taking cover. Another explosion went off loudly toward a front corner of the building, outside. Omari had apparently thrown another device, a timed one, into that area when he had shot the recovering guard on his way toward the place where he and the boys needed to wait for the primary rescue team to appear.

That was the perfect additional diversion for Hamid and Masoon to be able to get inside, locate the office door where the girls were being held, and move in its direction, as yet unseen by adversaries. At this point, every second counted.

Walid and Mafulla both knew what Hoda could do to the brains and minds of enemies, but for some reason, it had never occurred to them that Phi as advanced as Masoon and Hamid might also have that skill, developed to the nearly same level, as well as other powers that were just as strange. But they did, and they were using such an inner projection of force as they entered the large building.

Greta Estand and Dieter Himmel were rushing together down a hallway from the front of the building toward the back office when they were suddenly stricken with a mind-bending, excruciating blast of pain that made them both cry out. Dieter dropped his weapon and it clattered loudly onto the concrete, while he grabbed his head with both hands, bent over and unable to think. Greta bent down to one knee but held on to her luger, putting her free hand to her forehead and pressing it, desperately trying to do anything that would relieve the sharp, throbbing agony that had come on so unexpectedly.

She looked up but couldn't see anything except a thick swirl of dark smoke. And yet, in reality, there was no smoke. Dieter had the same experience as he sought to shake off the horrible searing pain and to glance over toward Greta. He saw only black and dark gray smoke revolving all around him. Greta even smelled it. In fact, the acrid burst of it assaulted her senses. She felt dizzy. A thought suddenly flashed into her mind through one small crack left open by the ongoing, screaming pain: The building around them, their own place, must be on fire. She had to get the hostages out, to extract them from this apparent rescue attempt, so that they could still be used to gain the scrolls. But she felt frozen in place, as if she couldn't move. And it was suddenly harder to think. Her mental activity felt like it was being slowed down or partly suppressed by something.

Loud gunfire could still be heard in the building. Paki and Amon were keeping a couple of the Black Widows pinned down and busy in the front of the old factory space. Their palace guard driver had brought the truck closer while all this was going on. He had made the reasonable assumption that, with everything happening in the building at this stage of the assault, no one would be paying much, if any, attention to the outside. He positioned the truck so that there would be good access to it, whether the teams came out the back or the front. A rear exit was the plan but, as he knew, plans can change. He backed up the truck with its rear doors open, and stood beside it with his gun in position. He would be able to cover them, if that was needed, before hopping back in and driving away with the teams and the rescued hostages.

Ara had managed to wiggle out of her ropes enough to finish the job, and she was now untying Cabar, who was saying to her, "Quick! Quick! I think it's the palace rescuing us!"

"You're right! Hold still and I'll get you loose!"

"Ok!"

"In a second, follow me, and I'll get us out so they can see us!"

"Ow!"

"Sorry!"

"It's all right. That was tight. Thanks."

"Yeah."

The second that Ara got the last knot untied and pulled the rope away from Cabar and the chair, the newly freed girl stood up. Ara said to her, simply, "Let's go."

They both then turned toward the door, but at that moment, a strong hand grabbed Ara and the assailant shoved the barrel of a black German pistol into her face. The woman snarled, "You're coming with me!"

Ara struggled and shouted, "Let me go!" Cabar just lunged at the woman in an effort to push her away from Ara, but the angry German flung her against the wall next to them and knocked the breath out of her. The Black Widow then practically dragged Ara from the room and around a hallway corner no more than five seconds before Masoon emerged from behind another corner and saw the office door and, through it, Cabar slumped on the floor. He heard Ara's shouts coming from nearby, but at this point couldn't see her.

He called out, "Hamid! In the room! Over there!" He pointed and his friend rushed through the door to pick Cabar up off the floor. At this point, Walid, Mafulla, and Omari were at the back door. The two younger boys stayed just outside, and their older friend went in and stepped over the inert body of the defeated guard.

Masoon ran around the corner of the hallway in pursuit of Ara, and in the next hall he saw two adversaries and the girl. One was running with her, away from him, with a gun pointed at her head. The other was standing low in a crouched position facing him, with her weapon aimed right at his chest and her finger on the trigger, preparing to fire, point blank.

35

Backup

Those of us who are blessed with basically normal vision, within a wide range of strength or weakness, tend most of the time to take this sense for granted. Sight is our normal way of greeting the world each morning and moving through it during the day. If we're very lucky, we might smell our breakfast before we see it, but then seeing it, we know for the first time exactly what we have awaiting us.

There's a strange old expression: "Familiarity breeds contempt." But look up the word 'contempt' in any standard dictionary, and you'll find something like "The feeling that a person or thing is beneath consideration, or worthless, or deserving of scorn." And it's only the most cynical, negative, and judgmental of people who would assume or otherwise believe that the mere fact of becoming familiar with anything would make us disregard it, or disparage it, or find it worthless or even deserving of scorn. Familiarity does breed something, but not contempt. It breeds unawareness. The most familiar things around us and about us tend to be things that don't draw out attention or explicit awareness. They become more or less transparent to our minds. We may look and experience through them or with them, but we typically fail to pay them much notice.

That's how it can be with vision. Most of us are so busy seeing the world around us every moment of the day, with eyes wide open, that we rarely take time to ponder vision itself or appreciate it as the remarkable phenomenon it is. And, at least in humans and other higher animals, but likely even more broadly than we might imagine, it's both a physical and a spiritual thing. Yes, light waves pass into the eyes and onto the retina. This has chemical and electrical results that go through the optic nerve and elicit neural events in the physicality of our brains. But our act of seeing isn't simply a chemical and electrical process of any known form. At least within this world of embodiment, those physical elements and events convey the necessary conditions for vision, but do not themselves fully explain the viewed and felt texture of what's seen, or of the seeing itself. There's almost a magic in the richness of all sense experience that, it appears, can never be fully explained or expunged by scientific description. Plenty of scientists and philosophers have tried, and none have succeeded. The chemical and electrical states of the brain appear to be one sort of thing, and the inner experience of attentive conscious awareness seems to be something altogether different.

Envision, then, an ordinary, embodied person awake in the middle of the day, moving about and doing things. Now imagine all conscious bodily control and sensory awareness removed from him or her in an instant. With that held stable, now propagate the light waves that normal vision would require into those currently unseeing eyes. Let the optic nerve be stimulated in all the standard ways by these waves, and imagine the brain's neurons undergoing their normal chemical and electrical changes, with the one difference that it's suddenly as if nobody's home to see the sights that would otherwise be sparked and conveyed by all this. In the absence of any connection with conscious soul or spirit, the chemistry is simply chemistry, the electricity is what it is, and vision doesn't take place at all.

Now, imagine that you're a highly trained assassin. You can be the one running, with a pistol held tight against the neck of a young lady over whose body and life you're seeking to retain control in the developing chaos of the moment. Or you can be the one crouched, with both hands on a gun that's practically a natural extension of your arm and hand at this point in your life, your right index finger just beginning to exert pressure on the trigger, a thin-shaved second away from firing point blank into a large, oncoming adversary who has just appeared from around a corner. You're focused and are about to eliminate this target. Then try to imagine that the full connection, whatever it may be—magical or metaphysical—between your soul and your senses, is suddenly severed. There's no sight, no smell, no touch, no taste, no hearing, no proprioception, nothing tethering you to the world around you any longer, across every sensory dimension. It's all vanished in an infinitesimal instant. You suddenly can't see or hear or smell or feel your body, or anything else. The lights are out in every possible way. The shock from this would probably be so great as to collapse that body, right then, into an inert pile of physically joined, but yet spiritually disconnected, parts falling, collapsing, and then splayed out on the unfelt floor beneath.

Masoon stopped for a moment, suddenly, as he had done just that to both his adversaries. He had pulled the plug on their sensory awareness, completely and instantly. He had to then jump around the first body on the floor and grab the monumentally startled Ara, as she stood, frozen and bent over after an otherwise iron grip had released and fallen from her arm and the violent woman who had just been dragging her down the hall had limply sprawled onto the floor beside her, with no muscular control remaining. Her body was now still, apart from several small twitches and minor contractions caused by the nerves and muscle fibers that were no longer under her control.

Before Masoon had seen Cabar, moments earlier inside the office and slumped against the wall, a car had slowed down on the street out in front of the building and a passenger, seeing the guard standing by the truck and holding a weapon, had waved to him. "Excuse me! Excuse me! I believe we're lost."

He had waved them off with a gesture indicating that he couldn't speak then, but the car stopped and the lady looked shocked and shouted, "Watch out to your right!" The guard turned momentarily and she quickly raised a gun to the window and shot him where he stood, at quite a distance. He fell to the ground. Backup had arrived. The car pulled up beside the truck and three women hopped out, guns held up, as they ran toward the far side of the building.

Inside, Greta Estand and Dieter Himmel were completely disoriented and momentarily unaware as to what was happening around them. Dieter's gun disappeared from beside his feet, and Greta was caught off guard as hers felt as if it had been suddenly twisted away from her, but by no one she could see. She lashed out, despite her continuing and monumental headache, flailing her arms around to feel for something or someone to fight for her now vanished weapon. Her hand hit something but she couldn't see what. The smoke continued to swirl around her as if she was in the worst part of a burning building, and she began to cough loudly, gagging for breath.

Greta remembered her knife and pulled it out, using it to jab the air all around her for any hidden opponent that she might be able to slash. She heard Omari's footsteps coming toward her and threw the knife in his direction, although she still could see nothing beyond the smoke. But there was no smoke. Omari could see her plainly, and her throw was eerily accurate, based merely on the sound of his approach, but he still easily dodged the knife as he shot her in the chest, then taking Dieter down as well. She fell, but screamed out, "I'll kill you!" And she improbably rose up to her knees and began to lunge toward him, again, in his exact direction. Another shot, then another, and a final bullet stopped her blind rage and attack.

Walid had heard the outside gunshot that came from up front, beyond the building, and at the same time, or a moment after, he and Mafulla both heard Omari's gun firing inside. Mafulla then moved into the door instinctively, his weapon also out and ready.

But Walid turned back toward the outside to look around the corner. Masoon had just grabbed Ara and was on his way with her back down the hallway that led toward the rear door. Hamid had bent down and picked Cabar up from the floor of the office and was carrying her toward the door. Paki and Amon were still in the front of the building at this point, on guard for any action there. They were just holding their positions as they had been instructed to do, regardless of what they might see or hear, until they got the final signal to leave the way they had entered, unless for any reason that door was blocked or too dangerous.

No one was aware of the backup that had just arrived to assist the Black Widows who had been guarding Ara and Cabar. It was too late, at this point, for them to save any of the original guards who had communicated to them the plan underway. Once they now saw and surmised what was going on, the focal goal for each of the newly arrived combatants was to keep the girls there to trade for the scrolls, or else to just get the scrolls directly, however that could happen. Never had so many Black Widows been stopped on one day, or actually ever, but the backup that was now present had the potential to reverse the outcome of all the action. Their main advantage was surprise. The three of them ran toward the back corner of the building and Walid saw them at exactly the same moment they saw him.

The difference was that, because of their extensive and expert training focused on the needs of assassination, in particular, they were all three on a hair trigger, prepared to shoot first and think later. The most advanced and talented of the entire group was actually now one of the three making their way toward the prince with guns already in position to fire.

Walid was certainly no stranger to dire circumstances or dramatic confrontations. In his short life, he had been exposed far too many times already, throughout the remarkable string of recent months, to such dramas where life and death seemed to spin like a coin on its edge, ready to fall one way or the other at the very next moment. Instinct told him what he now faced quicker than any conscious reasoning could process and leap inferentially to the full significance of the situation. Keen awareness displaced discursive thought entirely, and he now lived, rather than intellectually drawing, the conclusion that could have been reached in normal ways only with a great deal more time on the clock. And it happened before he could even begin to raise his gun.

Back at the palace, Sab Maayuf and King Ali felt it the moment before it transpired in the world. And they sent whatever intervention they could, full force, in Walid's direction. Hoda experienced the very same thing, and did the same in response. Layla felt it, too, but with less intense focus, and with a delay that kept her response from being as instantly reactive. Her thoughts were so focused on Hasina and Mafulla at the moment that this threat on the prince came to her more slowly, and as if indirectly.

Khata just let out a scream. She wasn't back at the palace yet, but still in the truck transporting her there. She had put her hands to her mouth as an overwhelming sensation coursed through her body and soul. But she couldn't repress the agonized sound that spontaneously came from deep within her soul and up her throat, out into the cab of the truck, and almost caused the driver to lose control of their vehicle.

She wasn't even aware of that danger. She was elsewhere, behind the factory, sharing Walid's eyes and his heart in this one moment, and feeling it all as even he could not at that precise instant.

Shapur Adi felt a jolt and stopped still where he stood and said, without knowing why, "Oh, my!" He froze for a moment and then began to look around, but for what he had no idea. He was only certain that something somewhere was happening, or about to happen, that was badly and deeply wrong.

His brother Reela, sitting alone in his office at that very moment, looked up from his desk and with something like an electric surge throughout his spirit and flesh said aloud, "No!"

Walid's mother, Bhati, was at the site of an ancient holy spot in Memphis, Egypt, at a distance from Cairo and what was happening there. She was in the company of a good friend who shared her love for antiquity and the spiritual traditions of Egypt. They were looking over a ruin where a temple used to be, and in that moment, Bhati took her friend's hand suddenly and said to her, "My son."

Jabari's monkey, Manny, started screeching as loudly as anyone had ever heard him, and he ran back and forth, desperately, wildly, and frantically. His eyes were bulging and his hoarse screeches suddenly became like a scream.

Paki realized that something was about to happen that should not. Amon had the same awareness, but not quite as strongly. Yet, when Paki looked over at him, he got up instantly with his friend, leaving their cover and running as fast as they could toward the back of the building, abandoning the plan they'd been given.

Bara El-Ari had actually passed out on the floor from sheer terror at what was happening all around her. Elam was still covering most of her body with much of his and continued to grip her tightly, holding on to what seemed to him at that moment his greatest and only real hope. But as Paki and Amon ran past them, he was utterly oblivious to what was playing out just a short distance away at the back corner of the building. And he could have no idea as to how so much was so soon to be changed.

Every moment of any temporal flow in our physical universe reflects a near infinity of events, a fine-grained lavish profusion of wild activity on the most miniscule scale, and with such a dense fecund enormity that no created mind could ever fully contemplate even a small fraction of it. There is no calm in this world. No true stillness exists. There is no form of physical changelessness. There is no gap between things, no truly empty spaces holding any events or objects at an invisible, intangible arm's length. All is connected and endlessly vibrant, dynamic, and moving. Everything is linked into and affected by everything else in an immense web of energized reality, and in more ways than we can imagine. And so, when anything happens, the ripples from it can extend eternally forward, sideways, up, down, and even, perhaps, backwards in time, insofar as we can use such spatial images at all.

Destiny isn't always beautiful when seen from our side of the great divide between this dimension and the next. It can appear horribly, terribly tragic beyond measure or description. But the king had always said that things aren't often what they seem—and yet; and yet. Some lovely, wonderful things are cut down, it seems, before their time. Some seeds never have a chance to grow. Some plants don't have a full season to blossom. Some blossoms won't have occasion fully to bloom. And it simply doesn't seem fair. It doesn't seem just or right. And especially when callous and evil intent has intervened, which was the thing that had bothered Mafulla so often throughout the most recent days of his life when he pondered it all too much. But the king had helped him with this, not long ago. And still, there were some things that, if they happened, even the king's deepest and most heartfelt reassurances might never be able to ease the pain.

The world was on the precipice of one of those things at this very moment. And as Mafulla suddenly turned around inside and ran back toward the door, he had no idea of it, yet. But he would emerge into the glare of the sun just in time to see something play out that would strike horror into his heart in a way he had never expected or even allowed himself to imagine.

There was more than one hostage situation going on in that place. The friendship that is love gives hostages to fate and relinquishes power over its own heart. The result can be either wondrously transformative, or else completely decimating. And yet, even the worst can potentially be an agent of positive metamorphosis in the end. But where and when is it the end?

These three Black Widows may have encountered the phenomenon of extended proprioception before, and unsuccessfully, in terms of their aim. In this world, failure teaches and enlightens and corrects if embraced properly. For at this moment, they together seemed to account for its possibility in their pattern of firing. Maybe it was just happenstance. Who knows? But it couldn't have been deliberately contrived any better. Their initial salvo could not be dodged, even by an advanced young Phi who was as well trained and talented as Walid, the former and meant to be future King of Egypt. But everything in our world is temporary, except real love. So anything else can be lost. And such loss has been continually confronted and lamented by artists and poets since the earliest days of history and before. No one expected the loss that this sudden and otherwise unexceptional rescue mission would involve. And it would be lamented and remembered, perhaps, forever. Two good souls would be saved. But one heroic spirit would be gone from out of this world, and henceforth for the rest of its future yet to come.

Mafulla saw it happen. He saw his friend from behind and just caught sight of the armed assailants as they suddenly come into view. And he witnessed in that instant the rapid firing of their guns with deadly aim. But before he could manage to react at all, Omari, Hamid, and Masoon all rushed out and emerged from behind him, weapons blasting forth at the three Germans in response. He then joined in, focused now on the surprised adversaries and afraid even to look at Walid, who fell, suddenly and violently propelled backward and downward from the spot of ground where he had stood.

Masoon and Hamid had just left Ara and Cabar right inside the door and told them to stay there, no matter what they heard, until someone came back for them. The two of them now cringed and covered their ears at the fierce noise of the desperate attack and the massive counterattack that could not reverse what had just been done.

The Black Widows each received three or four shots to the head and torso and they fell, as well. One still had the consciousness and control to aim her gun at Mafulla, but somehow, despite what had just happened, the fallen Walid managed to get off one miraculous shot at that last second to put her down and save his friend, before the utter darkness overcame him and the gun fell from his unfeeling hand.

He had been knocked down off his feet, as he stood ready to die, in what seemed with certainty of heart to be an unstoppable moment. And as Masoon and Hamid now dove down to him, Hamid pulled the Stone of Giza from his pocket and desperately shoved it into Walid's limp hand, wrapping his loose fingers around it. Then the doctor quickly looked for his wounds to assess what they faced, and to see if it was something the stone could help heal, or whether there was too much damage already, as had happened with Walid's father, so sadly, and they were perhaps simply and woefully too late.

Hamid checked the boy's head and neck and torso. And he looked again. He tore cloth in his frantic efforts as if it were paper. But he couldn't find the entry wounds, and there would surely be many. These women would all have hit their target multiple times from such a short distance. Utter perplexity began to overcome Hamid, and it momentarily got in the way of his reasoning. It even temporarily brought him to a stop in his rapid examination of the prince.

"Walid!" Mafulla yelled. "Walid!" He scrambled toward them.

"Prince!" Hamid then said aloud, as well, toward Walid's head.

"Omari! Check the shooters!" Masoon shouted as he dove down to put his hands on the motionless boy.

Omari ran over to the women and, after removing their weapons, began to look for any vital signs on each one. Paki and Amon had just dashed out of the door as well and stood there in a momentary thoughtless shock, just taking in the scene in front of them. "What happened?" Amon asked, to no one in particular.

Paki said, "Is the prince?"

"Oh!"

"What?" Mafulla exclaimed at about the same time as Masoon said the same thing.

"Oh," There was a faint groan, or some such sound, and a twinge of movement. Everything stopped. Everyone was afraid to move or breathe.

"You're alive? You're alive!"

"What? What happened?" Walid groaned.

"Praise God," Hamid said. He looked at Walid's face and his

half-closed eyes and said, "I thought you were gone! I thought you had been shot many times! I saw you being shot! And you fell from the bullets hitting you! You fell back, but there are no entry wounds!"

"Oh." Walid groaned again. "I, I felt a hit, a huge hit, on my entire body, like a car ran into me, and I fell backwards and I think I hit my head and sort of passed out for a second and came to and saw the woman's gun aimed at Maffie and I got off a shot and then passed out again, I think."

"Where were you shot? Where do you feel the pain?"

"I feel pain all over, but not so much, and the most in my head, in the back of my head. It's throbbing. I have no idea what happened."

Hamid and Masoon began to rip off more of Walid's clothing to find wounds, and could not see any. Masoon said, "What in the world?" He glanced all around. "I don't get this. I've never seen such a thing."

Mafulla looked back toward Omari and the women, and suddenly his eye was drawn to a mark in the sand. He walked over and bent down and said, "Here! In front of where Walid was standing, between him and the Germans but close to him, there are deep ruts in the sand."

"What?" Hamid turned quickly toward him.

"Marks in the sand where I didn't see anyone standing. Walid didn't go this far, and the women were where they are now. Look!"

"Stay with Walid," Masoon said to Hamid. "You're the doctor. Let me see what this is."

"Over here," Mafulla said and pointed down to the sand.

"Many of us passed this way," Masoon said.

"Yes, and I see lots of footprints all facing the door, but look at this."

"Prints coming from the door, in addition to Walid's, and that go beyond his. It could be Omari. He just walked over."

"But not across that exact spot, and look," Mafulla gestured again. "It's like the footsteps stopped going in that direction and turned back toward Walid, and look at this sand lumped up, as if a foot pushed off from it and shoved the sand up."

"Like the way it would look if someone had suddenly shifted direction and … jumped with all his might from there," Masoon reflected.

"Oh! Look!" Mafulla said, and bent over a few feet away, beyond and beside where Walid now lay on the ground." He reached over and picked up something from the sand and handed it to Masoon. "Oh, man."

At this point Omari, Hamid, and Walid were looking at Masoon, and over to Mafulla, and back to Masoon. The general held up an item that none of them at first could see, at least to know what they were seeing. And then he said, "The ring."

"What?" Walid said.

"The Ring of Gyges," Masoon answered. The ring that our new friend was wearing and that he used, when we entered the building, to become invisible and do things that none of us would be able to do."

"He became invisible?" Walid asked with surprise.

"Yes, on my suggestion," Masoon answered.

"But I thought."

"I asked him to do it."

"And that's the ring?"

"Yes, it is."

Hamid said, "It was in the sand? Right there?"

"Yeah," Mafulla answered.

Masoon walked over and began waving his arms back and forth right over the sand, covering an area on all sides of where the ring had just been found. "Nothing," he said.

"What?" Hamid asked.

"There's no body here. Invisible doesn't mean intangible."

"And now he isn't wearing the ring, anyway."

"What in the world?"

"Wait. This is how it was in the palace. But there was no ring then. If he was still alive, he'd be here."

"If he was alive, and didn't have the ring on, we'd see him."

"That's true."

"But … what?"

Then Walid knew. And he spoke the words. "He's gone. He's gone again. And he saved my life."

"What?"

"He jumped in front of me and saved my life. He took all the bullets. He saw what was going to happen and jumped between the shooters and me so that … he could be my shield. He knocked me down and chose to sacrifice his life."

"Unbelievable," Mafulla said. "But that's got to be right."

"He gave his life," Masoon commented.

"I don't know what to say," Walid muttered, astonished.

Hamid then said, "No greater love has any man than this, to give his life for his friends." This apt quotation of a famous passage from a great spiritual document resonated in all their hearts and struck them deeply in that moment of full realization.

And they all stood and remained still and deeply reverent where they were, and marveled in astonishment as they contemplated the thing that had just happened.

36

A Report to the King

Walid was the first through the door. King Ali stood up and walked to him, hugging him tightly, and saying, "Welcome back!"

"It's good to be back, Uncle—I mean, Your Majesty!"

"It's a great relief to see you."

"You, too."

"Now. Sit. Please."

"I'm glad to."

Walid sat down, and then so did the king. Ali said, "I was quite concerned for your safety at one point. I could tell that death was near to you and quickly approaching."

"It stared me in the face and then took Oz, who gave his life for mine."

"Yes."

"He jumped in front of me just as three assassins were shooting at me from close range. He took all their bullets."

The king nodded his understanding. "I knew the moment it happened, but not until that very instant. We had a special connection, he and I." Ali let out a deep breath and said, "I suppose this is why he came back. This is why your father sent him."

"Wow. I had no idea."

"You did the right thing to honor your father's wish, as our former enemy conveyed it to you, and accept Oz as transformed, and even as one of us."

"I had no idea that something like this was going to happen."

"I know."

"It's just hard to take it all in."

"Yes. But tell me more of what brought this to be. I don't yet have all the details."

"Masoon had asked him to use the Ring of Gyges and he was invisible when it took place. So I didn't see him or know what was going on when he threw his body into mine and knocked me over and took all the damage and death they had meant to deal out to me. He had already bravely done several things to make the rescue possible, but I had no idea he was anywhere near me when I faced what was likely so far the worst danger of my life."

Mafulla walked in at that point and said, "Your Majesty!"

"Mafulla! It is good to see you back, safe as well!"

"Did Walid tell you?"

"Yes, about our new friend's heroic action."

"But he already knew," Walid said.

"Oh."

"Not all the details," the king explained.

Masoon and Hamid then came in close behind Mafulla. "Majesty," Masoon said, and Hamid bowed.

"Where are the others?"

"They're still changing clothes downstairs," Masoon said. "They were all a bit of a mess."

"Any injuries?"

"Miraculously, no serious ones, except to a driver, who survived what could have been a fatal gunshot wound, thanks to the stone. Otherwise, there were only a few bruises for several of us, and the slight injury to the back of the head that the prince took when Oz saved him."

"It knocked me out, completely," Walid said. "I have a nice lump that still hurts like crazy."

"And then he came back to consciousness just long enough to shoot one of the Germans who was about to shoot me," Mafulla said. "I'm alive because he had perfect timing."

"And then I passed out again."

"We thought he was gone," Masoon said. "We were sure he had taken several bullets from fairly close range, and such professional assassins don't miss from that distance. It was only Oz Ali's fast action that prevented a terrible tragedy."

"Yes. Indeed. And the necessity of his sacrifice was also tragic," the king said, while everyone nodded in agreement. "Those who have strayed from a proper path in life, like the assassins, can create a massively disruptive force in the world."

"You speak the truth as always," Masoon said.

"And wisely," Hamid commented.

At that moment, Hoda and Kissa came into the room at a quick walk, and Kissa ran up to Walid to hug him. "You're safe!"

"Yeah, thanks to our former enemy, the man once known as a monster of legend!"

"What?"

"Oz Ali saved my life and gave his to do so."

"No!"

"He was a hero today. And thanks to him, we not only rescued Ara and Cabar, but we all came back with them, and basically unharmed, except for our driver, who's also now fine."

At that moment, Hasina came in right in front of Layla, and the young lady ran to Mafulla, throwing her arms around him. "I was so worried!"

"Probably concerned," Mafulla said in clarification, and made a face.

"Worried!" she replied.

"But, we don't do that around here. The king doesn't approve of it."

"Oh, all right. I'm really sorry, Your Majesty. I was extremely concerned and almost enough as to constitute worry, but one small step short, I suppose." Everyone smiled at her reply.

"That's fine," Ali said. "Concern is fully acceptable."

"Well, Walid, I was most concerned about you," Hoda said. "Because I saw you in a hazy vision and you were in front of those women. I knew they were about to shoot you where you stood, and I felt the approach of a dramatic end, but sent you love and power and hope."

"And it paid off," he replied, "despite the dramatic end."

"It paid off," she repeated the words. "But I'm so very sorry to learn about what happened to Oz Ali as a result of his action. I wish there could have been some other way."

"I do, too," Walid said, and he felt it from the heart.

"His transformation was indeed complete," Masoon reflected.

"It wasn't just words. It was fully real," Walid concluded.

"I knew there was a reason, a specific reason of some sort that he was back. But I thought he would be with us much, much longer," the king said. "I was hoping to include him in all that we do here, as a friend, and even a brother in our fellowship."

"Yes," Walid said, simply.

Ali continued, "He was a man of prodigious talents that had been corrupted and misused and squandered for so long. He had it in him to do truly great things for the rest of his life."

"And he did it all in a day," Kissa said.

"Yes, he did."

"It was the rest of his life."

"Yes."

"We also have some other surprises to report, beyond this one," Hamid said.

"Please, everyone sit. What are the surprises? Do tell me."

They all took chairs or sat down on a sofa, and Hamid began to answer the king. He first said, "Well, for one thing, in addition to all the Black Widows involved in the operation, all of whom are now deceased, there were some visitors in the building when we arrived."

"Visitors?"

"Bara El-Ari, her son Ebar, and Elam al-Buri, along with a woman from the German embassy were all there when the assault began."

"Ah. Yes. I've heard the story about the two older people, the famous love story. What in the world were they doing there?"

"Well, we had no idea. But then on the way back to the palace, Elam confessed to us what was going on."

The king looked puzzled. Hamid continued, "Bara apparently was indeed totally in love, but not with Elam. She was in love with the idea of everlasting life and beauty. She knew of the scrolls and had been seeking to obtain them for herself, or at least their contents, for her own personal use. She would employ their secrets for herself and her son, and then sell the recipe for immortality she believed they held, in order to support an endless lifestyle of luxury and indulgence."

"Oh, I see."

"When Elam returned to his home after the great first meeting with his long lost love at the Grand Hotel that was, of course, reported by the newspaper, he had some suspicions that there had been a break-in. There was no compelling evidence, he said, since he realized that, at his age, his memory as to where certain things had been left could be playing tricks with him. So he didn't say anything about it. Nothing was missing or left in a mess. And he subsequently put it out of his mind. But then his son mentioned to him the next day that a man had come around looking for scrolls in the shop. Elam asked his son what this man looked like, and the description he gave fit Bara's son Ebar perfectly, who, as you may or may not have heard, was nowhere to be seen during the great reunion at the hotel."

"Interesting. I had not heard that."

"Bara had told people that Ebar would keep busy elsewhere during the reunion. Everyone thought that it was because he wanted to give his mother some privacy in that special time. But he apparently kept busy looking for the scrolls. Elam didn't know what to think about any of this and just filed it away. He was so smitten with Bara that he was willing to overlook nearly anything, he told us."

"Ah, yes. Such is sadly too common."

"Indeed. And then, once she had him walking on air with infatuation for her, she sprang on him the surprising news that she had met the people who were seeking the scrolls and that she had entered into a partnership agreement with them."

"The same people who had attacked his son."

"Yes. It's amazing that this didn't show him exactly what he needed to know about her. But he was completely blinded by emotion. And she explained why she wanted the scrolls and of course in a way that would win over his cooperation in helping to get them back."

"Of course."

"She insisted that it was the one and only way that the newfound wonder of their rediscovered love could go on forever. And who was he, of all people, to think this was a bad idea? He was head over heels at that point. She dangled before him the prospect of returning to their youth and making up for all the lost years, and experiencing this giddiness and greatness without end."

"And why was she telling him all this?"

"To secure his active cooperation."

"And what was supposed to be the nature of this cooperation?"

"He was her secret weapon. Bara had come across one of the Black Widows by chance it seemed, in the Grand Hotel's dining room. And she heard her German accent and made bold to speak to the woman and a male companion who was with her. Elam recounted all this to us. Bara told them she knew that some Germans in town were seeking certain scrolls and that, if they would partner up with her, she could bring them a form of access that they could not otherwise even hope for, and she just wanted to read and copy the content of the scrolls, which they would then be free to take."

"I see."

"Then, the woman she was addressing revealed that she and the man with her were the seekers of the scrolls. And Bara assured them that she had unparalleled access to the items, an access she could share."

"How?"

"She told them the story of Elam and his ownership of the scrolls, and claimed that he was liked in the palace and would be allowed further access. She related all this to Elam later. So Bara and the Germans agreed to form a partnership. But the Black Widows had an alternate plan in place and wanted to see it play out first. And that was the kidnapping plot."

"So how did Bara get to the place the girls were held?"

"She was supposed to wait to hear from the Germans as they made their own play for the scrolls, but she became worried that they would betray her if they got the items first and without her help. She'd been told that a certain woman at the embassy could get a message through to the leader of the Black Widows and her associates at any time. So Bara assumed, rightly as it turned out, that this meant the woman knew where they would be. And the woman also knew they were here on a mission of some sort."

"Was the embassy staff member aware of the plan to kidnap Ara and Cabar?"

"Perhaps not that, in particular, but only that some sort of highly secret mission was going on."

"Did Bara know of the kidnapping in advance?"

"We're not sure of that. We actually don't think so. But she did know that some action was underway to get the scrolls from us, and she was afraid that, if it succeeded, she would never see the items she felt she had to obtain."

"I'm still a bit unclear. What exactly had she offered the Germans in this partnership that you mention?"

"A secondary plan and a guarantee. In case their scheme fell short, she promised that Elam would have access to the palace and to the scrolls because of his history of ownership and his new acquaintance with the prince and Mafulla and others. I don't think she spelled out to them how this was supposed to work, in any detail."

"Ah. Yes. I see."

"I think it was more hopefulness than a real plan on her part."

"You're likely right."

"Whether she intended to keep Elam in on the scheme or not is an open question for him now, as well as for us. But in any case, she convinced him to come along with her and Ebar to meet the lady from the embassy as she left work, and to help force her to take them to where the Widows were. And that's how they got to the factory."

"What sort of force did they use?"

"Simple threats, but serious ones, and a gun."

"So, where are they all now? What's happened to them?"

"They managed to talk their way into the building and were inside when our assault began. And then, during all the noise, violence, and chaos, Elam threw himself on top of Bara to protect her. She passed out. And, unknown to Elam at the time, Ebar had fallen suddenly, in his efforts to avoid the gunfire, and hit his head in apparently just the wrong way and, unfortunately, he died from the fall."

"That's too bad, indeed."

"Yes, and what Elam also didn't know was that Bara had been so frightened by the assault that, toward the end, she had a fatal heart attack right there on the floor and in his embrace."

"She passed?"

"Yes."

"And so, in her desperate search for everlasting life, the life she had was ended, apparently long before it need have been."

"Sadly, yes. And she seemed much younger than her years. Because of her vigor, there could have been many more years to come. But as is often seen, a selfish ambition seems to carry its own demise."

"What of the lady from the embassy?"

"Caught in the crossfire. Deceased as well."

"How unfortunate. Her involvement brought her an untimely and unexpected end."

"Indeed."

"And Ara and Cabar were completely unharmed?"

"Yes, Majesty, I'm pleased to say. We were blessed to get them free without incident. Oz helped us throughout. He played an important role, and not just at the end."

"Well, most people would say at such a moment, 'May he rest in peace.' But we know better."

"We do. So: May he continue to flourish, as intended, throughout all the endless opportunities of eternity."

"Amen. And may we all learn from his incredible example."

"Yes, indeed. Oh, and by the way, the two girls have been reunited with their families, and we've allowed Haji and Malik to visit Ara's home already."

"Good."

"Majesty, do we know that the threat is over now?" Masoon asked.

"We think it is. We're aware of no other elements that are in pursuit of the scrolls at present."

"That's a relief to hear."

"And I have some positive news of my own," the king said.

"You do?"

"Yes, and I think you'll all find it quite interesting."

"We could use more good news. Please, what is it?" Masoon asked.

"The scroll I brought from New York has now been used by Sab, and he's determined it was exactly what was needed to decrypt the coded passages in the main ancient scroll that King Gilgamesh left behind."

"And Sab has now read the scroll in its entirety?"

"He has. And he'll report to us all tomorrow morning on what's there. He's told me only that it's extraordinary and far beyond anything he had remembered from that time so long ago."

As if on cue, Sab Maayuf himself then walked into the room, announced by Kular. Ali said, "Come in, old friend. We were just speaking of you."

"Thank you very much, Your Majesty. Dear Walid! I'm delighted and happy beyond words to see you in the flesh. A guard told me that you had arrived back from the mission. I was so afraid that we had seen the last of you in this life!"

"Oz Ali saved me."

Sab just looked at Walid for a moment, and then said, softly, "Yes. I was aware of it. The power of love is without limit. Death can never diminish it. Nor can anything else." Everyone sat in silence and pondered these words.

Sab continued, looking at Walid, "I know that Oz regretted more than anything else, more than any particular action in his previous life, the fact that he was the one responsible for taking your father from you, and from us all. And ironically, on one level, his actions today prevented your being reunited quickly with our good Rumi. But Oz knew that your father wanted this life to be for you all that it can be. He knew that you have much more to do and be, and to experience here before your time of transition properly comes. Much goodness awaits your future action in this world. So Oz acted to save you and postpone that great reunion for another moment in the future, for when the time will fully have come."

Sab paused, and then added, "I know also that Oz had looked forward to his transformed life here on earth, to doing all that he should have done earlier—to helping others, and joining with us to build something for the good of us all. But, I know he also realized, in that precise moment of need on this day, that his sacrifice would be a foundation on which much could be built and much will be established. What you do henceforth, my fine young friend, will honor that sacrifice of love, an act that he, of course, never could have contemplated in his former life. But it became something that, in his new life, he did naturally and instantly, without a moment's hesitation when it was needed. Such is courage. And such is real love."

Walid nodded his understanding and agreement. "When I first saw him, back here with the king, I have to admit, my initial thought was that he certainly didn't deserve to live. Now, I feel even much more strongly that he certainly didn't deserve to die."

"Yes. Well said."

"He taught me with his sacrifice more than words can say about the power of transformative love in a life. You all have taught me so much about love," he said, looking around the room, and catching Kissa's eye for just a moment, "but I think that, today, I had the most surprising lesson of all."

All of those present took in what Walid said, and it struck a deep chord in their hearts. They had indeed all learned a great lesson from what had happened in this one man's life, redeemed and turned around by the power of love, and now from what occurred as it had finally displayed that power in a new and radically unexpected way.

The king then spoke. "I invite you all to stay for a simple, early dinner together. If there are any loved ones you'd like to have present, tell Kular and he'll send out guards to bring them here. It won't be anything fancy, but can be a time for us to continue to talk and unwind at the end of such a day. It will take us most of an hour to make preparations and begin to set out food, so, please, if you haven't done so already, there are a couple of guest suites here that you can use to clean up and change clothes, if you need to. The assistant butlers will take care of anything you may need."

There were murmurs of appreciation around the room. And then the king said, "Why don't we reconvene in the large dining room in exactly an hour? And, again, I gratefully thank you all for what you've done today. I'll see you at dinner in just a bit." He stood, on this last word, and everyone else rose as well, bowing and bidding him goodbye for the time being.

And Sab smiled, knowing that, within a very short time now, there would be much yet to be revealed.

37

Bringing the Truth to Light

"Hey," Walid said, as he walked into the breakfast room where he and Mafulla started most days.

"Hey back. How'd you sleep?"

"Pretty well, given all the excitement we had yesterday. I was tired."

"Me, too. Saving friends in distress is hard work."

"And we really didn't even get to do our jobs."

"Yeah, the exit team. We both almost exited."

Walid laughed and said, "True."

"I can't believe you woke up just long enough to shoot the creep who was about to take me out."

"Yeah, I'm glad I did. I mean, I'm not really glad to shoot anyone, ever, but under the circumstances, I'm happy I could help."

"Otherwise, breakfast would have been a solitary endeavor this morning."

"So would everything else."

Mafulla sipped his coffee and said, "I thought you were really a goner, for sure."

"So did I. You look like you're almost done."

"Always the first in to breakfast, my friend. Up early to start each new day. The sun and birds expect my companionship, even as I remain in the building. They know. They like it that I'm always here first."

"Almost always first."

"Yeah, what, once you were here before me?"

"Or twice."

"Ok, or twice. Maybe."

"I need to eat fast." Walid reached for a plate and started putting food on it. Then he said, "The big meeting's going to start pretty soon, right?"

"Yeah," Mafulla looked at his Reverso and said, "in about a half an hour." He then looked more closely and said, "Man!"

"What?"

"I got a scratch."

"Where?"

"On the side of my watch case."

"Ah. The wounded warrior."

"Yeah. Really."

"It can be buffed out."

"Seriously?"

"Yeah. The king's got a guy who can do it."

"Cool. Or maybe we can just put the Stone up against it."

Walid looked surprised and said, "I wonder if that would work."

"Who knows?"

"Wow. If it did, that would put every repair man in the world out of business."

"Only if everybody had one, or had access to one."

"Ok. True. And we've got the only one."

"Presumably."

"Presumably. I like that. Your vocabulary is a constant source of inspiration. You're a good influence."

"Indubitably."

"Ah, you see?"

'I do."

"But I've said that before."

"Yes. The compliment does oft recur. And I always appreciate it."

Walid laughed. "Yeah. Good."

"I'm ready to go."

"Ok. I can eat this on the way, or when we get there."

"Three figs and a biscuit—that's it?"

"For now. I want to be there early, not late."

"Should we take our coffees?"

"I think they usually have coffee at morning meetings."

"Ok then, let's go."

Mafulla and Walid got up, pushed their chairs in under the edge of the table, and left the room together as usual, walking down the hall in the direction of the large conference room. They were going to have a big morning meeting with the king and Sab Maayuf and others who had been invited by the king. It was supposed to be about some new revelations Sab was going to give them. What those would be, no one could guess. But he could do revelations like no one else. So the boys were intensely curious.

On their way down the hall, Walid stopped into Kular's office for a second to ask, "Has the king gone down yet?"

"Oh! Good morning, Prince! Yes, His Majesty has already gone down to the conference room. He was up early writing some letters, and just gave them to me to post when he walked out the door not five minutes ago."

"Ok, we'll go join him now," Walid said, as his eye drifted down to the stack of outbound letters piled on Kular's desk. The one on top was addressed by hand to "The Reverend Robert Archdale," followed by an address in the United States. Walid thought, "Oh, the minister in New York. Boy, is he going to be surprised!"

"See you soon, Kular," Mafulla said.

Then Walid added, " Yeah, we'll see you in a bit."

"I'll be in the back of the room. I'm going down in a minute, myself. But if we don't cross paths for a while, have a good meeting, Your Highness, and you, too, Mafulla."

"Thanks, Kular!"

So, Kular was coming. That was good, and interesting. He usually kept at work, doing his normal duties while meetings were going on. This must be a truly special occasion.

The boys walked down the hall, talking the entire way, and were surprised that, when they arrived, the room was already mostly full.

Everyone was early. There were Omari, Paki, and Amon sitting with the Sakat brothers, which was a bit unexpected. The brothers were rarely to be seen in the palace. But it seemed like everyone important in their lives was there, Walid gradually realized, as he looked across the room. There were Mafulla's parents, sitting over beside Reela. Walid pointed them out to Mafulla. And then he saw Sammi and Sasha standing near Shapur and Shamilar, looking around with expressions of complete fascination. When the best friend of the prince saw them across the room, he was quite surprised, and yet very glad at the same time, and he rushed over to greet them. Why would they be included in this particular meeting, and even the kids? He had no idea. This wasn't typical at all.

Walid at the same instant saw his mother come in by a different door. He didn't realize that she was back from her trip. He rushed over toward her with a huge smile and hugged her in the biggest, longest embrace ever. "Mother, you won't believe what happened while you were gone!"

"I want you to tell me all about it, as soon as you can," she said. "I'm so glad to be back. It was a great trip, but I knew that something big was happening yesterday, and managed to contact the palace and learn that you were Ok."

"Yeah, it's quite a story," he said.

"I'm sure. Isn't our whole life, these days?"

"Yes, it is!"

At that moment, Layla and Hoda came toward them, calling out Bhati's name, and offering their own warm hugs of greeting and friendship. Kissa and Hasina were right behind them, and were also eager to welcome Bhati back to town. Mafulla saw them and told his family he'd be right back as he hurried over to where Hasina was now hugging Walid's mom. And of course, the prince and Mafulla right away also got hugs from the girls, as they had hoped, in the general merriment of it all.

Mafulla then turned to his best friend, gave him the double eyebrow jump, and said, "Nice."

"Yeah," the prince replied. "Very nice."

Across the room, Set was standing with Khata and laughing with Haji and Ara. Bafur was right beside them, talking to Malik, and Jabari was just that second walking in with Manny on a bright blue leash. Walid was as surprised to see the monkey in the palace as Mafulla had been to see his parents and brother and sister there.

All the girls from Hoda's class were now in the room, along with all the boys from Khalid's class. And there was Khalid, and Ara's little brother Alim right in the middle of the room with her parents. Khata's mother was also sitting back in a corner with her daughter. This was a much bigger group meeting than Walid had expected. Usually, it was just Phi and maybe Naqid, and sometimes these days, Leem and Ibrahim Hadad, who already were sitting down toward the front of the big room. And, there was young Ben. This was also unanticipated, indeed. What sort of big and new revelations from Sab's reading of an ancient, secret scroll would be appropriately shared with such a wide group of people? Well, Walid thought, as he often did, the king must know what he's doing. He always does.

Some palace guards began to close the doors of the room, and everyone who wasn't already seated started finding chairs as Sab began walking up to the front of the room, accompanied by Masoon. The General spoke to him, and he laughed.

"We should sit down," Walid whispered to Kissa.

"Sure." She then squeezed his arm lightly and looked into his eyes and whispered back, "By the way, I love you."

This was a complete surprise to hear, all of a sudden, in such a context. But, of course, it was as wonderful as it was unexpected. Major flutters and a warm jolt of good feeling seemed to course through his soul. He smiled big and whispered back, "Shh. I love you, too." And they walked toward two chairs on the end of the back row closest to where they had been standing. And right after they were seated, the room grew quiet. Then, Sab began to speak.

From the first second, it was like they were all hearing a voice straight from heaven. He did have revelations, and huge ones. And they were big enough and deep enough to make sense of all that they had gone through since Ali and Walid had first arrived in town, together with their original group of friends from across the kingdom. But the insights were much bigger than that. What Sab said in the very first minutes opened many deep mysteries to each of them gathered in the room. They could barely contain their wonder and their sense of sudden understanding, and even a newly deep joy at what they were hearing. It was all far different from anything Walid had expected.

And then Sab smiled. And he paused. And he looked around the room. Walid then did so as well. And he felt like everything was right, just as it should be. He even felt the presence of his father, as if he was standing right behind him, and there was some sort of sense as of a hand on his shoulder. The prince felt affirmed and loved. And he felt truly, deeply prepared for whatever would be next. And that was good, because then something completely stunning happened, the most unexpected and surprising thing in his life—as if things could get any more astonishing than they already were. And it took a second, or actually, more than a few seconds, for it to even begin to sink in. There was first a shock of utter perplexity and even bewilderment, and then a huge realization.

"Uncle Ali?" He whispered. All of a sudden, his heart was pounding.

"Yes? What is it, my boy," Ali whispered back.

"Are you awake?" Walid turned and asked this with the driest mouth of his life. He could hardly get his bearings.

"Yes, I am. Are you?"

"I think so. But if I am, I just had the most incredible and amazing dream ever."

"You did?"

"Yes! Yes! It went on and on, with thousands and millions of details, and like it was going to last forever! I thought it was all really happening and I was so sure of it, of everything I saw and heard! It was so vivid, and so fully real!"

"Tell me of this dream."

"You were a king, the King of Egypt, and I was a prince! And for a short time, I took over for you, as king, and there were great friends and terrible enemies, and a powerful ring and a magical stone and a book and scrolls and a six thousand year old man that we actually know, old Sab was the man, and so many things happened!" His words just tumbled out in the darkness. And then, there was a moment of silence.

"I know, my boy. I know. I just had the same dream."

"You did? I don't understand. How is that even possible?"

"Many more things are possible than we realize. The world is full of unexpected marvels."

"But the things that I dreamed were so wonderful and scary and terrible and amazing and incredible!"

"Such is life, my boy."

"I remember most of it, so much of it, but I think, not all."

"Oh?"

"There was something really bad that happened at one point, I think, but that part's gone."

"Yes. Our minds can work that way."

"And the dream seemed to go on for weeks and then months—many months, longer than a year—and it was all about the greatest things ever! And I knew what people were thinking, and it was so strange. I saw and heard things happen even where I wasn't present, and it was so great and strange that I don't have words for it!"

"Dreams can come true."

"Can this one?"

"Yes. It can, and it will, I believe. I have a certain sense about it. It was a special dream. It will become true and real in every detail that we saw, and with many more twists and turns than we've yet seen."

"But, even the bad and scary parts?"

"Some things frighten us that shouldn't. What we have experienced in our dream will happen in the world as it should."

"But how do you know this?"

"I just do. It's been given to me to know."

"I wrote down notes. In the dream, I kept the diary that I started at the first oasis."

"Yes. I know. And the things you saw and heard and experienced and wrote about will all come true. They are true, or are soon to be true."

"You know this? You really know this?"

"Yes. And I know that something else will happen first, before the dream and the diary of the dream both play out in the world."

"What will happen?"

"We'll both sleep again, and this will be the most complete sleep of our lives, deeper than any slumber we've ever experienced. And in that sleep, we'll forget, at least for a time, this rich, immense, and elaborate dream that we've somehow shared, and even this talk that we're now having about it."

"But, why? I don't want to forget a single thing that I can still remember! It was extraordinary! It was wonderful!"

"We must forget so that we can fully and freely live the dream, here in the world, not knowing along the way what happens next, and often being quite surprised and, because of this, forced to draw on our inner resources and be brave and make choices from deep within our hearts."

"This is incredible."

"And it's true."

"But, Uncle, I don't want to forget any of the good or exciting stuff! I want to remember all these things I've seen, so that I can recognize the people and the things that happen and know how to respond!"

"Ah, but remember," the old man said, "within the dream, as I just now experienced it, and as I'm sure you did, as well, we could not know from one day to the next, or often from one moment to the next, what would come to be. We were continually balanced on the edge of the uncertain, stepping into the unknown, and we were constantly surprised."

"Yes, we were."

"And that's how we made our choices, always making our way into the unknown."

"That's how it felt, for sure."

"So if we're to live that great dream truly and in detail, the overwhelming and fantastic dream we've just shared, it must be lived and experienced in exactly that way."

"Ok. Ok. I think I see what you mean."

"Good."

"I guess you're right. I mean: That's how I lived it and saw it all, too. But how could I have lived through, in a dream just now, weeks and months and over a year … in just part of one night?"

"That's one of the many mysteries of dreams, and of time. Often, our dreams are partial and fragmented. Sometimes, they're wonderfully full."

"But, we really can't remember after tonight? We can't know?"

"The best stories in life are told initially by those who have no idea what comes next." Ali smiled in the darkness and said, "The best lives are lived the same way."

"Oh."

"We can plan and hope and believe, but it's best, it's needed, in order for us to be fully who we are, that we not know all that lies ahead as we step forward into our future."

"Are you saying that we need what you sometimes call the gift of uncertainty?"

"Yes, that's correct. You remember well."

"But I woke up before I saw how it all turns out. I didn't see the end. What will happen to me, and to you?"

"Wonderful things, my boy, amazing, marvelous things will happen, things more astonishing than you can imagine or even dream."

"Are you sure?"

"About this, there is no uncertainty. I'm absolutely sure. And in that certainty, I have been given a blessed and peculiar gift on this one dark night, along with the unexpected gift of the dream that I've just shared with you. But, now, let's go back to sleep. And the sooner, the better, because then the countless great things in and beyond our dream can begin."

"But first, I have to ask a question, one more question."

"Anything. I'll answer if I can."

"Am I really a prince, The Prince of Egypt?"

"Yes. You are."

"Am I … Phi?"

"Yes, indeed. And that, of course is a second question."

"Oh! In the dream, there's someone who always catches me when I do that."

"Yes, there is."

"Will there actually be a Mafulla?"

"Yes. There already is. He's real."

"And Kissa?"

"Oh, yes. Yes, indeed. She's waiting for you now. Her soul is ready to meet yours. I can promise you that. So we must sleep. And then, soon, we can both meet up with her and the glorious destiny that awaits us all."

"I don't think I can possibly go to sleep again, now, after that dream and after what you've just said. My heart's beating so fast."

Ali quietly laughed and replied, "Oh, I'm certain of one other thing. You'll get drowsy soon, even now, as I speak to you, despite your amply justified excitement. Your heart will begin to calm and you'll feel the tug of slumber pulling you into the cleansing transition that's needed in order for the next stage of our adventure to begin."

There was a silence then for a few seconds and Walid said, "Uncle, as usual, you're right." He yawned and added, "A great sleepiness is already coming over me this very moment, just as you say."

"That's always the way, my boy. Life gives us what we need, and prepares us for what's next, even when it doesn't seem that way. We're prepared beyond our awareness. Always have faith that you'll be given what you need."

And, within a minute at most, they were both asleep again, in the deepest and most complete repose of their lives. And all these memories from the spectacular dream were totally erased, as Ali had known they would be, as if by a magnificent transformation and, indeed, even a new birth into the world they were now to enter.

And Walid and his uncle lay still, completely unconscious, and aware of nothing, until the moment a man came running up to their tent and pulled open the flap and said, "Ali! Ali!"

"Yes?"

"Faisul is gone! And three camels are missing!"

And with this, our story can truly begin.

APPENDIX

The Diary of Walid Shabeezar Acting As King

I begin this part of my diary just as the most shocking thing has happened. This has been the most difficult time of my life, no close second. Uncle Ali fought the monster, Juan Osvaldo Santiago, and they both just disappeared. I know Uncle Ali used the Ring of Phi. But I don't know what happened to him. None of us do. And it's my job to carry on in his proper role until he, hopefully, returns. When I've been able to, I've continued to write down things I've learned and other thoughts along the way. I've divided up this overall diary into chapters, from early on, because I feel like my journey, since crossing the desert, has unfolded in a series of adventures, or stages. This is the latest stage.

∆ ∆ ∆

People often press us to do what they think is right. We need to be open to advice but resistant to pressure, and then do what we believe is best.

It's possible to live like there's no mystery in life. But why anyone would want to do so is a real mystery to me.

What people forget about social status is that how you get somewhere is in the end more important than where you are.

Your status never matters as much as your soul. I'm the king right now—as hard as it is for me to believe. But that hasn't changed me. I am who I am, regardless of what I'm called.

We're defined by inner character, not outer circumstances.

Power is never what we think. It's meant to be, ironically, subservient. We imagine it in terms of control. We should think of it in terms of provision, possibility, and practical service.

We're always better off with the advice of people we trust, than just going it alone. Partnerships bring power and possibility.

△ △ △

People can surprise you. Even good people can surprise you in good ways.

I've come to think that human nature is more complicated than we often suppose. Still, there are some powerfully simple elements in it that can guide us well.

One of the ongoing challenges in life is to cut through complexity and find the simple truths underneath.

People often speak of the battle of good and evil within each of us. It seems to me that it's when these two forces are at peace, and not when they're at war, that the danger is greatest. There's a complacent intertwining of these elements that's subtle, self-justifying, and insidious.

That's my new word for the day: Insidious. Yeah, I got it from Maful-la The Great.

△ △ △

Khalid talked about obsession in class today. It's a strange thing. It can lift people up and bring them down. It can fuel mastery and achievement, and also pridefulness and self-destruction.

Any fanatical fixation is dangerous. Obsession promises great transformation, but most often leads to big trouble.

Obsession is a form of prolonged imbalance. Temporary imbalance, we can deal with; prolonged, it can create a great fall.

We also talked about loyalty. I would have said that it's simply a good thing, but Khalid convinced me that its value is always proportional to its object and its degree. Loyalty to the wrong people or causes, or even loyalty to the right things but in the wrong degree is harmful. Devotion in the right way, with the right object, is great.

Loyalty should never blind us to new information or noble feelings that could conflict with it in a specific situation. When it's operating properly, it strengthens us, and others, and never weakens us.

Santiago was obsessed. And look at all the terrible consequences that caused for other people and now, most likely, for him.

△ △ △

When challenge comes your way, will you rise to the occasion or fall on your face? I've come to realize the importance of preparation.

We can prepare for greatness. And we should.

We can be prepared deliberately and wisely for great challenges, great opportunities, and great things in general. That's what Uncle Ali was doing for me in the desert, and it's what he's been engaged in ever since—preparing me for whatever I'll have to face in life, including a time like this.

You don't have to just hope you'll be brave when confronted with danger. You can prepare to be brave. Courage in fact grows only in the right soil. We can be prepared or unprepared for the choices we face—and in either case, the outcome may be very different.

△ △ △

I came across a great quote today from the famous artist Michelangelo. "Lord, grant that I may always desire more than I accomplish."

People think that to be happy, they have to get all their desires satisfied. But he's implying that this would be a bad thing. We need desires that reach beyond our accomplishments, because that gives us room for learning and growth and hope. It's like we're meant to be ever developing, never stagnant, and always aiming to achieve more than we've already accomplished. That doesn't mean we can't appreciate what we already have and where we already are. It just means that we're always to be moving forward, doing the next good thing, and ever becoming what we can be.

You're either learning-and-growing, or you're stagnating-and-dying. If you're not climbing up the hill of life, you'll be slipping backwards down it, and soon.

I like to stretch to try new things. We all should.

△ △ △

I understand for the first time the full amount of work a king has to do every day. What's interesting is that I have lots of help—actually, a huge amount—but I still see or hear about nearly everything. Uncle Ali told me a lot about the job as he was doing it, but really, I had no full idea how much responsibility attaches to the role of king. And I'm sure this is true for running any large enterprise, as well.

It seems to be a general truth in life that, from a distance, people see the power and status of high office, but they rarely imagine all the work that a position of great responsibility involves.

Everyone comes into the world to make a difference. We should seek to help others find their path. And maybe, in so doing, we'll find ours.

I have to read some extremely detailed reports in my new, temporary role. After one very complicated agricultural study today, I had to sit and think a bit about the ideas of boredom and interest. And I've come up with some conclusions.

Nothing in the world is intrinsically boring. A spirit of curiosity can see something interesting in anything, however well hidden that gem might be. Boredom is a poverty of spirit, rather than an intrinsic result of certain circumstances.

If things don't spark our interest, we can sometimes spark it ourselves by asking good questions, or taking a new perspective on whatever it is that we face. When in doubt, dig. Dig deep enough and you'll always make a discovery.

The important question isn't whether things are interesting, it's whether we are interested. So much of life comes back to inner attitude and inner disposition.

Maybe there's something like a spectrum: Totally bored, merely uninterested, attentive but unmoved, mildly interested, truly engaged, utterly fascinated, completely obsessed. Wisdom avoids the extremes.

∆ ∆ ∆

I've come to see curiosity as one of the most important qualities for living a full life.

Curiosity and courage: two vital attributes. And the first really requires the second, or else, it's just idle.

∆ ∆ ∆

Sometimes things happen so fast that it's hard to get your head around *all the possibilities for what might come next. But nothing demands inner calm like outer chaos. I'm glad Uncle Ali taught me about the oasis that can be within us to cultivate and use.*

Choice is rarely a sure thing. We hardly ever know as much as we'd like to know as we make crucial decisions about things that matter.

When the stakes are high, you can't let yourself freeze up with anxiety, or by second-guessing your choices. No one is expected to be perfect. We're just called on to do the best we can, and move forward.

∆ ∆ ∆

Mafulla and I had an interesting conversation about dreams today. He was reading a book on ancient views about dreaming. It said that some people believe that dreams are portals to divine insight. There have been views that God speaks to us in our dreams. But there's also a modern view that our dreams are places where our unconscious minds wrestle with things we've consciously been thinking about, but maybe haven't figured out yet, or made peace with, or solved. It could be that both things are involved, at one time or another.

Maffie's dreams have often told him, or shown him, something important happening at a distance. I wonder if dreams can ever show us the future in all or most of its coming details? Well, why not?

We spend nearly a third of our lives asleep. Some people keep dream journals so that they can learn better from that time. Most people forget their dreams within an hour or two after waking up, but many claim that if you write down your dreams, starting the minute you come to consciousness, you can remember a lot more. And then you can learn later on from reading what you've written, day after day. Dreams certainly can have a form and logic of their own. And dream interpretation isn't always simple, or easy. But it may be well worth the effort. Why shouldn't we benefit in this way from that third of our lives where our experience is so different?

Dreams can sometimes show us the path ahead. We should pay attention to what they can teach us.

Maybe some things can come to us only when our guard is down and our conscious beliefs, prejudices, and assumptions aren't up and working. There's a kind of passivity in sleep that may allow deeper truths to enter our unconscious minds where, perhaps, we can find them later.

∆ ∆ ∆

Until recently, I didn't even know what monetary policy is, or tax policy. But I've been reading stuff about all that, and about economics more generally. I was going over a recent report and saw in it a reference to something Uncle Ali had written about taxation. I found that policy paper and read it, too, and it made a lot of sense. He wrote about capitalism and what he called a well-regulated free market. As we move toward developing the foundations of democracy in the kingdom, we have to make the right decisions about how our system of economics can support our vital goals of independence and self-governance. People need both knowledge and resources in order to be able to attain those worthy goals.

Some things, only the government seems big enough to provide, and of the right nature to administer it, like a national road system. But in other things, the government should try to stay out of people's way as much as it can, while still protecting the safety, opportunity, and freedom of all. It's a real balancing act and people won't always agree on what it takes to get it right.

Uncle argues well that governments should not own what he calls the means of production—major industries and such things. A national government isn't exactly like a business. It's different. Of course, the central government could hire lots of business people and have them as officials running businesses that the government would own, but what would be the point? That would just introduce another layer of administration that's unnecessary. People should be free to start and run their own businesses with minimal interference from the government, as long as this is compatible with the safety of all.

Creating regulations that both safeguard and empower is a form of art. It's challenging, and it's fulfilling when done right.

Government regulation is necessary. What an individual business owner perceives to be in his personal interest might diverge dramatically from what's in the greater interests of the community. And, at a certain point, lines should be drawn to protect the overall environment and the social fabric from extreme forms of damage.

The society that provides for the possibility of thriving business should also make clear the rules under which business should be run, for the good of all. The more enlightened we are, the freer we can be.

And taxation is important. Done right and responsibly, it isn't a matter of the government taking from the people. Especially in a democracy, the government represents the people. Taxation is ultimately just the people themselves deciding how resources should be gathered for large-scale social goals that are vitally important. Those things that we need to do together, and not just for the profit of private individuals, have to be paid for, and taxation does that. But it should be minimal on those who would feel it the most, and something like an increasing responsibility for those who can most afford it, and so would feel the pain of it the least. The rich are those who have benefited the most from the common structures of a society, and it only makes sense for them to provide proportionately more for those extra benefits.

Uncle wrote about what he called "progressive taxation"—that those who are at the very top of the economic pyramid should contribute a greater percentage of their wealth to help provide for the good of all. They feel the difference less; they reap the greatest overall societal benefits from their work, given the common structures and services that allow for such work; and they're in a position to use a larger portion of their bounty for the good of all. And this, of course, will also rebound to their benefit in many general and specific ways. If their tax dollars are used well, they will end up living in a healthier and more prosperous society, overall.

Countries where most people are poor or struggling, and a very small percentage of the society is immensely wealthy, will not flourish over the long run. That's what Uncle Ali believes, and it makes sense to me. People should reap the rewards of their talents and good work, but not so as to weaken and destroy the social fabric around them.

Uncle wrote that some people object to such a view like this: If taxation is proportionately higher for the wealthy, then their motivation to use their talents and leverage to create and build more businesses will be eliminated, to the detriment of all. But here's my question: Why should personal financial profit be anyone's only motivation to create and build in the first place? It can be a good and proper motive, but so can lots of other things. Making great things just feels good, and answers to a deep spiritual need we all have.

For most people, money is power—the power to buy and provide, the power to have options in life, the power to do and to be. But we only need so much power, and more than that becomes almost abstract, and nearly irrelevant *to how we live. Uncle Ali wrote that opponents of progressive taxation on income assume that a desire for greater and greater money and power is the only motivation that would keep people creating and building. And that may indeed be true for some people—unwise, unenlightened, and corrupt souls who've narrowed their focus and forgotten many of the proper values in life. But why should we want to encourage such people as these to be the top leaders of business in the first place? We should want the top of our society, where the most money and power is to be found, to be populated with people who have broader motivations than just their own personal financial profit by itself, as healthy as profit can be. But such profit is only a part of a much larger puzzle. People should benefit financially for the great work they do, and prosper. There's no question about that. But a country's tax policy should both protect that, and protect the broader needs that exist for the good of all.*

If a sensible tax policy takes away the creating and building motivations from unwise, unenlightened, and corrupt people, then I guess we all would benefit! Make way for the enlightened, the socially conscious, and the more broadly concerned! Business at its best is a spiritual endeavor that changes the physical world.

I've got to think about all this a lot more. I'm fourteen, and not quite ready to create long term tax policies, so I hope for this reason as well as a million other more important ones that Uncle Ali gets back soon. I've never thought much about national economics at all, but I'm glad I read what Uncle wrote. He expresses his views clearly and well. I strive for the same.

Writing helps us to think. Writing about all this is helping me to absorb it and reason it through. If anyone else ever reads this diary, I hope they're not bored by all the details I go through here in my ruminations.

More people my age should think about the things I'm wrestling with today. What sort of society do we want? And what can be done to make things better, overall? What should we do? What can I do?

The worst thing we can do is to cocoon ourselves in our small private lives and forget about the larger community we depend on.

We often feel like we've been born into a world that runs itself. But that's not true. We need to learn how to run it, and run it well.

Preparation and true engagement are keys to doing most things well.

For a democratic way of life, we all have to prepare ourselves to contribute to a well-functioning society. And we should also help prepare each other.

∆ ∆ ∆

Today, I heard somebody say, "It's a stressful time." And I knew what he meant. But, in a sense, a situation has to be perceived as stressful in order to be stressful, at least, in a psychological or an emotional sense. And, to some extent, that perception is up to us.

Maybe this is how to say it: A situation can't really be stressful for you unless you believe it is. And this is the sort of belief that, in principle, you can control, and even withhold.

Faith dissipates stress like the sun burns off fog. Wisdom, at its best, is immune to the worst forms of stress and worry.

∆ ∆ ∆

Almost nothing is as good as it seems or as bad as it seems. So we should all just calm down. How many times do I have to remind myself of that? Lots!

Wisdom often comes to us in words, but stays with us in actions. It's supposed to be lived. It's not about clever words but good lives.

Knowledge is in the mind. Wisdom is in the heart.

We're meant to possess knowledge. Wisdom is meant to possess us.

Few things never fail us. Wisdom is one of those things.

A life without wisdom is barren, regardless of the fireworks it contains.

Wisdom and love go together. You can't have one without the other.

△ △ △

What am I supposed to do if Uncle Ali doesn't ever come back? I can barely even consider that possibility, after losing my dad. It would be just too much—to do without him, too, for the rest of this life. But I have to be strong and of good hope. I can walk whatever path is presented to me.

What does anyone do when he suddenly finds himself in a surprising position, with more responsibility than he ever could have imagined? I guess, in a sense, that's much of life for all of us.

Being alive in this world as a person my age, or older is, in a sense, always a surprising position, when you really think about it, with more responsibility than we ever could have imagined as kids. I mean, when you're really young, you barely understand the concept of responsibility at all, and then when you're older, you suddenly find yourself with more of it than you know how to handle. I guess the answer is wisdom and virtue, and especially, the chief virtue of courage. All we can do is have courage and move forward wisely.

Courage is the baseline of a life well lived. It isn't ever defeated.

Whatever the question about life might be, the answer always involves wisdom and virtue.

We only have to handle one day and one decision at a time.

Life itself, existence in this world, is in its own way a surprising position to be in. Nothing is stranger than the mystery of existence. Once you absorb that fully, then I think you can deal with anything.

My head's spinning with all the ways things could go, from this point on. But there's a famous old saying that's relevant to my anxieties: The coward dies a thousand times, the courageous only once. I need to dial down my endless scenario envisioning and deal with what's in front of me now. We're never given more than we can handle, because if that more ever comes, we're no longer here to be crushed by it.

∆ ∆ ∆

Mafulla cracked me up this morning saying there should be a movie made about us. I guess that, really, a movie made about almost anyone could be interesting and maybe even fascinating, if it was made well enough. All of us have rich inner lives, and unexpected things happen to us. Everyone has hopes and dreams and disappointments and successes. But Maffie and I have certainly had a string of unusually crazy adventures since we met. I wonder.

∆ ∆ ∆

Sab is the original Utnapishtin, The Faraway, in the famous Epic of Gilgamesh, and Meskhenet is his wife, the people who talked to the original King Gilgamesh about everlasting life, in about 2,700 BC. I had to write that down. It may be one of the strangest and most surprising things ever.

What's it like to live for thousands of years? I can't even begin to get my imagination around that. How many generations of friends do you gain and lose? Does that affect how close you allow yourself to get to people? What does it mean for accomplishment and for patience? I feel like it's so different and alien a thing, but aren't we all meant for everlasting life? Not here, of course, but somewhere? And, really, does it matter where? But maybe it does. Maybe eternal life can be supported only by natural laws and conditions for existence that are in some way different from what we have here—circumstances in which physicality and movement and action are in some ways similar to, but also interestingly different from, what they are in this world, at least, at this stage in its history.

Some people believe that everlasting life would eventually bring massive tedium and infinite boredom, but I don't see why. I mean, there aren't really any finite limits on creativity, in principle, or on imagination. And as long as that's going for us, why should we need only limited time available to us? I think the opposite—that everlasting life would be eternally fascinating, if you do it right.

Does everlasting life imply everlasting work? I'm sure vacations would still be possible. But imagine if you were thinking about going somewhere and then realized, "Yeah, it's nice, but I've been there a million times already."

How many adventures are possible? How many new realizations can you experience? How many intriguing things are there to learn? Will a spirit of curiosity endure forever, or does it eventually ebb? Can love and wisdom grow forever? My bet is that any pessimistic answers to these questions are just due to a lack of imagination, which is easily understood, given our current circumstances and limitations.

On good days when Uncle Ali was around, I remember occasionally thinking, "I could live like this forever." That's a sign of happiness and contentment. It shows I've found my path.

I talked about eternal life one day with Mafulla and his dad. Shapur said that he knows he'd never get bored in all of eternity, as long as his memory was no better than it is now. He said he usually doesn't remember what he had for breakfast yesterday or most of what he did the week before. He concluded that maybe eternity would never get old as long as you have a suitably bad memory. He cracks me up.

Eternity: A lot to think about.

∆ ∆ ∆

Seneca spoke about how we invest the time that we have. I like the concept of investment in this connection. Some people invest time in personal growth and in other people. Some invest it only in money and power, and maybe fame. Some invest it in creativity.

How you invest your time shows your values better than anything else. You can say anything, but what do you do?

A wise Jabari quote: "A life that looks like it hasn't accomplished much on the outside could be really rich and full on the inside." And I guess we can flip that insight. A life that looks like it's accomplished a lot on the outside could be really poor and empty on the inside.

Where our treasure is, there will our heart be also, and our time. What we spend time on shows what we most deeply value.

We should never judge lives by external standards alone. An outwardly quiet existence can be full and amazing within.

Good Khalid quotes today. Here they are, as I remember them: Attitude is almost everything. Live with love. Work with passion and joy. Choose happiness—It's up to you, and each of us.

△ △ △

The events with Santiago, the new Oz Ali, are almost beyond words. I've learned in this situation so much about love and forgiveness and the possibilities for redemption. I understand personal choice and transformation in new ways. And I'm humbled by his sacrifice.

Greater love has no man than this: that he lay down his life for his friends.

Love gives and seeks to serve. And in the end, that's the royal road to happiness, I think, and fulfillment.

In the end, love can conquer all.

Acknowledgments

This has been an unbelievable journey for me, getting to know Walid, Mafulla, Ali, Kissa, Hasina, Hoda, Layla, and all the others. They've enriched my world immensely. I hope they've had the same effect in yours. I wonder if we'll ever hear more from them. I hope so.

One neighbor of mine, Ed Hearn, has read each of the books in the series as I've written them, and before I showed them to anyone else outside my family. He's been extremely encouraging and a rock solid source of support. In his mid-sixties as I write this, he's a man ranked at the top in the world in such sports as shot put and javelin. I've begun to wonder if he might be a member of a particular society.

And, speaking of that, it recently came to my attention that a Swiss watchmaking firm adopted as their brand emblem a few years ago a stylized rendition of a certain Greek letter, historically used to name a famous mathematical ratio and a particular clandestine society of remarkable individuals. By engraving this letter on the backs of watches sold openly all over the world, they may be making a statement. Are they suggesting that a specific existential identity is perhaps more widely available than we might guess? Or do they think that certain individuals will be drawn to these timepieces, whether or not they're aware of the symbolism? I certainly was. I took off one of those watches the other day while writing this book, and set it down on the dark desk pad in front of my computer screen, and there on the back was a large engraving that I had never before connected with the subject of these books. So, for years before I knew what it represented, I had been wearing the sign of Phi. Interesting, isn't it?

I want to thank all the good people who have been so helpful to me as I've written down the movie in my head that became these books. Thanks also to all those who allowed me to talk about the stories with an enthusiasm that I could not tone down. It's been great.

Tom Morris
Wilmington, NC

Afterword

The Mysteries of Life

First, there was *The Oasis Within*, a short tale about a series of deep conversations and surprising events that took place as a group of men and camels crossed the desert in Egypt in 1934. Then there was *The Golden Palace*, the official Book One to a series of subsequent stories about these remarkable individuals collectively entitled:

Walid and the Mysteries of Phi

Then came *The Stone of Giza*. Next was *The Viper and The Storm*. Then, *The King and Prince*. Next: *The Mysterious Village*. And there was *The Magic Ring*. Finally: *The Ancient Scroll*. This is Book Seven in the official series. If you've read these books, I hope you've loved every one of them. All the volumes together present a sprawling account of action, adventure, and ideas set in and around a richly reimagined Cairo, Egypt in 1934 and 1935, with a few sojourns farther abroad. They all contain tales about life, death, meaning, love, friendship, the deepest secrets behind everyday events, and the extraordinary power of a well-focused mind. The events they relate interact with many classics of philosophy and literature from around the globe. And you can discover in these books the outlines of a powerful worldview and a profound philosophy of life.

To find out more, visit **www.TomVMorris.com/novels** or go to **www.TheOasisWithin.com.**

The prologue and companion book to the series, *The Oasis Within*, as well as any book in the series, will be available for large group purchases at special discounts. To find out more, contact the author through his oldest and most reliable email, **TomVMorris@aol.com** or through his website. Tom is also available to speak with book groups via email, Skype, or any other means that would help in the discussion of these stories. Make a request, and speak to the author.

About the Author

Tom Morris is one of the most active philosophers and public speakers in the world. A native of North Carolina, he's a graduate of The University of North Carolina (Chapel Hill), where he was a Morehead-Cain Scholar, and he holds a Ph.D. in both Philosophy and Religious Studies from Yale University. For fifteen years, he served as a Professor of Philosophy at the University of Notre Dame, where he was one of their most popular teachers. You can find him online now anytime at **www.TomVMorris.com.**

Tom has been honored with the University of North Carolina's Distinguished Young Alumnus Award, as well as with honorary doctorates in recognition of his work. He has been a George A. and Eliza Gardner Howard Foundation Fellow, through Brown University, and a Fellow with the National Endowment for the Humanities.

Tom is also the author of over twenty-two pioneering books. His twelfth book, *True Success: A New Philosophy of Excellence*, launched him into an ongoing adventure as a philosopher working and speaking throughout the world. His audiences have included a great many of the Fortune 500 companies and dozens of the largest national and international trade associations. His work has been mentioned, commented on, or covered by NBC, ABC, CNN,

CNBC, NPR, and in most major newspapers and news magazines. He's also the author of the highly acclaimed books *If Aristotle Ran General Motors*, *Philosophy for Dummies*, *The Art of Achievement*, *The Stoic Art of Living*, *Twisdom*, *Superheroes and Philosophy*, and *If Harry Potter Ran General Electric: Leadership Wisdom from the World of the Wizards*, as well as many others. His most recent books include the philosophical prologue to the current series, *The Oasis Within*, and the subsequent books, *The Golden Palace*, *The Stone of Giza*, and *The Viper and The Storm*, as well as the current volume. He just may be the world's happiest philosopher.

And when the time had fully come …
Galatians, 4:4

Φ

www.ingramcontent.com/pod-product-compliance
Lightning Source LLC
Chambersburg PA
CBHW030419310726
48979CB00009B/1524/J